A LITJOY EDITION

The Love Curse of Melody McIntyre

Robin Talley

ROBIN TALLEY

HARPER TEEN

An Imprint of HarperCollinsPublishers

The Love Curse of Melody McIntyre

The Love Curse of Melody McIntyre

ROBIN TALLEY

An Imprint of HarperCollinsPublishers

For Darcy.
It's okay if you don't love musical theater when you grow up, but
you can never say your moms didn't try.

BEACONVILLE HIGH SCHOOL

presents our
spring musical production

Les Misérables

Based on the novel by Victor Hugo

Director
Ms. Jennifer Marcus

Music Director
Ms. Michelle Qiao

Technical Director
Mr. William Green

Conductor
Dr. P. J. Benjamin

Stage Manager
Melody McIntyre,
class of 2021

May 1–9, 2020

Beaconville High School Performing Arts Wing

Beaconville High School Theater Rules
Stored on BHS performing arts department shared drive
Created by: Billy Yang, stage manager, class of 2007
Viewable to: All cast, crew, and directors
Editable by: Current SM ONLY

This document was created following our production of the Scottish Play in spring 2007. Henceforth to be referred to as The Production That Must Not Be Named. If we stick to the rules below, hopefully, *hopefully*, we'll never have another show like it.

Rule 1:

All standard theater superstitions are to be strictly followed within the performing arts wing. No one can ever whistle, actors may only be told to "break a leg" (never "g**d l**k"), there is to be no giving of flowers to anyone before a performance, etc.

And for God's sake, no one is EVER to say the real name of the Scottish Play out loud under ANY circumstances. We don't care if you're studying Shakespeare for your English APs. We don't care if you're trying to come up with a cute ship name for your favorite characters, "Mackenzie" and "Bethany."

No matter the circumstances, you are NEVER to say *M*cb**h* out loud. Seriously. We cannot stress the importance of this enough.

Rule 2:

Before rehearsals on a new show begin, all cast and crew must pay tribute to the fire memorial plaque in the theater lobby. What form this tribute takes is up to your team. For our next show, we've decided to pay tribute via intense silent prayer to whatever deity each of us may or may not believe in, but anything should do the trick as long as you do it with sufficient gusto.

Rule 3:

A new superstition must be created and strictly adhered to for every play and musical produced on the main stage (see <u>A Brief History of BHS Theater Superstitions</u>). This new superstition will apply to that show and that show only. We highly recommend applying lessons learned from whatever went wrong last time around (which in the case of The Production That Must Not Be Named was everything).

Rule 4:

If any superstition is violated, the offender must perform the appropriate countercurse as soon as possible, or the entire cast and crew will face the consequences.

Rule 5:

The above rules are not to be taken lightly. Trust us, curses aren't something you want to mess with.

PROLOGUE
November

Scene 1—Tech Booth, Beaconville High School Theater

MINUTES UNTIL OPENING NIGHT CURTAIN CALL: 75

I tap the button, and below me the entire audience draws in a quick, happy breath.

A pale beam of light just appeared at the top of the scaffolding we built on stage left. I hit that cue at the perfect moment, and now the audience is primed and ready. The light was the signal they needed to get invested in this scene, and now they'll hang on every word while the actors do their actor thing.

Man, I love my job.

"*But soft!*" Liam calls from downstage center. Another collective happy breath goes up as the audience recognizes the line. "*What light through yonder window breaks?*"

"Stand by, sound M." My voice is steady as I call the cue into the headset. Smooth and professional. I've only been stage manager for three months, but I've already got the smooth-and-professional headset voice down.

My best friend, Dom, nods silently in the seat next to mine, his finger hovering over the go button.

Below us, Liam launches into his first big speech. Up in the booth, we wait.

It'll take him a while to get to the cue, so I take a moment to squint down at the stage, making sure his doublet's still intact. One of the sleeves somehow got snagged during the opening fight scene, which Liam isn't even *in*, and Rachel spent the whole Lady Capulet scene frantically attacking his shoulder with a needle backstage. If it gets any worse, we'll have to tell David to give his speech in the next scene *really* slowly so the costume team will have time to work on it again. Romeo isn't supposed to look bedraggled yet.

Liam finally gets to the cue line—"*Her eye discourses; I will answer it*"—and at the exact moment he says *it*, I say, "*Go!*"

Dom presses the key right when he's supposed to, on the *g* in *go*. The sound of a dog barking pipes out onto the stage, and the audience members sit up, startled, just like *they're* supposed to. The outside world just intruded on Romeo and Juliet's private moment, reminding them both of what they're risking if they get caught. The audience is appropriately unsettled.

I want to grin, but I don't let myself. Dom hasn't missed a cue all night, and neither have I. It's still early, though. We've got plenty of time to screw things up.

The great dream of my life is that opening night will come off perfectly, but that *never* happens. It's the first rule of theater. Besides, we ran into so many crises during the rehearsal process for this show that I stopped counting. Odds are, *something's* bound to go wrong between now and curtain call, and it'll be something worse than a torn doublet. Stage managers can always sense disaster in the making.

"Hey, Mel?" Gabby's voice chirps in my ear from backstage, and my usual roster of anxieties surges. Did Tybalt's sword break again? We already had to fix it twice during tech. Or is one of the nervous ensemble freshmen puking in costume? They all know they're under strict orders when it comes to puking attire.

But then Gabby says, "Should I stay stage left in case Christina needs to look at my script again, or can I check on the Greek chorus?" and I relax.

"Check on the chorus," I tell her. "Christina has no business looking at your script during a performance anyway. The actors had to be off-book weeks ago. If she forgets a line tonight, she's on her own."

Over the headset, Estaban starts singing "On My Own" from *Les Mis* in a high-pitched voice, and I struggle again not to laugh. Sure, that's arguably the best song in definitively the best musical ever written, but I can't risk getting distracted with gorgeous melodies tonight.

"*Oh, Romeo, Romeo!*" Christina sings out on the stage below, her face settling into the same over-the-top smile she always wears onstage, whether she's Juliet or Mrs. Potiphar or a backup Delta Nu. "*Wherefore art—*"

"My cough drops?" Estaban says into the headset. Gabby and

the others laugh from backstage, and next to me, Dom chuckles silently into his hand.

This is the first show where Christina's gotten a lead, and during rehearsals she quickly became infamous with the crew for demanding that cough drops be placed in her palm whenever she held it out. For the first week Gabby actually did it, unwrapping Ricolas and running up to the stage, until our theater teacher, Ms. Marcus, took us both aside. It was Christina's responsibility to deal with her own cough drops, she told us. And as assistant stage manager, Gabby's job was to make sure we put on a good show, not to enable the actors' laziness.

(Okay, I'm paraphrasing Ms. Marcus rather than directly quoting here, but the point is . . . *actors*. They're the *worst*.)

"*Ahem*." A throat clears behind me.

When I turn around, Will—Mr. Green, I mean; that's what I'm supposed to call him at school—frowns from his perch against the back wall of the booth. He's our technical director, and he doesn't approve of non-show chatter on headset. I'm the only one who's really supposed to talk, except when the other crew members need to acknowledge my cues or tell me about some problem backstage.

It's hard to resist, though. We've all seen this show a hundred times in rehearsals, and besides, we just upgraded our headset system. There are a dozen of us on the intercom tonight—all the crew heads and a few of the assistants, plus Gabby and me, plus Will. Basically, everyone I actually like in this school is connected via microphones attached to our heads right now. The urge to go off-topic is strong in us all.

But Will's right. We need to stay focused. The Greek chorus is about to enter.

"Stand by, sound N," I say into the mic, nodding at Will so he'll know I understand.

Dom hovers his finger over the button and wiggles his eyebrows at me. I bite my lip and glare back. Ever since the invited dress rehearsal, he's been trying to see if he can trick me into laughing during a standby. No one's allowed to talk on the headsets when we're in standby, not even me, but Dom says I'm too much of a stickler for the rules.

I haven't cracked yet, though, and I'm not going to. Sure, this is my first full show as stage manager—and I'm only a junior, which makes me the youngest SM in the history of the Beaconville High School performing arts department, thank you very much—but rules exist for a reason. In a standby, the crew's attention should be focused on hitting each cue at precisely the right moment. If one person loses track, the whole show could fall apart.

Besides, professionalism is any good stage manager's number-one character trait. If I can put on an almost-perfect fall play—and, better yet, a *totally* perfect musical this spring—I'll be on track to get into my dream stage management program for college, and that'll set me up to get hired as a professional SM after graduation. First stop, the Beaconville High School theater tech booth, last stop, Broadway.

But only if I can get this right.

"*Henceforth I never will be Romeo!*" Liam proclaims, throwing his arms up in one of those patented actor flails that make audiences lose their minds.

"*Go,*" I say into the mic.

Dom presses the button.

This sound cue is short—just a few seconds of recorded music to cover the Greek chorus's entrance from the wings. Ms. Marcus wanted to bring out actual musicians, but Dr. Benjamin flat-out refused to deal with all the parent permission forms and extra rehearsal scheduling it would've taken to get a few horn players onstage for a tiny fragment of a song.

Rachel—who happens to be my girlfriend, in addition to being the best costume crew head our school's had in years—was glad Dr. Benjamin won that argument. Otherwise she and her team would've been stuck sewing three more costumes for just one scene. She wouldn't have actually minded the sewing part, but band guys at our school are notoriously terrible at standing still and letting themselves be measured, and they're always cracking vaguely creepy jokes about woodwinds.

As the music winds down, Alejandra and Malik and the rest of the actors in the so-called Greek chorus file on from stage right. The most complicated set of light cues in the entire show is about to start, and my heart's already racing. But when the music ends, I tap the button for the first cue, right on schedule.

"See, Mel? You got this," Dom mutters as light slowly fills

the stage. He's keeping his voice down, but his mic is still on, which means the crew can hear him through the headset. Even when he's being a nice, reassuring friend, which is most of the time, Dom craves an audience. "Nothing can knock you off your game. You're the cue-calling master."

"All hail our fearless leader," Fatima says from backstage.

The others giggle into their headsets. I smile over at Dom and summon up my most relaxed expression. My friends call it my Stage Manager Calm. A good SM is utterly unfazeable. Or pretends to be, at least.

It was the cast's idea to stage the second half of the balcony scene this way, with a Greek chorus full of Capulets and Montagues trooping out onstage to watch and silently judge while Romeo and Juliet moon over each other. The idea is that they aren't *really* there, they're just hovering on the edges of our heroes' thoughts, imaginary stand-ins for the risk they're taking by even having this conversation. While the young lovers are busy declaring passionate, lifelong devotion based on having flirted for approximately thirty seconds at a party, their families are shaking their heads at their inanity, both metaphorically and literally.

The conceptual flaws here are many—for one thing, the whole point of the balcony scene is that it's an intimate moment between Romeo and Juliet *alone*, and for another, a Greek chorus by definition *can't* be silent—but it's not my job to point out things like that. *My* job is to make sure the audience understands what's happening onstage. And since it's really hard for a dozen teenage actors to convey mass imaginary silent judgment, we're doing it with lights.

We came up with a plan for the scene that I now realize is . . . a little on the complicated side. The brightest pools of light will switch back and forth, often, between Liam and Christina at the balcony and their "families" on the opposite side of the stage. The SM always runs the light board on our fall plays, which means it's up to me to hit the button at precisely the right moment every time to keep that light dancing from one end of the stage to the other while the actors do their thing. Some of the cues are really close together, so it's going to be tricky, but if I get it right, the audience should be able to follow along. And if I screw up, they'll be baffled, trying to figure out why all these extra people are hanging out in Juliet's backyard during the most iconic two-person scene in dramatic history.

Honestly, though—this is why I love technical theater. The actors can prance around reciting iambic pentameter as much as they want, but even they know they'd be helpless without us. Sure, it's hard—I'm stuck calling cues for the crew all night, *plus* keeping up with these complicated lighting changes on my own, but I wouldn't have it any other way. *I'm* in charge of everything that's happening.

It'd be easier if I didn't also have to follow along with every word of the script as they're saying it, though. I'm the only person in this building who has to know exactly what's *supposed* to be happening onstage at every second, even when the actors screw up.

"What's going on with Christina's hair?" Fatima asks over the headsets. Now that the Greek chorus is in place, there isn't much for the run crew to do while this scene is playing out. I'm the only one who has to worry about much of anything right now. Well, me and the cast, I guess. "Did she put on some industrial-strength gel? I can practically see my reflection in it."

"Don't even ask," Shannon says, the eye roll clear in her voice. "I begged Ms. Marcus to let me order her a wig."

"Maybe you'll get lucky and the spring musical will be *Tangled*." Dom laughs. "Except I bet she wouldn't even let you get wigs for that after *Midsummer*."

Shannon laughs too. Ms. Marcus declared an official ban on wigs freshman year after the crew had to spend three hours untangling fairy hair from the bedazzled headdresses the parent committee donated in the last week of *Midsummer* rehearsals.

"Hey, has anyone noticed Malik's looking particularly luscious in his doublet this evening?" Estaban sounds extremely chipper, even though he really ought to be focused on polishing Liam's sword. He's only two scenes away from stabbing Tybalt. "And, sub-question, does anyone know if there's an update on the heterosexuality situation over there?"

I fight again to keep from laughing—objectifying cast members *during* a performance is definitely unprofessional—but no one else bothers.

Will hears the chorus of giggles and catches my eye, slashing a hand across his throat. I nod again, and I'm about to tell the others to cut it out when I hear the crash.

The sound is loud in the ear that's attached to my headset, but I didn't hear anything from the house. A couple of people in the front rows of the audience jumped, though, so they must've heard it too.

"Is everything secure backstage?" I sit up straight in my seat, trying to place the sound and follow along with the script at the same time. It could've been a backdrop coming down from the rigging, but I can't be sure. "Gabby, can you find out what that noise was?"

"Thank you, finding out . . ." Gabby's trotting footsteps echo through the headset.

"It was the curse!" Estaban stage-whispers.

Dom and I trade eye rolls. I don't even bother looking back at Will.

"It wasn't," I say, genuinely calm this time. "It can't be— we've followed every rule. It was probably the flat from Act One coming loose."

More shuffling footsteps echo over the headset before Gabby answers. "Yep, Mel's right. It was the flat."

"All right," I say. "Gabby, can you put Michael and Caroline in charge of fixing it, and Bryce, can you guide them through what they need to do?"

"Definitely," Bryce says from her perch by the fly system backstage. "Sorry, Mel. I don't know what happened. It worked fine during tech."

"I told you, it's the cuuuuuuurrrse!" Estaban says again.

Fatima giggles. "It'll wreak its vengeance by yanking down all our scenery!"

"I thought it already wreaked its vengeance when the computer ate half my sound files during midterms." Dom drums his fingers on his chin and winks at me. "Are we *positive* no one said the real name of the Scottish Play in that production meeting when we kept talking about getting fries at *Mc*Donald's?"

"It's fine, everyone." I glare at Dom again. We don't have time for jokes, or curses either. Not with the fastest light cues in the show only a few lines away. "Just please make sure Michael and Caroline get it cleared out so it's not a trip hazard."

"Maybe the curse only hit us *mildly* this time," Fatima offers. "It could be saving up the real goods for the musical."

"Ooh, don't even go there," Bryce says.

"I wouldn't call it *mild*," Jasmin adds. "I was within inches of a concussion when I fell off that ladder last week."

"You mean when you fell on *me*," Gabby says. "*I* came within inches of breaking both wrists."

"Only because you were standing right—"

"Quiet, please," I say, and the giggling cuts off immediately. The crew knows I don't say *quiet* without good reason. "Stand by, lights fifty-three to sixty-four."

There's no point in me calling each individual light cue out loud, since I'm the one running them anyway, but I need the crew to be in standby so I can concentrate. I press the button for the first cue in the series, and the light goes out over the chorus side of the stage just as a new one comes on above the scaffold.

"*Juuuuuu-liet!*" Beth sings from offstage. The audience laughs. Beth's always funny, even when she's hiding in the wing. I stay away from actors as a general rule—us crew types prefer to stick together—but there's no denying some of them are good at what they do.

I hover my finger over the button for the next cue. Two lines from now, Christina's going to exit and I'll need to make sure the audience can see the Greek chorus judging her and Liam even more harshly than they already were. And another round of ominous non-band music needs to play, to emphasize it even more. "Stand by, sound O."

Dom dutifully holds his finger over the button as Christina steps into the wing.

"Sound, *go.*"

Dom hits his key and I press my button at exactly the same time. The lights and the sound come on at once, and the mood onstage shifts exactly like it's supposed to.

Dom holds out his hand without looking up, and we high five with silent smiles.

Liam has a short speech while he's waiting for Christina to come back on, so I get ready for the next light cue. I can't see Christina from here, but I've been backstage enough in rehearsals that I can easily picture her anxiously tugging on her hair.

I've never understood it. Why would anyone *want* to go out there in front of everyone? Why put yourself through that when you could be back here with us, making the *real* magic happen?

Don't get me wrong. I love theater more than life itself. I just don't get why you'd choose to stand in a spotlight saying the same words over and over with everyone you've ever known watching and gleefully hoping to catch a mistake. Sure, people will clap for you in the curtain call, but I've been to enough shows to know that audiences will clap for *anyone* who runs out and bows.

It's like they all think they're going to be the Next Big Thing. Sure, our performing arts department is the real deal—some of our shows have won awards, and there's even a senior at our school, Odile Rose, who's already semi-famous. She got to skip school for a month and fly off to Iceland to film a three-episode arc on the *Game of Thrones* prequel.

But it's not like that's going to happen for *everyone*. The high point of most of my classmates' acting careers will consist of trying and failing to make Shakespearean dialogue sound natural right here in the BHS auditorium.

Up in the booth, though, no one's looking at us. We have the best seats in the house—at the back, far above the stage, where we can see the movements of every actor, every prop, and every piece of scenery. We can open our wide glass window when we need to hear the sound clearly and close it when we want people to stop bothering us. We've got our own secret stash of junk food and soda, and there's a row of beanbag chairs for when we have to crash after twelve-hour tech days. If it weren't for us running the lights and sound and sets—not to mention the dozens of crew people who built the awesome plywood castle set everybody's standing on, sewed Beth into her floppy white headpiece, and shouted lines to Liam every time he forgot them in rehearsal—no one in the audience would understand any of this witty Elizabethan banter.

"*I do beseech thee . . .*" Christina says, and I sit forward to listen. Beth's about to interrupt her mid-sentence, which makes cues like this especially tricky for me. The light needs to change at the exact moment Beth comes in. If I get it right, people will laugh. If I screw up, there'll be awkward silence.

I press the button, and the light shifts just as Beth singsongs her line. "*Maaaaa-dam!*"

The audience laughs. So far, so good.

But I'm coming up on a bunch of other short, quick cues, all in a row. Christina and Liam are done with their speeches and they're going back and forth now, almost like normal dialogue. Meanwhile, the Greek chorus is eyeballing them ever more viciously.

My next cue comes on a joke, but it's, you know, a Shakespeare joke, so once again we kind of have to tell the audience it's funny. I flex my finger and lean in to hang on Liam's every word.

"Mel?" Rachel's voice from backstage is sudden and sharp in my ear.

That's weird. We're still in standby for all the light cues. Rachel's mic should be on mute.

For her to get my attention right now, there must be a serious emergency. But what? Gabby's right near the wardrobe area. If there was an emergency with a costume, Rachel should've quietly gotten her attention, not called out to me. "What is it, Rachel?"

There's a sharp tap on my shoulder. "Ms. McIntyre!"

It's Will—uh, Mr. Green—gesturing frantically at the light board. Crap, I nearly missed the cue.

I press the button, half a second too late. A few people laugh half-heartedly as the far side of the stage lights up. Behind us, the house manager steps into the booth and whispers something in Will's ear.

Well, the show must go on. It'll be a little while before the next cue, so at least I can find out what's happening with the costumes.

Dealing with clothes is my least favorite part of theater, after actors. Come to think of it, costumes and actors have a lot in common. They both take up a lot of space, and they both give us constant headaches.

"Okay, your turn, Rachel," I say.

"Oh, so I get a *turn*." There's sarcasm in her voice, which is weird. She doesn't sound at all worried about whatever emergency is happening. "Thanks for allowing me to *speak*."

Dom shoots me a confused look across the sound board. I shrug, trying to push past my worry. I still have to follow along with the script, but I try to listen to the headset at the same time. "What's wrong?"

"A lot of things are wrong." Her words come out clipped. Abrupt. "Which you'd know if you'd ever talk to me when we *aren't* in the middle of a show."

What?

My eyes zoom across the stage to what little I can see of the wings. Beth's feet are visible under the curtain where she's hiding to call out her offstage lines, but there's no sign of Rachel.

That's when I remember—she texted me right before the show. I forgot all about it the instant the curtain went up, but the memory's surging back now. The way her texts kept popping up on my screen, one after another.

I didn't have time to open them then. We were already two minutes late for places by the time I even saw them on my phone.

Dread pools in my stomach, and with it, a new certainty:

This is the disaster I've been waiting for.

I look over my shoulder for Will, but he's stepped out of the booth with the house manager. His headset is down around his neck, and they're both gesturing to the lobby. A moment later they're moving down the hall, leaving the booth door open behind them.

"*Maaaaaa-dam!*" Beth calls out. The audience laughs again.

"Rachel, let's talk after curtain call." I try to sound as smooth and professional as always, but there's a tiny tremor in my voice. I pray the others can't hear it.

"No, let's talk now. It's the one time I can count on you to pay attention."

Footsteps sound behind us. I turn around, ready to beg Will for help, but it's not him.

It's Rachel.

She switches off her mic and steps into the booth. Dom's eyes widen and he whips around to face the stage, probably trying to turn himself invisible.

It's not as if either of us can leave. The next light cue is seconds away, and there are more sound cues not long after. Besides, an SM can never abandon the booth during a show, not without an earthquake, zombie apocalypse, or equivalent disaster.

But Rachel doesn't even seem to register Dom's presence. She's staring straight at me, panting. She must've run here from backstage.

She's wearing show blacks like the rest of us—a nondescript black long-sleeved shirt, black leggings, and black sneakers, designed for going unnoticed by the audience in case she needs to step onstage—but unlike most of us on the crew, whose primary goal is to disappear into the background, Rachel always looks stunning. She has piercing blue eyes and long black hair that she wears in a thick braid during shows. It's currently coiled forward over her shoulder, the tail hovering above her crossed arms like a snake ready to pounce.

Next to her, I look completely inadequate. My skin is white bordering on pasty thanks to spending the past week effectively locked in a windowless tech booth, and my rumpled show blacks are spattered with crumbs from my potato-chip dinner. Not to mention the dark circles under my eyes, the complete lack of makeup, and the messily-pulled-back, not-recently-washed frizz of hair that's my standard look during performance weekends.

"You're supposed to be backstage," I tell Rachel, keenly aware that our friends can hear every word I'm saying. SMs aren't supposed to switch off their mics during shows.

Should I break that rule now that this—whatever *this* is—is happening?

"Costumes are fine. Liam's doublet is fixed." Rachel stares down at me, and I slowly rise from my seat to face her. It feels like facing a guillotine. "Mel, we have to talk."

"This isn't the right—"

"It'll *never* be the right time. If I wait until after curtain call, you'll be consumed with your postshow to-do list, and then you'll be dead to the world for the rest of the night until you get up at the crack of dawn to come back here and start the whole thing all over again."

She's not wrong—show weeks are hell, everyone knows that—but I still don't understand what's going on.

Plus, the ear that's attached to my headset is registering a *lot* of coughs and cleared throats from the other crew members. Rachel switched off her own mic, but she's close enough that *my* headset is transmitting her voice loud and clear.

"Mel," Dom whispers.

I turn back just in time to hear Christina say, *"A thousand times, good night!"*

Shit.

I lunge down and press the button just in time.

When I turn around again, Rachel is drumming her fingers on her arm. "Are you ready to talk to me?"

Not really, I want to say. We're still in standby for the next batch of light cues.

But Rachel knows that. She knows this show backward and

forward, just like all of us. And she's standing here anyway, clearly expecting something from me.

Whatever it is, I should be able to give it to her. Stage managers are experts at multitasking. There's no reason I can't put on a perfect show and be a perfect girlfriend at the same time.

Right?

"*Mel!*" Dom whispers again, louder this time. Shit.

"Stand by, sound, um . . ." I look frantically down at my prompt script, but the words swim.

"P," Dom mutters, pressing the button before I've managed to say *go.* Another dog bark pipes out, louder than the last one.

"What's going on, Rachel?" I ask, frustration seeping into my Stage Manager Calm.

"Do you seriously not know?" She stares at me. "Or are you just acting innocent? Jesus, I don't even know which would be worse."

Oh, God. I must've really screwed up.

Dom's eyes are locked on the stage, his face impassive. The rest of the crew's got to be listening, too, but none of them are so much as breathing into their mics anymore.

"I've been trying to talk to you about Hannah since yesterday, but you keep ignoring me." Rachel shakes her head. "And you know what? It isn't even about her. It's about how you didn't listen to me. I *told* you I didn't want her there, and you called her anyway. Obviously, what *I* thought never really mattered."

"This is because I called *Hannah*? Don't be ridiculous, I did that to *help* you—"

"I told you *not* to, and you did it anyway. How was that helping?"

"Come on! You needed to get the costumes finished, and you did!"

"We could've gotten them finished without *her*. I told you that, but you didn't care. All you were thinking about was how much you love being in charge. Like always."

Someone on the headset sucks in a breath. I shut my eyes and try not to think about how many people just heard what Rachel said.

Yesterday was our invited dress rehearsal. A few of the costumes for the party scene needed last-minute fixes, and some of the girls in the cast wound up having to go on in their jeans while the costume crew sewed frantically backstage.

It was clear they needed more hands, so I called a few people who I knew could sew. One of whom happened to be Hannah, who happens to be my ex.

It wasn't a big deal. As SM, it's my job to make sure everything gets done. I wanted opening night to be as perfect as it could possibly be. We *all* wanted that.

And yeah, I knew Rachel didn't exactly love the idea, but it's not as if there was any risk of Hannah and me getting back together. She was on the costume crew freshman year, but now she's gotten super popular and started going out with some basketball player. Rachel had absolutely nothing to worry about, and I told her that.

Or at least . . . I *meant* to tell her that. Come to think of it . . . I was really busy practicing the light cues, so maybe I didn't actually . . .

Hmm.

"*I have forgot why I did call thee back.*" Christina giggles. Crap—I missed Liam's lines. I whirl around and press the button, and the light comes up over the Greek chorus so Alejandra and Malik and the others can look alternately amused and/or offended at Romeo and Juliet's preteen-level flirting.

The cue coming up next is the fastest in the whole show. I have to switch the light back again before Liam says his next line or the audience will lose track of what's going on. I hover my finger over the key.

"It's not like I'm *surprised*." Rachel drops into the empty chair next to mine. I don't dare meet her gaze, but I can see her in my peripheral vision, staring down at the stage vacantly. "People warned me. They said you'd rather be everybody's boss than somebody's girlfriend. I should've known there was a reason you go through exes so fast. Relationships with Melody McIntyre never make it for long."

Rachel pauses. It's dead silent. On the headset, and on the stage too.

Damn it! I missed the cue. I have to put the light back on Liam so the audience knows to pay attention, and—

I hit the button just as he finishes saying, "*Let me stand here till thou remember it.*"

Now the light's on him, but he's already done talking. There's supposed to be another pause in the dialogue while the Greek chorus reacts, but their side of the stage is totally dark.

None of the actors move—no one knows if they're supposed to—but a few laughs bubble up from the house. Even the audience has noticed that the cues aren't lining up.

Damn it! I hit the button again and the light shines on the chorus, their expressions looking slightly pained. I press it again as Christina takes a breath and starts her line. She's out of the moment now, though, and she garbles her words.

And—what the *hell* is Rachel talking about? I haven't gone out with *that* many people.

I try to catch Dom's eye. He's still looking straight ahead, like he's totally absorbed in the play, but there's a slight red tinge creeping in around the base of his neck.

"I . . ." I swallow. My hands are trembling as hard as my voice. "I don't know what you're talking about."

"Of course you do. What's embarrassing is, I told them they were wrong. Everyone was saying, you know, 'Oh, be careful with Mel, she's got somebody new every week,' but I told them things were different with you and me. Only now it's—"

"No one would've said that!" I'm not following along with the script at all anymore. "I haven't gone out with anyone all year except for you! And last year it was just, like, three people—or maybe, I don't know, unless you count prom, but—"

Now Dom's looking my way. He shakes his head slightly.

"*'Tis almost morning; I would have thee gone,*" Christina calls from the stage. There's another lightning-fast cue coming up. Another single-line delivery from Liam.

I get ready to press the button. I can't let Rachel take over my head.

But I can't just let this go, either.

"There's nothing between me and Hannah." I speak quietly, even though it's pointless. Our mics are designed to be sensitive. The crew can hear me, whether I'm whispering or shouting. "I've never cheated on anyone. I would *never*."

"It isn't about that. I told you what I wanted, and you didn't even bother to tell me you disagreed. You just overruled me, like you always do. Everything has to be your call, regardless of how anybody else feels. God, Mel, I didn't even know she was *coming* until she showed up and I stood there stammering like a complete fool."

"Look, I didn't mean to—"

"Did you know I had a crush on you all last spring during *Joseph*?" She's stumbling over her words now. "When you used to come sew after rehearsals, I kept trying to work up the nerve to tell you."

No. I hadn't known.

I'd been putting in time in the costume closet last spring because I needed to learn more about wardrobe if I wanted to get promoted to SM. I was strong on set design and construction, but my costume skills were sorely lacking, and a stage manager needs to be proficient in every department.

But that was when I started liking Rachel, too. She was

hilarious, and incredibly talented, and so much fun to hang out with. When we wound up at the same drama camp over the summer, it was easy to slip from flirting over sewing machines into sneaking kisses behind bolts of brocade.

"Mel?" Rachel twists to face me. I fight to keep my eyes on the stage. "Are you even listening?"

Christina finishes her line, and I press the cue for the light to shine on Liam. He just has to deliver a few words, and then I'll wait a fraction of a second so the audience can feel the full weight of them—it's another one of those cues where the timing has to be precisely right, or else the meaning of the moment won't come through—and then . . .

"Well, you don't seem to care what I'm saying, so whatever." Rachel's talking fast now. She almost sounds like she's choking. "I guess this is it."

My finger falters. Did Liam finish his line?

I hit the button, too hard, and it clicks twice. The lights flash onto the chorus side of the stage, then back to Liam and Christina again before anyone's had time to say anything.

More laughs from the audience.

"*Damn* it!" I say, not even caring who hears as I slam the button down again.

Too late, I realize I shouldn't have done that. The light board is programmed. Every cue in the show is in the system, in order. It's supposed to be easy—all I have to do is hit the button when the cue is supposed to go up and the lights will come on, like clockwork.

But now the board is two cues ahead of where it's supposed to be. Or is it three?

Oh, *God*.

Onstage, the actors are trying to keep the scene going, but I've completely lost track of what's happening. The worst possible thing that can happen to a stage manager.

The lights are all wrong. The audience won't have a clue what they're supposed to be looking at.

Ms. Marcus will demote me for sure. I won't get to SM the spring musical. I'll be lucky if she even lets me on the run crew.

"So I guess we're broken up now." Rachel's voice is thick and heavy as she rises from the seat beside me. "That's what you wanted anyway, right? You've probably already got your next hookup planned. Have fun hanging all over whoever it is at the cast party. I just hope they know they're disposable."

No, this isn't what I *wanted*! And—*disposable?*

Oh my *God*.

I've had bad breakups before. Isabelle dumped me in the middle of the dance floor at homecoming freshman year. Jess and I shouted at each other over video chat so loudly the night before the *Steel Magnolias* opening that my dads came running into the room thinking I was being murdered. Tyler and I got in a huge fight when we were painting scenery for the winter showcase and spent the next week getting side-eyed by the rest of the set crew every time we got within thirty feet of each other.

But nothing like *this* has ever happened. No one's ever made me feel so . . . small.

"You know what? Screw you, Rachel." The sound of Gabby's voice shocks me out of my stupor. She sounds shaky, too—but even more than that, she sounds pissed.

Rachel's already halfway toward the booth door, but she freezes. Even with her headset down around her neck, she can hear Gabby too.

"Sorry, Mel," Gabby's saying in a rush. "I know we aren't supposed to talk during standby, but it doesn't matter what happened between you and her—she can't pull this crap in the middle of a show. Shut up and go away, Rachel, you're messing things up for everybody. Mel, the actors kept going, so just hit G-O and let's see where we are."

My reflexes kick in and I hit the button automatically—and somehow, it works. The lights go up exactly where they're supposed to, and in exactly the right moment.

I turn around. Rachel's gone.

"Breathe, Mel." Dom leans in and looks at the monitor. "You're on LQ sixty-two, and sixty-three is on the next line. We're all good. Breathe."

I nod and exhale, slow and steady.

The rest of the show flows normally. I get the next cue right, and the one after that, too. Will comes back into the booth, whatever crisis was happening in the lobby having apparently been resolved. As far as I can tell he doesn't know about what happened earlier, but he'll find out soon enough. There's no such thing as keeping secrets from the technical director.

The actors run through their lines, and they flub a few words here and there, but I'm the only one who notices. Liam's doublet stays intact, Malik and Julio get stabbed to death, Liam and Christina make out and kill themselves, and finally it's curtain call. We get a standing ovation, and everyone on the stage and on the headsets is crying because they're happy, and I'm just crying because I'm crying.

I screwed up. I screwed up *everything*. The show, Rachel . . .

And all my friends witnessed my complete failure.

I put the house lights up, and Dom shuts his laptop. He keeps giving me sympathetic looks, silently gesturing for me to come with him to meet the others backstage, but I can't deal with sympathy. I don't deserve it. I wave him on without me.

Alone in the booth, I pull off my headset, yank my hair loose from its messy ponytail, and shut my eyes.

Our theater's cursed. That's the rumor, anyway. Strange things have been happening here for years. *Unexplainable* things.

I've never been sure I *really* believed it. I enforce the rules that are supposed to keep us safe, of course—but that's my job. I'm the stage manager, and this is my theater. Here, I'm the one in control.

After tonight, though, I can't help wondering if I've got that right. Maybe there's more going on here than I realized.

Maybe I'm *not* the only one in control.

Beaconville Theater History

Stored on BHS performing arts department shared drive

Created by: Billy Yang, stage manager, class of 2007

Viewable to: All cast, crew, and directors

Editable by: Current SM ONLY

Inferno Horror

Hundreds Injured in Beaconville Theater Fire

Beaconville, Apr. 13, 1906—The Beaconville Theater was the scene of a terrible fire Friday evening. Police confirmed that over two hundred were injured. Fire escapes were not in position at the building, according to police, and most victims were trapped inside when the staircases became jammed.

The fire began during a performance of Shakespeare's *Macbeth*. The leading lady had just begun to perform a scene at stage left when audience members noticed her staring into a corner of the curtain above the stage. Moments later, the blaze became apparent to the audience, and the actress turned to the crowd and called out, "Ladies and gentlemen, please stay calm."

She lifted her arms as though to say more, but before the crowd heard anything further, a piece of burning wood fell from above and knocked her to the ground.

The theater burned to the ground overnight, leaving nothing behind but ashes.

—Screenshot from the Library of Congress website. Article originally appeared in the *Beaconville Journal*

Scene 2—Stage, Beaconville High School Theater

DAYS UNTIL SPRING MUSICAL OPENS: 164

"It was the curse." From her perch up on the step ladder, Jasmin aims the power drill at the top of the scaffold and unscrews the beam in three easy, practiced motions, passing it down to where Dom's waiting below. "It's the only explanation."

"I don't know how you can be so sure." Dom stacks the beam gently on the wheeled dolly. We need to save this wood for a future show. Hopefully the spring musical, if the teachers picked one that'll give us an excuse to build something cool. "I don't know how much time you've spent on YouTube, but things go wrong in theater a *lot*. One school did *West Side Story* and forgot the gun for the finale. Chino had to throw a shoe at Tony."

"Things go wrong here more than they do anywhere else. *Something's* up, and it could ruin the musical." Fatima carefully wraps a light cable around the fixture on the pipe, then holds out her wrench so Gabby can loosen the C-clamp. The two of them are sitting on the edge of the stage striking the electrics on the pipe we flew in from overhead. It's the first time Gabby's gotten to work with actual tools, and she's grinning like the true theater dork she's turned out to be.

Gabby's a freshman, and back in September, she thought she wanted to be an actor. She auditioned for *Romeo and Juliet* but didn't get a speaking part, and when Ms. Marcus saw how disappointed she was, she suggested Gabby come on as my assistant stage manager instead. She turned out to be fantastic at it—she's super organized and responsible, and she's up for anything, from sweeping the stage to calming Malik down when he freaks out and forgets half the Queen Mab speech. We've all been trying to teach her stuff, the way the older crew members taught us when we were freshmen, and today Fatima volunteered to do the lights with her, since that's a pretty easy job for a newbie.

The whole cast and crew are required to help on strike day, but we give the cast a call time that's thirty minutes later than ours so we can do all the fun power-tool stuff without them getting in the way. Then we give the actors easy, boring jobs, like folding costumes and counting props.

"Are we positive the musical's not *Phantom*?" Dom asks as Jasmin hands him another beam.

"We are." I wheel in a new dolly from the wings. The one Dom's loading is almost full. "Whoever at the district office was in charge of getting the performance rights failed utterly, so my money's on *Into the Woods* or *Sweeney Todd*. Ms. Marcus is obsessed with Sondheim."

"Who isn't?" Gabby grins up at me.

"Hey." Fatima elbows her, gently but firmly. "Focus. Lights."

"Sorry." Gabby turns hurriedly back to her C-clamp.

"Where's Ms. Marcus now?" Jasmin asks as she unscrews the last beam.

"In the shop with Mr. Green. She said they'd be back once the cast gets here so they can announce the musical to all of us at once."

"Perfect." Jasmin passes the beam to Dom and dusts off her hands. "Because, Mel . . . there's something we need to talk about first."

A weird silence falls on the stage. The rest of the crew is still wrapping cords and unscrewing furniture and sorting scraps, but no one reacts to what Jasmin said. I'm the only one who even seems surprised she said it.

Uh-oh. That's . . . not a good sign. I raise a quizzical eyebrow, but Jasmin holds my gaze without giving anything away.

This doesn't make sense. Jasmin's my closest friend, after Dom, and we tell each other everything. We sign up to work as partners on every class project, so she spends a lot of time at my house, and she eats dinner with us so often my dads always joke about putting out a plate for her even when she *isn't* there, just in case.

It's extremely unlike her to talk to the others behind my back.

"Um." I force a laugh. "This sounds ominous."

"Yeah . . ." Dom scratches the back of his neck, his eyebrow quirking under his scruffy dirty-blond hair. "Pretty sure you're only supposed to say *we need to talk* if you're breaking up with someone, Jazz."

But his laugh sounds just as forced as mine, and I strongly suspect he already knows what Jasmin's going to say. The others, too.

The crew's been talking about me. That much is clear. This is either an intervention or a mutiny.

Stage Manager Calm. Stage Manager Calm.

"It's about the superstition for the spring musical." Jasmin climbs down from the ladder and reaches into the wing for her messenger bag.

"Oh, okay." I sigh in relief.

We usually pick the superstition for the next show during strike on the show before it. During *Joseph* strike, we realized nine different people had gotten hit by swinging doors in rehearsals, resulting in at least two near-collisions and one emergency orthodontist appointment, so for *R&J*, the rule was that everyone on the cast and crew had to knock twice before they could come into the auditorium. It seemed simple enough, until Dad begged me to give him earplugs for the days he came in to help with set construction because all that knocking made his teeth hurt. Dad's sensitive, auditorily.

Jasmin pulls out her phone, taps the screen a few times, and passes it to me. "We've done some analysis, and we have a proposal."

I take the phone, trying to keep a relaxed smile on my face. Jasmin's pulled up a note titled "Things That Went Wrong on *R&J*." I scroll down the list, but it's nothing I don't already know— Liam's doublet tore, a backdrop fell even though it should've been secure in the fly system, a sword kept breaking, the bottle of fake poison kept spilling even though Estaban triple-checked every night that it was sealed, Beth got scarlet fever even though we'd all thought that had been eradicated in the nineteenth century and barely recovered in time for tech, et cetera, et cetera, et cetera. And, of course, the lights went screwy during the balcony scene on opening night.

I turn my hands down on my knees so my friends won't notice that reading that last bullet made my palms break out in sweat. I've been trying not to think about what happened with Rachel, but it's been impossible. We both had to show up at the theater for every performance after opening. She's here today, too, but she's back in the costume room, sorting clothes and probably thinking about what a horrible person I am.

I can't remember how long the despair lasted after my last breakup. It's all a blur, and I guess it doesn't matter anyway. The only thing I know for sure is that *this* breakup is significantly worse.

The whole time Rachel and I were going out, I honestly thought I was doing everything *right*. Until she walked into the booth, held up a metaphorical mirror, and showed me, for the first time in my life, what I'm *really* like.

Selfish. Bossy. Inconsiderate. . . .

"Thanks, this is really helpful." I nod toward Jasmin's phone, trying my hardest to act unfazed. "When you put it all in a list like that, you can see what a miracle it is we made it to strike without anyone dying. Ha. Send the list to me and I'll put it on the shared drive, okay?"

"That isn't all." Jasmin sits down next to me on the stage. Fatima, Estaban, and Bryce glance at each other and come over quietly to sit beside her.

It's obvious they planned this. The four of them are crew heads, just one tier down from me in the tech hierarchy. They have a lot of power, and the team is used to listening to them.

Dom and Shannon are still hanging back, though, and since they're *also* crew heads, that's comforting.

"We thought back over the last couple of years, and we noticed a correlation." Estaban points at Jasmin's phone. "More things tend to go wrong on shows when, uh . . ."

"When you're not single," Jasmin finishes for him, still looking right at me.

I wait to see if this is a joke, but no one laughs. Not even Dom.

Jasmin starts ticking things off on her fingers. "All the worst things that've happened have been when you were in a relationship, Mel. Like when that red dye bled into all the white costumes in the laundry during *Joseph*, and the time half the *Fiddler* cast got mono—"

"It wasn't half the cast, it was, like, three people!" I gape at her, but she still isn't laughing. "And—what are you *saying*, exactly? That I screw up more when I'm dating someone?"

"It's not about you screwing up." Jasmin shakes her head. "Everybody screws up. Besides, a lot of the bad stuff didn't have anything to do with you, not directly. Which means it's got to be the curse."

"Wait." I gaze back and forth between the four of them. They're all nodding. "You think the theater curse is triggered by me *dating* someone?"

"We just think it's a possibility." Fatima holds out her hands palms up. She's still holding the wrench. "It's a theory worth testing. Especially with the musical coming up."

"It's a theory that makes *no sense* at all." Dom finally comes over to join the rest of us, sitting down on the stage and sighing. At least *someone's* speaking up for me. "We already start a new superstition for every show, and we've *been* following them. Ever since she got named SM, Mel's made everyone who broke a rule do a countercurse within seconds and things *still* go wrong."

"So this should be the new superstition for the musical, then. If it doesn't work, it'll prove we were wrong." Jasmin shrugs. She sounds so reasonable I can barely think of a way to argue. "If Mel stays single until the cast party and the show still has a million problems, we'll know it doesn't matter if she's with someone or not. But if it *works* . . ."

"Then what, we force our stage manager to take a vow of chastity until she graduates?" Dom shakes his head. "How would *you* like to live under that rule?"

"*We're* not the ones whose relationship drama messed up a performance." Jasmin glances over at Gabby, as if she's looking for backup. Gabby turns to me, her lips pressed together uncertainly.

"Okay, but Mel is, like, this school's patron saint of serial monogamy." Dom holds out his hands and ignores the other crew members' chuckles, even though it's clear from the way he's smirking that he's proud of that witticism. Though I'm not sure how *I* feel about that title. "She *likes* going out with people. Which, let's be honest, is true for most of us. This doesn't seem fair."

"Well," I start in, "it's not like I *have* to be dating someone in order to survive."

Jasmin gives me a pleading look, the beads in her box braids clicking together as she shakes her head. "I know. Mel, I'm sorry, it's really nothing personal. It's just—the musical could be a disaster if we don't take drastic measures."

I nod. I get it. I know Jasmin well enough to know she wouldn't do this if she didn't think it was important.

"We agonized about whether to even bring this up." Fatima sits forward anxiously, laying her hand on my forearm.

They're sincere, that much is evident. They really *do* think my love life has been screwing us over.

I don't know . . . maybe they're right. My relationships during shows have a definite tendency toward drama. This is the first time I've broken up with someone during an actual *performance*, but it was bound to happen sooner or later.

Besides, after what happened with Rachel, I'm willing to try anything. And it's not as if I *want* to date anyone—I'm broken-hearted. Plus, if our theater really *is* cursed, maybe this will solve it. Who knows?

I'd do anything to make the spring musical go perfectly. It's my junior year, the time when colleges pay the most attention to your extracurricular record, and pulling off a stellar musical would be huge for me. For the rest of the crew, too.

"Wait a second." Gabby raises her hand. "I don't get how this works. Is it just that Mel's not allowed to date anyone? What if she only hooks up with somebody one time? How particular is this rule, exactly?"

Estaban laughs, and some of the freshmen and sophomores do, too, but I can't help smiling at Gabby's thoroughness. It's exactly the kind of question a good stage manager *should* ask.

"Valid point," I say. "Are we playing by Disney rules here? Is a kiss enough to activate the curse?"

"Only if it's the kiss of *true love*." Shannon makes her voice high-pitched and squeaky from center stage, where she's unscrewing the legs from a prop chair. "Is that from *Snow White* or *Sleeping Beauty*?"

"*Shrek*, actually, I think." I smile at her, and the others laugh. "But yeah, it would probably have to be something more intense to get a curse's attention."

"Something like falling in love." Jasmin nods. "That seems logical. You can flirt with people or whatever, but no getting in deep."

"Until the musical closes," Fatima adds. "So for now, just, you know . . ."

"Keep it in your pants?" Estaban suggests, and everyone laughs again.

"No problem." I smile. If I act like I'm entertained by this whole thing, maybe it'll start to seem funny. Maybe I'll forget that I *was* deeply in love until three days ago. "Once the musical starts, I won't have time for love anyway."

"Give yourself a little more credit, Mel." Shannon laughs. "You fall in love more easily than anyone I've ever met."

"Ha," I say, because the others are laughing.

But . . . is that true?

I shrug it off. It doesn't matter now. Besides, the others are starting to nod along. Even the junior crew members who'd been quiet until now.

I guess that means they all believe it, and once the whole crew believes something, it has to be true, or the glue that holds us together as a team will fall apart.

All right. So be it. If I fall in love, the musical's doomed.

"Mel?" Jasmin points to the phone sticking out of my pocket. "Will you put the new superstition on the shared drive?"

I nod, slowly. "Yeah. As soon as Ms. Marcus announces what the musical is. But, um . . . I'd just as soon not tell the actors, if that's okay."

Everyone nods immediately.

"Hell, no," Jasmin says. "The last thing we need is them getting another excuse to think every problem is the crew's fault. We'll come up with a decoy superstition for them."

Dom raises an eyebrow. "Are you sure about this, Mel? You don't have to—"

I nod. A good leader is decisive, and a good leader listens to her team.

Besides, my heart is currently shattered in a million pieces. There's no way I could put it back together in time to fall in love before the musical opens.

Dom sighs, then glances at his watch. "Okay. Should we go clean out the booth while we're waiting for the cast?"

And not have all these eyes on me anymore? Heck yeah.

I stand up. "Let's go."

Beaconville Theater History

Stored on BHS performing arts department shared drive
Created by: Billy Yang, stage manager, class of 2007
Viewable to: All cast, crew, and directors
Editable by: Current SM ONLY

New Beaconville High School Performing Arts Wing to Open

Students at Beaconville High were thrilled on Wednesday when they were given their first opportunity to tour the new performing arts wing on their campus.

"This is awesome!" senior stage manager Billy Yang told the *News* reporter who joined their tour. "Look at that fly system! And the booth equipment is a thousand times better than what we've been using in the old auditorium. I can't wait to do our first show here!"

BHS is renowned for its theater program. Student productions have won statewide awards, and some of the program's alumni have gone on to careers in the performing arts, both as actors and in behind-the-scenes roles.

The new performing arts wing was made possible due to a budget enhancement and gifts from a large number of alumni. It includes a state-of-the-art, 1,200-person-capacity theater; a black box theater for more intimate performances, which will also double as classroom space for the performing arts department; a "scene shop" with tools for constructing sets and props; a dance studio; and a choir room.

Local historians have noted that the new performing arts wing stands directly on the grounds of the former Beaconville Theater, which was destroyed by a tragic fire in 1906 and later was found to have violated building codes. The land had been the property of the city of Beaconville and was vacant before being annexed by the adjacent high school last year.

"We don't see the location of the new performing arts wing as disrespectful in the least," school superintendent Evan Newton told the *News*. "In fact, we've set up a memorial to those injured in the 1906 fire. There's a plaque in the lobby of the new building's auditorium. It's very tasteful."

Students and faculty seem to feel the same way. In memory of the tragic fire, they've decided that their inaugural performance in the new auditorium will be the same play the Beaconville Theater company was performing that night—*Macbeth*.

—From the *Beaconville Neighborhood News*, January 3, 2007

Scene 3—Tech Booth, Beaconville High School Theater

DAYS UNTIL SPRING MUSICAL OPENS: 164

Dom and I climb the steps through the theater until we reach the wide, empty tech booth at the back.

The booth is my favorite place in the entire performing arts wing. Maybe the entire world. I'm effectively trapped in here from tech week through closing on every show we do, but that's okay. This is a sacred space.

Right now, though, all I want is to collapse into a sacred beanbag chair and crack open a sacred Diet Coke—but that's not an option during strike. We have too much to do. Besides, the actors are due soon, and if we're not on the stage when they get here, we might miss the announcement of what the musical's going to be. At this point, I honestly think I'd cry.

"You're really sure about this?" Dom asks, rooting around in the papers stacked on the desk. "You know, the whole *love curse* thing?"

I laugh. It sounds funny when he puts it that way. "I mean,

I'm not *sure* about anything, but it's obvious *they* are, and that's what superstitions are really about—team unity."

"Unity's great and all, but . . ."

"Besides, being single for a while sounds *amazing*." I reach up, fully intending to grab a bottle of spray cleaner from the shelf, but I find myself tipping forward and collapsing into a beanbag instead. "It's not like anybody'd want to go out with me after what Rachel said anyway."

I shut my eyes. I hadn't meant to say that last part.

"Mel." There's a crush of polystyrene to my left. I open my eyes to see Dom in the beanbag chair next to mine. "No one believes that stuff. I like Rachel, or at least I used to, but what she said that night? It was total crap. No one really thinks you're like that."

"Dom. You just called me the patron saint of serial monogamy."

"I was being ironic." He sighs. "Look, for what it's worth, I heard Rachel feels really bad about what happened. Estaban said she was crying in the costume closet when he went in to grab gaff tape."

"Great." I scrub my face with my hands. "It's just—why do all my relationships have to end in giant disasters? Epic scenes, my own crew rising up against me . . . what am I doing wrong?"

Dom stretches his arms over his head, chuckling. "Well, speaking from *personal* experience . . ."

I roll my eyes. "Please don't."

"I'm just saying, they don't *all* end that way. When we broke up during *Fiddler* rehearsals, it was really chill."

"I know, but A, that was ninth grade, and B, you were the exception, not the rule. Most of my breakups don't result in me getting a new best friend, they result in major suffering. Look . . ." I meet his eyes so he'll see I'm serious. "For real. I think there's something wrong with me."

"Yeah, there is. You got named SM and became an obsessive-yet-beloved dictator, exactly like every other SM before you."

"You're the worst best friend ever."

"Hey, I try. Also . . . okay, look, there's something I've got to tell you, and it isn't exactly going to change your perspective on that front, so . . ."

I sit up abruptly, which is hard to do in a beanbag. "Is it about this love curse thing?"

"Uh . . ." He shakes his head. "From your point of view, it's probably worse."

I look over my shoulder. "Is someone *else* coming in here to dump me?"

"There's just something I've been thinking lately." He scratches the back of his neck.

I honestly have no idea where Dom's going with this, but he's making me super nervous. "Spit it out."

"Well . . . when it comes time for the spring musical . . ." He turns to stare down at the patches on his jeans. His next words come in a rush. "IthinkIwannaaudition."

It takes me several seconds to decipher that. When I finally piece it together, I can only pray I heard it wrong. "*What?*"

He glances up, smiling sheepishly.

"Dom." I glare. He looks off to one side with a distinct combination of guilt and excitement on his face. The last time I saw him make that expression was right after he told me he was going to homecoming with my ex-girlfriend. "You want to be an *actor*?"

"I . . ."

"Tell me you're kidding."

"Um . . . I'm sorry, Mel. I—"

"We're crew! We don't *act*!"

He doesn't answer.

"I can't *believe* this!" Show after show, Dom and I have worked together, plotting the sound effects and analyzing the set designs. His presence in the booth next to me was the only thing holding me together during tech on *R&J* when everything kept breaking. Now all of a sudden he wants to go *on*stage? "Dominic Connor! That's a line we don't cross!"

"I think I . . . kind of want to cross it, though?" He shrugs, still with that wide, faux-apologetic grin. "If I can get a halfway decent part, it'll beef up my extracurriculars for college applications now that I'm not playing volleyball."

"Being a crew head looks *great* on applications!" I keep waiting for him to hear how ridiculous he sounds, but his goofy grin refuses to fade. "Besides, don't you *want* to do sound for the musical? There'll be so many voices to mix, plus the orchestra, and there will be effects too—it's going to be really hard, and you get to be in charge of all of it. Colleges will be super impressed."

"I don't know. . . ." He shrugs again. "Mr. Green said I might want to think about auditioning this time, and I thought I'd just . . . give it a try."

"*Will* told you to audition?" I cover my face with my hands and groan. What's happening to the world? "He's the *ultimate* crew guy! He wouldn't want you to join the dark side any more than I do!"

Dom laughs. "This is real life, not Jedi training."

"You know what I mean!"

"Come on, we know plenty of actors who are cool." Dom starts ticking them off on his hand. "Malik, and Alejandra, and Sebastian, and—"

"I'm not saying *all* actors suck, just the vast *majority*."

"Way to be dramatic." He laughs again.

"Anyway, it doesn't matter. *You* aren't one of them. You're a geek, like me. You know everything there is to know about sound technology."

"Plenty of actors are geeks. And I only learned to do sound so I could edit videos for the Badgers."

Dom started a band in middle school with Malik and two other guys called the Honey Badger Liberation League. Malik was the lead vocalist, and Dom played drums and did all the organizational stuff. I guess officially they're still together, but it's been months since they've practiced. They mostly did classic rock covers—Prince and R.E.M. and U2 and even older songs. Sometimes they played on teen band nights at the community center, but mostly they posted stuff on YouTube. They still have a small but very dedicated following of girls who post comments on all their videos with a lot of exclamation points and emojis.

"Well, there's nothing wrong with that," I tell him. From the determined set of Dom's lips, I'm starting to suspect I won't win this argument, but I'm not giving up that easily. "If you wanted, you could try a different department, like lights or sets."

"I already tried all the departments. You and Mr. Green made me, remember?"

"Oh. Right."

Dom had been a starter on the volleyball team when he broke his ankle halfway through the season freshman year. He was my lab partner in bio and I knew he was depressed about not being able to play anymore, so I recruited him to help paint sets for *Midsummer.* Not too long after that we started going out, and soon he was hanging around backstage often enough that Will asked him to help with lights, then sound. He helped some with costumes, too, and he wound up being the only guy on the hair and makeup crew for *Fiddler* that spring. He got really good at pinning on everyone's hats so they wouldn't fall during the bottle dance scene.

"Come on, being a crew head on a musical is what we've always wanted!" I lean forward earnestly. "You can't change sides on me like this!"

"Look, this doesn't have to be a big deal. I might not even get cast."

"You'll get cast." I probably shouldn't say that, since I'm supposed to be objective about auditions, but it's the truth. Dom's been singing backup to Malik in their band for years, plus he did church choir as a kid. He's no Jonathan Groff, but he can carry a tune. Ms. Marcus will probably put him in the featured ensemble and give him a funny part with a few solo lines.

He must sense that I'm on the verge of giving up, because Dom climbs to his feet, cheerfully humming "Those Canaan Days."

I smile a little in spite of myself. "*Joseph* was last year's show."

"They won't really make us learn all-new songs, though, will they?"

"Oh my God. Tell me you're not—"

"Relax. I'm kidding."

"*Oh Romeo, Romeo!*" The shout carries up all the way to the booth. It's Julio, doing an exaggerated trill on every word. "*Wherefore art thou Ro—*"

"Right here, baby!" someone else yells—it sounds like Andrew Hernandez—and then there's the unmistakable thump of bodies falling onto the stage. Without bothering to get up, I surmise that Andrew just jumped on Julio, pretended to kiss him, and knocked them both flat.

The actors have arrived.

"If someone gets a concussion during strike, do you still have to write an incident report?" Dom asks.

"I always have to write an incident report." I sigh and climb up after him, leaning down to peer through the window. Julio and Andrew are still lying in a pile at center stage, right in the middle of the circle of power tools the crew was using a few minutes earlier. Looks like no one's injured. Yet.

"I sense a techie watching us!" Andrew calls. "Or a vampire. I can never remember how to tell the difference!"

I raise my eyebrows at Dom. "Tell me again why you want to be one of *them?*"

"Hello, everyone!" Ms. Marcus calls from the wing. That's enough to make me forget all about the actors.

The musical! They're about to announce the *musical!*

Dom and I trade glances. Seconds later we're racing out of the booth and down the steps. He beats me—longer legs—and I'm panting when I reach the stage.

It's crammed full. The actors take up most of the space, as usual, and a thick cluster of them have gathered upstage right, already buzzing with excited whispers. The crew's hanging on the periphery, but a quick glance at their faces makes it obvious that my friends are even more excited than the cast.

Musicals are a *big deal* at our school. At least, for everyone who doesn't care about baseball season.

And even if I don't get to be SM again—even if I've got a stupid love curse hanging over my head—there's no denying it. I can't wait to get started.

A Brief History of BHS Theater Superstitions—Spring Musicals Edition
Stored on BHS performing arts department shared drive
Created by: Riley Feldmann, stage manager, class of 2008
Viewable to: All cast, crew, and directors
Editable by: Current SM ONLY

In the wake of last year's disastrous performance of the Scottish Play, the Beaconville High School stage manager is hereby responsible for tracking, and enforcing, all superstitions during the rehearsal and performance period for any and all shows, from auditions through strike. All offenses must be dealt with via immediate performance of a countercurse, also to be enforced by the SM.

Newly established superstitions must be added to the list below and preserved for posterity's sake.

Also see the related doc "A Brief History of BHS Theater Superstitions—Fall Plays Edition."

Show	Superstition
Cinderella (2008)	All cast members must walk out of the dressing room backward when returning from intermission (matinees excepted).
Shrek (2009)	Anyone caught kissing in the black box must shout "Sorry for the PDA!" up to the rafters.[1]

Little Shop of Horrors (2010)	DO NOT TOUCH THE PUPPET AFTER DARK WE REALLY THINK IT MIGHT TRY TO EAT YOU THIS IS NOT A JOKE.
West Side Story (2011)	Immediately before the house doors open on each performance night, Colleen McCormick (ASM) must stand center stage and shout "Buttheads!" as loudly as possible.
Beauty and the Beast (2012)	Bill Jusino (sound crew head) must say "pug snout" to the portrait of Abigail Adams in the hall before every rehearsal.[2]
Once Upon a Mattress (2013)	All male principals must chant in unison before each rehearsal, "I recognize the textual and sub-textual misogyny in this musical and I promise to always strive to do better in my life than these jackass characters." Members of the ensemble and crew, as well as non-males in any of the above groups, are welcome to join them.
A Funny Thing Happened on the Way to the Forum (2014)	The first actor to make the audience laugh in each performance is given an extra flower at the end of the show.[3]
The Little Mermaid (2015)	All run crew members must wear glitter eye shadow at all times. (This superstition is irrelevant of gender. Mermaids are WAY beyond the binary.)
Sunday in the Park with George (2016)	No one can say the word *forget* onstage or in the choir room unless reciting it as a line in the script (*forgot* is allowed, though).

Legally Blonde (2017)	All cast members with naturally blond hair must apologize to the SM during tech for said blondness.
Fiddler on the Roof (2018)	Aquafina bottles are banned from all backstage areas. (Other water brands are technically allowed but we advise taking this as an opportunity to switch to reusable bottles anyway. Climate change is real, people!)
Joseph and the Amazing Technicolor Dreamcoat (2019)	Julio Ramirez (actor) isn't allowed to fist-bump anyone.[4]
Les Misérables (2020)	Melody McIntyre (SM) must not fall in love.

---

1 There was some debate as to whether this superstition was limited to kissing or whether holding hands, nuzzling, or other forms of PDA qualified. As a general rule, better safe than sorry.

2 Based on the number of problems we encountered on this show, we recommend considering in the future banning superstitions that are obviously derivative of Harry Potter; we suspect they may be less effective due to lack of originality. Any allegations that the problems were caused by Bill shirking his duties are malicious lies spread by actors. The SM can personally verify that Bill took his responsibility on this front very seriously and never missed a single "pug snout."

3 This superstition was cast only; the crew did not believe this worked, so we started a separate superstition of eating XXtra Flamin' Hot Cheetos in the booth every night, just in case.

4 It's a long story.

Scene 4—The McIntyre-Perez Living Room

DAYS UNTIL SPRING MUSICAL OPENS: 164

Oh my God. Oh my *God*.

My heart's racing so fast I can't stand still.

"Mel? Are you feeling all right?" Gabby hovers tentatively in the doorway. I gave her a ride back to my house since she lives in the next neighborhood over and her parents are both working late. We've done that a few times when we had a rehearsal run long. Her family just moved here and they're still paranoid about crime rates in the "big city," even though Beaconville is very much a suburb.

"I feel *fantastic*," I tell her just as Pops sticks his head in from the kitchen.

"She's home!" he calls around the corner. "And Gabby's here too!"

"Hi, Mr. Perez," Gabby says in her most polite voice. "Hi, Mr. McIntyre."

"Hello to you both!" Dad comes out of his office, brushing

off his jeans. He owns a contracting company and wears jeans every day, but he's weirdly fastidious about them. "Gabby, it's so nice to see you again. And please, call us Sean and Charlie. More importantly, congrats on the show, we saw it every night and—"

"Dad, Pops, you won't *believe* what the musical is." I'm still bouncing on my toes. "Guess. Come on, guess."

"Ooh, do you think it's *Rent*?" Pops asks Dad in a stage whisper.

"Mayyyybe," Dad stage-whispers back. "Remember how that used to be her favorite show?"

"Remember how she sang it in her crib during naptime?"

"She did?" Gabby smiles. "Which songs?"

"'Take Me or Leave Me,' mostly," Pops says. "She liked it because it has the word *baby* in it."

"I forgot about that." Dad snaps his fingers and catches Pops's eye. "She cried unless we played the soundtrack every night during dinner, remember?"

"No, you two." I glance at Gabby. "Please don't be cheesy right now."

But Pops is already snapping his fingers, too.

The next thing I know, they're singing. Dad takes Maureen's part and Pops takes Joanne's, and they're trying to outdo each other on the high notes.

My parents are *so embarrassing.*

To make things even worse, Gabby's laughing. She joins in when they get to the chorus, singing along, except she won't say *damn* (Gabby doesn't believe in cursing) so she changes it to *dang,* and now *I'm* laughing too, which just isn't fair. They shouldn't make me laugh at a time like this. I haven't even told them what the musical is yet!

"All right." Pops finally switches to normal speech. "We should probably stop torturing Mel or she'll never let us talk to her about those colleges."

"You could have also *never started torturing me in the first place*," I point out.

"Where's the fun in that?" Dad grins. "So, what's the musical?"

I geared up the video on my phone before I got out of the car so I'd be prepared for this moment. I clear my throat and, when both my parents are standing at attention, I hit play.

The music surges out. "*Dun DUN!!!! BAH-pah-bah!*"

They both recognize the opening notes to the overture right away and start to laugh. Gabby pretends to conduct the orchestra, sweeping her hands out dramatically with every note, and I seriously consider doing an interpretive dance but decide against it.

"*Les Mis!*" Dad grins. "Will must have finally given in."

"Or Ms. Marcus overruled him." Pops starts air drumming along as the music builds, clashing his pretend cymbals. My dads are the heads of the performing arts department parent committee, but they were already friends with Will before I was born. That's why I call him by his first name. He used to babysit me, and even now that he's been my teacher for two and a half years, it still feels wrong to call him "Mr. Green." He comes over and makes dinner for us all a few times a month, which is good because he's a much better cook than either of my dads.

"Ooh, you know who should play Éponine?" Dad says to Pops, totally ignoring the degree to which I'm about to burst into pieces from delight. We're only about to put on *the greatest musical of all time*, and I'm not getting over that thrill anytime soon. "Odile Rose."

"You think her schedule will allow it?" Pops raises his eyebrows. "One of the parents in the Facebook group said she might have to miss graduation if she gets that movie role."

"Oh, that's too bad," Dad says. "Especially after she already had to miss doing the fall play her senior year."

"Dad, Pops, please stop obsessing," I say, but they aren't even looking at me. "We didn't need her in *R&J*. Christina did fine."

Odile's schedule is so weird, the joke is that she just happens to go to school with us here in Massachusetts for part of the year. Her parents set up some kind of special arrangement with the district where she's allowed to miss school for weeks, sometimes months, at a time. And if the rumors that circulated during the last week of rehearsal are correct, she's also being considered for a role in a Martin Scorsese movie. It makes most of us on the crew roll our eyes, but the truth is Odile's going to walk every red carpet in Hollywood someday, and we all know it.

Up-and-coming teen ingenue Odile Rose is what the *Variety* article I read called her. As though everything about that phrase isn't a built-in cliché.

At school, though, Odile never says a word to anyone. She

stars in our shows whenever she happens to be in town, but it's obvious she thinks she's better than all us high school peons. She's a year ahead of me, so I've never really spent much time around her, but I've heard plenty of stories from the upperclassmen. Apparently she just sits in class every day, staring blankly at the whiteboard with her perfect hair and vacant eyes. In rehearsals last year, she said her lines when she was supposed to and spent every other minute sitting off in a corner with David Patel and Sebastian Santos, the best two actors in our school other than her. (They also happen to be the only two high school students she's ever deigned to interact with.)

"Do you remember her in that Super Bowl commercial?" Pops asks Dad. "She made me cry."

"You cry over *everything*," I remind him. "No offense."

"Ooh, I remember that," Gabby says, which is unfair, because this is the second time tonight she's taken *their* side. "She was incredible."

"See!" Pops points to Gabby in triumph. "Validation. Thank you. Gabby, I now officially like you better than my own daughter."

"Oh my God, Pops. *Seriously.*"

"Did you not see the ad, Mel?" Dad reaches for his phone. "Here, I'll pull it up."

"I've seen it." I edge away. I have no idea why everyone's so obsessed with Odile. Sure, she can sing and stuff, but I hate how everyone acts as though that makes her God's gift to the universe. I know performing's a skill, but the work *I* do is hard too, and no one ever fawns over the tech crew. "We don't need Odile. All she does is make the other actors nervous, and that's a nightmare for us to deal with. Besides, it's not like she's *that* much better than everybody else."

Dad and Pops exchange a look. Even Gabby casts me a doubtful glance.

"Anyway, I haven't told you the best part yet." I wait until they're all looking at me expectantly. "I get to be SM again!"

"Woo-*hoo*!" Pops shouts. Dad lets out a low whistle.

I beam up at them. I'm no less excited than I was when Ms. Marcus first told me the news. I've had wild, crazy fantasies about the day I'd get to stage manage *Les Mis*, but I thought it would be years from now.

My obsession with the show started in sixth grade, when I found the cast recording in a pile of Will's old CDs. Since then, I've read the original 1,500-page novel and seen every adaptation I could find. A couple of years ago, my dads took me to see the musical in New York as a surprise birthday present, and I thought my heart was going to explode from glee before the prologue even started.

Stage-managing this show will be the high point of my school theater career. I can already picture myself talking about it in *Backstage* interviews years from now—how I got my start calling the cues for one of the most complicated musicals known to theater before my seventeenth birthday.

"Congratulations, honey," Dad says. "I can't say I'm surprised, but you certainly deserve it after how hard you've worked."

"And Gabby said she'd be ASM again," I add, not wanting her to feel left out.

"You sure you want to do that?" Pops asks her. "If you thought our daughter was a fierce taskmaster on *R&J*, I can assure you she'll be even worse now that she's working on a show she actually likes."

"Don't worry, *Les Mis* is my favorite too," Gabby says. "I saw it on tour three times. I even dressed up as Enjolras for Halloween."

Pops grins. "I retract my concern. You're clearly very well suited to partner up on this."

"Plus, Will said we get to build a *turntable*." I wait for Dad to get excited about that part too, but his smile's fading. I don't know what his problem is. The original Broadway set for *Les Mis* was built on a turntable—a floor that spins, basically, for quick, dramatic set changes. It was so iconic they copied it for *Hamilton*. "And he's bringing in a professional sound mixer."

"We're incredibly excited for you, sweetie," Pops says.

"Although one of us isn't exactly looking forward to how much work installing that turntable's going to be." Dad juts his chin toward my phone, which is still playing the last few notes of the overture. "But I'll worry about that later. For now, you know what? I'm making that my new ringtone."

"What, you're just going to be walking around construction sites with *dun-DUN* blaring out of your pocket?" Pops asks, but Dad's already started the download.

"Why not? I'll tell anyone who asks that my daughter's

the stage manager for the world's most beloved musical, and I couldn't be more proud."

"Okay, well." My ears are probably turning red. "Gabby and I need to go upstairs and start working on the audition forms."

"Of course," Dad says. "Make sure you put at the top, 'And if your name is Odile Rose, don't bother auditioning, just name your part.'"

"Dad. Look. She'll probably be off in Antarctica filming another Oscar-winning role by the time we start rehearsals. Besides, Ms. Marcus said it's really important for me to go into the audition as a professional and not show favoritism to anyone, or—"

"Melody. Look. I'm being facetious."

"Good," I say, with a firm nod.

But as Gabby and I start up the stairs, I have a distinctly unprofessional thought:

That all our lives would be a lot simpler if, on audition day, Odile Rose is as far away from the Beaconville High performing arts wing as she can get.

ACT 1
February

Spring Musical Audition Form

The Beaconville High School Performing Arts Department is pleased to present *Les Misérables*. Auditions will be held Monday after school. If you'd like to audition, sign up at the bulletin board outside the choir room no later than noon Monday.

At the audition, you will be asked to sing sixteen bars of a song of your choosing. Please bring sheet music if you would like the pianist to accompany you. If you do not bring sheet music, you may perform a cappella.

Please complete the form below and return it to the stage manager, Melody McIntyre, when you are called in for your audition.

First name: _____ Last name: _____
Grade: _____ Email: _____
Phone: _____

Parents'/guardians' names: _____
Parents'/guardians' phones: _____
Parents'/guardians' emails: _____

Allergies: _____

Audition song: _____

Please list your current weekend and after-school activities:

	Monday	Tuesday	Wednesday	Thursday	Friday	Saturday	Sunday
Activity							
Times							

Please specify any conflicts (travel, major events, etc.) you will have this spring, particularly in April and May, when the rehearsal and performance schedules will be most demanding:

_____

_____

_____

_____

_____

The cast list will go up Wednesday afternoon. Break a leg!

Scene 1—Beaconville High School Choir Room

DAYS UNTIL SPRING MUSICAL OPENS: 87

"There are ninety-two names." I show Ms. Marcus the photo I took of the sign-up sheet. "Should I start sending them in?"

Ms. Qiao winces, but Ms. Marcus shakes her head, all business. "Let's give it another few minutes."

"How many times do you think we're about to hear 'On My Own'?" Ms. Qiao taps something into her phone.

I try not to snicker. "On My Own" is Éponine's big song in the second act of *Les Mis*, and anyone who's ever taken a musical theater class knows you're *never* supposed to audition with a song from the show you're hoping to get cast in.

Ms. Qiao's the choir teacher, so she's the *Les Mis* musical director. She's in charge of making sure everyone knows how to sing their songs. Ms. Marcus is the *director* director, so she's in charge of everything else.

Casting the show is up to the two of them. I'm only here to

show people in and out and keep things running more or less on time.

We're holding auditions in the choir room, which feels enormous with just the three of us surrounded by huge, empty risers. Will isn't coming today, since auditions aren't a tech thing, and none of my crew friends are around either. Only the stage manager is in this weird in-between place. I'm officially part of the crew, but I spend a ton of time with the actors, too.

Today was an early dismissal day, but even so it'll take us forever to get through everyone. I should probably text my dads. They get annoyed if I don't tell them when I'm going to be late for dinner.

But I don't mind the idea of auditions taking us late into the night. In fact, whatever the opposite of minding is, that's me right now.

I'm the only student who gets to be in the room for auditions. Ms. Marcus has already reminded me about twenty times that I have to keep everything I see and hear totally confidential, and that I have to be impartial, even when the auditioners are my friends. I promised I'd show her exactly how professional I can be.

"What's the gender breakdown, Mel?" Ms. Qiao asks. "Just roughly."

"I'd say about three girls for every boy."

Ms. Qiao and Ms. Marcus exchange a look, and I know what they're thinking: it's going to be really hard to find enough guys with decent singing voices to put on *Les Mis*.

This happens with every show we do, to some degree. There are always more talented girls than guys, and most shows have more male characters than female characters, because theater's always been pretty sexist. To get around that, our teachers usually wind up casting a lot of girls in male roles, but that's hard to do with *Les Mis*. It would be almost impossible for a girl to sing most of the principal male roles, except maybe Gavroche. The big solos are written for specific voice types.

The main characters are these two guys, Valjean and Javert. Javert is a police officer, and he's chasing Valjean because Valjean stole a loaf of bread. But it turns out Valjean's a good guy, and he starts helping out this poor woman named Fantine and her daughter. Then in the second half of the show there's this mini revolution, because it's France, and we meet a bunch of new characters like Marius and Éponine, and there are dramatic battles, so we'll get to build an awesome barricade set.

Mostly, though, people like *Les Mis* because of the singing. There's no dialogue in the whole show, just music, and the songs—the solos, obviously, but the big group numbers, too—are *gorgeous*. Which means you have to cast people who can sing beautifully all night long, or the whole show will fall apart. Valjean especially has to be excellent, since he has, like, eight big solos. But if a girl tried to sing them, she'd hurt her voice for sure.

The women's parts are a lot smaller. Fantine and Éponine are the only ones who really have a lot to do, and both of them die after just a few songs. The other big female character, Cosette, is kind of boring, and her part can only be sung by a soprano anyway.

As much as I love *Les Mis*, I know it's going to be hard to cast. But, well—that's why I'm not an actor. It's ridiculous that you're limited in which characters you can play based on the way your throat is shaped. As a crew member, I can learn any skill I want to, and if I work hard enough, I can do it well.

"Better give them a five-minute warning." Ms. Marcus sips her tea. I set the timer on my phone and stride out into the hall, my binder tucked under my arm.

"Five minutes to start, everybody!" I yell.

Dozens of nervous faces turn my way. Almost every actor in the school is here, and a lot of the choir people, too. The only ones missing are the actors like Liam, who know they can't sing and don't want to embarrass themselves trying.

I don't let myself make eye contact with any of them, even though I know almost everyone here. Everyone who does shows at our school knows each other, or knows *of* each other, at least a little bit. But today, it's my job to be impartial.

Which isn't easy when I spot Dom by the bathroom door. His face is so green I'm worried he's about to puke. I want to go tell him that he doesn't need to be so nervous—that it's going to be all right. Instead, I carefully lift my gaze to an empty spot on the wall over his head.

When he told our friends he was auditioning, they gave him crap about it for weeks, but none of them seemed as shocked at the news as I was. Jasmin even offered to help him practice. I asked her later if she felt betrayed, but she laughed and said she didn't see it that way—she saw it as getting a loyal spy who could tell us what the cast really talked about when we weren't around.

"And anyway, he'll come back to our side," she'd added while we waited in line for our cafeteria sweet potato fries. "Once he sees how much actors suck."

"Try to relax, everyone." The door at the end of the hall opens and Will steps through. "It's the school play, not the guillotine."

A few people laugh, including me, but everyone's hanging on his every word. Will has that vibe about him—he's very obviously an authority figure, but he's the kind of authority figure who everyone likes because he tells non-awkward jokes and has a gold-tipped frohawk. He's one of the only openly gay teachers at school, too.

"I'll be spending the rest of the afternoon hiding in the scene shop, but Ms. McIntyre, is there time for me to make a quick announcement first?" he asks. I nod, glad to be consulted. "Great. For those who don't know me, I teach the stagecraft classes, and I'm also the theater's technical director. And welcome, everyone, to auditions for our spring musical, *Les Misérables*."

Before he's even finished saying the title, Malik's already stomping his feet. Some of the other actors break out into whoops and cheers, too. I clap harder than any of them, then stop myself—is clapping unprofessional?

"This show will be expensive to put on." Will rubs his hands together, his eyes gleaming, and I already know what he's going to say next. "So, folks, that means it's bake sale time."

A few people groan, but most of us laugh. Will is notorious for his bake-sale obsession.

"Everyone on the cast and crew will need to take part." Will glances at me, and I nod and pat my binder. "Ms. McIntyre has the sign-up sheets. Does everyone know Ms. McIntyre, by the way?"

I blush and shake my head. Should have thought to introduce myself.

"Well, this is Melody McIntyre." Will strolls over to stand beside me. "She's the stage manager, which means everyone on the tech crew answers to her. The actors do too, especially if Ms. Marcus and Ms. Qiao aren't around. Mel's the person to talk to if you're interested in joining the crew, and she's also the person you should go to with any questions. Unless you need an excellent recipe for cherry soufflé, in which case, I'm your guy."

There's more laughter, and I can't stop myself from grinning. But just then my timer rings, so I duck back into the choir room.

"Are you ready?"

"Ready, Melody." Ms. Qiao slides gracefully onto the piano bench. "Send in the first sign-up."

I nod and step back into the hall. Will's already gone. I overheard him telling my dads you couldn't pay him enough to sit through *Les Mis* auditions, but that's probably because he's so old he's forgotten how to have fun.

"Hi, everybody." I raise my voice so they can all hear me. "We're going in the order you signed up, so look at the sheet and see where your name falls. Make sure you're in the hall when I call your name, because if you're not here, you forfeit your audition. Any questions?"

No one moves. No one even blinks. A freshman sitting across the hall looks like she's about to cry.

"And relax." I try to sound reassuring. I'm going to be working with this cast for the next three months, and it'll be a lot easier if they like me. "The teachers are really nice, and all you have to do is sing sixteen bars. Then you can chill out and eat Cocoa Puffs until the cast list goes up on Wednesday. Wicked easy, right?"

A few people laugh. The anxious freshman across from me cracks a tiny smile.

"Give me your audition form as you're going in. If you have sheet music, you can take it to Ms. Qiao at the piano when you get inside. Okay, last chance to ask questions."

No one says anything, and I realize I'm torturing them by talking so much. Crap. I flip over the sign-up sheet. "First up is Imani Miller."

A freshman—not the one across the hall who looked like she was about to cry, but another girl who looks like she's *also* about to cry—steps forward, her legs wobbling. I smile, take her form, and lower my voice.

"Good idea," I whisper. "Going first, you'll get it out of the way while everyone else is still stressing."

She smiles faintly and nods.

I open the door and lead her into the room. The teachers both smile warmly, and Ms. Marcus gives Imani a little wave.

"Break a leg," I whisper. Then I raise my voice, reading off her audition form. "This is Imani Miller, freshman, and she'll be singing—'On My Own.'"

The teachers' smiles stay as firm as ever as Imani wobbles over to the piano. She hands Ms. Qiao her sheet music, and the two of them talk quietly. Imani manages to compose her face as Ms. Qiao launches into the opening notes.

It's actually a really good audition. It's obvious Imani's been practicing. The teachers clap when she's done, and Imani smiles, as though she's finally allowing herself to breathe.

The auditions go faster than I expected after that. Sixteen bars of a song isn't very long, and most of the actors have come prepared. Three girls in the first half hour sing "On My Own," but they're all pretty good, and there are plenty of other songs in the mix, too. Even the girls who aren't great singers are clearly trying hard, and that counts for a lot.

The guys are more all over the map. Some of them don't even really sing, they just talk along to the music, which you absolutely can't get away with doing in *Les Mis*. Still, a few of them are solid. Julio Ramirez, who was Tybalt in *R&J*, sings "Gaston" from *Beauty and the Beast*, and he manages to both sing really well *and* be darkly funny at the same time. And David Patel, about whom I know nothing except that he's a good performer and he used to date Odile Rose, sings a song from *The Scarlet Pimpernel*. He has a strong stage presence from the moment he walks in the door, and his voice is incredibly deep and rich compared to every other guy we've heard.

Dom's up next, and I work hard to keep my face neutral as I take his form. I wouldn't let him tell me which song he was auditioning with, since I was afraid I'd accidentally give him some sort of hint about what the teachers were looking for. Though, come to think of it, I don't actually know what the teachers are looking for.

"This is Dominic Connor, junior." I keep my voice totally flat as I read. "He's singing 'Hotel California.'"

"Nice to see you stepping onto the other side of the fence, Dom." Ms. Marcus smiles. Dom tries to smile back, but his face has turned from green to white.

Once Ms. Qiao starts playing, though, he launches into the song with no hesitation. I expected him to sound fine, but actually, he's good. *Really* good. He's swaying a little because he's nervous, and his twisty facial expressions are a tiny bit much for the song, but he still sounds better than I've ever heard him. His voice is clear and full for the whole sixteen bars. He must've been practicing this song for weeks.

How did I not know he'd been working so hard on this? What else has been going on when I wasn't paying attention?

As I lead him out of the room, I catch the teachers trading a look. Ms. Marcus jots something down on Dom's audition form, then crosses it out and writes something else.

Could she be thinking about casting him as one of the *principals*? Dom isn't an obvious choice for *Les Mis*—he sang a rock song to audition for a musical from the 1980s, for one thing, plus he's kind of skinny and quirky for a powerful role like Valjean or Javert—but he's obviously willing to put in the effort, and we haven't seen that many other guys yet with strong voices.

The next few auditions pass quickly. Christina's pretty good, but she's better at acting than she is at singing. Her friend Leah goes next and she's a lot better. Malik's turn comes after that and he's good, *really* good, but he's still not *as* good as Sebastian Santos was when he used to star in all our musicals. Too bad he's off at Northwestern now, or we could bring him in as a ringer.

"Let's take a quick break," Ms. Marcus says after Andrew Hernandez finishes singing "The Music of the Night." "Three minutes?"

"Five minutes," Ms. Qiao says, standing up and flexing her fingers.

When I go out into the hall, Dom is already gone. The people still waiting sit up straight when they see me, but I wave apologetically. "At ease. The teachers are taking a break."

There's a chorus of groans, but all I can do is shrug and smile again as I turn toward the sign-up sheet. A tall girl is reaching for it with a pen in her hand, despite the giant sign that says ALL INTERESTED STUDENTS MUST SIGN UP BY NOON and the line I drew after the cutoff with NO MORE SIGN-UPS written under it.

"Hey." I tap her shoulder. "Auditions are closed."

"Oh, I'm terribly sorry." The girl steps back. I recognize her semi-British accent before I recognize her face, but when I do, I nearly trip over my own feet trying to put more space between us.

She looks different than the last time I saw her. But then, she always does, since her hair's usually got fresh dye for some new role or another. When she first came back from Iceland in December, it was standard Hollywood-issue blond, but when I spotted her walking through the cafeteria by herself a week ago, she'd gone auburn.

Today her hair's dark brown, with loose curls and messy tangles framing her face. Her white skin is lightly tanned even in February, her eyeliner's perfectly straight, her belted pink shirt-dress probably cost more than Pops's car, and somehow, she's prettier than I remember.

She glances at the pen in her hand and lowers it, giving me a sheepish smile. "I can see how this looks. I'd already put my name down, but I was curious about how many others had signed up after me. I like to audition toward the beginning if I can, because . . . oh, I suppose it doesn't matter, does it? I'm sorry to take up your time, I'm sure you're very busy."

I shake my head. I should be the one apologizing. Her name's been there all afternoon. *Odile Rose*, written in neat, curving blue ink, right under *Nicholas Underwood*.

I wonder what the brunette look is for. A *Vogue* spread? Some kind of celebrity Instagram challenge? Whatever it is, it's working for her.

I smile back at her. Then I remember that she's Odile Rose and we don't need her in this show in the first place, and I let my face go blank.

"Sorry, I saw that you signed up already." I shrug, doing my best to talk to her the same way I'd talk to any other actor. "My mistake."

"Oh, no, you're just doing your job." She meets my eyes, and, ugh, now I'm blushing. Blushing in front of actors almost definitely qualifies as unprofessional behavior. "Good SMs are always sticklers about the rules. Congratulations on the position, by the way. I knew Ms. Marcus would pick you after you did those incredible sets last year for *Joseph*."

My blush deepens. Actors don't usually notice things like who designed the sets, much less remember them a year later.

But even with Odile's rotating palette of hair colors, I'd always remember *her*.

I was still in eighth grade when she did her first musical at BHS, but my dads and I had been coming to see the shows here for years. I was doing middle school shows back then, and I remember how huge the high school stage looked. It's funny to think about now that I've moved scenery across it hundreds of times.

Odile was only a freshman then, but she'd been in *Annie* on Broadway the year before. Still, I didn't really get why everyone was *so* excited about the phenomenon that was Odile until that night when I watched her play Elle Woods in *Legally Blonde*.

It was the first time—and the last—that a freshman had gotten the lead in a BHS musical, and Odile carried that whole show on her slim shoulders. She'd bleached her hair platinum, and she sang song after song after song—it's one of those shows where the main character has to sing pretty much all night—and nailed every one. Her big solo at the end of the first act got a standing ovation, and during the curtain call the audience literally screamed when she came out to bow.

What stuck with me about Odile that night, though, wasn't the way she held the high notes (though *wow*, did she ever hold those high notes). It was how *happy* she looked at the end.

During the show, she'd been acting—her character is supposed to look sad or overwhelmed or falsely confident for most of it—but in the curtain call, we got to see the real Odile for the first time. And the real Odile looked absolutely *radiant*. There wasn't a drop of sweat on her, even though she'd spent the past two and a half hours dancing under the blazing lights. She was grinning so wide she looked ready to burst into a blaze of light herself.

She just seemed so . . . *delighted*. As though getting to do what she loved onstage was the biggest thrill imaginable. For a split second, I almost understood the appeal of acting.

Then the actor who'd played the UPS guy took off his shirt and waved it around over his head, and the audience started screaming all over again, and Odile stepped back into the line with the rest of the cast, the bliss on her face already fading into a standard pasted-on curtain-call smile.

And I remembered why acting was the worst job in theater.

"Is it true that you designed the whole set by yourself?" she asks me now. "That's what Wes told me."

I scratch the back of my neck. "Er, yeah."

"It was really beautiful."

"Oh, um. Thank you."

"I loved those huge paintings upstage, with the hieroglyphics." She sounds so earnest I'm not sure how to respond. "I used to sit in the house when I was waiting to go on and just stare at them. The patterns were mesmerizing."

My mouth drops open. *Mesmerizing* was exactly what I'd been going for. The panels I'd painted had hung onstage through the whole show, and I'd imagined audience members studying every angle of the patterns during scene changes, but I'd never pictured the actors looking so closely. Especially her.

"Um, well. Thanks. I had a ton of help executing it. I was inspired by a set for *Aida* from this one theater in Austria, actually, so, um, it wasn't totally . . ."

I order myself to stop telling Odile all these details she didn't ask for and probably couldn't care less about.

Besides, why do I keep stumbling over my own voice? I'm clear and succinct when I talk. When you're doing a show, there's no time for unnecessary syllables.

"I love it when there are actual paintings onstage." Odile doesn't seem to have noticed how flummoxed I am, but a few of the others have turned around to watch us. I scratch my neck again. I can't believe she's still standing here, talking to me about set design. "I did a show once with this amazing painted backdrop of a cityscape, but after previews they switched it out for a projection. I don't know why—maybe a critic complained? The projection was nice, but there's something about paint. It's just part of theater to me. Like the smell of sawdust, you know?"

I nod—I agree with her, vehemently—and try to place which show she's talking about. We've never done a show with a cityscape behind it. Maybe . . .

Ohhh. Wait.

There's a cityscape in the Broadway set of *Annie*.

"Projections can be really hard to work with," I say, because I want her to think I know as much about theater as she does, even though I have a feeling that's not true. "I saw a show once where this giant blinking message suddenly popped up on the scrim that said 'Error—Restart.' The whole audience started laughing right in the middle of this serious scene about cancer."

Odile winces sympathetically, and she looks like she's about to say something else when a voice comes in over her shoulder.

"Mel?" Alejandra's gripping a piece of sheet music in her hand. Odile turns around and brushes her hair behind her ear, a move that looks precisely calculated to show off the pale pink manicure that perfectly matches her dress. Or maybe it's not calculated at all, and she just naturally exudes glamour.

I need to stop wondering about stuff like that. I despise uncertainty of any kind. "What's up, Alejandra?"

"Could I ask you a question? About my music for the audition? How do I know exactly when to start singing after the piano—"

Only then does Alejandra notice who I'm talking to. The new hair color must've thrown her off, too, but now she steps back, her eyes widening, as though Odile's a tiger who just escaped her enclosure at the zoo. "Oh! I didn't mean to interrupt."

"Odile! *There* you are!" Christina's voice comes out of nowhere. I turn around to see her charging toward us, Leah right on her heels. "We saw that you were auditioning later and we hoped we'd catch you. We're *so* glad you're going to be in town to do the musical with us! Aren't we, Leah?"

"We are!" Leah chirps, smiling her most fawning smile.

Oh, God. I so don't have time for sycophantic actors.

But Odile is beaming at the girls, showing precisely the right number of teeth. It's clear she's forgotten all about me, so I roll my eyes and turn back to Alejandra, trying to focus on the sheet music she's holding out.

She's singing "In My Own Little Corner" from *Cinderella*. It's a good song choice. Alejandra was excellent in *R&J*, and rumor has it she's been singing brilliantly with her church choir for years, but she's always been too nervous to sing a solo so she's never auditioned for a musical before.

"After I introduce you, just take your music up to Ms. Qiao and she'll help you figure it out," I tell her. "Don't worry, she makes it really easy. She'll probably play one note, and then she'll let you start and follow your lead."

"Melody?" Ms. Marcus sticks her head out the door.

Crap! I forgot to set my timer!

"Sorry! Oh my gosh, I'm so sorry!" I jog to the door.

Ms. Marcus laughs. "Relax, you're not late. But we're ready, so let's get this show back on the road."

I nod and turn to the sign-up sheet, all business. "Henry Qualls, you're up."

Henry, a sophomore, sings a song from *Hamilton*—not very well—and then it's Alejandra's turn. The teachers both beam at her while she smiles nervously. And just as I suspected, she sounds fantastic.

I call more names after that, and Ms. Marcus and Ms. Qiao keep smiling as we sit through the same songs over and over again. It's starting to feel like a never-ending parade of "On My Own," Disney, and *Phantom*. Plus, two different girls who try, and fail, to sing "Defying Gravity," which . . . no. No one should ever try to sing that song without about fifteen years of vocal lessons behind them.

Then there's a long string of auditions where no one seems to be trying at all. People who sway on their feet so much it's impossible to focus on their voices, or who sing so quietly we can barely hear them over the piano, or who forget the words (how can anyone forget the words to just sixteen bars of music? Seriously, how?). I'm starting to see why Ms. Qiao and Ms. Marcus weren't as excited going into auditions as I was.

After the afternoon's third rendition of "Let It Go," I'm yawning in my seat when Ms. Marcus taps my elbow with her pencil. I jump up to escort the latest girl out and look down at the sign-up sheet.

"Nicholas Underwood," I call.

No one answers. A few people start giggling. I try again. "Nicholas Underwood?"

A white guy I vaguely recognize—he's a fellow junior, and I think we once had English together—lifts his head and slowly climbs to his feet, his phone in his hand. He's really tall, with a broad chest, and his arms are all muscly. Maybe he plays a fall sport.

He tries to walk past me without looking up from his phone. When I hold out my hand, he finally glances up. "You need something?"

I blink. His tone's astonishingly rude for a guy who, as far as I know, has never been in a show here. "I need your audition form, Nicholas."

He passes me the paper and turns down to study his sheet music. "It's Nick, actually."

"Okay. I'm Mel. I'm the stage manager."

He shrugs without looking up, like the fact that I have a name couldn't possibly be less relevant to his life. How very *actorly* of him.

"Good luck, Nick!" a senior girl calls from across the hall.

I sigh. "You mean 'Break a leg.'"

Nick winks at the girl, then turns to me with a smirk. The girl looks contrite, though, and I realize I know her. Her name is Selah, and she's been in the ensemble for all the shows I've worked on. *She* knows the rules. "Whoops, sorry, Mel. Should I do the countercurse?"

"No, it's okay since rehearsals haven't started. Always better to be in the habit, though."

Selah nods, and I nod back to show her we're all good. It's never smart to be casual with theater superstitions, though. It's like how you shouldn't drive through a red light even if there aren't any cars coming. Rules exist for a reason.

I take Nick's form and lead him into the choir room. From the way Ms. Marcus and Ms. Qiao nod, it's clear they both recognize him. "This is Nick Underwood, junior, singing 'How Glory Goes.'"

Nick looks a little confused when I sit down, like it hadn't occurred to him I'd stay in the room, but I meet his gaze, impassive. He breaks eye contact first, which is pleasantly satisfying, and goes over to Ms. Qiao with his sheet music. I settle into my seat and prepare to tune him out.

But when he starts singing, I sit back up again.

Nick Underwood is good. *Really* good.

I glance at Ms. Marcus. She's staring right at Nick, her face blank as usual, but she's got to be registering this. His singing is up there with the best we've heard all day.

Plus, he isn't swaying around or making weird faces, like most of the other guys have. He's standing with his feet planted, and his hand gestures and facial expressions actually seem to go with the song—as though he's really playing the character who's singing. And since that character is trapped in a cave and about to die, it's doubly impressive.

When his sixteen bars are done, Ms. Marcus writes something

on his audition form and Ms. Qiao looks up from the piano.

"Thank you, Nick," Ms. Qiao says. "That was a very interesting song choice."

Nick grins at her. There's a thin sheen of sweat on his forehead. "Thank you, ma'am."

Ms. Qiao looks like she wants to say something else, but instead she turns my way and nods. I stand up to show Nick out.

He doesn't look at me as I hold the door for him. He's already taken out his phone. I sigh and check my list for the next name.

Gulp.

"Odile Rose," I say, trying to sound as neutral as possible, even though every head in the hallway has already snapped up to watch her walk by.

I can kind of see why. Odile walks with her chin lifted, as if she's *expecting* you to watch her make her way down the hall. As if that's just what *happens* when you're her.

The words stick in my throat when I introduce her to the teachers. It feels ridiculous—they already know exactly who she is. "This is Odile Rose, senior, singing 'I'm Not Afraid of Anything.'"

The teachers smile warmly as Odile takes her music to Ms. Qiao. And when she starts singing a moment later, the whole room changes. As though we've all been transported to another space altogether.

Odile's voice is *stunning*. That's all there is to it. The last time

I heard her sing was on closing night of *Joseph* last year, and I remember her being fantastic then, but either she's gotten better or I'd forgotten what she really sounded like. As though she was born to sing.

Her voice is beyond powerful, and her performance is somehow straightforward and dazzling at the same time. She's playing her character, but she isn't showy and dramatic about it the way Nick was. It doesn't feel like she's *acting* at all. She simply *is* the character, reflecting on her life with this deceptively plain, pretty song.

I feel unbelievably lucky to be getting this private performance. It's as if the teachers aren't even here—as though she's singing just for me. The whole world is the two of us, and the rest of humanity's tucked off into the wings.

When she finishes, she has that same glow on her face she had years ago, the night I first saw her. The same pure, shining delight.

And I get why she looks so happy. That's how theater makes me feel, too. When everything goes right—when the sets are stunning, when a perfectly executed sound mix elevates the voices to sparkling, when we haven't flubbed a single cue—*this* is what it feels like.

I didn't know how that felt three years ago when I first saw Odile perform. But *she* did.

Today she isn't standing in a pool of perfectly calibrated light, or gazing out from an elaborate set. She isn't wearing a costume or stage makeup, or singing into a microphone that carries her voice to every corner of the room. Yet somehow, everything about her radiates drama. The *best* kind of drama.

It's obvious why she keeps getting bigger and bigger roles. When Odile's in front of people, her very essence shimmers.

And as her song ends and the last notes of the piano fade, she looks right at me, still smiling. The emotion is so strong, so overwhelming, I have to look away.

I can't afford to be dumbfounded by the Odile phenomenon. I have work to do.

Besides, she's probably straight.

"Thank you, Odile." Ms. Marcus smiles and studies her audition form. "Based on your song choice, I'd guess you're most interested in playing Fantine. Is that right?"

"That's right." Odile beams at Ms. Marcus. I keep my eyes focused carefully over her left shoulder.

Huh. I was sure Odile would want Éponine. It's the most ingenue-y role in the show.

"And you wrote on here that you don't have any conflicts in April or May, is that right?"

"Yes, ma'am." Odile bobs her head. It's interesting to see how different she is with the teachers than with the rest of us. When Christina and Leah came up to her in the hall, she gave them that carefully calculated smile, but here she's surprisingly relaxed and cheerful.

"It must be a nice break for you to be in town long enough

to do the musical." Ms. Marcus smiles back. "I know you've been on the road a lot this year."

"I can't wait." On the last word, Odile's voice shifts into a high-pitched squeak, and I almost want to laugh. She sounds like anyone else who's excited about being in the play.

But why would she be excited about *this*? Odile's performed on *Broadway*. Who cares about the Beaconville High spring musical?

But Ms. Marcus is still smiling at her, and as Odile smiles back, a silent understanding seems to pass between them. And I think I sort of get it.

Auditioning for our teachers is probably a lot more fun than auditioning for Martin Scorsese.

I do my best to act nonchalant as I show her out of the room, but my hands falter when I reach down to flip to the next page on the sign-up sheet. I grimace when I hear myself stumble over my words again. "Ah. Um. Tasha Barnett?"

Somehow, we make it through the rest of the afternoon. Some of the singers are good, some are terrible, and a lot are in between. But not a single person is remotely on the same level as Odile.

I call more names, I walk people in and out, and I give everyone exactly the same smile—the one that isn't supposed to let on what I'm thinking.

But as I show the last actor of the day out the door and Ms. Qiao cracks her knuckles and climbs to her feet behind me, that smile Odile—the *real* Odile—was wearing when she finished singing for us here in the choir room still lingers in my mind.

And I can't stop thinking about how much I want to see her smile that way again.

Spring Musical Callbacks

Please note, we're holding callbacks for the role of Jean Valjean <u>only</u>. The full cast list will be posted Friday, and many students have already been selected for other roles. So don't worry if you tried out but you don't see your name on this list!

Students listed below should report to the choir room at 3:00 p.m. Thursday:
Dominic Connor
David Patel
Malik Sexton
Nicholas Underwood

No advance preparation for the callback is necessary. See you Thursday!

Scene 2—Beaconville High School Cafeteria

DAYS UNTIL SPRING MUSICAL OPENS: 85

Malik studies my clipboard. "How many shifts do we have to take?"

"Just one, but Will's making a special batch of brownies for anyone who signs up for extras."

"Count me in." Malik scrawls his name down next to two time slots and passes the clipboard to Adam, who signs up for another two shifts.

Bake sale recruitment is one of the easiest jobs on any show. Everyone in the cast and crew is supposed to bring in food on different days and we set up tables to sell it during lunch periods, with three people working at a time. We've all got our favorite recipes down by now. Gabby already asked me to sign her up for two shifts with her grandmother's special frosted Rice Krispies treats.

I'm about to head over to one of the sophomore actor tables to get more sign-ups when I hear, "Mel! We need you!"

Hearing I'm needed provokes a Pavlovian response, so I'm already all the way across the room before I realize it's just my friends at our usual table. "Wait, do you actually *need* me, or are you trying to distract me from getting sign-ups?"

"Here, we'll all sign up right now, and you can stay and talk to us while we pass this around." Jasmin takes the clipboard and scribbles down her name before passing it on to Shannon.

"We wanted to make sure you got in on the hookup pool before the freshmen and sophomores see it." Fatima holds out her tablet to me. She runs the betting on every show, and the competition can get fierce. It's open to the whole crew, and the winner—whoever correctly guesses the most verifiable actor hookups between the first rehearsal and the cast party—gets a gaudy trophy at the beginning of strike, courtesy of the props team. Dom won it for *R&J*, having accurately predicted that Liam and Christina would have at least four known hookups and two public blow-out fights before opening, and the trophy's been sitting on the top shelf of his locker ever since. It has seventeen layers of iridescent paint, a disturbing row of googly eyes, a half-dozen glittery unicorn stickers, and a pair of giant plastic red lips glued on top.

"I don't know if I should enter this time. It seems kind of unprofessional." But I study the list on Fatima's screen anyway. Julio Ramirez and Aaron Crane currently have the top odds for the most dramatic relationship of the *Les Mis* run. "Also, I'm pretty sure Julio and Aaron already hooked up during *R&J* so I'm not sure they count."

"It counts as long as they're not in an actual relationship." Tyler slurps a hefty spoonful of strawberry yogurt and points at the screen. "Besides, the *R&J* hookup was just a rebound. I saw Julio fighting with Tom in the locker room one day and the next, he and Aaron were sucking face backstage."

"It's too bad about Tom," Jasmin says. "He was really into Julio. They were picking out matching tuxes for prom."

"Well, I hope Julio isn't too depressed to be funny," Shannon says. "He's going to get Thénardier, right, Mel?"

"I have no idea." I shift in my seat, even though I'm positive the answer is yes.

"Of course he will." Jasmin waves her hand dismissively. "He and Beth always get the funny parts."

"I heard he's way over Tom anyway," Shannon says. "Besides, Tom wasn't *that* into him. He never got over Sebastian graduating."

"Tom and Sebastian were never even a real thing," Jasmin tells her.

"Wait, are you sure? I thought . . ."

Shannon trails off mid-sentence, to my relief. Hearing all this speculation about who's going to hook up with whom is actually kind of depressing. It's a stark reminder that I promised, way back in November, that *I* wouldn't fall for anyone at all.

Not that I *want* to date anyone. When I remember how badly I screwed things up with Rachel, all I want to do is hide under a very large rock and never come out.

But the pain of that breakup isn't quite as raw as it was the day my friends first brought up what Dom still calls my "love curse." I'm on board with the plan, of course—whatever my crew needs from me, they'll get, and I always do what I say I'll do—but I can't help being a little jealous that everyone but me gets to have a showmance.

I glance around for my next bake sale sign-up target. Our cafeteria table stands right in the middle of the theater cluster. It's mostly a junior crew table—in general, actors sit with actors, the crew sits with the crew, seniors sit with seniors, et cetera—and I guess it also qualifies as the ambitious junior crew table, since by now most of us have risen in the ranks to crew head or higher. Besides Jasmin and Fatima, there's Shannon, Kevin, Tyler, and Bryce. Rachel used to sit with us, but she moved to Estaban's table after we broke up. Dom usually sits here too, but he's MIA. Maybe he'll abandon us altogether for one of the actor tables once the cast list goes up this afternoon.

I'll post the crew list at the same time. Most of the assignments won't exactly be a surprise—Will and I only had to move a few people around, since obviously Dom can't be sound head if he's in the cast, and we'll need someone to run the light board since thankfully I won't be doing that myself this time—and our team's a well-oiled machine. Everyone at this table is experienced, talented, and ready to put in the work.

That's when I realize a hush has fallen over our table and the others nearby, and I look up to see Odile walking past us. She isn't carrying a lunch tray—just a tiny purse that couldn't possibly contain food—but then, I'm not entirely convinced she eats. You probably aren't allowed to consume calories if you're in the running for a Scorsese movie.

"Make way for the ice princess," Bryce mutters when Odile's out of earshot, and my friends laugh. "Seriously, though, do you see the way she walks? As though she's expecting us all to fall down and worship at her feet?"

"You mean we don't have to do that?" Tyler says, faux-scandalized, and everyone laughs again.

Odile doesn't look at anyone as she crosses the room. Only when she's finally disappeared through the cafeteria doors does everyone start talking at regular volumes again.

"She seriously never speaks, does she?" Fatima frowns after her, tapping her lip.

"I heard she was talking to Mel at auditions." Jasmin points her milk straw at me, her dark brown eyes narrowing.

"Just a little." I squirm. "You know, actually, I'm not sure if she's all that—"

"What's going on, Mel?" Dom drops his tray onto the table next to me with a thud that makes his onion rings jump. His voice is shaky, and his face is sheet white. Bryce grabs his juice bottle to keep it from tipping over. "You said they were posting the cast list after school today."

"They are." I trade worried looks with Jasmin. I knew Dom was nervous about his audition, but I didn't think he was going to lose it completely.

"You never said anything about callbacks." He sits down heavily, grabs the apple off his tray, and takes a huge bite. I'm worried he's going to choke.

"That's because there aren't any callbacks," I tell him patiently. "We don't have them here."

"We do now," he mumbles around a mouthful of apple. A piece of peel shoots out from the corner of his mouth. Ew. "There's a sign on the board."

"Which board? The one by the black box?"

He nods and takes another bite. "Callbacks for Valjean, tomorrow after school. Me and Malik and two other guys."

I stare at him. "That's impossible. Ms. Marcus didn't tell me there'd be callbacks."

"Wait, you got a callback for *Valjean*?" Jasmin practically shrieks. "Oh my God, congratulations!"

Dom scowls at his lunch tray. "Thanks, *Jazz*."

"Oh, right. Congrats!" Crap. I forgot to get excited. God, I'm a horrible friend.

"What do I do?" Dom puts down his apple. He's talking so loud, people are turning to watch from other tables. "The sign said I didn't need to prepare anything, but what does that *mean*?"

"I think it means you don't need to worry." Jasmin's clearly trying to sound soothing.

"But what are we going to do when we get there?" Dom refuses to be soothed. "Just sing our audition songs again?"

I almost shake my head, but I stop myself in time.

I know how callbacks work from theater camp. They'll each

be asked to sing a song from *Les Mis*—the same song, with the sheet music in front of them so they won't have to memorize the lyrics. Probably one of Valjean's big solos, like "Bring Him Home" or "Who Am I?"

But I can't tell him that. I can't give Dom any information the other guys going into the callback don't have.

I stare down into my tomato soup.

Wait. What if I *am* supposed to tell him something, and the others too? As SM, shouldn't I be helping organize the callbacks anyway?

"I need to go see Ms. Marcus." I push back my chair.

"Wait." Dom turns to me with a desperate hitch in his voice. "You know about this stuff. I'm not asking you to put in a good word for me or anything. Just tell me what you think we're going to do. Please."

I can't risk it. "Sorry. I've got to go."

He stares at me with pleading eyes. His skin's starting to turn green again.

"Hey, don't worry, it'll be all right." Jasmin takes out her phone as Shannon puts her hand on Dom's arm. "I'm googling it. We'll help you figure this out."

"No thanks to our resident expert," Dom mutters, just loud enough for me to hear.

I try to shake it off as I wind through the hallways to the performing arts wing. I'm just doing my job. Dom will figure that out sooner or later.

The sign announcing callbacks is right outside the door to

the black box theater, in the same spot where the teachers usually post the cast lists. I take a photo so I can upload it to the shared drive. But the black box is locked, and there's no sign of Ms. Marcus.

Now I feel guilty about walking out on Dom like that. Not giving him tips about the callback was the right thing to do, I'm pretty sure. But if I were him, I guess I might not see it that way.

There are three minutes left on the lunch period, but I can't go back to our table after that, so I duck into the empty bathroom. I might as well glance at my Spanish notes in case there's another pop quiz. It's always good to be prepared even though I usually do pretty well in Spanish; it's one of the perks of Pops being half Puerto Rican. But the door opens behind me seconds later and a familiar, slightly accented voice floats into the room.

"Yes, yes, of course." Odile turns to shut the door behind her, speaking evenly into her phone. She doesn't seem to have noticed me. "No, no, this is a fine time. Yes, but it isn't a problem. Yes, yes, did you—you did?"

She pauses, listening to the person on the other end. I should probably edge out of the room—from the extra-smooth tone in her voice, I'm pretty sure this is a work call, and she probably doesn't want anyone eavesdropping—but she's blocking the door. I could go into a stall, but I'd have to come out before the bell rings or I'd be late for class. Besides, I don't want her to see and think I'm peeing.

"Oh, that's—" Odile pauses. She bends her head down, and I can see her profile as she swallows. Her eyes shut for a moment, and her lips almost look like they're trembling. But an instant later, when she opens her eyes and speaks again, there's a new lilting note in her voice, even though there's no trace of a smile on her face. "That's wonderful. Thank you so much for everything you've done. I know it's been a huge effort. Yes, yes. Yes, it's really brilliant news."

The warning bell rings. One minute until class.

Odile will have to get off the phone, right? She won't want to be late.

Unless whatever she's doing on the phone is more important to her than being on time to class. Whereas I can count the total number of times I've been late to class in my entire life on one hand.

The person on the other end must be talking a lot, because Odile is quiet for a long time. She nods, reaching up to finger the gold hoop dangling from her left ear. I'm debating whether to cough when she slowly turns her head, sees me, and lets out a little gasp.

"Oh, no, I'm sorry." She laughs into the phone, but it sounds ever so slightly forced. "Please go on."

I try to convey via silent gestures that I'm really sorry for eavesdropping. It involves a series of elaborate shrugs while alternately holding my hands palm up, pointing at my ears, and shaking my head, trying to show that I haven't actually heard anything she's been saying.

(Look, there are a lot of reasons I prefer to stay offstage.)

Odile watches me, still holding the phone to her ear, her

eyebrows creeping higher with my every movement. Finally she says, "Yes, thank you. Yes, I'll look for that email and be sure to let you know if I have any questions. I hope you have a wonderful afternoon. Goodbye."

She hangs up and stares at me in silence for a second. Then she bursts out laughing.

This isn't one of her calculated, glamorous smiles, where she shows precisely the right number of teeth and keeps her eyes wide the whole time. It's legitimate, eyes-half-closed-in-a-genuinely-unsophisticated-way, hand-clutched-to-her-chest, uncontrolled *laughter*.

"That was *awesome*." She raises her hand. "Here, tell me if you get this one."

She holds up four fingers, then pretends to crank an old-fashioned movie camera. My dads and I play charades every New Year's with Will, so I know all the signals. "Four words. Movie title."

Odile nods, then holds out both arms and starts spinning around in circles.

"Um . . . you're dizzy?" She shakes her head, then spins a little more emphatically, tossing her head from side to side. "Um . . . the Story of the Very Dizzy Teenage Girl with Perfect Hair?"

She pauses to let out an actual *snort* of laughter that makes me extremely pleased with myself. Then she shakes her head and cups one hand to her ear.

"You hear something?" I ask. "You hear . . . a sound?"

She nods and taps her chest the way opera singers do, which

makes me blush because now I'm looking at her boobs. She tosses her hand out to one side and pantomimes like she's singing a grand, silent aria.

"Opera?" I try to guess while she keeps belting out imaginary lyrics. "The sound of singing?"

Odile lets out an exaggerated sigh, then holds out her hands like she's strumming a guitar and does a mini-skip toward the sinks.

"Ohh! *The Sound of Music!*"

She nods vigorously, grinning. "Took you long enough!"

"Wait, I've got one." The bell is seconds away from ringing. I should be sitting in my seat looking over my Spanish notes, not doing impromptu charades with an ingenue in the bathroom. But I raise two fingers, then hold out my hands and draw them apart like a curtain opening.

"Two words." Odile grins. She doesn't seem in any hurry to leave either. "Play title."

I nod. Then I pantomime swinging a giant hammer over my head.

"Okay, I already know what this is, but I'm not going to say it because I want to see what else you'll do." Odile folds her arms. She's smiling even wider than she did after her audition.

This isn't her stage persona, or her professional-phone-call persona. The girl in the bathroom with me right now just might be the *real* Odile Rose.

I pretend to grab something, then pretend-stash it in my pocket. I hold out my fists and shake them, like I'm rattling the pretend-bars of a jail, then lunge forward and run in place for a while. Then I angle my hands above my head, trying to show that I'm wearing a massive pointed hat, and run in place again. I keep waiting to feel self-conscious, like I should stop, but the sight of Odile's grin only makes me want to keep going.

I'm doing *Les Misérables*, obviously. I'm trying to show Valjean stealing stuff and Javert chasing him, but I probably just look like an untrained clown.

"This is surprisingly easy to follow," Odile says. "I want to see more characters."

I point to her, then hold out my ponytail and form pretend-scissors with my other hand, like I'm about to chop it off.

"Hey!" She giggles. "Don't mock Fantine's pain."

"Ha! I got you to say it." I grin.

She grins back. "I could've watched that all day, though. I want to see you do 'Castle on a Cloud.'"

I grab an imaginary broom, and I'm pretending to sweep up the paper towels under the sinks when the bell rings.

My heart speeds up. I'm never late, to *anything*. But Odile doesn't seem particularly concerned about getting a tardy on her record.

And, well . . . I guess the damage is already done.

"I'm, um, sorry for listening in on your phone call." Now that we're talking with actual words, my self-consciousness makes a belated appearance and I reach back to pat down my hair. It's long, dark brown, and frizzy, so I usually just pull it back with a plain band unless I'm going to a dance and have the patience to spend an hour with a blow-dryer and several palmfuls of gel. That doesn't usually bother me, but next to Odile, with her salon-perfect waves, I feel inadequate. "Was that your, um—" I try to think of a Hollywood-type job title. "Your agent?"

"Oh. Yeah." Her smile fades a little. "Don't worry about it, it wasn't—hey, is that the form for the bake sale?"

"Oh, yeah, um. Yeah." I hold out my clipboard. Why can't I just say *yes*? What is it about being in Odile's proximity that adds all these nonsense words to my dialogue?

"Can I sign up? I've never gotten to do one since I'm always out of town. Mr. Green is so nice, isn't he?"

"Uh. Sure." I hold out the form. "You only have to do one shift."

"*Your* name is on here three times." She smiles up at me.

"Yeah, um. I signed up before anyone else." I pat down my hair again. "Will—Mr. Green, I mean—he taught me to always write my own name down first whenever I'm recruiting. It's like putting a dollar in your own tip jar—people are more likely to sign up if someone's done it already."

"Smart." She smiles again. Glimpsing that smile—the real one—when there's no one else around to see it makes a warm feeling surge inside me, as though the sun just came out from the clouds. "Could I sign up for one of the same shifts as you? I've never done a bake sale before, so I won't know what to do."

"Um. I mean, it isn't exactly hard, but—" I stop talking when I see her smile falter. "How about Thursday?"

"Thursday's perfect." Her smile rises back into place as she scribbles her name down. "I'm sorry, I hope I didn't make you late for class."

"I mean, it's not like you held a gun to my head and ordered me to stay in the girls' bathroom." I laugh when I realize how ridiculous that sounded. "But, um, I should probably get to Spanish. In case there's a quiz."

"Me too. I mean, I'm going to physics, not Spanish, but . . ." She laughs again. "I guess it doesn't matter. Bye, Mel. See you soon."

She gives me that smile one last time before she turns to go.

I wait until she's gone before I plaster my hand over my face, but it still takes another full minute to catch my breath.

This show's getting more complicated than I realized.

LES MISÉRABLES TECH CREW LIST

We still have room for additional crew members in some departments. If you're interested in joining, please speak to the relevant crew head or to Melody McIntyre.

Department	Crew head	Assistant head	Crew members (list subject to change)
Stage management	Melody McIntyre, class of 2021	Gabrielle Piacine, class of 2023	N/A
Set	Fatima Pataras, '22	Daniel Horton, '22	Michael Coken, Lilyan Dilay, Caroline Graham, Kekoa Lauzon, Zack Nguyen, Reaiah Gerstein, Skylor Riggan
Sound	Kevin Lo, '20	Nena Curley, '22	TBD
Lighting	Jasmin Bennett, '21	Ellie Nagy, '22	Ezra Saxon, Anton van Dijkum

Costumes	Rachel Scott, '20	Devin Schmidtke, '21	Riya Florence, Clarisa Wright, Juan Molina, Ronee Penoi, Grant Moore, Joey Pytel, Holly Pounds, Ian Mitchell, Paul Villalovoz, Morgan Springborn, Ryan Amin
Props	Estaban Goodwin, '20	Jacob Matushek, '22	Matthew O'Hara, Lon Bailey, Victoria Jahn, Rayonna Feichtel
Hair and makeup	Shannon Kardas, '20	Han Thai, '22	Amanda Barber, Miranda Craig, Cameron Babb, Lindsey Thaniel, Preston Tekmenzhi
Publicity	Tyler Zumbrun, '21	Aya Aljoulani, '22	TBD
Flies	Bryce Teitelbaum, '21	Ben Levy, '22	N/A

Run crew (only needed from tech week through strike to handle set changes during performances)	Everyone in the set, costumes, and hair/makeup crews, plus Anjali Singh, Melissa Adler, Elijah Lackritz, Steve Nelson, Angela Schoonover, Erin Edmonds, Lexi Grenzner, and Kristen Lang		

—Printed list as of February 7, 2020. One copy tucked into Mel's binder and the other given to Ms. Marcus, ready to post that afternoon alongside the cast listing.

Also stored on the BHS performing arts department's shared drive.

Scene 3—Hallway, Beaconville High School
Performing Arts Wing

DAYS UNTIL SPRING MUSICAL OPENS: 83

I pause the video and drag the cursor on my phone backward. I want to watch the last few seconds again.

We're in the hall, waiting for Ms. Marcus to post the final cast and crew lists, and I've been watching an old video clip I found from when we did *Steel Magnolias* last year. It looks like it was shot from the house, and the quality isn't great, but it's zoomed in on Odile in the last scene, when she was sitting in the secondhand salon chair we'd reupholstered with iron-on vinyl. She'd sat in that chair and delivered a seven-minute monologue that had the entire audience, and most of the actors onstage behind her, in tears every night. Her character's daughter had just died, and the monologue was about what it was like when they turned off the machines.

I remember watching her from backstage. It's an incredibly moving scene, even when you've already seen it a dozen times in rehearsal. The whole crew was silent as we stood in the wings watching on closing night.

It's different seeing it this way, though. On the video, you can hear people in the audience crying audibly. Plus, when you're watching the scene straight-on instead of from the side, you can see how Odile's face changes subtly as she goes from line to line. You can hear it in her voice, too.

How does she *do* that? I know how to do everything *else* in theater—I can light a scene to make the audience feel angry or off-balance or scared or create effects that replicate pretty much any sound using nothing but a peanut butter jar and a baseball, or scour thrift stores to find the perfect representation of any character on a costume budget that's barely above zero. But I don't know how someone like Odile can do something like this. Just sit in a chair, talking, while hundreds of other people feel what she wants them to feel simply because they're in the same room.

"How much longer until they decide, do you think?" Dom blows on his fingers and rubs his knuckles. He's nervous. But then, so are the forty or so other actors and techs waiting in the hall with us. "The teachers have been in there for a while."

"They must've decided by now. They're probably just fixing typos or something." I switch off the video before he can see what I'm watching and double-check that I have my binder. My marked-up copy of the script is inside, just in case Ms. Marcus wants to talk to me about it. Gabby and I went through it at my house after school yesterday, looking for where the prop, sound, and light cues are going to be. I'd thought I'd have detention or something for being late to Spanish, but it turns out the rule is, you get one free tardy each semester. Who knew?

"The callback wasn't as bad as I expected." Dom reaches into his bag for a pair of fingerless gloves and struggles to pull them on. His hands are shaking. "Did I already tell you what song they had us do? It was 'Who Am I?'"

"Yeah." I spot Malik out of the corner of my eye. He's checking his watch and laughing at something Christina's saying. "Could you do me a favor and sign up for this bake sale shift with me on Thursday? I don't want to get stuck on my own."

He studies the form. "You're not alone. Odile signed up for the same time."

"You know what I mean. I don't want to be there with just *her*. She's all . . . you know. Intimidating."

Dom raises his eyebrows. "Since when are you intimidated by anyone? Much less an actor?"

"I'm not. I'd just rather not be one-on-one with her. It'll get all awkward."

Dom still looks skeptical, but he puts his name down.

While he writes, I flick my gaze from side to side. Does it look like I'm showing favoritism by standing next to him? No one's paying attention. Everyone's way too anxious. Besides, they already know he's my best friend, so does it matter?

Ugh, *why* did he have to go over to the dark side? It makes everything so . . . unclear. Messy, even.

We still haven't tried to talk about that painful moment in the cafeteria on Wednesday. It's easier to pretend things are normal. Dom's kept on sitting at our usual table, too, which helped.

"Anyway, yeah, that song," he says. "The hardest part was

having to learn it then and there. I've seen the movie, but only once."

"Ugh, that movie is crap."

"I know *you* hate it, but I haven't listened to the Broadway cast recording a million times like you have. It was a good thing Mr. Green sang it for us first or I wouldn't have had a clue how it was supposed to go."

"Wait—Mr. Green?" I can't have heard that right. "*Will? Will sang?*"

"Yeah." Dom blows on his fingers again. "Then Ms. Qiao made the four of us sing it together, which was incredibly awkward since, you know, we're competing against each other, but at least we got to read the words off the sheet music. And then we each sang it by ourselves. I don't know how I did, since I was so nervous. But everyone else looked nervous too, so who knows."

"It must've been so embarrassing to listen to Will sing." I can't get over that idea. I wonder if it was like when my dads sing around the house. They're notoriously terrible. "Was he awful?"

"No, he sounded good. A lot better than we did."

"Really?"

"Yeah. It was like when the guy in the movie sang it."

The black box door opens. The buzz of conversation in the hallway grows into a roar.

"What do you mean, the guy in the movie?" I ask, but Dom's eyes are locked on Ms. Marcus. She gives us all a carefully neutral smile as she steps up to the bulletin board. "What—Hugh Jackman? Are you seriously saying Will *sang* and he sounded like *Hugh Jackman?*"

But Dom's already caught up in the throng surging toward the bulletin board, where Ms. Marcus is smoothing out the cast list. I swear, she's as bad as any of us. She totally milks the drama out of moments like this. She tacks up the crew list next, then steps back to watch the chaos.

I hang back. As far as I'm concerned, it doesn't actually matter who got cast, since I already know none of the people I chose as crew heads and assistants auditioned. But I *am* curious, so as the first squeals come in from the actors at the front of the crowd, I hold up my phone over my head, zoom in, and take a photo.

When I pull my phone down to take a look, I notice that someone else is hanging back, too. Odile. She gives me a tiny wave and a tiny smile to go with it.

"Hi." She steps toward me as the other actors get louder.

There's a moan of disappointment from the front of the group that I immediately recognize as Christina's—she has a very distinctive disappointed moan. Malik's up front next to her, grinning and glancing back at Dom, who hasn't made it to the board yet.

"Are those the contact forms?" Odile asks. "Can I have one?"

She points at the stack of forms I'm holding on top of my binder. Why is this girl always asking me for forms? I usually have to force them on people. "Of course."

She takes a pen and textbook out of her backpack, bending forward to lean on it.

I look away. When she gives me back that form, I'll have her phone number. That feels kind of weird, even though it's literally my job to have everyone in the cast's phone numbers.

"Uh, so . . ." I glance down at the photo I just took. The crowd is getting louder, with more squeals and laments from the actors. Some of the crew members are starting to react too. I can hear excited chatter about production meetings and shopping trips. "You got Fantine. Congratulations."

"Oh, that's lovely. Thank you." Odile smiles up at me, and for a brief moment I feel that warm buzzy sensation I felt in the bathroom all over again. Then she turns back to the contact form, and I take a closer look at the cast list.

LES MISÉRABLES CAST

Thank you to everyone who auditioned. We were incredibly impressed with your talent, but there simply aren't enough roles for us to cast everyone.

Students we were not able to cast, as well as students cast as members of the ensemble, are welcome to join the tech crew. Please see Melody McIntyre for more information.

PRINCIPAL ROLES	
VALJEAN	Nicholas Underwood, class of 2021
JAVERT	David Patel, '20
FANTINE	Odile Rose, '20
ÉPONINE	Leah Zou, '21

MARIUS	Malik Sexton, '21
COSETTE	Alejandra Huston, '22
THÉNARDIER	Julio Ramirez, '20
MADAME THÉNARDIER	Elizabeth Meyers, '20
ENJOLRAS	Dominic Connor, '21
GAVROCHE	Lauren Breen, '23
BISHOP OF DIGNE / GRANTAIRE	Andrew Hernandez, '20

There's a list of featured ensemble members under the principals and another list of regular ensemble members below that. I try to scan them quickly.

"Hey, Mel, need help with anything?" Gabby's voice at my elbow catches me off guard.

I didn't know she was coming today, but I'm happy to see her. "Not right now, but I'll let you know."

"Hey, you're Gabby, right?" Odile leans around me and waves. "Congrats on being the only freshman on the senior crew team. That's going to look awesome to colleges later."

"Um . . . thanks." Gabby glances back and forth from Odile to me, like she suspects this might be a trick.

"Are you interested in sticking with tech theater?" Odile asks her. "Because if you're thinking about doing it as a career, like Mel, I'm still friends with the ASM at Boston Rep. I bet she'd be happy to talk with you about her job."

Now I raise *my* eyebrows. I would *also* like to talk with the

ASM at Boston Repertory Theater, which happens to be one of the best nonprofit theaters on the entire East Coast. But Gabby's eyes are already saucer-wide.

Also—how does Odile know I want to do this as a career? I've never told her that.

Has she been asking around about me?

"Mel? Who's In Joel Rass?"

I turn around. Dom's hovering behind us. "You mean Enjolras?"

I can't help correcting his pronunciation—it's *Ahn-Juhl-Rahs*, which Dom should know since he's taken four years of French— and it's only then that I notice how stricken he looks.

God, I'm the worst best friend *ever*.

"It's a *really* good part," I tell him. It's the truth, but I know he won't believe me, because it isn't Valjean. "The teachers wouldn't have given it to you if they didn't think you were awesome."

"It's almost at the bottom of the list, though." Dom shoves his hands into his pockets.

Come to think of it, I barely paid attention to who actually got which part. I glance at my photo one more time and see that Nick Underwood, who acted like a total tool in auditions, is our Valjean. Great. Well, maybe he'll rise to the occasion. The lead actors usually try to set a positive example for the others, especially the freshmen and sophomores who are brand-new to theater and petrified of everything.

"There you are, Mel." Ms. Marcus appears at my side. "Oh, hello, Dom. Congratulations! I can't wait to hear your version of 'Red and Black.'"

"Thanks," Dom mutters, looking at his feet.

"Mel, I was hoping you could take advantage of this crowd to encourage everyone to fill out their contact forms." Ms. Marcus gestures toward the group still alternately shrieking and groaning at the bulletin board. I see the back of Odile's head—she's finally making her way through to study the list herself. Having her out of earshot is both relaxing and, weirdly, disappointing. "We need them all back by the first rehearsal. Parent permissions too."

"On it." I pat my trusty binder. "I just want to talk to the crew really quick first if that's okay."

"Of course. We're going to have an all-star lineup—onstage and off." She steps back with another smile.

I'm making my way toward the front when I run into David Patel, smiling into his phone as he types a text. "Hey, Inspector!" I reach into my binder. "Contact form. Fill it out before you leave and earn my never-ending gratitude."

"Well, that seems like a good deal." He takes the form and turns his smile, which is really quite dazzling now that I'm paying attention, toward me. It's too bad he'll never be allowed to smile onstage in this show. His character is a major downer.

"David! *Congratulations!*" a familiar voice screams into my ear as someone jumps in from the side to crush him in a hug. "I knew you'd get Javert!"

I'm about to turn away and yell for the crew to assemble when I realize the girl with her arms wrapped around David is Odile.

Hmm. Major body contact. I wonder if they're back together. Though it's not as if I care, obviously.

"Hey, crew?" I wave my arm over my head and move to the far end of the hall, putting plenty of distance between Odile and me. "Over here."

The crowd starts to split, as it always does sooner or later, with the actors still hugging and crying in front of the cast list and the crew forming a circle around me. Three of the set guys are trying to get a group rendition of "Do You Hear the People Sing?" going, and I resist the urge to join in.

Some of the crew are still looking over their shoulders, eavesdropping on the actors. I hear snatches of the gossip, like "Christina's featured ensemble. I bet she'll get Factory Girl, but you know she wanted Fantine" and "I *knew* they couldn't find a guy who could pull off Gavroche" and "Who's that random junior who got Valjean? He'll look pathetic next to Odile."

There's more, a lot more, but I cut them off. This isn't the place to be having these conversations. Besides, what with Dom switching sides and Odile being nice all of a sudden, the way my friends and I talk about the cast is starting to make me squirm.

"Everybody needs to fill out a contact form before you leave here," I announce, writing quick mental bullet points for the rest of what I'm about to say. "And bring your parent permission forms home and have them sign everything tonight. We're the organized ones, so we should get our stuff turned in before the cast does."

There are a few chuckles. Gabby wordlessly takes half the forms off my stack and moves through the group, passing them out. She's the best ASM in ASM history.

"If you're interested in joining crew but your name isn't on the list we posted, start thinking about what department you want to help with," I go on. "We need every pair of hands we can get if we're going to stage this show in three months. And we need to pool our design ideas, too, so a week from today, there'll be a brainstorming lock-in at my house. My dads are ordering pizza, and I might even be able to convince Mr. Green to make brownies."

Someone laughs, and there are more excited whispers as the crew breaks into groups. Estaban asks me about the props budget, and I'm about to tell him we won't know the specifics until the first production meeting when I notice Dom off to one side of the hall, talking to Malik.

I have a distinct feeling that I need to intervene. I apologize to Estaban and jog toward them.

"Hey, you and me both, man," Malik is saying when I get there. "I didn't even know who this Nick guy *was* before the callback."

Dom doesn't look particularly comforted, and I don't blame him. I'm sure Malik means well, but he's in no position to commiserate with Dom. They both got good roles, but Malik's playing Marius, so he'll be spending twice as much time onstage as Dom. And since Malik's always been the lead singer of their band—the band *Dom* started—this whole dynamic probably feels uncomfortably familiar.

The thing is, though, I can see why the teachers did this.

As much as he annoyed me, Nick was the best of the guys we heard at auditions. He had a wider range than Dom or Malik, and he chose a better audition song. Plus he looks older and stronger, which is important since he has to age twenty years over the course of the show, and lift a bunch of heavy stuff.

And between Dom and Malik, Malik has more of a romantic-hero vibe, and Dom's a little more . . . unusual. I can totally see Dom leading a troop of misfits to their doom, just as easily as I can see Malik flirting with a cute girl through a gate.

I quickly file all that away under Thoughts I Won't Be Sharing with Anyone, Ever, and clear my throat.

"Contact forms," I announce, thrusting a sheet at each of them. "Fill them out right now and earn my unending gratitude."

"Your wish is my command, boss," Malik says just as Leah comes over to throw her arms around him and yelp in delight. Not far away, Fatima and Jasmin are bent over a tablet, eyeing Malik and Leah and quietly adjusting the odds on the hookup pool. I take the opportunity to steer Dom down the hall.

"I was the worst at callbacks," he starts lamenting as soon as we're a safe distance from everyone else. "The others got the good parts. I've never even *heard* of this Angel-whatever."

"Enjolras. And seriously, it's a *great* part." I struggle to think of how to explain the fabulousness that is Enjolras to someone with only vague knowledge of *Les Mis*. "He's Gabby's favorite character in the whole show, and mine, too, after Éponine. He's this fiery revolutionary, and he gets a really dramatic death scene. Plus, you get to wear an awesome vest. Look up a video of literally any performance of 'One Day More' and you'll get what I'm saying."

"Okay . . ." But Dom doesn't look particularly encouraged, so I take out my phone.

"Also, there are a bunch of smaller roles that didn't get listed on the cast sheet," I tell him while I look for a good video. "The Foreman, for one, and the chain gang soloists. And Young Cosette, but you wouldn't be Young Cosette, obviously." I laugh at that, but Dom is clearly not going to laugh at anything, so I plow ahead. "Anyway, you might get to do some of those other parts, especially in the first half of act one, since Enjolras doesn't actually show up for a while."

"He . . . doesn't?" Dom goes even paler.

Out of the corner of my eye, I spot Odile again. She's leaning down obligingly while Shannon peers at the roots of her hair. Probably already planning out ways to talk Ms. Marcus into getting her a wig. Sometimes I think Shannon forgets that there are actual human beings attached to the hair she's so obsessed with.

"Only because he's, like, an infant when the show starts. Because it jumps ahead twenty years and—never mind. Here, look." I find the video from the 1987 Tonys, hand Dom my phone, and hit play. "You can't miss him. Just wait for the drumroll and look for the vest."

"Congratulations to everyone in the cast and crew," Ms. Marcus calls from the other end of the hall, and everyone abruptly goes silent to listen. "The first rehearsal is a week from today, so please go to the performing arts department website tonight to download the script. I'd like you to read the whole thing before the rehearsal, and spend some time familiarizing yourself with the cast recordings, too. You can find all the songs online. Please resist the urge to watch the movie—I hope all I need to say is 'Russell Crowe' to convince you on that one."

Everyone laughs. Dom comes up and passes me back my phone, nodding slightly—to show, I hope, that he now understands why Enjolras is awesome. Then he winds his way back through the crowd.

"If you're interested in joining tech crew, please speak to Melody," Ms. Marcus adds. "I understand that the costume team particularly needs volunteers. Making all the costumes this show requires by opening night may be even more of a challenge than mastering all the high notes."

There's another laugh, and the crowd starts to dissipate. I linger to pass out more contact forms and answer questions. A few actors in the ensemble stop to ask about tech roles, so I chat with them about what departments they might be a fit for. Three girls volunteer to help with costumes right away, which should make Rachel happy.

"There you are, Mel." Odile's voice is bright in my ear as the last of the freshmen ensemble guys steps away. She's holding out her contact form. "You're way too popular. Every time I try to find you, you're talking to someone. Here, I hope I filled it out right."

"I, um. I'm sure you did." I flush. Ugh, *why* is it impossible for me to act normal around this girl?

"Er, Mel?" It's Alejandra, holding out her own completed form. Her eyes dart back and forth from Odile to me. "I wanted to ask—do you know when we need to have our parts memorized by?"

"Don't worry." I take her form. "Ms. Marcus will tell you when you need to be off-book, but it won't be for a long time. You'll probably already know all the lyrics by then anyway just from going through rehearsals."

"And congrats!" Odile smiles at her. "I'm playing your mom! I'm so excited to do this show with you."

Alejandra smiles back, but tentatively, as if she's not sure Odile's being sincere. "Thanks."

"Let me know if you'd like to practice together on one of our free afternoons. Sometimes I think it's easier to practice solos with an audience, even if it's just an audience of one."

Alejandra audibly gulps. "Er . . . all right."

David comes by and starts talking to Odile again, and more people stop by to ask me questions. A *lot* more. They ask the same things over and over, about rehearsal schedules and production meetings and whether power tools are scary.

I don't mind. It's a lot easier than it will be once we get deep into rehearsals. During our last two weeks on *R&J* I couldn't set foot in the performing arts wing without being besieged with frantic questions and desperate pleas for help.

And I don't mind that either. It's always nice to be needed.

Besides, this is what I love about theater. We're going to make something amazing together. We're a team, and we trust each other to do whatever it takes. We're making something bigger than any of us could ever have done alone.

Just as long as none of us does anything to screw it up.

The Scottish Play: What Went Wrong
Stored on BHS performing arts department shared drive
Created by: Billy Yang, stage manager, class of 2007
Viewable to: All cast, crew, and directors
Editable by: Current SM ONLY

Attention, future Beaconville High School SMs: This list must be preserved for posterity. Our mistakes are being recorded so you don't have to repeat them.

During the spring 2007 production of the Scottish Play, the following unexplainable events occurred:

- On opening night, an actor, in character as Lady [Scottish Play], while performing the sleepwalking scene with her eyes closed, walked off the stage and into the orchestra pit. We're told we were lucky she only broke one bone. She's still in a cast and doesn't feel particularly lucky.
- During tech, a plastic dagger that was branded as "retractable" did not, in fact, retract. Fortunately, that actor only needed a few hours at urgent care, but the actor on the other end of the dagger will probably need therapy for life.
- During the second night of the show, an actor developed a never-previously-present allergy to her witch makeup and had to perform with her face broken out in hives.

(We all agreed it actually added to her performance, but nevertheless she was very itchy.)

- On closing night, the hazer set off a smoke alarm and we had to evacuate the theater twenty minutes before intermission. Never mind that the hazer had worked fine during tech, three dress rehearsals, and three performances before that.
- During the matinee, a cable detached from one of the many scraggly trees in the set just as it was being flown in for the second act. The audience thought it was part of the show and cheered. It was not part of the show. That tree was heavy. Witches could've died.
- On closing night, the scrim came down early during a fight scene and the cast had to break character to run out from under it. The audience didn't notice, which depending on your point of view may or may not be a bad thing.
- During strike, a member of the run crew fell backward into the trap, which apparently wasn't fully secured, even though I had personally checked the lock right before the show started. Fortunately, she was okay aside from a bruised butt.

To conclude: be careful in this theater. Be very, very careful. Something is deeply wrong here.

And to the curse overlords, if you're reading this over my shoulder: we're really sorry we bothered you. Please take it easier on future SMs than you did on me.

Scene 4—Beaconville High School Cafeteria

DAYS UNTIL SPRING MUSICAL OPENS: 77

"Three dollars for a cupcake?" Dom frowns down at the price card I'm writing out. We're at a wide table at the back of the cafeteria, getting ready for our bake sale shift. "Exactly how spectacular are these cupcakes?"

"Pretty darn spectacular." I fold the price card and set it in front of the tray. "Dad and I spent hours on them. We even made the frosting."

"I'd pay three dollars for a cupcake with homemade frosting." As if to prove the point, Odile fishes around in her purse, pulls out three singles, and drops them into our cash box, then takes a strawberry cupcake and sets it next to her Ziploc full of baby carrots. "I'm selling my snickerdoodles for two dollars a bag. They're my aunt's recipe, and seriously, they're life-changing."

I don't argue with her, but I strongly suspect Odile's never eaten a cookie in her life, and I'll be astonished if she actually takes a bite of that strawberry cupcake. Last I heard, ingenue diets didn't include baked goods.

"Is the credit card thingy on your phone working?" Dom asks as he straightens the trays. Half the table is covered in brownies, since those are always the biggest sellers. Dom, who's worked almost as many bake sales as I have, brought in what looks like twenty batches of Duncan Hines.

"Yep." I pull out the jar of complimentary jelly beans. Will brought in huge bags of them. He's a big believer in generating future ticket sales with memories of sugar. "Flip the sign."

Dom stands up—he's the tallest of our group, so he's in charge of dealing with the BAKE SALE OPEN / BAKE SALE CLOSED sign on the wall—and as soon as he flips it to OPEN, a whoop goes up from the nearest table of jocks and the line starts forming.

"Give me the biggest brownie you've got, drama club dude," the first basketball player says, holding out a five-dollar bill to Dom.

The line moves fast, like bake sale lines always do, and we fall into a natural rhythm. Dom does food service, using his long, gangly arms to reach across the table and swipe up the cookies, cupcakes, and brownies. I handle the money, making change and swiping credit cards on my phone.

I hadn't expected Odile to be much help, but she turns out to be good at sales. She speaks in a sweet voice I've never heard her use before, and she smiles exactly the way she did when she played Elle Woods. Between her *Us Weekly*–approved bone structure and the way she somehow manages to make every athlete at the school feel like she's their best friend, she guilts half our customers into leaving their extra change in our donations cup.

Before we're ten minutes into the lunch period, the cash box is stuffed, and Dom's already reaching under the table to restock our inventory. The line has gone down, but I know from bake sales past that it'll pick up again when we get closer to the end of the period.

"How are we doing?" Odile nods toward the cash box and stretches her arms over her head.

"Pretty, um . . . we're doing pretty well."

I can't help staring at her. She's as resplendent as ever in her bright orange leather jacket, artfully ripped skintight jeans, and ankle boots. I feel like a slob next to her in my black sweatpants and hoodie. I spend so much time in show blacks that I forget I have other clothes.

"If the other shifts earn this much, we'll have enough to cover the costumes and the turntable and even a little extra," I add, sitting up straight and tearing my eyes off Odile's arched back. "Maybe we can afford some wicked cool new lighting stuff."

Dom smiles, but I can tell from the vacant look in his eyes that I've already lost him. Sound geeks always think lighting is boring and vice versa. At least, I *hope* it's just a sound-versus-lighting situation, and not a new case of Actor Brain.

(Actor Brain isn't a character flaw or anything, since it's not as if they can help it. When you start to talk about tech stuff, actors' frontal lobes suddenly acquire a soft layer of fuzz that blocks all interest and understanding.)

"Do you have any specific wicked cool lighting stuff in mind?" Odile asks me.

"Um, yeah. I had this one idea, but it won't be cheap so I need to make sure we have enough in the budget." Why am I talking about this? Odile probably just asked to be polite. But suddenly I can't shut up. "I've always thought it would be amazing if, when Javert sings 'Stars,' we had a star drop—you know, one of those drapes with a million tiny lights that look like actual stars."

"That *would* be amazing." Odile pulls the bottom part off her cupcake and smooshes it down onto the frosting. Pops does that too. He calls it his cupcake sandwich. "And it would be really inspiring for David, singing up into those lights."

"You think?" Hmm. I always thought actors got their inspiration from having people look at them. "Will says it won't be easy, though."

"Will?" Odile wrinkles her forehead. "Do you mean Mr. Green?"

"Oh, yeah—sorry, I always forget to call him that. He's friends with my dads, so I've known him a long time."

"Wait, *dads*, plural?" Her eyes widen. "Oh, wait—did your dads help at the *Joseph* strike?"

"Indeed." Dom nods gravely. "Once you've spent some time around Sean and Charlie, Mel suddenly makes a lot more sense."

"Hey." I stick out my tongue at him. "No making fun of me. At least *I* know how to pronounce your character's name."

"I think I've got it down now. I watched some tutorials."

"Now I remember." Odile lays two fingertips on my elbow.

"Your dads are the ones who run the parent committee, right?"

For a moment, I seem to have lost the ability to speak. Or use any other part of my body not directly connected to my elbow, where her fingers are still resting.

"That's them," Dom says after an uncomfortable pause. I make a mental note to thank him for not trying to tease me that time.

"Uh-huh," I say, but it comes out more like a squeak. "Dad's the president. Um. Sorry if you've seen them do anything embarrassing."

Odile takes a big bite of her cupcake sandwich. Okay, I guess she does eat baked goods.

"I have no room to talk about embarrassing parents," she says, wiping crumbs off her mouth. "My dad wears this Santa suit every Christmas—not that he dresses up like Santa, mind you, it's a literal *suit*, a jacket and pants, that's bright green and covered in Santa heads. He found it in a bargain bin and he wears it every year because he enjoys humiliating my sister and me."

Dom laughs. I'm kind of jealous of how relaxed he is around Odile. He's talking to her as though she's anyone else at school.

"So, Mel, how much do you need to raise for the star drop?" she asks as I reach under the table for the bag of jelly beans.

"It's a couple thousand to rent one. More than we'd make in a bake sale—we'll need to sell a *lot* of program ads too. But I haven't proposed it to Ms. Marcus yet, so we'll see if she even wants to do it. She might not trust me with lighting after the way I screwed up on *R&J*."

"You did?" Odile frowns.

"Big-time." I sigh. "Long story."

"Stop beating yourself up, Mel." Dom pats my arm. "It was Rachel's fault. Besides, it'll be funny a few years from now."

"Oh, you mean the balcony scene?" Odile furrows her eyebrows. Her voice is astonishingly warm. "My sister was at the show that night. From what she said, it was a three-second blip and everyone forgot about it by the time they got to *Parting is such sweet sorrow.*"

"She clearly remembered it enough to tell *you* all about it," I point out.

"Come on, stuff like that probably happens all the time when you're shooting fancy TV shows, right?" Dom grins at Odile.

"It happens *everywhere*." Odile's smile is warm, too. I can't help smiling back. "On opening night of *Legally Blonde*, all the stage lights went out in the middle of the second act right when there were thirty of us onstage ready to go into 'Bend and Snap.'"

"Oh, God." I groan. "That's an SM's worst nightmare. Did anyone get hurt?"

"Not at all. The crew brought up the work lights so we could see, and they got us back to the right cue really quickly. Up until then we had to dance in the dark with only the backup lights, and the audience could barely see us. They must've thought it was a moody lighting effect, and we all had to act like it was *supposed* to be that way. My cheeks were aching from having to hold that exact smile without laughing."

"You know, I always wondered about that." I tilt my head. "You had to smile through that whole show, practically. *Did* it make your face hurt?"

"A little." She laughs again.

"You saw *Legally Blonde*?" Dom asks me. "Weren't we still in middle school?"

"Yeah, but my dads always used to bring me here to see the shows, even when I was a kid."

"That's wonderful." Odile sounds as though she really *does* think it's wonderful. "I don't think my parents have ever seen a musical except the ones my sister and I have been in."

"Wow. Seriously?" I'd assumed she had stage parents who'd pushed her into the business.

But Dom jumps in before I can ask more about her family. "Did you like doing *Legally Blonde*? I've seen clips from when it was on Broadway, and it looked kind of cheesy."

"It was, but that's all right." Odile shrugs. "As long as you embrace the cheese. Plus, it was the most dancing I've ever gotten to do in any show."

"It has that one really funny song in the trial scene, right?" Dom asks. "What's it called? Something about is he gay or is he European?"

"*That* song!" I thump my hand down on the table, harder than I mean to. I haven't thought about that song in years, but now it's all rushing back. "I hate it *so much!*"

"Whoa, okay." Dom holds up his hands. "Sorry. Didn't know it was a touchy subject."

Odile doesn't say anything, but she's staring at me, clearly waiting for me to say more.

Legally Blonde ends with a big trial scene, where the main character decides the male star witness must be lying about having an affair with her female client, because he's gay. The whole cast then sings this ridiculous song about how the guy might not *actually* be gay because he could just have, like, affected manners or whatever, since he's from some unspecified European country.

"I know it's just supposed to be goofy." I pause, struggling to think of how to explain it. "But when I came to see that show, I was still trying to figure out if I identified as gay or bi or something else, and that song actually made me kind of worried. It made it sound as if figuring out how you identify is supposed to be really easy, so I thought I was neurotic for even thinking about it in the first place. *Now*, obviously, I know that's not how it works at all. I know I'm bisexual, and I don't sit around worrying about it anymore like I did when I was a kid. And I know exactly how uncool it is to have a song that's so completely wrong about everything in a show, and to perform it in a *school*, of all places. And, I mean, besides, what kind of legal defense *is* that? They're trying to say the guy can't *possibly* have had an affair with that lady just because he has a boyfriend. As if no one on the jury's ever *heard* of sexual fluidity."

When I stop talking, Dom's staring at me as though I've been speaking another language. But Odile's lips are slightly parted, and her eyes are wide. "Wow. I always knew that song bothered me, but I didn't know why until now."

"I think this may be the first time in history anyone's ever had a serious conversation about the subtext of the lyrics in *Legally Blonde: The Musical*," Dom says, but neither of us laughs.

"Maybe I should just be glad there's a musical that even *has* a gay character." In the distance, another table of jocks is heading our way, so I try to talk faster. "Maybe it doesn't really count if he's only in it for a joke, but *Les Mis* doesn't have gay people at all. Unless you count fanfiction about Grantaire."

Odile laughs and pulls a baby carrot out of her bag. "Yeah. It's too bad *Les Mis* doesn't have more women. Well, it's too bad for a lot of reasons, but it's also unfortunate that it's so hard to come up with believable girl/girl fanfic."

Well, *that's* an interesting thing for her to say.

"For real." I nod emphatically. "I guess you could do Éponine/Cosette, but with the power imbalance it's just—"

"Brownie time!" a very tall, very wide football player shouts as he strides toward the table, holding out a twenty-dollar bill. "Hand 'em over!"

"Of course." Odile smiles up at him. It's her sunny smile, the one she used with the actors who came up to fawn over her at auditions. Nothing like the soft, subtle smile she wears when we're talking for real. "How many would you and your friends like? If you buy five, you get a free snickerdoodle."

The football player melts under Odile's gaze. I can relate. "A *free* snickerdoodle? Wow."

I busy myself with the cash box as Dom reaches for the brownie platter, the three of us sliding back into our rhythm.

When the football players finally move away, Dom pulls out what's left of the jelly beans and slides them across the table, passing five to me and five to Odile. "Okay, until someone else comes over we're playing jelly bean 'Never Have I Ever.'"

I groan. "We can't play that game in the cafeteria. It always winds up being about sex."

Dom raises his eyebrows, and that's when I realize I just said the word *sex* with Odile right here.

"We'll keep it strictly PG." Dom's lip quirks up. I can see him resisting the urge to make fun of me again, and I try to show I'm grateful with a quick appreciative head-bob. "Well, maybe PG-13. Odile, do you want to start?"

She frowns as she carefully lines up her jelly beans. "I don't think I know how to play this game."

"It's easy." Dom holds up a jelly bean to demonstrate. "You have to eat one if someone says something you've done. At the end, whoever still has jelly beans left wins. I'll start. Let's see . . . never have I ever had a surprise party."

"Ugh." I reach for a jelly bean. "My dads gave me one for my thirteenth. It was the worst. I *hate* surprises."

"Of course you do. You hate anything you can't be in charge of." Dom laughs.

"I *love* surprises." Odile reaches for a jelly bean too.

"You've had a surprise party?" Dom asks her.

"What? Oh, no." She drops the jelly bean. "Sorry, I'm already losing at this game! Mel, you go next so I can get the idea."

I laugh. "Never have I ever, um . . . been late to rehearsal."

"Borrr-ing." Dom pops a jelly bean, but Odile keeps her hands in her lap. "Come on, you've *never* been late to a single rehearsal in your life?"

She shrugs apologetically. "On my first show, the director taught us that early is on time, on time is late . . ."

"And late is unacceptable," I finish for her, grinning. "The first rule of theater."

"Okay, I've got one." Odile raises her hand. A group is coming toward us from one of the actor tables in the middle of the room. Malik and Leah are in front, but they're moving slowly. "Never have I ever sung along to a really embarrassing cast recording in the car with the windows down, and had a cop pull up and stare at me judgmentally."

I'm already laughing at that image, but Dom holds out a jelly bean. "Okay, two things. One, that is so specific there's no way you would've said it if you *haven't* actually done that yourself, which is against the rules. Which means you need to eat a jelly bean even though it's your turn."

"Shoot!" Odile laughs and pops a jelly bean in her mouth. "Can we say this round doesn't count since I've been so incompetent the whole time?"

"Fair." Dom passes out an extra jelly bean to each of us. "And two, which really embarrassing cast recording?"

But I'm positive I already know. "It's *The Sound of Music*, right?"

"Yes!" Odile grins and swallows her jelly bean. "I was at a traffic light and didn't notice he'd pulled up. I was singing Rolf's part in 'Sixteen Going on Seventeen'—it's one of my favorites—and I glanced out the window and he was looking right at me. I'd just gotten my license and I was frantically trying to remember if I'd broken any laws, but when I turned around he was laughing. He waved at me and drove off when the light changed."

I slap the table as I laugh, making my jelly beans jump. "I don't know what I love most about that story. That you thought you were going to get arrested for belting a cheesy sexist show tune, or that *Rolf's* lines are your favorites."

"Like *you've* never done something like that." Dom tosses a jelly bean in his mouth as the table's worth of actors reaches us. "You probably sing 'Climb Ev'ry Mountain' in your sleep. Anyway, remember, it's my turn after this. Hey, Leah, what can I get you?"

But Leah's looking at Odile, smiling the same simpering smile she did when she came up to her during auditions. "Hi, Odile! I'm so excited we're going to be doing this show together."

Odile smiles back. Her sunny smile again. "Hi, Leah! I'm excited too! We get to sing together in the epilogue. It's going to be so much fun."

Even her voice is different now. The casual warmth that was there when she was talking to Dom and me has been replaced by a cool, smooth, even tone. Generic ingenue.

"You know, has anyone ever told you, you should really start a YouTube channel?" Leah asks. "For your singing, I mean. My dad still has the video he made of *Joseph* if you want to use it. You were incredible on 'Pharaoh Story.'"

Odile's smile never fades, but I can see her fingers tensing up around her jelly bean. "That's so sweet of you to offer. Thank you. If I need it, I'll text you for sure."

Leah beams and buys a snickerdoodle. The others buy stuff too, forking over money that we're going to turn around and use to buy costume pieces for them to wear. It might not be a very efficient system, but at least everyone gets sugar out of the deal.

Malik lingers at the table after the others have gone back, biting into one of Odile's snickerdoodles. "Oh my God," he moans. "This is the best cookie I've ever tasted."

"See, Mel?" Odile sounds like herself again now that Leah's not fawning over her anymore. "Life-changing snickerdoodles! And *you* doubted me."

"I never said that!" I blush. I didn't say it *out loud*. Can Odile read minds?

"Crap," Dom mutters next to me. "Whatever you do, Mel, don't look to your right."

I freeze. "Stage right or audience right?"

"Stage—no, wait, I mean—"

But I've already seen her. Rachel's hovering by the door, looking hesitantly in our direction, as though she's debating whether to approach us.

"Uh-oh." I slink down in my seat, wondering if I could somehow crawl all the way under the table. "Is she coming over?"

"Looks like she thought better of it." Malik's very obviously trying not to laugh. He, like Dom, appears immune to the disease of Acting Weird in the Presence of Odile Rose. "You can emerge from your self-imposed exile."

"Yeah, she's leaving." Dom pats my shoulder. "You're safe, Mel."

"Safe from what, exactly?" Odile asks, her eyebrows raised.

"Mel's allergic to her exes," Malik explains around a mouthful of snickerdoodle. "Hey, are you playing jelly bean 'Never Have I Ever'?"

"Not true!" I can't just let that stand. "I'm not allergic to all my exes."

"Well, clearly not *all* of them." Malik smirks and reaches for a jelly bean. "Hey, I've got one. Never have I ever hooked up with anyone within a ten-foot radius."

I groan and shut my eyes. Malik's one of the few actors who *don't* usually make me want to tear my hair out, but in this particular moment, I could kill him.

When I open my eyes again, Dom is laughing, popping a jelly bean in his mouth. I don't turn to look, but I can *feel* Odile watching as I do the same thing while Malik goes on smirking.

She doesn't say anything. I wish I knew what she was thinking.

I guess it doesn't really matter. It isn't a secret that Dom and I went out a million years ago, and there's no reason she'd care anyway. Besides, she's probably already back with David.

But I don't turn to meet her eyes. And a few minutes later, when the lunch bell rings and we start packing up the leftovers, I still can't bring myself to look.

There's something about Odile that makes me feel strange.

Like I'm not myself. Like I'm out of control, and I really, really, *really* don't like feeling out of control.

But I have a strong suspicion this whole situation is only going to get worse.

From: Melody McIntyre

To: All directors and crew heads

Date: Thursday, 2/13, 10:20 p.m.

Subject: Notes from Production Meeting #1

Date: Thursday, 2/13

Start: 3:05 p.m.—*End:* 4:12 p.m.

In attendance: Fatima, Kevin, Jasmin, Shannon, Rachel, Estaban, Tyler, and Mel

Important dates coming up:

- First rehearsal: Friday, 2/14
- Crew party (brainstorm design elements): Saturday, 2/15, Mel's house

Set updates:

- Fatima and Mr. Green ruled that we can repurpose the ship railing from *Little Mermaid* for Javert's suicide bridge, so that's one less thing we have to build (score!).
- We'll definitely use the trapdoor for Valjean and Marius's escape into the sewers and Javert's suicide. We might also use it for the Thénardiers during "One Day More"—Ms. Marcus wants to test it in a blocking rehearsal first.

Props updates:

- The team is modifying leftover swords from *Shrek* to look more nineteenth-century.

- Estaban and Jacob went on an IKEA trip and came back with many, many candlesticks, plus cups, plates, silverware, etc. There were no silver candlesticks so the team is currently experimenting with wrapping a gold set in foil vs. spray-painting a glass set silver. They got LED lights for the scenes that require candles to actually be lit. (Reminder: actual fire of any kind is STRICTLY PROHIBITED in the performing arts wing, for obvious reasons.)

Lighting updates:
- We'll use two follow spots.
- Jasmin is working with Mr. Green on window gobos for the sewer scene, "Master of the House," "On My Own," and maybe "A Heart Full of Love."

Costume updates:
- Rachel, Devin, and Ronee have the first of many planned trips to Goodwill scheduled for Saturday to scour for peasant dresses, military jackets, and accessories.
- We need to ask all cast, crew, and parents if they have vests they can donate. We'll alter them beyond recognition into nineteenth-century student attire, so no one should donate a vest they hope to get back in one piece.

Hair/makeup updates:
- Shannon is experimenting with blood options and is currently

leaning toward a mixture of chocolate syrup and strawberry syrup (needs to be edible in case it accidentally drips into the actors' mouths).

- We may need to use an alternative blood mixture for the barricade scenes, because it's unclear if syrup will run fast enough down Enjolras's face when he's dead and upside down, plus Éponine may also wind up needing to actively bleed. The team is looking into this too.

- We need to know if Nick plans to shave his chest for fake tattoo purposes. Han drew the short straw so she'll ask him and report back.

- Shannon is checking on whether we should black out any of the Thénardiers' teeth. Beth and Julio eagerly voted yes but fortunately it's not their call.

Sound updates:

- The professional sound mixer is booked! Rukmini Raman will be here from tech through closing. Thanks for the hookup, Mr. Green.

- We have twelve working mic packs on a good day, so we need to plan how we'll do handoffs among principals and other soloists. Kevin's working on it.

Publicity updates:

- Official show T-shirts should be in by the beginning of April for all cast, crew, and musicians. Aya is harassing people to get their sizes.

- Tyler is offering a prize of a customized Bitmoji to anyone who submits their program bio to him by the end of February. Tyler has excellent Bitmoji game so please spread the word.

Thank you, everyone! —Mel

—Also stored on BHS performing arts department shared drive.
Created by: Melody McIntyre, stage manager, class of 2021
Viewable to: All crew and directors
Editable by: Current SM ONLY

Scene 5—Beaconville High School Choir Room

DAYS UNTIL SPRING MUSICAL OPENS: 76

Valentine's Day.

What a stupid, pointless, utterly banal holiday.

"No flowers in the choir room." I point at the huge bouquet of roses Christina is cradling in her arms as though it's a human child. "Leave them in the hall with your coat."

"But—"

"Ms. Marcus's orders." Gabby cuts her off neatly. "And you've got to pay tribute to the memorial plaque in the lobby before you come in. We're using the jelly beans left over from the bake sale, so take one from the bag and set it on the shelf under the plaque."

Christina rolls her eyes but doesn't argue, grabbing a jelly bean and flouncing away to carefully deposit her unnecessarily gigantic display of the crass commercial approximation of romance in the hall.

Not that I'm bitter or anything.

Ms. Marcus likes to schedule first rehearsals the Friday after casting. It gives everyone time to get in their permission forms and study the script before we all come together. And this year, that Friday happens to fall on Valentine's Day.

It's actually kind of convenient. This way, I'm so busy I barely have time to think about the fact that I'm single and flower-less.

Two of the new costume team members trot in after Christina, fortunately sans flowers, and I show them where to stash their phones. Once rehearsals start, Ms. Marcus has a strict no-phones-backstage-or-onstage-or-really-anywhere-remotely-near-the-stage-or-even-in-the-choir-room policy, so Gabby and I hung a bunch of over-the-door shoe organizers by the entrance. We always have the first rehearsal in the choir room so we can read through the script and focus purely on the text before everyone starts obsessing over blocking.

A delighted buzz slowly fills the room as more and more people arrive. Soon there's a thick cluster of actors talking and laughing in the middle set of risers. The crew's gathered in smaller groups around the periphery of the room, but they're no less buzzy.

The first rehearsal is the last time the cast and crew will mingle. Up until tech, anyway, but it's best not to think about tech until you don't have a choice in the matter.

In my opinion, the first rehearsal is also the most fun part of a run, when everyone's still happy-anticipatory. By final dress we'll all be stressed and overwhelmed, the cast prone to anxious bouts of tears and the crew sloppy from sleep deprivation. We've got to relish this new-show energy while we can.

"Mel!" Speaking of energy, Dom bounds through the door and wraps me in a hug, even though I literally just saw him in precalc. "It's the first rehearsal! Are you so excited? I'm so excited!"

"I'm excited, for sure." I laugh.

"*I'm* excited!" Gabby pipes in. Dom releases me and turns to hug her, too. She giggles, her light brown cheeks flushing.

"Did you pay tribute to the plaque?" I ask him.

"I did." He holds up his copy of the script, which I'm pleased to see he's already scribbled notes all over. "Also, I took your advice and watched more videos last night. I've decided that what my character may lack in quantity, he makes up in quality."

"Heck yeah." Gabby grins. "And did you see what your vest looks like?"

"Just you wait." Dom takes off his jacket. Beneath it he's taped strips of red and yellow construction paper to his Boston College sweatshirt. It's a decidedly amateurish but still recognizable imitation of the vest Enjolras wears in the second act.

Gabby and I both crack up. I don't even mind that Dom's being a total *actor* right now.

"You win the prize," I tell him. "No one else has come in costume. Well, unless you count Lauren's newsie hat, but I'm pretty sure she wears that every day."

"Go me!" Dom pumps his fist and steps aside to let Ms. Qiao pass him. Even *she's* smiling today. "So, the only thing about this Enjolras guy—and don't get me wrong, I'm not complaining, because he gets to do a lot once he finally shows up—but, well, he seems kind of, ah, one-note? Like, I didn't see a ton of, you know, complexity?"

I'm about to offer to loan him the novel with all the Enjolras scenes marked in Post-its when Gabby fakes a gasp and clutches at her heart, tossing her loose black curls behind her.

"How dare you!" she cries. "Enjolras is not *one-note*. He's *passionate*! He's a *revolutionary*! He's fighting for *justice*!"

Dom holds up his hands, laughing. "Sorry! Clearly I stand corrected!"

"Besides, if you want character complexity, this may not be the show for you," a voice stage-whispers from the other side of the door.

I groan. "It's the first rehearsal, Mr. Green. No complaints allowed."

Will steps inside, carefully balancing three giant Tupperware containers. Gabby rushes forward to help him. "Right you are, Ms. McIntyre. I promise to be cheery from now on. Look, I come bearing snacks! Cranberry popcorn and apple chips with cream cheese. You have napkins, right?"

"Of course we have napkins," Gabby says, understandably offended he'd even ask.

"Of course. I never doubt the preparations of the stage management team." Will claps Dom on the shoulder as Gabby carefully transfers the food over to the table we set up by the whiteboard. "As for the rest of us, shall we venture to the barricade?"

"*To the barricade!*" Dom yells, loud enough for everyone to hear.

The actors start laughing. "I'm with you, man!" Malik yells at the top of his voice.

Soon there are more shouts. "To the barricade! *To the barricade!*" Some of the guys even stomp their feet.

I can't help smiling, but still, oh my God. *Actors.*

"Okay, everyone," Ms. Marcus says, "I appreciate your enthusiasm, but the chess team can probably hear you in the next wing. Mel, are we waiting on any principals?"

I haven't seen Nick or Odile yet, but before I can say so Odile ducks past me silently, sliding her phone into a shoe pocket without needing to be told. She gives me a small smile and a wave, and I smile back, ever so slightly flustered.

Okay, so it's *possible* I'm getting a crush. A small, nonthreatening one. It's the equivalent of having a crush on Anna Kendrick or someone else equally unattainable. Except Odile's prettier than Anna Kendrick.

"Just waiting on Nick," I say as Odile glides to an empty spot on the bottom riser next to David.

"Well, we can't exactly start without our Valjean." Ms. Marcus is still smiling, though. On first rehearsal day it's hard not to stay in a good mood. "Let's give him one more minute."

David leaps to his feet, like he's going to go hunt Nick down then and there, Javert style. Someone starts humming "The Confrontation," which earns another round of laughs and foot stomps, and Ms. Marcus gently pushes David back into his seat. "Save it for opening night, Inspector."

I don't realize Rachel's come through the door until she's

clearing her throat in my ear. "Hi, Mel."

"Oh. Hi." I straighten up. Yesterday after school was our first production meeting, also known as The First Time I Had No Choice but to Talk to Rachel Scott Since We Broke Up. I knew *that* would be awkward, but being so close to her right now is somehow worse.

"Listen, I didn't want to say anything yesterday with everyone else there, but . . ." She clears her throat again. "I wanted to thank you and Mr. Green for keeping me on as costume head. I know things have been kind of uncomfortable since . . . But anyway, I'm really excited to get to work on this show. I love *Les Mis*."

"I remember. You said you'd always wanted to design non-revolting corsets for 'Lovely Ladies.'" I try to replay the conversation we had last summer about *Les Mis* costumes in my head, but all I can think about is her effectively announcing over the headsets that I'm a slut.

"Do you think there will be time to take any cast measurements today?" she asks, oblivious to my stress. Which, come to think of it, she always kind of was.

"Oh, are you the costume girl? Here, you can measure me right now." Nick smiles broadly from the doorway, holding his arms out to each side. I half expect him to start flapping them and making airplane noises. "Put me in something cool, and whatever you do, don't make me wear a wig."

"Costumes and hair and makeup are two separate departments." Rachel plucks the phone out of Nick's outstretched hand and slides it into an empty compartment in the shoe bag.

Nick whips his head around to face her, his mouth falling into a shocked little O.

I grin. There *is* a reason I liked Rachel. She takes crap from no one.

"She's right," I tell Nick. "But by the way, if the hair and makeup crew decides you need a wig, you'll wear a wig."

Nick lowers his arms, and he looks like he's about to say something either snarky or flippant when Ms. Marcus interrupts us. "Nick, Rachel, welcome. Time to take your seats. You can join us too, Mel."

I avoid making eye contact with either of them as I go to my seat next to Gabby, where I'd already laid out my binder with my blocking script and mechanical pencil at the ready.

Nick wedges into the front riser between David and Odile, giving the two of them a totally different smile than the one he gave Rachel and me. He actually looks sincere. Maybe even nice. Odile meets his gaze for a second, then turns down to her script as Christina simpers into a seat on her other side.

Ms. Marcus goes through some admin stuff about rehearsal schedules, then gives us a mini speech about the history of *Les Mis*. No one speaks while she's talking. No one even moves. We're all in a theater hush.

It's finally starting to sink in that we're doing this show. *This show.* In a couple of months, we'll build a barricade, and not long after that the auditorium will be filled with people, listening to a full orchestra play "Do You Hear the People Sing?" while sixty voices ring out in perfect harmony.

It's awesome. I'm not going to lie.

Ms. Marcus leads the actors through some warm-up exercises and assigns the ensemble solo lines, and then we start the read-through. Gabby and I take turns reading the stage directions, which is fun.

Dom gets to read the first solo line of the show. He looks happier than I've ever seen him, which is unfortunate since he's supposed to be talking about how hellish prison life is. But he's so glow-y it's hard to hold it against him.

The reading goes pretty quickly once we start, since without the actual music, the show isn't nearly the three-hour epic it's supposed to be. Most of the actors aren't really acting yet, much less singing, but just hearing the words read out in the voices that are *going* to sing them is still kind of amazing.

I make notes in my binder as we go. I can already see places where we'll have to carefully choreograph what the crew's doing backstage.

When Malik, Alejandra, and Leah start reading "A Heart Full of Love," a few of the younger actors start giggling behind their hands at the romantic lyrics. Some of the crew members do too, until I look their way and they go quiet. But a moment later, as the lyrics venture into the way-over-the-top territory—seriously, Marius and Cosette's flirting is *significantly* more painful to listen to than Romeo and Juliet's—Nick starts chuckling. Loudly.

It's *so* unprofessional. This is his first show as a principal, but he should still know that laughing during a read-through is one of the rudest things you can do. I knew Nick was a jerk to me and

Rachel, but I didn't think he'd be this uncool even to his fellow actors.

When we finally get to the last song of act one, "One Day More," Ms. Marcus lets the cast sing the final chorus. This song involves a lot of triumphant yelling, so the sound of all sixty-odd cast members booming out the lines together is nearly deafening. Even Odile joins in for the finale, despite the fact that her character's dead during this song. I almost want to join in myself.

Ms. Marcus declares a break, and everyone pounces on the food. I set the timer on my watch so I can call the group back on schedule and try to think of how I can most productively use the break time. I could show Gabby how I've set up my blocking script, but she's talking to Jasmin and Dom, and I don't want to interrupt cross-generational crew bonding.

"Mel?" Ms. Marcus calls. "Do you have a second?"

"Of course." I hurry over.

She gives me instructions on how to make the rehearsal schedule for the next week, and I jot down notes in my binder. Making rehearsal schedules is a lot of work, but it's fun—it's like a logic puzzle, figuring out who needs to be where and when. Plus, she already gave me the list of who's going to be in all the featured ensemble roles, which is cool, since the actors don't know that themselves yet. I like that she trusts me to keep it secret.

Ms. Marcus calls Fatima and Jasmin over next, and I'm halfway back to my seat when I hear Gabby say, "Wait, *what* do you want?"

Something in her tone makes me turn and look. She's

standing in front of Nick and Christina, her hands on her hips, making a face like she just bit into something sour.

"Should I spell it for you?" Nick says. "L-A-T-T-E."

"Stop," Christina mutters beside him, but she's giggling. Nick turns to her, grinning in that way guys like him do when they've made a girl laugh. As though that's equally as impressive as climbing Mount Everest or hitting every note in a Sondheim show.

"What's going on?" I step forward. I don't want to undermine Gabby's authority, but I really, really, *really* don't like Nick's tone.

"He wants me to go get him coffee." Gabby turns to me, then back to Nick. "I was about to tell him I'm not an errand girl. I have to stay at school until rehearsal's done, just like you do."

Nick's smile fades.

"Gabby's right." I fold my arms across my chest. "The crew isn't here to do the cast's bidding. You want a drink, you get it yourself—after rehearsal—like the rest of us."

I glare at Christina, remembering all those cough drops. Most of the actors are decent to the crew, but there are always a few who think we're here to be their servants.

Usually it's not the leads, though. Liam brought *me* dough-nuts during *R&J* tech.

"Hey, okay, okay." Nick's smile widens as he holds up his hand in a mock salute. "Whatever you say, boss lady. Don't put me in a time-out, all right?"

Behind him, Christina giggles. "Mel, I thought you were coming over to tell us we were breaking one of the superstitions.

Is there one for this show yet?"

"Yeah, actually . . ." Julio leans over from his seat. "We need one now that rehearsals have started. If we don't have it by the end of today, *that's* bad luck by itself."

"It is?" Leah looks alarmed.

That's the first I've heard that, and I'm pretty sure Julio's making it up, but I go with it. We're still keeping the whole love-curse thing a secret from the cast, and we need a decoy superstition so they don't start asking questions. "Yeah, we should come up with something."

"Or the evil curse spirits will get us," Julio stage-whispers.

Dom starts humming the *Twilight Zone* theme music from a few risers over, which makes me snort, but Leah and Christina are both darting their eyes back and forth, as though they can't figure out whether to take this seriously.

"Plus . . ." Beth leans in, stage-whispering just like Julio. "Remember how we were supposed to do *Phantom of the Opera* originally? Well, *I* read that if you say you're going to do *Phantom* and then you back out, your new show gets cursed by the *real* Phantom as revenge for spurning him. He'll send Andrew Lloyd Webber's personal thirteen horsemen of the apocalypse after you."

"Okay, no, wait." I have to intervene now. Some of the ensemble girls have their hands over their mouths, like they're genuinely frightened by this inanity. "That's completely *not* true. I've never heard a single story about the thirteen—"

"Should we even be talking about this?" Christina asks. "Isn't it bad luck to say the number—um, the number one-three?"

I've never heard that rule, either, or at least nothing that's theater specific, but I might as well take advantage. "Okay, look, here's the special superstition for this show." I hold up a finger so they'll know I'm serious. "No one can say that number. Not in rehearsals, not in the auditorium, not anywhere. If you say it, you'll have to, um . . ." I try to think. Countercurses are supposed to be the opposite of whatever you did to bring about the bad luck. What's the opposite of saying *thirteen*? Well, seven is supposed to be a lucky number. "Spin around backward seven times."

"While yodeling," Beth adds. Everyone laughs. "Seriously, yodeling is good for the spirit. Plus it's a solid vocal warm-up."

I nod agreeably. If a countercurse is funny, people are more likely to do it.

"Sorry, I didn't catch that." Dom cups his hand over his ear. "Which number are we not supposed to say?"

"I'm not falling for that," I tell him while Beth and the others snicker. "Spread the word, everyone. I'll put it on the shared drive tonight."

"But what if we have to write it down?" Julio points to his script. "Like, what if Ms. Marcus tells me I'm supposed to steal exactly *thir*—I mean, twelve-plus-one coins out of Nick's pocket? Can I put it in my script as a blocking note or will Andrew Lloyd Webber come chasing after me on a horse with a chandelier? Or what if I'm doing my calc homework and the answer is *exactly* thir—I mean, um—"

I hold up my hand again, trying to look stern even though everyone's laughing harder than ever. "You know how this works, everybody. We have superstitions for a reason."

When I get back to my seat, Gabby's sitting with her arms crossed, still fuming. "We should call him Nick the Dick," she whispers as I take the seat beside her.

"Ha. I like it."

"Hey, Mel, do you have a second?" Will asks from behind us.

At the sound of my first name, I snap to attention. Will *never* calls me that at school. I twist around. "Sure?"

"Good." He lowers his voice to a whisper and beckons for me to lean in. "I have a suggestion."

"Cool, what?"

"You may want to downplay the superstition talk." He fiddles with the tape measure in his hands, drawing the tape out and rolling it back in again. "It isn't always a great idea to make a spectacle of these things."

I shift in my seat. Obviously I can't tell Will about my need to hide my love curse from the cast, so I shrug. "It's tradition. And it's good for team unity, right? We all have a common enemy—the curse."

"Sure, but . . ." Will tilts his head and scratches his chin. "You might want to avoid using that word, too. When you start throwing it around, that's how rumors get going. Imaginations run wild. Notions are planted."

"But it's my job to enforce the rules."

"It's only a suggestion." He holds up his hands. "Just . . . the subconscious is a heck of a thing. We've got enough problems on this show without everyone worrying about some boogeyman."

"But we just got started. There aren't any problems yet."

"There will be." Will starts ticking things off on his fingers. "We're going to have a hazer, twelve wireless body mics, a flying bridge, a giant barricade made of falling-apart furniture, rolling carts, a starter pistol—assuming we can get Coach Mulhern to lend it to us—a trapdoor, *and* that godforsaken turntable. It's a recipe for accidents. If you want to keep your team safe, *that's* what you should be focusing on. Make sure they learn to be careful and follow the rules—the ones that actually matter—and that they trust you enough to always do *exactly* what you say."

I sigh. I hate getting lectured. "Okay, okay."

The act two read-through goes faster than the first half did. The actors have hit their strides, and there are fewer lyrics in this act anyway, since a lot of it is battle scenes. Most of the principals die off—except Odile, who already died back in act one—but Ms. Marcus lets them sing the very end again anyway. Considering that they've had exactly zero music rehearsals and we don't have any instruments today, it sounds surprisingly good.

"Principals and featured ensemble members, come up when I call your name," Ms. Marcus says when they're done. "Everyone else, you're dismissed. Dom, you're up first."

I sit back to watch the squeals as she tells the actors which ensemble solos they're getting. All the male principals have extra parts except Nick and David, and some of the girls get multiple parts, too. Christina gets to be Factory Girl *and* one of the student revolutionaries, plus she's understudying for Fantine, and she looks simultaneously thrilled and terrified when she gets the news.

"Convict Number One!" Dom cries, skidding toward Gabby and me. "I get to open the show! More singing for me!"

"Since when are you even that into singing?" I ask him. "I thought you always said percussion owned your soul."

"I changed my mind. Singing can have, like, half of it. Also, you weren't kidding about my awesome death scene. I'm going to keel over and make all the poor fools in the audience cry. Do you think I could talk Ms. Marcus into having Convict Number One die onstage too?"

"Um . . . I doubt it."

"Congrats, man." Nick claps Dom on the shoulder, dude-bro style. "I heard you're opening the show with us."

"Yeah!" Dom grins at him. "It's gonna be awesome."

Nick grins and claps him again before going over to join Malik and Julio, probably to dude-bro with them, too.

"Ugh." I groan as he walks off. "That guy is every obnoxious actor stereotype come to life in vivid and horrifying detail."

"Eh, he's not that bad." Dom shrugs. I'm about to tell him about how he tried to send Gabby on a beverage run, but he's already turning around to call out to Malik, "Hey, wait up!"

I follow the others outside. The hallway is packed and noisy, with sixty-plus actors and the whole crew too slowly making their way out. Ahead of us, some of the guys are goofing off at the far end of the hall. Dom jogs up to join them.

"Pick me up like this," Malik is saying, slinging his arms around Nick's neck. "Bride-over-the-threshold style."

The others laugh, and I sigh wearily. They're talking about the sewer scene, where Malik's character is unconscious and Nick is supposed to carry him around the stage, but I don't see why they have to do that tedious straight-guy thing where they act like it's hilarious to even think about making physical contact with each other.

"Or I could sling you over my back." Nick bends down like he's going to pick Malik up around his knees. Malik jogs backward out of his reach, and the others keep laughing.

"You could carry him up on your shoulders," Julio calls.

"I'm supposed to be totally passed out, though," Malik says.

"Try piggyback. And you can, like, pretend to sleep on his neck."

"Bury your face in his hair," Andrew says, which makes them all laugh harder than ever.

That's when I remember what Will said, about being careful. There are no teachers out in the hallway, so I'm in charge. "No unsupervised stunt practice," I call.

"Sorry, Mel." Malik grins sheepishly. "Won't happen again."

Nick doesn't say anything. He's still laughing.

"Melody?" Ms. Marcus steps out into the hall. "A quick word?"

I hurry back to the choir room. "Of course."

"Thank you. I'd like to look over the notes you made during the rehearsal."

I take out my binder and we go through them quickly. She nods approvingly and gives me a few more things to add to my list. I tell her my idea about renting a star drop, and she nods, tapping her chin.

"It'll depend on how much we wind up needing to allocate to the final costume budget," she says after a moment, "but it's a wonderful idea. Go ahead and work with Fatima and Jasmin on the research and let me know what the rental costs would be, and we'll take it from there."

"Awesome. I will, thank you."

"And now . . ." She reaches into her bag with a flourish and produces a thick metal ring loaded with keys. "This is for you."

I squeak. "Seriously?"

She's giving me the keys to the theater.

I've never been this close to them. The previous SMs wouldn't let anyone else so much as touch them, and during *R&J* I was still too new to the role to be allowed my own set. I had to text a teacher every time I needed to get into the performing arts wing after hours.

"This one goes to the house, this one to the costume closet, this one to the prop room . . ." Ms. Marcus goes through each key as I do my best to commit it all to memory. "They're yours until strike. Remember, you can never loan them to *anyone*, under any circumstances. I know I don't need to tell you how important that is."

I nod somberly. "You have my word."

Gabby's by the door as I head out, taking down the shoe bags. "What's the homework tonight?" she asks as she passes me my phone.

"I'm writing up the rehearsal report, but you can have the night off. Maybe do some *actual* homework, if you want."

She scrunches up her face. "Is it wrong if I'd rather do theater paperwork than read about isotopes?"

"If it's wrong, I don't want to be right."

"Party's still tomorrow night, Mel?" Estaban calls from the hallway. Odile walks past him, her chin lifted, and he steps back to make room like she's the Duchess of Sussex or something.

"Yep!" I call back. "Seven, my house. Bring your scripts!"

Estaban waves, and Gabby leaves after him. The last of the others are trickling out. I spot a few more bouquets of Valentine's flowers piled up around the door, but I do my best to ignore them. The last thing I have time to think about right now is romance.

I don't actually need to leave through the auditorium exit— my car's all the way on the other end of the parking lot—but I can't resist going the long way so I can try my new key in the main door.

It fits. This theater's officially my domain now. With or without the stupid curse.

CAST LIST—ALL NAMED ROLES

Name	Role 1	Role 2	Role 3	Role 4	Role 5
Nick Underwood	Valjean				
David Patel	Javert				
Odile Rose	Fantine				
Malik Sexton	Convict 2	Marius			
Leah Zou	Éponine				
Alejandra Huston	Cosette				
Julio Ramirez	Convict 3	Man 2	Sailor (nonsinging)	Thénardier	
Beth Meyers	Sex Worker 1	Madame Thénardier			
Dominic Connor	Convict 1	Enjolras			
Lauren Breen	Gavroche				
Andrew Hernandez	Convict 5	Bishop	Grantaire	Brujon	*Understudy— all male principals*
Christina Leasure	Factory Girl	Feuilly	*Understudy—Fantine*		
Aaron Crane	Convict 4	Foreman	Combeferre		
Katelyn Landwehr	Pimp	Joly			
Madison Rogers	Old Woman	Jean Prouvaire			

Imani Miller	Courfeyrac	*Understudy—Cosette & Gavroche*		
Peyton Tiu	Woman 1	Lesgles	*Dance captain*	
Jillian Waldrep	Bamatabois	Claquesous		
Briony Olson	Woman 4	Sailor 1	Montparnasse	
Kadie Akins	Sailor 2	Urchin		
Selah Levi	Laborer	Woman 3	Sailor 3	
Kyle Marckini	Man 1	Fauchelevent		
Uri Lee	Constable 1	Sentry 1	*Understudy—Madame Thénardier*	
Tasha Barnett	Constable 2	Woman 2	Sentry 2	*Understudy—Éponine*
Bruce Dickerson	Army Officer	Major Domo		
Chad Syring	Babet			
Connor Kukovec	Farmer	Beggar		
Johanna Depto	Sex Worker 2	Onlooker 1		
Paige Dickert	Sex Worker 3	Onlooker 2		
Josefina Penoi	Young Cosette			
Taylor Kellerman	Young Éponine	*Understudy—Young Cosette*		

Prepared for distribution by hard copy and email to all cast, crew, and directors following first rehearsal.

—Also stored on BHS performing arts department shared drive.

Created by: Melody McIntyre, stage manager, class of 2021
Viewable to: All cast, crew, and directors
Editable by: Current SM ONLY

Scene 6—The McIntyre-Perez House

DAYS UNTIL SPRING MUSICAL OPENS: 75

"Hey, you two!" I step out onto the porch to hug Fatima and Jasmin. "Thanks for coming! You can head on down to the basement. The schedule's up on the wall, so assemble your groups and start brainstorming. Make sure you pull your teams into separate corners and don't let them talk too loud, because we don't want anyone's ideas to influence the other teams until we merge for the cross-team debrief."

"Nice to see you too," Jasmin says, but she's laughing. "Don't worry, I'm sure you'll stop us before we break any rules."

"Is Mr. Green here?" Fatima tries to peer behind me into the kitchen, where Dad is opening a bag of chips. Pops is hiding in the pantry. "I watched a bunch of videos about turntables yesterday and I still have no idea how to actually build a set that fits on one."

"Not yet, but he will be soon."

They go downstairs, where the speaker's already blaring the

original *Les Mis* concept album. The people who take French are trying to sing along with Gavroche, badly.

"Is that the last of them?" Dad asks, stepping out onto the porch and rubbing his arms.

"No, there are still a few stragglers."

Pops comes out too, pulling on an old Harvard sweatshirt. "How long do you think before it's warm enough to eat out here?" he asks, gazing fondly at the dining set on our front porch. We have a comfy couch and table and chairs, but we don't get to use them for most of the year.

"A couple of months, at least." Dad turns to brush snow off the railing. "Sometimes I really don't like living in New England. Speaking of which, Mel, I hit send on your registration. Another summer at the Providence Theater Institute."

"You didn't!" I wrap my arms around his torso in a massive hug-from-behind. He straightens up, laughing. "I didn't know camp sign-ups were even open yet!"

"Yeah, you've been busy." Dad grins. "So we decided to look it up on our own."

"You're so awesome! Thank you!" I can't stop grinning. "Another summer of getting to do nothing but eat, sleep, and breathe theater."

I wonder what shows PTI will do this year. I've been crossing my fingers every summer for *Les Mis*, so now I don't even know what to hope for. *Spring Awakening? Dear Evan Hansen*, if they can get the rights?

"That's actually something we've been meaning to talk to

you about, Mel." Suddenly Pops has his serious face on. My good mood evaporates in an instant. "This isn't the time, but we might as well mention it now and we can discuss it later."

Uh-oh. "What?"

Dad moves over to stand next to Pops, the two of them opposite me on the porch. Whenever they make a point of talking to me as a united front, I know they're going to say something I won't like.

"We know you love working on these shows, and going to drama camp," Pops begins.

"And we're thrilled you got the stage manager job," Dad says. "But it's spring of your junior year, and it's time to start thinking seriously about college."

"I've *been* thinking about it. I told you my plan, remember? Ms. Marcus thinks I'll get in to UMass Amherst. They have the best technical theater program in the whole state."

"Yes, well, UMass is a great school." Pops folds his arms across his chest. "But—"

"But what? Pops, please don't try to act like UMass isn't good enough just because *you* went to—" I point to his crimson sweatshirt.

"That isn't what I was going to say at all." Pops sighs.

"Listen." Dad holds out his hands in his best look-how-reasonable-I'm-being move. "We don't have time for a big discussion about this. All we wanted to say, Mel, is that we should talk more about college."

"And it's not that we don't want you to look at theater

programs," Pops adds. "You should definitely apply to UMass, but there are a lot of other great schools you haven't even considered. You have excellent grades, and there are plenty of colleges where you can major in an academic field and do theater as an extracurricular."

"What do you want me to do? Study engineering just so I can say I did? I already *know* what I want to do for my career. There are *thousands* of professional stage managers. People do this their whole lives!"

"We believe you, sweetie, we really do, but keep in mind that you're sixteen years old." Pops still has that maddening I-know-better tone in his voice. "You're too young to make a decision like that. When I was sixteen, I wanted to be—"

"A rock star. I know." I roll my eyes. "Just because *you* had unrealistic goals doesn't mean I—"

"Hey, relax, everybody," Dad jumps in, which is a good thing because Pops's eyes look like they're about to bulge out of his head. "Let's talk more when—"

"Sorry I'm late." Gabby bounds onto the porch. She isn't really late—it's seven on the dot—but on time is almost-late for stage managers. "Do you need help with anything, Mel?"

"Hi, Gabby, it's nice to see you." Dad smiles at her. Pops does, too, but I can tell he's still fuming. "Charlie and I were just going inside. We'll talk later, Mel."

After the door closes behind them, Gabby tilts her head to one side. "Are you all right?"

"I'm fine."

"You're sure?"

"Totally."

"Okay, good. Because, listen, there's something I've been meaning to talk to you about . . ." She trails off.

"Sure, what's up?"

"Well . . . I'm kind of worried about the whole curse thing."

"What, my love curse?" I laugh.

"I didn't mean that. Although now that you mention it, maybe." Gabby shakes her head. "The whole thing at the rehearsal yesterday, about the actors not saying the number thirteen—that's not a real rule, is it?"

"Nah. It's just a decoy, because we don't want the actors to know Jasmin's theory about my personal dramas. They already try to blame the crew whenever anything goes wrong, and we don't need to add fuel to that fire. Plus, I mean . . ." I tuck a curl that's sprung loose from my ponytail behind my ear and glance around to make sure no one's coming up the walk. "It's actually a little embarrassing, so the fewer people who know, the better."

"I get that, but . . ." Gabby frowns again. "It's just—we're *lying* to the actors, aren't we? Telling them they can't say that word or bad things will happen? I thought you always said that in theater, everyone has to trust each other or the whole show will fall apart?"

I have said that. Many times. Hmm. "Well, yeah, but . . . that really matters for the *crew*. We have to be honest with our fellow techs. The cast's on a need-to-know basis."

"Okay . . ." Gabby tilts her head again. "I guess that makes sense."

A car door slams behind us, and we turn to see Rachel climbing out and waving goodbye to her mom. I quickly change the subject.

"You and I are just floating between the groups for most of tonight," I tell Gabby. "Stage management isn't really supposed to come up with ideas, but we can jump in if anyone needs help figuring out what's feasible or whatever. Later we'll do a group debrief and put on the concert video for inspiration."

"Can't we watch the movie instead?" Rachel asks as she climbs the porch steps behind us. She's carrying two tote bags, both of which appear to be stuffed full of fabric samples and thrift-store finds. I have to give her credit for coming prepared. "The costumes are way better than in any of the stage versions."

"We're *not* watching the movie." I cut her off. "Ms. Marcus expressly forbade it."

"I thought that was because the singing was bad?" Gabby asks. "Does it matter for costumes?"

I want to ask whose side Gabby's on, anyway, but Will interrupts us.

"Anyone call for brownies?" he booms from the sidewalk. "I put in my customized brainstorming fuel. Or you can call them pecans, take your pick."

"You're hilarious, Mr. Green." Rachel smiles.

"I try, Ms. Scott, I try."

"Fatima's freaking out about the turntable," I tell him. "She has a bunch of questions."

"Then let's go talk shop."

I lead the way to the basement. Rachel finds Devin and the rest of the costume team, and Will goes over to confer with Fatima while I set out his brownies. The pizza my dads ordered isn't here yet, so everyone descends on the food table.

"Just a reminder, everybody . . ." I smile at my friends as they throw elbows to get to the brownies first. Smiling and admonishing at the same time is a big part of stage management. "You're supposed to be *brainstorming*."

"Come on, boss!" Estaban holds a brownie triumphantly over his head. "You can't expect us to brainstorm without sustenance!"

Bryce shoves an entire brownie into her mouth. "I just had, like, eight hundred new ideas," she tries to say, while crumbs fly from her mouth.

"Yeah, we're good, Mel." Jasmin laughs. "You can relax. Look, we've already got a whole list of ideas."

She shows me the lighting team's notebook, where, sure enough, there's a long list of scribbled bullet points.

I love my crew. We're always diligent and organized, even when we're scarfing down chocolate.

"Besides," Estaban adds, helping himself to a second brownie, "it's been a week since they posted the cast list, and we haven't had a single crisis yet. That's got to be some kind of record."

"True," Shannon points out. "We made it through one whole rehearsal unscathed."

"That's because Mel's averting the curse gods for us single-handedly." Jasmin grins.

I laugh. "Or maybe our luck's finally changing."

"Ack! Don't say that!" Estaban shakes his head fervently, brownie crumbs falling onto his "I'll Sleep After Strike" sweatshirt. "You'll tempt the spirits!"

The others go back to their groups, and I reach down to set up the concert video so it'll be ready after the debrief. That's when I hear Pops's voice at the bottom of the stairs.

"Come on, the gang of teenage ruffians is down here." Pops likes to make fun of my friends because the theater crowd at his high school all wore black eyeliner and smoked clove cigarettes. "I'm sure they'll be glad to see you. Mel, we've got one more!"

"We do?" As far as I know, the whole crew is already here. I weave a narrow path through the groups only to find my father standing at the foot of the stairs next to Odile Rose.

She's wearing black leggings and a T-shirt with "Young, Scrappy & Hungry" printed across the front, and she's carrying a giant food container and a purse with a fancy label. She's got less makeup on than usual, and from the way her fingers are clasped in front of her, she actually looks a tiny bit nervous.

"Oh, um. Hi." I glance over my shoulder at the crew behind me. A few of them are eyeing Odile, and the conversations in the room are dying off.

Actors don't step into our midst voluntarily. Even Dom knows to keep his distance from crew-only gatherings now that he's crossed over.

"Oh, I'm sorry." Odile's slight accent has never sounded more adorable. She bites her lip as Pops retreats back up the stairs. "I think I misunderstood. Is this party just for the tech crew?"

"Uh . . . kind of?" I don't know what to say. Having an actor around changes things for us. Sure, *I* might have a mild celebrity crush on Odile, but for my friends, having her here is very much contrary to the spirit of what we're doing tonight.

This party's for *us*. We'll probably spend a significant chunk of it complaining about the cast. That's just kind of what we do, the same way they complain about us.

Besides, Odile probably only showed up because she thought *her* friends were coming. Now that she knows the truth, she's bound to hightail it out the door.

Sure enough, she glances around behind me at the increasingly quiet room and says, "Well, I don't want to be in the way."

"It's all right," I say, but I can feel all the eyes on us.

"Could we . . ." Odile fumbles with the strap of her fancy purse. "I'm sorry to take you away from the party, but do you think we could talk in the hall?"

"Oh, um. Okay." I signal to Gabby to get the conversations going again and follow Odile back up the basement stairs. I guess to say goodbye.

"This is a bit awkward." Odile tucks a lock of wavy hair behind her ear. God, she's cute. "I don't have a ride home. My parents dropped me off, but they were on their way to the hockey game with my sister."

"Oh . . ."

"I can get an Uber." But she doesn't reach for her phone.

"I mean, or you could stay for a while." I don't know exactly why I say it, but when I see the way Odile's lips curl up into that soft smile again, I'm glad I did. "I mean, there might not be a lot for you to do—the crew's brainstorming with their departments. But Gabby and I don't have departments either, so you wouldn't be the only extraneous person here. I mean, not that you could ever be extraneous, but—um. You know, uh, you know what I mean." There I go again. Why can't I form proper sentences in this girl's presence?

"Really? I won't be in the way?"

She'll definitely be in the way, but I shake my head. "We'd love to have you. Also, there are brownies."

"I do like brownies. But I was hoping for another one of those cupcakes you made."

"Um." I giggle. Ugh, I *never* giggle. "The brownies are better. Mr. Green made them."

"Even so."

Now I'm blushing. Ugh ugh *ugh*. I turn away before she can see and lead her back down the stairs.

It turns out Odile's food dish has an enormous lasagna in it from the good Italian restaurant downtown. I put it on the table next to what's left of the brownies and back away carefully to avoid getting trampled as three dozen hungry techs pounce on it. When they figure out who brought the food, some of them shout thank-yous to Odile, but a few just look at me quizzically, as if they can't quite wrap their brains around the idea that our resident ingenue brought carbs to the crew.

All I can do is shrug. Odile's ways are as mysterious to me as they are to them.

She heads for an empty corner, and I go over to the lighting group so I can talk to Jasmin about the star drop. They all get quiet when I walk up, casting glances back at Odile.

"What's *she* doing here?" Ellie whispers. "I mean, I like lasagna, but it's weird."

"She thought it was an actor party, too," I explain.

"Why would she think that?" Jasmin doesn't bother to whisper. That's probably fine given how loud the room is, but I still kind of wish she'd lower her voice, just to be polite. "We didn't tell the actors we were doing this. Unless *you* did."

"I didn't. She probably just overheard some of us talking at rehearsal. It's no big deal."

"I don't know." Jasmin shakes her head. "Something doesn't seem right."

"Okay, well, *anyway*." I shrug. "Who here's heard of a star drop?"

"A—wait, seriously?" Ellie's eyes widen. "Can we get one? No way!"

"It depends on the budget, but I hope so." I grin, glad the subject's sufficiently changed. Even Jasmin's gaping at the idea.

We talk about logistics for the next ten minutes. We could keep going for another ten at least, but I'm supposed to be circulating, so eventually I say goodbye and move on to hair and makeup. Shannon's already got her team sketching out ideas for how to gather David's long hair into a Javert-ish ponytail and experimenting with cocoa powder to see how dirty they can make each other's faces, so it's clear they don't need my help. Though I notice a few of them are casting uncomfortable looks Odile's way, too.

Gabby's sitting with Estaban and the props team, looking over their sketches, and Rachel's crew is going through the fabric bags. Fatima's group is gathered in the far corner, talking to Will about the turntable and munching lasagna.

I glance at Odile. She's sitting on the floor with her purse beside her, a thick paperback open on her lap.

Well, I don't want her to feel like we've abandoned her.

"Homework?" I ask as I approach.

She flips over her book so I can see the cover, and I laugh. She's reading *Les Misérables*.

"I haven't read that all the way through since ninth grade." I slide down the wall to sit beside her, leaning over so I can see which edition she's got. It's the newest translation, and it looks well-thumbed. "I should warn you, there's fifty random pages about the Battle of Waterloo halfway through."

"I actually kind of like that chapter. I lived in the UK for a few years, and we were taught to view Waterloo as a victory for humankind. It's interesting to see the French perspective."

Wow. I don't know anyone else who's actually read the entire book. "Oh. I guess that makes sense."

A sudden burst of laughter makes me glance back into the room. The set crew, halfway across from us, is doubled over.

"He's a lot better-looking than Newt Scamander, that's for sure," Caroline says, to even more laughter.

"I'm telling you, Malik's gonna be the hottest Marius of *all time*," Daniel says. "It's like if Idris Elba went back in time thirty years and started singing 'Heart Full of Love.'"

"Too bad Leah's got that giant stick up her ass," Skylor adds. "I always want to root for Marius and Éponine."

"She's still better than Christina," Daniel says. "If she'd gotten Éponine, you know she would've changed the song to 'On *Your* Own' and it'd be all about how she's way too good for Marius anyway."

More laughter. Next to me, Odile shuts her book and rubs her fingernails softly over the worn paper edges.

Maybe it's kind of inappropriate, the way we talk about actors. But they're annoying when they talk about us, too. The other day I overheard two freshmen in the ensemble say the only people who'd ever voluntarily sign up for stagecraft were the ones who'd already flunked out of the *real* theater classes.

When I turn back to Odile, though, she's smiling. Maybe she didn't hear the set team after all.

"So you've read the whole book?" I ask her.

"A couple of times. But I'm slammed with make-up work this semester, so I'm just rereading Fantine's sections now. I'd forgotten her tendency to ramble."

"Yeah, I guess life spent an awful lot of pages killing her dream." I worry for a second Odile will get offended by me trivializing her character's suffering—Fantine's story is sad, but once you've seen the show a few times, you forget how gravely upsetting it all is—but to my surprise, she laughs.

Every time I make Odile laugh, I feel like I should get a gold star.

"Are you disappointed you'll be the first death in the show?" I ask her.

She shakes her head. "It'll be nice, honestly. After everything I have to do before that, I'll be more than ready for a break."

"Ha. I've got to admit, I'm a little worried about how many characters we have dying onstage this year."

"Worried? Why?"

"Well, between this show and *R&J*, our body count is through the roof. It's like we're tempting fate. Our theater doesn't have a great track record when it comes to morbid stuff."

"So . . . you really believe in all the superstitions, then?" Odile raises her eyebrows.

"I don't know if I literally believe in *all* of them, but it's my job as SM to enforce it all regardless. Good teams always play by the same rules."

Odile nods. "True, but I also think you can never prepare for *every* possibility. That's one thing I love about theater—so much is unpredictable."

I laugh. "You love it when things go wrong?"

"No, but I *do* love how everyone works together to pull things off, no matter what. I did a show once with food poisoning, and it wasn't fun when it was happening, but it made a great story I could tell later. And it worked, because everybody came together and *made* it work."

"Wait. You went on with *food poisoning*?"

"Yep. The ASM kept a bucket backstage for me, and I'd step off into the wing to, you know."

My jaw drops. "You left to puke *during* a scene?"

"A couple of times." She grins. "The hard part was holding it until I'd gotten through my lines."

"You're joking."

She shakes her head. "I wish I was!"

"Wow. I guess I should add *puke bucket* to my list of backstage necessities. Did you not have an understudy?"

"I did, but the director really wanted me to do it."

"Couldn't you have said no?"

"Huh. That never actually occurred to me." She pauses. "I guess I'm old-school. If my director wants me to do something, I do it. The show must go on."

I nod. "I say that all the time."

"Of course you do." She laughs. Another full, *genuine* laugh.

That makes twice in one night. It feels like I just won a marathon.

"That's why I'm skeptical about the rituals. Which doesn't mean I don't follow them," she adds, when she sees me getting ready to interrupt. "I promise, I'll never whistle or say 'good luck' or anything else like that. The first rule of theater is whatever the SM says, goes."

Interesting. I don't know anyone else in theater who doesn't believe in any superstitions at *all*. Even Will refuses to say the real name of the Scottish Play.

"So, did you read the book for a class the first time?" I ask her, to change the subject.

"Sort of. I did an independent study unit on it in eighth grade, but it was my idea. I'd just seen the musical for the first time and I was obsessed. Plus, I'd always really liked the Disney *Hunchback* movie, so I wanted to read all the Victor Hugo."

"Ooh, I love that one. That 'Hellfire' song is so creepy. I can't believe they put it in a cartoon."

"Me neither!"

"For real! By the way, how'd you get your teacher to let you do an independent study in middle school?"

She strokes the book's spine. "I was homeschooled for most of eighth grade. I got to design the curriculum myself."

"Ohhh." Now I get it. She must've been in eighth grade when she was in New York doing *Annie*. "Was that fun, being home-schooled?"

"Not really." Her smile is fading.

There's another burst of laughter, from the lighting group this time. When I look up, though, Jasmin isn't laughing with them. She's watching us, and she looks uneasy.

"It must've been fun working on Broadway, though," I say. My phone buzzes with a text, but I'll look at it in a minute. "That's always been my dream. I mean, not the acting part obviously, but I'd love to SM there someday."

"You'd be great." Odile smiles, but it isn't the wide, open smile she had before. "It wasn't for me, though. It's so different from regular theaters. No one really talks about working hard to put on a good show. It's all about making money."

"Oh. That . . . doesn't sound so great."

"There you are!" Will strides up to us with two brownies balanced on a plate. "Nice to see you, Ms. Rose. Ms. McIntyre, I thought you were circulating between the groups."

"Right. I am." I climb to my feet, bracing myself awkwardly against the wood-paneled wall. Odile stands up too, a lot more gracefully. Jasmin's still eyeing me, and a few of the other crew heads are looking our way too. "Actually, it's probably a good time to put the movie on, if people are starting to wind down."

Will glances up at the schedule on the wall and passes a brownie to Odile. She reaches for it, but doesn't take a bite.

"Didn't you want to have a group debrief before starting the video?" Will says.

"Right . . ." *But I kind of want to keep talking to Odile instead.* "But I think it's too soon. Maybe we should take a break and watch the recording for a while instead. Then we can debrief at the end when all the groups are feeling more solid about their ideas. What do you think?"

"Well, I . . ."

"There you are, Mel." Jasmin charges toward us. "We need to talk about the star drop."

"Okay." I glance reluctantly at Odile. Jasmin sees, and her eyes narrow.

"Also, the set crew wanted your thoughts on the barricade." Jasmin glances over her shoulder, and I see Fatima a few feet back. She's talking to Rachel, but they're both watching us. Are they waiting for Odile to lash out with her evil actor claws or something?

I sigh. "Okay, let's go ahead and debrief. We can all talk then. And . . ." I glance back at Odile. "Maybe then we can put on the video. As long as everyone finishes their worksheets."

Jasmin frowns, but Will holds up his hands in front of him. "You're the boss, Ms. McIntyre. If you want to voluntarily change a schedule for the first time in sixteen years, that's your prerogative. I'm just in this for the food."

I ignore his low-grade mockery and Jasmin's pointed looks and call out for the crew's attention. We gather in a circle on the floor, and I start my timer. The debrief lasts exactly fifteen minutes. I call on the crew heads and take notes and answer questions and do everything else I always do at these meetings.

And through it all, I keep casting glances into the corner, where Odile is slowly turning the pages of *Les Misérables*.

The instant my timer goes off, I start the video. Then I stand up, ready to head back into the corner where Odile is still lingering with her paperback while the overture plays.

"Mel." Jasmin steps in front of me. "Do you have a second?"

"What's up?"

"I tried to text you, but . . ." She lowers her voice. "People are talking."

"If this is about Odile crashing the party, it's not like she *meant* to—"

"It's not about the party, it's about the curse." Jasmin raises her eyebrows. "Remember?"

"What? I mean, sure, I remember, but that has nothing to do with Odile being here."

"Mel. Come on. It's obvious you're into her."

I start to laugh, but Jasmin's face is still stony, so I answer seriously. "She's hot, sure. I admit it. Even *you've* got to admit that, and *you're* straight."

Her expression doesn't change. "Mel."

"What? I promised I wouldn't fall in love during this show, and I'm not going to. My point is, it doesn't matter that she's hot. If you haven't noticed, she's about twenty miles out of my league."

"It's only—"

"We're supposed to trust each other, right?" I hold Jasmin's gaze, so she can see I'm serious. "I promise, if I was anywhere close to falling in love, I'd know. Besides, I wouldn't do that to you and the others. I'd never do *anything* that could hurt this show."

Jasmin stares back at me for a moment. Then she nods. "All right. We trust you."

"Good." I unfold my arms, give her a nod back, and walk away.

Right up to the corner where Odile's still sitting.

So what if I can't fall in love? There's no rule that says I can't still have fun.

"Hey." I clear my throat. "Do you want to, um . . . go somewhere?"

Odile doesn't smile, but there's a light in her eyes. "Uh-huh."

I hold out my hand to help her up. As she takes it, her fingers squeeze mine for the briefest moment.

And—oh. Oh, *no*.

I could shut my eyes and stay in exactly this spot, exactly this moment, for the rest of my life, and be perfectly happy forevermore.

But that's not an option. *Not an option.*

I let go of her hand as soon as she's on her feet.

What I told Jasmin was the truth. I'm nowhere close to falling in love with this girl. Okay, so I don't know the exact words for what *is* happening here, but I won't cross that line.

I know what I'm doing. I *always* know what I'm doing.

But when Odile smiles at me again, there's a brief moment when I'm not so sure.

UNREAD TEXTS ACCUMULATING ON MEL'S PHONE, SATURDAY NIGHT

Gabby:
Where'd you go?

Dom:
How's the crew party? It's weird not being
there ☹

Fatima:
Mr. Green says he doesn't know the turntable
dimensions yet so I don't know how big to
build the barricade

Jasmin:
Everyone's talking about you leaving with her

Jasmin:
Just so you know

Shannon:
Please help me explain to the freshmen why
we can't put REAL dirt on the actors' faces

Estaban:
Jacob had a cool idea. Do you know if we can use part of the set budget?

Fatima:
Hey, are you here? Someone told me you went somewhere with Odile?

Estaban:
If we get a few rubber chickens cheap I bet I can borrow my mom's butcher knife and we could have Beth and Julio chop them up for real onstage

Estaban:
It'll be hilarious, they can be throwing all these rubber chicken parts into the soup pot

Shannon:
Wait did you really leave with her?

Estaban:
Gabby said you might have a safety concern but we can just get them to be careful

Estaban:
WAIT I just heard a rumor, is it true you're
not answering my texts because you're
running around with Odile Rose?

Gabby:
Seriously, I can't find you. What's going on?

Scene 7—The McIntyre-Perez Front Porch

DAYS UNTIL SPRING MUSICAL OPENS: 75

"Want to go outside and talk?" I ask Odile when we're halfway up the stairs. "You brought a coat, right?"

She nods.

I think about setting my timer so I'll know when the video is done, but we should only be gone for a few minutes. I felt eyes lingering on Odile and me as we walked past the others, and I gave Gabby a little wave on our way out. She waved back, unsmiling.

I shake all that off as Odile and I climb up to the empty first floor. My dads must have retreated upstairs. We grab our coats from the rack and step out onto the porch. It's February in Massachusetts and thus frigid, with patches of snow still dotting the lawn, as we sink down into the patio cushions.

There's so much moonlight pouring into the yard that I decide not to bother turning on the porch light. At the last second I remember the blanket we keep in the basket under the table, so I pull it out, but it feels rude to spread out a blanket over my lap without offering Odile anything, so I just lay it on the table. My phone buzzes with another text, but I only slide it deeper into the pocket of my jeans.

I expected things to get awkward between Odile and me once we were alone, but now that we're sitting down, the conversation picks up easily. As if we've been doing this for years.

At first, we talk more about *Les Mis*. I find out why she wanted to play Fantine (she thought it was a more mature role than Éponine) and why she wouldn't want to play Cosette even if she were a soprano (we both agree that the Marius/Cosette romance in the musical is absurd, and he'd obviously be happier with Éponine). Then things get quiet, and out of nowhere I find myself apologizing.

"I'm sorry about the way my friends acted." I didn't mean to say this—it feels like I'm betraying my crew, kind of—but it's hard not to say what I'm thinking when I talk to Odile. "We aren't used to actors hanging out with us. Especially actors like you."

"Please, don't apologize. The cast here is even worse when they talk about the tech crew. It makes me miss other theaters."

"What, you mean professional theaters?"

"Yes, but community theaters too. Everyone there has this overriding sense that we're all in this together. The cast and crew are friends, most of the time."

"Wow. Really? Is it like that in TV?"

"Well, no. TV's different."

"What about movies?"

"I don't know. I've never done one before." She shrugs. "I guess I'll find out this summer."

"What's happening this summer?"

"I'm doing a shoot in London."

"For a movie? Oh—wait." That's when I remember the bathroom phone call. "You got the part in that Martin Scorsese movie?"

She nods slowly but doesn't smile.

"Wow! Congratulations!" I clap my hands. "I can't believe I'm sitting on my porch with a real movie star!"

She laughs, but it isn't the full, solid laugh I earned back in the basement. This one is short and almost fake-sounding. Like she's . . . acting. "Thank you."

"Oh—are you, um." I'm suddenly conscious of just how cold this porch is. I grab the blanket and pull it up over my shoulders. "Are you not . . . happy about it?"

"I am, of course." She shrugs. "But it's more terrifying than anything else. I'm positive I'll get there and everyone will see in an instant that I have absolutely no idea what I'm doing."

"That can't be true. They wouldn't have given you the part if you couldn't do it."

"You'd be surprised. Meanwhile, my agent's already trying to leverage it into other roles. Last year she wanted me to do more theater, and she was always after me to set up a YouTube channel of singing clips, but now all she can talk about is movies and TV. There's a Netflix series she wants to put me up for, but I'm not sure that's what I want."

"What *do* you want?"

My phone buzzes. More texts. I'm about to reach for it when Odile clears her throat. "So is *Les Mis* your favorite musical of all time?"

It's obvious she's trying to change the subject. But I go with it, since she's changing it to one of my favorite subjects ever, and she's gazing right at me with those deep brown eyes.

"Probably, but I have a bunch of other favorites." I tick them off on my fingers. "*Spring Awakening* is incredible. And *Hamilton*, even though that's such a cliché. How about you?"

"*Hadestown* might be my all-time favorite. When I was a kid, though, it was *The Lion King*."

I don't even try to hide my delight. "Me too! I even named my cat Nala. What's your favorite straight play?"

"I'm always going back and forth. I really enjoyed *Steel Magnolias*, actually. I didn't know much about the show before we did it here, and I still don't know much about the South other than what I learned when I was researching it, but it was a lot of fun to be part of."

I like that she says *to be part of*, not *to star in*. Even though she was literally the lead. "I liked that one too. Ms. Marcus only picked it because of the all-female cast, though. We never do shows with enough good parts for girls."

"Can you believe some of the guys had the nerve to complain?" She rolls her eyes. "They should really stop talking now that we're doing Shakespeare and *Les Mis* in the same year."

"True." I laugh. My phone's still buzzing, but I tuck it away.

We'll go back in soon enough. "Were you sad you didn't get to play Juliet?"

"I wish I could've been in the show, but I'd rather have played the Nurse. There's so much more you can do with that role."

"Really? But Juliet's the ingenue."

"Ugh, I despise that word."

She shudders, and I laugh again. Odile really is nothing like I thought.

"It must've been fun going all the way to Iceland for that *Game of Thrones* show, though, right?" I ask her.

Her voice goes smooth and flat, the same way it did when she thanked me for congratulating her before. "Sometimes."

"You . . . don't sound all that convincing."

"Well." She gives me that subtle smile again. "It turns out Iceland's a long way to go by yourself."

"Your parents didn't go with you?"

"Not this time. When I was younger, one of them would come when I worked out of town, but now I'm eighteen, so it's legal for me to not have a chaperone." She glances out into the moonlight shining across the lawn.

"Isn't that kind of cool, though?" I wonder if I sound naive. Odile's been in this business since she was a kid, and the only acting I know anything about is the kind that happens in our school auditorium. "Being experienced enough that you can do it on your own?"

"I don't know." She shivers.

"It, uh . . ." I offer her the blanket, and she looks at it longingly for a moment, then shakes her head. She's wearing a puffy gray coat, the kind rich people buy at Neiman Marcus, so maybe she really doesn't need it. "It doesn't sound as if you like doing TV and movies very much."

"No, it's not that. It's just that I . . ." She draws in a breath and meets my eyes, her chin trembling. It's the first time I've ever seen her look so open, so vulnerable. It feels like another victory.

Then she bends forward and bursts into tears.

"Oh crap! Oh no, I'm so sorry!" I don't know what to do. If one of my regular friends suddenly started crying, I'd hug them, right? But I've never hugged Odile. I settle for awkwardly patting her shoulder while she sobs into her hands. "Oh my God, I'm so sorry I said that. Can we please go back in time and pretend I didn't? Can we be in Harry Potter so I can grab a Time-Turner?"

Odile doesn't move, but I can hear her laughing even while she's crying. She mumbles something I can't understand.

"Sorry?" I realize my hand has gone still on her shoulder, and I pull it back. But I hate to just leave her there, so I spread the blanket over her back instead. "I didn't catch that?"

"I said, yes, please." She sits up, turning her back to me and wiping her eyes. "I mean—you didn't say anything wrong, it's just—I'm so sorry. I haven't yet told anyone I got this movie, except my family, and I—" She pulls a tissue out of her pocket and blows her nose. "Sorry. Oh, this is so embarrassing."

"Hey, no, it's okay." I push the blanket up over the shoulders of her expensive puffy coat. Then, instead of pulling away, I lean into her back, trying to hug her without really hugging her.

She just seems so *alone*.

"You, um . . . you can talk to me, if you want to," I say. "If you just need to tell someone what's going on."

"I don't even *know* what's going on." She turns toward me, and my face shifts onto her shoulder. When she starts talking again, her voice wobbles into my ear. I didn't know her voice *could* wobble. "All of this used to be fun, you know? I loved doing shows. But Iceland wasn't fun at all. I'd signed so many nondisclosure agreements I was barely allowed to leave the hotel. Not that I wanted to leave anyway, since it was so cold and dark out. And I had to stay up all night to film my scenes, so when it *was* light out, I was inside, sleeping. And I couldn't stop thinking about how I was missing part of my senior year to do it."

"Yeah, that . . . that does sound kind of miserable."

"It was." Her voice is starting to smooth out again. I hope she's feeling better than she was, but selfishly, I also kind of hope that she keeps wanting to tell me things that matter. It makes me want to tell her things that matter, too. "It's all so different from how I thought. I got into this because I like to sing, and now all of a sudden I'm in this movie about spies murdering each other. I have to take lessons on how to use a *hunting* knife. They haven't finished the script yet, but I think I have to stab someone."

"Ew."

She leans back, and I tilt my head against the back of the couch. We're sitting side by side again. I lift my chin off her shoulder, but I don't move to put space between us. My phone keeps buzzing in my pocket.

"Why'd you agree to do the movie?" I ask her.

"Agreeing or not agreeing never seemed to be a question." She shrugs again. The gentle lift of her shoulders makes her skin glow. When *I* cry, my whole face turns into a red streaky mess, but the only clue that Odile was crying a few minutes ago is a slight shine to her eyes. "Everyone kept telling me I could get film work if I tried, and it just seemed to be assumed that that was what I wanted. That that's what *anyone* would want. My agent was so thrilled when I got invited to audition, I could hear her bubbling over the phone. There was never a conversation about whether I *should* do it, only whether they'd pick me."

"Were your parents excited too?"

"I suppose?" She pulls the blanket farther onto her lap and runs her fingertips across the seam. The movement makes me want to reach out and grab her hand.

But that's a dangerous thought. I should shove it deep in my jeans pocket, too.

"They've never really understood how any of it works." She shakes her head. "I gave up trying to talk to them about it in any serious way a while ago. Last year I was debating whether to change agents, but they never talked to me about how to handle it—I had to figure everything out on my own. My mother's a doctor and my father's a lawyer, and as far as they're concerned, *real* jobs are the kind you go to school for. All they ever say about my work is that I have to keep my grades up no matter what."

"Ugh, I know what you mean. My dads want me to major in biology or something, even though I've told them over and over that I'm going to be a professional SM. Studying something else is pointless when I already know what I want to do with my life."

Odile's eyes flick back toward me, and I'm glad the moonlight is too dim for her to see my cheeks flushing. At some point we must've started sharing the blanket, because it's spread out across both our knees now.

"I thought they supported you doing theater," she says. "They help with the sets, don't they? And the parent committee?"

"Yeah, it's not as if they're anti-theater. They just don't seem to get that this isn't some random fun after-school activity for me. It's my whole *life*."

Odile nods, her expression solemn. *Wow*, her cheekbones are really quite striking.

"They know you're bi, right?" she asks. "Sorry, I suppose that's a silly question."

I laugh, but it's a nervous laugh. We're in uncharted conversational territory now. "Yeah, it wasn't exactly difficult. I think the first time I told them I had a crush on a girl, I was about six."

She smiles. It's a soft, unsure smile, and it makes something inside me uncoil.

"I haven't had that particular chat with my parents," she says, quieter now. "I think they suspect, but they've never said anything. I doubt they will unless I bring it up."

Yep. This conversation now feels actively treacherous. Even

so, I take a deep breath and ask. "So you're queer?"

"Something like that. I'm not totally certain of the details yet."

Well, that's awfully fascinating.

I want to ask if she's ever hooked up with a girl. I want to ask *really, really badly.* But I've already asked one question that felt impossible to voice, and I don't know if I have another one in me.

Odile's looking right at me, her eyes roaming across my face. Suddenly, the desire to kiss her is so strong I can't believe I haven't already done it.

There's something going on here. Something I don't have a name for. It's thrilling and frightening at the same time.

I lean forward, and she meets my eyes, and—

The curse.

I jerk to my feet. She turns away just as quickly, coughing into her hand.

"I'm sorry. I, um—" I try to think fast, but my brain doesn't seem to be functioning. "I thought there was a bug."

Great. Very convincing, Melody.

Odile covers her face with her hand. "I should apologize."

"No, you shouldn't." I sit back down, making sure to leave a solid foot of space between us.

All right. So this *isn't* a regular crush. I've had plenty of those, and they've never felt like this.

The problem is, I don't know the word for what I *am* feeling. Maybe it's nothing more than a very strong crush with a healthy dollop of physical attraction on top.

Better safe than sorry, though. Especially with my friends right inside.

"*I* should apologize," I say. "I . . . I didn't really think there was a bug."

Odile lowers her hand and rolls her eyes. It's a surprisingly genuine gesture coming from her, and if I didn't feel so pathetic about what just happened, I'd be pleased. "You're kidding."

"It's just that I, um . . ." I bite my tongue to keep from saying *I have a love curse, but I really like you anyway* out loud. Odile doesn't believe in superstitions, and if I start trying to explain the nuances of Jasmin's theory, she'll probably forget all about whatever miracle made her want to open up to me in the first place. "I'm sorry. I have no explanation for what just happened. The bug thing was the best I could do under the circumstances."

"Mel . . . can I ask you something?"

"Of course."

"Exactly how many of your current friends are also your exes?"

I blink. I don't know what I was expecting her to ask, but it wasn't that. It feels like another abrupt subject change, except . . . maybe it's not. "Um. I mean, not *all* of them. I never went out with—uh, Gabby."

I'm trying to make her laugh again, but it doesn't work. Instead, her piercing brown eyes catch mine and hold on. It feels impossible to hide from those eyes, and I have a weird, sudden certainty that no matter what image I'm trying to present at any given moment, Odile can see right through it.

"Well, I feel like a bit of a fail," she says, sounding charmingly British as she folds her hands in her lap. "I've only ever dated one person in my life."

"That's *impossible*," I say, because once again I am incapable of verbal restraint in this girl's presence.

She tilts her head, half smiling. "It must be, because it's the truth."

"David Patel?"

She nods. Well, that answers my question about whether she's hooked up with a girl yet. "Are you and him broken up for good?"

She nods again. "Since last summer."

"But you're still friends, right?"

"Of course. He's really my only friend at school, now that Sebastian's in college."

"Your *only* friend? But you're the most famous person at BHS! You walk around the halls like a queen!"

She laughs and scrunches up her face. It's a delight to see her look so normal. "You make me sound like a snob."

"Sorry. I don't really think you are." It's the truth. Now, at least. "Besides, all the actors like you."

"Some of them, maybe." She shrugs again. "But . . . sometimes I wonder if it's really *me* they like."

I nod. Most of the actors at our school seem to be in one of two camps when it comes to Odile. Either they're terrified and keep their distance, like Alejandra, or they fawn over her, like Leah and Christina. Probably hoping she'll hook them up with her agent or give them their big break.

"I've never really been sure of how school, well . . . works." Her voice is slow and serious, and the shine in her eyes has faded. "I always feel like I'm acting, even when I'm only trying to get through the day. I've traveled so much over the past few years that it's hard to get a foothold. Whenever I'd finally get the hang of things at school, I'd leave town for weeks at a time, and when I came back, I'd have to start over from scratch."

"That sounds really rough."

"I finally just stopped talking much. That way everyone can ignore me. Besides, no one ever seemed to want to really talk to me in the first place. Most of the seniors think I'm weird." She shrugs again, staring down at her Converse sneakers.

"*I* don't think you're weird." I lean down to meet her gaze so she'll know I'm serious. "I think you're—"

The front door swings open behind us, and I slam my mouth shut. Which is good, because I was about to say something *super* awkward.

"Mel? Is that you?" Dad sticks his head out. "You must be freezing out here. Gabby's looking for you, if—oh, hello."

"Hello, sir." Odile stands up smoothly, her whole demeanor shifting in an instant. She holds out her hand. "It's so nice of you to have me over. I'm Odile Rose."

"Of course you are." Dad smiles and shakes her hand. "Sean McIntyre. My husband told me he let you in, but I didn't realize you were out here too."

"Yep, she is." I stand up, trying to intervene before Dad can embarrass me. "What were you saying about Gabby?"

"She came upstairs a while ago. I thought you'd gone to your room, but she checked there and she said she couldn't find you."

"Huh, I wonder why. She could've just texted me." But when I reach for my phone, I see a bunch of texts from Gabby, and my other friends too. Odile and I must've been sitting out on the porch for longer than I would've guessed.

"Wow. Okay." I put down my phone. Dad's eyebrows are lifted. "Well, I guess I'll go downstairs and get everyone started on the, um . . ." I can barely remember my own agenda now. It's almost as if I *didn't* spend weeks planning out every minute of this party. "I'll just go see where things stand. Do you want to join us, Odile?"

"I probably shouldn't." She smooths back her hair. She looks cool and detached again. Like when she was walking down the hall to her audition. "I'll call an Uber."

"No need for that." Dad jingles his keys. "I'd be happy to give you a ride."

"Oh, you don't need to go to the trouble."

"I was about to make a run for more chips anyway. Besides, it'll be nice to get out of the house. No offense, but kids your age are easier in small numbers."

Odile smiles the same wide, bright smile she used on the football players at the bake sale table. "Then thank you, I appreciate it, Mr. McIntyre."

"Please call me Sean. And by the way, Odile, we'd love it if you could join us for dinner next Monday." *What?* Dad doesn't look my way, so he doesn't see me trying to frantically communicate a loud *No!* with my eyes. Whatever this crush thing I have on her is, I've got to rein it in before it gets worse, and her coming over for dinner will *not* make that easier. "Charlie and I don't cook much, but Will—Mr. Green—is coming over, and you haven't lived until you've tried his braised carrots."

"Whoops!" I say, hoping he'll pick up on my tone. "You forgot, Dad. Next Monday's when Dom and Jasmin are coming for the mentorship dinner."

"That's perfect!" Dad grins. "Sorry, Odile, I should explain—Mr. Green feels strongly about shepherding the next generation of theater professionals, so Dominic and Jasmin have been coming over for the past couple of years to talk shop. But it's only fitting that we have another actor join in now that Dom's switched teams on us. I'll tell Mr. Green; he'll be delighted."

I pray Odile will say no, but she's already smiling at him. "It's very kind of you to invite me, Sean. I'd like that."

Dad gets his coat, and Odile gives me one last soft glance. A minute later, they're gone.

I start down the basement steps, trying to plan out what I'm going to say to the crew, but focusing is impossible. For the first time I can remember, I don't want to work. All I want is to still be sitting out on that cold porch again, sharing a blanket with Odile Rose.

TODAY'S SCHEDULE
MONDAY, FEBRUARY 17

Time	Called	Task	Location
3:00–3:45 p.m.	Full cast	Music rehearsal: "Epilogue"	Choir room
3:45–4:30 p.m.	Thénardier & Madame Thénardier	Character work	Auditorium
3:45–4:30 p.m.	Marius, Cosette, Éponine	Music rehearsal: "A Heart Full of Love"	Choir room
4:30–5:15 p.m.	Marius & Cosette	Character work	Auditorium
4:30–5:15 p.m.	Éponine	Music rehearsal: "On My Own"	Choir room

Note: End times are approximate. Actors should be prepared to stay later if needed.

Written on the portable whiteboard in Mel's handwriting and stationed at the entrance to the performing arts wing.

Scene 8—Beaconville High School Choir Room

DAYS UNTIL SPRING MUSICAL OPENS: 73

"Very good, everyone!" Ms. Qiao forces a smile as Jasmin trills out the last few instrumental notes on the piano. She plays for rehearsals sometimes, partly because it's good practice but mostly because she enjoys getting to observe the actor drama. Early rehearsals, especially when the entire cast is here, are actor-drama central. "Let's go through that last chorus together one more time and then we'll incorporate a few solos."

"Mel? Are you ready to check this?" Gabby whispers, holding out a stack of purchase orders she collected from the crew heads at lunch.

"Sure." I reach for the papers while the cast struggles through the chorus. Ms. Qiao likes to start music rehearsals by having everyone practice as a group. The problem is, most of the cast doesn't know the lyrics yet, so they're staring straight down into their music stands, and their voices get drowned out. They're still working on enunciating, too, so words get lost here and there.

The principals and some of the featured ensemble members are on the bottom riser, and a few of them, Christina and Leah in particular, keep glaring at the people behind them who are messing up.

They need to stop doing that. We're all supposed to be one team, and we have to support each other.

But it'll all come together by opening night. Right now, the song sounds ragged and uneven, but in two and a half months it'll smooth out. It has to.

I flip through the pages in the stack Gabby gave me, checking each one off as I go. As I pass them back to her, a movement on the front row of risers catches my eye. Odile, turning the page in her script, half a second before everyone else does the same thing.

I look away before she can notice me watching her. I've been doing my best to act like nothing's changed between us since the party, but it's too late for that. I've finally met the *real* Odile, the one with actual fears and vulnerabilities and tear ducts, and I don't know how to go back.

But I have to. I've got a love curse to worry about.

"Very good, everyone." Ms. Qiao lifts her hands as the chorus winds down, glancing back at the whiteboard agenda I put out at the start of rehearsal and clicking her tongue. "Let's take a quick break, and then we'll do an abbreviated version of the solos. We'll pick up with Fantine's 'Come to Me' reprise. That'll give us a sense of how the transition to the group portion will sound. Nick, Odile, Leah, will you be ready?"

Odile nods. She looks as calm as she has all afternoon, but beside her, Nick is shifting his weight from foot to foot, and Leah looks absolutely petrified. These will be the first solo rehearsals of the show, and if I were them, I'd be petrified too.

Ms. Qiao dismisses us for the break, and as I'm setting my timer, Dom plops down in the empty seat on the other side of Gabby. "Hey, you two. Mel, can I borrow the nail clippers?"

"Sure." I haul out the tackle box from under my chair and pull out the clippers, plus an alcohol wipe.

"Wow. What else do you have in that box?" Alejandra asks. She and Malik, it seems, have followed Dom over to our corner. Jasmin came over to sit with us, too. *That* isn't a surprise, but actors don't usually hang out with us during breaks. Or at all. "Is it like a traveling pharmacy?"

"It's her SM kit." Dom stretches his arms over his head. "She's got first aid stuff, breath mints, mechanical pencils, mini Sharpies, paper clips, highlighters, condoms . . ."

"Condoms?" Alejandra's eyes widen.

"Yeah, they're the best way to seal up mic packs. Plus I've got rulers, Post-its, rubber bands . . ." I open the tackle box again so she can see. Inheriting the official BHS SM kit was one of the high points of my career to date. "Needle and thread, lint roller, clear nail polish, hair ties, tampons, full water bottle, screwdrivers . . ."

"Screw*drivers*?" Malik asks. "As in, more than one?"

"Well, yeah. You always need a flat-head and a Phillips on hand, at least."

"For sure," a familiar voice echoes above us. Odile's come over to our corner, too. "During the first *Steel Magnolias* stumble-through, the sink fell apart in the middle of a monologue. Estaban came onstage and screwed it back together, and we didn't even have to pause the scene."

The others look astonished, probably at hearing Odile say so many words that aren't in her script, but I smile up at her. "I remember that. I'd wanted to use glue, but I got overruled."

"Clearly, they should've listened to you to begin with." Odile grins.

That's when I spot Jasmin watching us through narrowed eyes. I stop smiling, but Odile doesn't seem to notice.

"SMs always have whatever you could possibly need," she's telling Malik and Alejandra. "I did a show once where the direc-tor had the whole cast go barefoot onstage, and my friend got a splinter in the middle of the first act. As soon as he exited, the ASM was standing in the wings with tweezers in her hand. She had him all set by his next entrance. That was when I first learned you can count on the tech crew for absolutely anything."

"Hi, Odile!" Christina bounds up while everyone else is still staring at her, dumbfounded. I'm pretty sure this is the first time an actor at our school has *ever* said anything that nice about the crew. "You sounded amazing during that rehearsal. I learned so much about how to use my chest voice just from standing next to you."

"Thank you, you're so nice to say that." Odile's smile shifts completely as she turns to Christina, her lips spreading into that

sunny look I've come to think of as her feigning-happiness costume.

"Maybe you two should go somewhere and compare notes."
Jasmin glances from Odile to Christina to me. "I bet you have a
lot of acting tips to share, Odile."

She shifts her sunny smile to Jasmin. "That's nice of you to
say, but I don't, not really."

That's when we hear the whistling. It's soft and half-hearted,
but still—it's whistling.

Everyone turns around at once. Even Christina looks stunned.
So far—knock on all the wood ever—rehearsals have been running pretty smoothly, but to straight-up whistle in the middle of
the performing arts wing is *seriously* tempting the curse's wrath.

Yet I'm not surprised at all when I spot Nick sitting on the
top riser, peering down at his script and whistling the tune to his
"Epilogue" solo.

"Hey, no whistling," Malik calls before I've even said anything.

Nick stops, but he glances around, looking confused. "Come
again?"

"You can't whistle in rehearsal," I tell him. "Do the countercurse before break ends."

"The *countercurse*? Are you serious?" Nick laughs.

"She's serious," David says from the far corner of the room,
where he's talking to Leah. "You have to do it, man. Spin around
three times and tell the theater you're sorry."

"We aren't even *in* the theater," Nick protests.

"We're in the performing arts wing and in rehearsal," I tell him. "That qualifies."

"I seriously can't whistle in the choir room?" His voice sounds a little raspy, like he's so astonished he's getting called out that he can't even form the words to argue properly.

"It's one of the oldest theater superstitions," I explain. "Back in the day, stagehands whistled cues to each other up in the rigging. If you wandered on the stage whistling, a stagehand might think you were cueing them and drop a sandbag on your head."

"Are there sandbags in here?" Nick cranes his neck toward the fluorescent lights.

"Doesn't matter. You've gotta do it." Dom crosses the room and climbs onto the riser next to Nick. "Here, I'll do it with you."

"I will too." Now Malik's hoisting himself up.

"Let's all do it!" Julio claps his hands and thunders up the steps to join them. David heads over, too. Soon there are a dozen actors all spinning and apologizing in unison, and it's actually pretty funny. Even Nick is laughing, and the curse is officially countered.

With perfect timing, my phone starts buzzing. "We're back, everyone!" I shout.

The actors climb to their places. Jasmin goes to the piano bench, giving me another pointed look. I pretend not to notice, but when she turns toward her sheet music, I shift in my seat.

A few of my friends have been acting weird since the party, but Jasmin most of all. She texted me all through yesterday, asking what Odile and I were doing out on my porch for so long.

I told her the truth—that we were just talking, and that we're getting to be kind of friends, and that she isn't as bad as the other actors—but I couldn't tell if she believed me.

I didn't tell her, or anyone, about our almost-kiss. My friends don't need to know *everything*. Besides, an almost-kiss isn't the same as an actual kiss. And neither an almost-kiss nor an *actual* kiss means anybody's falling in love with anybody else. I've been in love enough times to know what it feels like, and I've kissed enough people I *wasn't* in love with to know what *that* feels like, too.

When love hits you, it hits you all at once, and nothing's ever the same again.

"All right, let's pick up at the start of the solos," Ms. Qiao tells the cast. "Don't worry too much about the harmonies, we'll work on those later. Fantine, are you ready to kick us off?"

Odile nods. Ms. Qiao tells Jasmin where to come in, and Odile lifts her chin and parts her lips. The ensemble is supposed to stay silent during her solo, so for the next few bars the only sounds in the room are Jasmin's piano playing and Odile's voice soaring.

Before we're even a few notes in, I'm already breathless. The group's been singing all afternoon, but now it's as though we've stepped through a portal into a different rehearsal altogether.

So far, most of the cast has been shuffling along through the song, mostly just trying to get the words right, but Odile is already singing like it's opening night. Fantine's dead by this point in the show, and in this song she's coming back as an angel-slash-ghost to tell the dying Valjean he's going to heaven because he was nice to her (it sounds weird when you put it like that, but in the context of the show it's really moving). Odile's fully in character, and her voice is passionate and powerful, ringing out with beautiful precision.

I can already see her onstage, a spotlight surrounding her like a halo, her voice filling the hushed, packed theater. Tears on the audience's faces. And on mine, too, up in the booth. I'll be the one calling the cues, making her light shine, but she'll be glowing all by herself.

There's a short instrumental break after Odile's solo. Ms. Qiao smiles a genuine-looking smile for the first time all afternoon. Then the music picks back up and she nods at Nick.

He clutches his music stand and squints down at the script. As soon as he starts his first line, it's obvious something's wrong. I have to force myself not to wince, and I'm not the only one. It's a good thing he can't see the rest of the cast on the risers behind him, because if I were him and I saw all those grimaces, I'd cry.

Nick is *bad*. There's no other way to put it. The light rasp in his voice from earlier is still there, but it's much worse now that he's trying to sing. I glance at Ms. Qiao, but her face is perfectly neutral.

Odile and Leah have to sing the next part of the song together, so they come in after Nick's line is over. They aren't really singing in harmony the way the actors do on the cast recordings, but they both have beautiful voices and they sound good together.

But when Nick joins them for a short three-way solo, I swear it sounds like he's actually *croaking*.

Dom's jaw is on the floor. Christina's staring at Nick with horror in her eyes. I want to signal them to be slightly less obvious, but there's nothing I can do without being even more obvious myself.

"Nick," Ms. Qiao says quietly, gesturing for Jasmin to keep playing as she talks. "It's all right."

Now he really *does* look like he's about to cry.

He mouths the words for the next line while Leah and Odile sing without him. Finally he gives up and just stares down at his sheet music, his face crumpled.

The rest of the cast finishes the song without him. When they reach the end Nick slumps into his seat, and Ms. Qiao quickly dismisses everyone and goes over to talk to him.

"Looks like Nick the Dick won't be walking the red carpet anywhere but the asshole awards," Gabby whispers next to me. I bite my lip to keep from laughing. "What happened?"

"I have no idea. He was good at auditions. Maybe he's sick."

Ms. Qiao leads Nick out through a side door. I'm about to tell Gabby she can leave for the day when I feel a light touch on my elbow.

"Hey." Odile's smiling at me.

"Heyyyyy." I grin like a giant dork. This makes twice now that she's come over to me today. "Are you, um . . ."

"Were you going to . . . ," she says at the same time. Then we cut ourselves off, and we both laugh.

Gabby coughs awkwardly. "So, is it okay if I—"

"Oh, sorry!" I spin back to her. "You can leave. The teachers are only working with a couple of the principals after this, so they don't need us for the rest of today."

"Okay, cool." Gabby gives us a tentative smile and turns to go.

Now it's just Odile and me in our little corner. No one else seems to be paying attention to us as they pack up and move toward the door, not even Jasmin. Odile tucks a curl behind her ear, and she looks like she's about to say something more when we hear a yell from the front of the room. "Watch out, you're gonna hit him for real!"

The threat of physical injury is the kind of thing my ears are fine-tuned to hear. I jump up to see a cluster of guys messing around near the whiteboard while the rest of the cast stands around, watching.

With Ms. Qiao out of the room, I'm in charge. "Hey, everybody," I call. They either ignore me or don't hear. "Hey!"

"Nah, go ahead," Julio's saying. I step forward through the crowd until I can see inside the knot of people gathered. It's Julio, Andrew, and a few of the ensemble guys who got cast as Thénardier's gang. It looks like they're trying to rehearse the robbery scene, which they definitely aren't allowed to do without a teacher around. "Just do, like, a stage punch, you know? Then maybe I should take a swing at you, and—"

This is stupid. The fight in this scene hasn't been choreographed yet, and it's not safe to mess around with moves you haven't practiced.

Plus, it's bad blocking. Thénardier isn't supposed to fight with the members of his own gang.

"Stop it." I raise my voice, but the guys are already scuffling. Before I can do anything else, there's another shout.

"Hey! *Hey!*"

That's not a playful shout. That's a distress cry.

I spring forward, the crowd parting for me instantly.

Julio is sprawled out on the floor, holding his face. Andrew's crouching next to him. Everyone's gone silent.

This is my fault. I should've *made* them stop.

"Step back!" I tell the others. I can hear footsteps running toward us, and I pray it's a teacher. "Julio, can I see?"

Reluctantly, he pulls his hand away from his face. His chin is streaked with blood. Some has dripped onto his shirt, and there are bright red drops on the floor, too.

"What happened?" I turn back to Andrew, but he looks as stricken as I feel. There's a patch of blood on his knuckles.

"It was an accident." Julio shakes his head. "It's not his fault."

"I started to throw a punch." Andrew's shaking. His face has gone completely pale. "A stage punch, I swear—but I guess there was something wet on the floor, because he slipped, and then— and then he was on the ground."

"What did he slip on?" I study the tiles, but I can't see any water.

"Back away, everyone, back away." Ms. Qiao pushes through the crowd behind us. "Melody, find Ms. Marcus and tell her to call Julio's parents. You have their numbers, right?"

I nod and try not to think about all that blood on the floor as I run toward Ms. Marcus's office in the black box.

This doesn't make any sense. There wasn't anything he could've slipped on. And all that blood . . .

The curse.

It can't be. We've followed every rule.

Except . . .

Odile's face flashes in my mind.

No. *No.* I haven't done anything wrong. What's happening now is scary, but it isn't my fault. It *can't* be.

But—oh, God . . .

What if it is?

LES MISÉRABLES PRELIMINARY BLOCKING DIAGRAM AS OF 2/18/2020—"LOVELY LADIES"

Stored on BHS performing arts department shared drive

Created by: Melody McIntyre, stage manager, class of 2021

Viewable to: SM, ASM, and directors

Editable by: Current SM ONLY

(C1)(C2)(C3) Ensemble Customers 1,2,3 (F) Fantine

(E1)(E2)(E3)(E4) Ensemble Sex Workers 1,2,3,4 (P) Pimp

(SW1)(SW2)(SW3) Sex Worker 1,2,3 (soloists)

(S1)(S2)(S3) Sailors 1,2,3   (OW) Old Woman

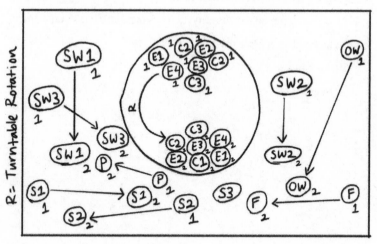

—*Preliminary blocking diagram, sketched quickly in Mel's binder prior to blocking rehearsal.*

Scene 9—Beaconville High School Performing Arts Wing

DAYS UNTIL SPRING MUSICAL OPENS: 72

"They're sure it's laryngitis?" Estaban shoves three chips into his mouth at once, then tries to talk around them. "My mom got that. She had bronchitis, and she couldn't get out of bed for three days. But I just saw Nick in the cafeteria and he looked fine to me."

"That's because he *is* fine." I groan. "Or he *should* be. Except he went to a hockey game Saturday night and yelled for three hours straight, and his voice gave out."

"You're serious?" Fatima starts laughing. "The weekend before music rehearsals started?"

"For the show where he's the *lead*?" Estaban holds out the chips bag to Fatima and me. The three of us are walking at the front of the crew group, winding our way through the hall on the way to rehearsal. "That takes serious balls."

"Or a serious lack of brain cells." I grab a couple of chips. "He doesn't belong in this show at all. Get this—he didn't try to sing at all after the game. He didn't even do the warm-ups all the actors are supposed to do before rehearsal. If he had, he'd have known he was having issues and he could've warned the teachers."

"He didn't care if he screwed everyone over by not being able to rehearse." Gabby shakes her head. She and I are clearly the principal Nick despisers in our crew.

"*Everyone* knows singers are supposed to protect their voices." I'm so exasperated I can't even eat. The chips crumble in my clenched hands. "He was probably shouting in the cold at all those hockey guys because he's jealous they're better at sports than him. I heard he only played in one football game all season."

"I bet that's why we're stuck with him," Bryce says. "Football wasn't working out so he decided to come bother the theater people instead."

"Lucky us," Gabby says. Everyone laughs again.

Nick's doctor put him on vocal rest for a week—no talking or singing, so his voice can recover from this ridiculous hockey-induced situation—so we had to rework the entire rehearsal schedule. I'll be in the auditorium today for the first blocking rehearsal, on "Lovely Ladies," the song where Fantine sells her hair and becomes a sex worker. The rest of the crew is going to the scene shop so they can work on sets and other fun stuff with Will, and Gabby's headed to the choir room with Dom and Malik and the others to rehearse the music for the café scenes.

I check over my shoulder again to make sure Dom's still behind me. He's been quiet today, by Dom standards. Maybe he's nervous about his solos.

Rachel's walking next to him. She's been quiet too, but when we reach the scene shop, she pauses and leans toward me. "I meant to tell you, Mel—the rehearsal pieces are hanging up by stage right. Try not to let the cast destroy them."

"Thanks. I'll do what I can."

Being civil with Rachel has been easier than I expected. It helps that she's a total pro. I've barely had to think about costumes since rehearsals started. Yesterday Ms. Marcus asked me to include a note in the rehearsal report about wanting to use a few pieces today, so during lunch Rachel and Devin went into the long-term basement storage room two levels under the stage to dig out a few old skirts and accessories. That storage room is the one part of the performing arts wing I don't like—I'm always positive a spider's going to spin a web on my head in the time it takes me to navigate through decades' worth of falling-apart set pieces—so it was a relief to know I could trust Rachel and her team to handle it.

Maybe Rachel and me getting along is a good sign on the whole curse front. So far, things don't look like they're going *too* badly on this show. Julio just needed a couple of Band-Aids after that weird accident yesterday, no stitches or anything. And anyway, that couldn't possibly have had anything to do with my crush-or-whatever on Odile.

I *have* been trying to avoid her, though, just to be safe. Today after lunch I spotted her coming out of the bathroom, the same one where we once played musical theater charades, but before she could see me, I turned around and walked in the opposite direction. It was especially tricky given that I really did have to pee. Spanish wound up being *highly* uncomfortable.

"It was amazing," Gabby's telling Jacob as the others meander into the scene shop. They must've changed the subject while Rachel and I were talking. "They took me around the *whole* theater. It was like a two-hour tour!"

"Which theater again?" Jacob asks.

"Boston Rep! I was there so late my mom got annoyed."

"You got a tour of Boston Rep?" I interrupt.

Gabby nods, grinning. "Odile set it up for me. The ASM knows her from a show they did together a long time ago. Her name's Cheryl, and she gave me a private tour of the whole backstage, and the shop, and everything. It was incredible!"

"Wow." I'm jealous, but more than that, I'm happy for Gabby. "That's awesome!"

"Odile set that up?" Jasmin raises her eyebrows.

"Yeah, she's really nice, it turns out." Gabby's positively beaming.

"Surrrrre she is." Bryce laughs. "When she's done being a stuck-up diva."

The others laugh and nod along. I want to jump in to say that Gabby's right, but Jasmin's eyeing me again. Maybe it's better if I stay out of this one.

The crew veers off into the scene shop, and Gabby and the still-silent Dom head for the choir room. When I push open the auditorium doors, the cast is still trickling in, but the stage is empty.

I always love the sight of a bare stage. It's full of possibilities. And today it's even better than usual, because the bare stage means we're about to start blocking.

Blocking might be my favorite part of this job. It's when the director tries out different ways of moving the actors around on the stage so the scenes will look interesting and the audience can understand what's going on. I watched some videos last night to see how other productions blocked "Lovely Ladies," and I sketched out a quick diagram to practice how we might do it on our stage with the turntable.

Today I'll sit beside Ms. Marcus in the front row of the house, taking notes and drawing diagrams while she directs the cast. The actors will do their best to remember what they're supposed to do, of course, but the SM is the only one making a written record. Ms. Marcus is way too busy making actual artistic decisions to keep track of every logistical detail.

Blocking rehearsals can be kind of brutal, though. There's a lot that needs to happen in a scene like this one, and it isn't easy to get everyone onstage at the right time and in the right place. Plus, we don't actually have the turntable yet, but we have to block the scene as if we do. I make a note to ask Will about the coordinates so I can tape out where it'll go before our next rehearsal.

I go over to the wing where Rachel hung the rehearsal costume pieces—long skirts for some of the girls, a cane for Jillian, a pirate hat for David that's shaped kind of like his official police inspector hat will be—and start passing them out to the actors. It's supposed to be easier for them to get in character if they have temporary costume pieces to work with, but in my experience, actors tend to lose all self-control as soon as you hand them anything, so it's a mixed bag.

As I expected, once the rehearsal pieces are in their hands it doesn't take them long to get silly. Ms. Marcus isn't here yet, so that doesn't help.

"Attention, everyone!" I find myself shouting just a few minutes later. "That isn't how we treat props in this theater! From now on, only David's allowed to wear the pirate hat."

"I'm not *wearing* it." Technically, Julio's telling the truth. He isn't *wearing* the hat. He's spinning it around the tip of his finger like a basketball.

"You can't touch another actor's prop." I do my best to act stern. "It's the first rule of theater."

"It isn't a *real* prop." Adam swipes the hat from Julio and tosses it to Kadie, who catches it with a giggle. "There aren't any pirates in *Les Mis*."

"It could be a prop in a future show. Next year we could do *Peter Pan*, and what are you going to tell Ms. Marcus when it turns out our only pirate hat's turned to mush?"

Kadie tosses the hat to Alejandra, who wasn't even going to be in this scene until yesterday. Ms. Marcus added her to the ensemble for this number so she could get over her stage fright before she comes back on later as Cosette. She catches the hat immediately, pops it onto her head, and makes a hook hand. "Arrr!"

Julio swipes it right away. "Aye, lass, ye better walk the plank!"

"Come on, people!" I try to say, but it's clear I've lost control of the situation. I'm also laughing along with everyone else. That doesn't exactly make me seem more authoritative, but I can't help it.

David plucks the pirate hat out of Julio's hand and sets it at a jaunty angle on his head. He's kind of on the short side, which adds to the effect. He looks like he's just stepped out of a theme park ride. "Give me an eye patch and a parrot and let's go hunt some fugitives!"

Beth sneaks up behind David and snatches the hat, stashing it deftly behind her back. David feigns outrage and chases after Beth.

"Ahoy, matey!" Odile, who I somehow didn't see come in, reaches out as Beth runs past and grabs the hat, perching it on her head and hunching forward in an impressively pirate-like pose. Everyone laughs again, including me.

"All right, everyone." Ms. Marcus claps from behind us. "Odile, return the hat to David, please."

Odile grins sheepishly, but she doesn't seem to mind being the only one to get in trouble for something that everyone else was doing too. "Sorry, Ms. Marcus."

I hurry down to my seat as Ms. Marcus directs the cast to their positions. She gets started right away, and the blocking diagram I'd sketched out before rehearsal quickly becomes inaccurate when she adds in more ensemble girls than I'd expected, but that's all right. I can already tell the stage is going to look fuller this way, and that'll add to the sense of chaos in the scene.

Halfway into our first run-through of the song, Ms. Marcus

asks me to call a hold so she can move the ensemble farther down-stage. That's always fun because I get to shout "HOLD!" at the top of my lungs and watch everyone freeze, but she gets them into their new positions fast.

Finally, she calls for a break, and I set my timer and take off for the bathroom. Three different people stop me with questions about the new rehearsal schedule on my way out, but when I reach the auditorium doors, the hallway's empty. Or so I think, until I hear a faint giggle.

"Do you feel it?" Odile's voice echoes from the end of the hall.

"Yeah," a girl answers. More giggling.

My heart thuds as I step closer. All I can see is the dim out-line of two people lying side by side.

"Hi, Mel." Odile lifts her chin and gives me a tiny wave. There's a fresh set of giggles from the figure next to her.

As my eyes adjust to the dim light, I can make out the shape lying on the hallway floor beside her. It's Alejandra. They're both on their stomachs, their faces turned toward each other.

But there's at least a foot of space between them, which . . . is good? I guess? I'm so confused right now I don't know what to think. I'm supposed to be keeping my distance from Odile, but that doesn't mean I'm happy to see her lying on the floor with someone else.

"Oh, hey, Mel." Alejandra giggles again. She's got one arm tucked under her stomach. This whole situation is only getting more bizarre. "Yeah, you're right, I totally feel it now."

"See?" Odile laughs. "My voice teacher showed me this once and I swear it changed everything."

"Showed you what?" I probably shouldn't interfere with what I'm starting to suspect is some bizarre actor ritual, but I sit down cross-legged next to Odile anyway.

"I couldn't figure out how to breathe from my diaphragm." Alejandra pushes herself up onto her elbows. "Ms. Qiao explained it to me, but I still didn't get where my diaphragm actually *was*."

"But if you lie on your stomach and breathe, you can feel it pushing into the floor." Odile rolls over onto her side. "Try it, Mel, you'll see."

"Er, maybe later." I'm climbing back to my feet when Dom's voice echoes down the hall.

"Hey, everybody." His footsteps are heavy on the tile floor. "Do you have a second, Mel?"

"Yeah." It's nice to be distracted from this too-many-feelings weirdness. "Are you all on break too?"

He nods, then waves to Odile and Alejandra and leads me around the corner to an empty hallway. "How much is left on your break timer?"

I glance down. "Two minutes. How's music rehearsal?"

"Okay." He fidgets and looks back around the corner. "Did Gabby tell you she's getting a cold?"

I pinch the skin above my nose. "Yeah. I just hope she doesn't have to miss any rehearsals. The schedule's already screwed up thanks to Nick being a fail, and I *really* don't have time to train a new ASM." Dom gives me some side eye, and I hastily add, "And

I hope she feels better soon, obviously."

"She said it isn't bad. Might just be allergies. Also . . ." He shifts his weight from one foot to the other. "Maybe I should wait until later to bring this up, but . . ."

"Uh-oh. That sounds ominous."

"It's just . . ." He glances around again, probably to make sure no one's close enough to hear us. "She told me about how Odile came to the party the other night."

"Ohhh." Shit. "I'm sorry. I swear, we didn't actually invite her. If I'd known she was coming I'd definitely have asked you too."

"It isn't that." He glances back around the corner again.

"Then what is it . . . oh." I sigh. "You've been talking to Jasmin, haven't you? Look, this isn't going to trigger the curse, I swear."

Dom shakes his head. "I'm not worried about the curse. But I am kind of worried about *you*."

"What? Why?"

"Look, you can be honest." He lowers his voice so far I can barely hear him. "I won't tell Jasmin, or anyone else."

I don't like this. "What are you talking about?"

"You can tell me if you're, you know. With her." He tilts his head toward the corner. "Or if you want to be."

"I—I'm not." I swallow. "I don't."

"Well, she's into *you*. That much is obvious to anyone with eyes. And ears."

"No, she isn't!" I say, but his words have already sent such a huge thrill through me that it's hard to focus on denial.

"Um. Mel. It's hard to take what you're saying seriously given that enormous smile on your face."

"Sorry." I try to make my face completely blank. "I was, um, thinking about something else."

"Sure." He rolls his eyes. "Anyway, I can *tell* you like her. A lot. The way you act together—it's different from how you were with Rachel. Or Tom, or Tyler. I don't remember seeing you look this happy with anyone, actually, as long as I've known you."

Wow. Could he be right? "I don't . . . Look, I'm honestly not . . ."

"Please don't lie to me. It's really not cool." He trails off, and that's when I realize he hasn't smiled once in this conversation. Dom's always joking around, always over the top, but right now he's dead serious. "As far as I can tell, Odile's awesome. I'm not surprised you like her. I just . . . don't want you to get hurt, okay?"

I cross my arms. "Out of curiosity—because I'm telling the truth, there's nothing going on between me and her—but, what do you mean? About getting hurt?"

"Look, you . . . you tend to get in over your head without realizing it sometimes. Things can get really intense really fast when you're involved. You might not know how bad things are until it's too late."

"Okay . . ." I'm not sure what he's getting at, exactly, but I nod. "Thanks for the warning, I guess."

He shrugs. "What are best friends for?"

I smile, trying to lighten the mood. "Do you really still want to be my best friend even now that you've abandoned me for the actors?"

"Hey, you abandoned me first. Remember how you wouldn't talk to me during auditions?" Now he does smile, a little, his words softening into a joke.

At least, I'm *pretty* sure that was a joke.

My timer buzzes. "Got to go."

"Same." He scrunches up his face. "We're doing 'Red and Black' next."

That's his big solo. I grin. "You're going to be amazing. I can't wait until we block that scene. It'll be all you strutting around looking fanatical and cocky."

He cracks a smile, finally. "I've got to admit, that sounds good."

We have to go in opposite directions, so we wave before I jog back toward the auditorium. When I get there, Ms. Marcus is onstage with Katelyn, Beth, and a couple of the other girls who are playing the featured sex workers.

"We need to hold for another five or so, Mel," Ms. Marcus calls when she sees me come into the house. "Doing some quick character work before we get back into the scene."

"Okay." I take my seat at the front-row table, trying to think of what I can do with an extra five minutes. I should probably go over my blocking notes from the first half of rehearsal and see if I need to clean anything up before I share it with Ms. Marcus at the end of the day.

"Sorry about earlier." I recognize Odile's soft voice in my ear and forget all about my blocking notes. "I think it was a little awkward."

"Oh, no, no, it's okay." I turn around, grinning like a doofus. She's slipped into the seat right next to mine, and it's making me feel strangely warm and gleeful. As if being around Odile turns me into a different person entirely. "I was just confused because I'd clearly stumbled into some sub-territory of actor land that I'll never understand."

Odile covers her mouth with her hand like she's trying not to laugh, and I wonder, too late, if that was unprofessional of me to say. For a second I almost forgot she *was* an actor. I guess I've started thinking of her as just plain Odile.

"Sorry." I try to backpedal. "For some reason it's impossible for me to talk to you without pouring out every thought that's in my head. It's highly inconvenient."

Oh my God, did I seriously just say *that* out loud, too?

Odile tilts her head, giving me that fraction of a smile again.

"Like . . . right now." Well, I've already dug myself into this ditch. Might as well stick around. "Every word I say seems to be getting progressively worse. I'm incapable of shutting up whenever you're within three feet."

"I feel like this is something I should take advantage of." She rubs her hands together, and I burst out laughing.

Mischievousness. It's such an un-ingenue-like trait. Or maybe I just need to recalibrate my expectations of this particular ingenue.

Except for the part where I'm trying to avoid her.

Come to think of it, though, maybe it's okay this once. The

rest of the crew isn't here to see us talking.

But it still feels like I'm betraying them. And what if flirting with Odile really *is* dangerous? What if someone else gets hurt, like Julio did?

Except . . . Julio got hurt because the guys were being immature and I didn't make them stop in time. Not *everything* has to be about the curse.

I turn to smile at her. "Now I'm getting nervous."

"Hmm, what secrets do I want to extract from an unwitting Melody McIntyre . . ." Odile smiles, full and real, and I grin back at her. "There actually *is* one thing I want to know. We started talking about it at your house, but we didn't get very far. If you'd rather keep it to yourself, though, just give me some kind of hand signal and I'll back away before you start spilling."

I already know I'll answer any question she asks. Mainly because I don't want her to back away. "Totally. What?"

"How many people in the performing arts department have you dated at some point in the past?"

"I told you, it's not *that* many." I blush, then try to think. "You already know about Dom. Also, Rachel. I'm, uh, guessing you heard that story."

She nods, flushing ever so slightly. "It's the first one I heard when I asked around about you."

She asked around about me? My blush is only getting deeper. "Anyway, also, you probably heard I went out with Tyler, too. And Hannah and Tom usually play in the pit orchestra, so they'll probably be here starting with the sitzprobe, but I don't think that's enough to qualify them as actually being *in* the performing arts department, at least not at this exact moment, so—"

"Wait." Odile holds up her hands. "I didn't hear about Tyler. Are you talking about Tyler Zumbrun? The guy who got written up in the *New York Times* for winning a bunch of national graphic design awards when he was a freshman and only joined the theater tech crew because he liked listening to the *Be More Chill* cast recording? *He's* your ex, too?"

"Er . . . yeah." It's kind of neat that Odile knows who's who among the crew. Most actors can barely tell us apart. "Technically, he's my ex twice. We were a thing for a while and we broke up, but later we got back together. And broke up again, obviously."

"You should draw me a chart so I can keep track." She eyes my binder. "Like that blocking diagram."

Of course Odile knows a blocking diagram when she sees one. My other friends, even on crew, go cross-eyed when they see my paperwork. "You want me to draw a blocking diagram of my exes?"

"Yes! It would help me keep the list in my head."

I want to ask why she wants to have a list of my exes in her head. Instead I pull a piece of scratch paper out of my binder— the blank side of an old flyer, because trees are friends to all—and sketch an empty rectangle with my ruler.

"I'll have myself enter at upstage right." I draw an *M* with a circle around it and label it as position number one. "Oops, wait, I forgot to write out the key first. Hang on."

Across the top of the page, I start writing my exes' names with the first letter marked in a bubble. I quickly realize I've gone out with two people whose names start with *T*, so I add a second letter to their bubbles. The list is longer than I realized it would be, but so far Odile's just watching me in silence.

"So starting with ninth grade, Isabelle was my first real significant other." I add a bubble for Isabelle, *I*, and a new bubble for myself above it, then draw a line showing myself moving from my entrance at upstage right to stand behind Isabelle at position number two. Since upstage is at the top and downstage is at the bottom, my bubble looks like it's actually on *top* of Isabelle's bubble, which is mildly awkward, but it's too late to change that. "She's not a theater person, though. She was part of my jock phase, freshman year. Dom was after that, in the spring, during *Fiddler*—he was part of my jock phase too, now that I'm thinking about it—and after that was Jess. You know Jess Cushwa, right? Used to be on the debate team? They graduated last year. But I went to homecoming with them when I was a sophomore."

Odile nods, her eyebrows knitting together. "Okay. I'm trying to follow. We're up to, what, fall of last year?"

"Yeah, during *Steel Magnolias*. Actually, maybe I should add a separate key at the bottom for the shows we were doing. That's how I keep track of everything in my head anyway. I'll put the shows in boxes instead of circles, with lowercase letters so it's easy to follow."

Odile nods again and glances up at where Ms. Marcus is still talking to a few of the actors onstage. Everyone else is milling around, talking or reading over their scripts.

I erase a line I drew at a bad angle and start over. Odile looks down at the paper quizzically. "Are you stalling because you don't want to tell me who the rest of your exes are?"

"No!" I can tell she's teasing, but I draw faster anyway. "You only want people from school on this, right? Because I don't know if I have space for everyone from theater camp."

"Wait, how many . . ." Odile lifts a finger and softly touches her bottom lip as she trails off. Hmm, maybe I shouldn't have mentioned camp. "Actually, never mind."

The diagram winds up being a little awkward, because I have to convey that I went out with Tyler twice, so I have to draw a movement arrow for him, too. And there are a couple of people I went out with when I wasn't doing shows, so they don't have any boxes by their circles, which makes the whole thing frustratingly asymmetrical. When I'm done, my paper looks like this:

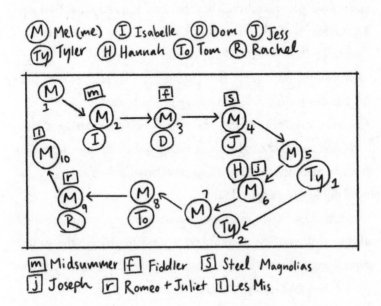

239

Odile tucks her hair behind her ear. "Wow, that's . . . wow. Okay."

Yeah. Now that I'm looking at it, I've moved around this diagram a *lot*.

I should probably play it cool, but once again all the rules I usually try so hard to follow fly away in Odile's presence and my mouth spews out exactly what I'm thinking. "Do you think I'm a slut or something?"

"What? No!" She sits up straight, her eyes flashing. "I'm so sorry if I made you think that. I *hate* that word. But no, I was just thinking about how I'm a *lot* less popular than you."

"Um, that's the opposite of true. You're legitimately famous. You're the most popular person in the entire *school*."

Her smile fades, and I suddenly remember how just a couple of days ago she was telling me about how isolated she feels. I swallow, trying to think of something else I can say to make up for it. "Well, if it makes you feel any better, I'm a virgin."

Oh my God, I *really* need to work on my self-control. I clap my hands over my face and cringe into my seat.

But Odile only laughs. "Saving yourself for marriage?"

I look up and laugh too. It feels good to let out the tension. "Er, no. Just for, you know. True love or whatever."

I'm blushing again. Hard.

"Um." I scrunch my shoulders up around my ears, trying to play this off like it's no big deal. I need to change the subject, fast. "I guess this is now extremely obvious, but I meant what

I said about how I can't shut up around you. Anyway, fair's fair—I just revealed a bunch of embarrassing stuff. Now it's your turn."

"Fair is fair, huh?" she says, to the tune of the witch's rap from *Into the Woods*.

"Now *you're* the one stalling." I straighten up in my seat, giggling.

God, I still can't believe being around this girl makes me *giggle*. It doesn't bother me as much as it did last time, though. Especially when she tucks a curl behind her ear and smiles at me.

"There's too much embarrassing stuff about me." She laughs. "I don't even know where to start."

"Yeah, right. You've probably never done anything embarrassing in your entire *life*."

"I wish. Okay, how about this—the first time I got a phone call from my agent, I was so nervous I almost threw up."

"Wow, you have a lot of experience with vomit, don't you?" She laughs again. "Apparently."

"I'm surprised you were nervous, though. When I heard you on the phone in the bathroom that one time, you sounded like the most confident person ever."

"Yeah, well . . ." She turns back to face forward. Ms. Marcus is talking to Kadie by the wing and David is stage center with Beth, spinning his pirate hat and watching Odile and me. Hmm. "I have different voices I use for different occasions. Sometimes it feels like I'm different *people* for different occasions."

That makes me forget all about David. "What do you mean, different people?"

"It's something I started doing when I was younger." Her smile is gone now. "When I talk to people in the business, I'm bright and airy. When I talk to my parents, I always make it sound as though I've got everything under control, even when I have no idea what I'm doing. And at school, I never know what to do, so I usually don't do anything at all."

That sounds exhausting. "So . . . which mode are you using now?"

"None of them." She meets my gaze and holds it. "For some reason, whenever I'm with you, I forget to put on any disguise at all."

"All right, let's get started," Ms. Marcus calls out. "Actors, stage center, please."

Odile gives me one last soft smile, then climbs out of her seat and heads for the stage. I try to smile back, but I'm pretty sure it comes out as a generically terrified facial wobble.

I want to drop my face into my hands, but I can't do that. Not in front of half the cast.

But . . . oh, shit. Oh shit oh shit oh shit.

I thought I was safe.

I thought I knew how I felt about Odile. I thought I was in control of what happened next. I thought there was no way in hell I was actually in danger of falling for her.

Suddenly, I'm not so sure I've ever been in control of anything.

From: Melody McIntyre

To: All directors and crew heads

Date: Monday, 2/24, 6:45 p.m.

Subject: Rehearsal report

Today's rehearsal:

- 3:01 p.m. to 3:45 p.m.: Music rehearsal, "Stars"
- 3:01 p.m. to 3:42 p.m.: Blocking rehearsal, "At the End of the Day"
- 3:45 p.m. to 3:52 p.m.: Break
- 3:53 p.m. to 4:45 p.m.: Blocking rehearsal, "Prologue"
- 4:46 p.m. to 5:42 p.m.: Blocking rehearsal, "The Runaway Cart"

Tomorrow's schedule:

- 3:00 p.m. to 5:00 p.m. (later if needed): Blocking rehearsal, "Red and Black / Do You Hear the People Sing?"; music rehearsal, "Prologue" (Valjean only)

Actor report:

- Absent: Taylor (excused)
- Late: Julio (5 minutes—excused), Nick (3 minutes), Aaron (3 minutes), Noah (2 minutes)
- Principals now off-book include Beth, Alejandra, David, and Odile. All other principals and most ensemble members are still on-book.

- We reminded all actors that the off-book deadline is March 15.

Set updates:
- The crew got through a LOT of construction this weekend (THANK YOU, EVERYONE!!!).
- The set team will be testing the preliminary turntable design tomorrow. NO ACTORS are allowed in the auditorium until we give the all clear.

Costume updates:
- The team had an excellent thrift-shop haul and has made solid progress on altering pieces and adding trim. However, there's still a LOT of work ahead of us.
- We're seeking parents and others who can follow a simple pattern to help make aprons for the factory scene (period-appropriate aprons are impossible to find in thrift stores). The work can be done at home and we'll provide all materials. If anyone has leads on people who might be able to help, contact Rachel.

Lighting and sound updates:
- All lighting and sound crew members have been temporarily reassigned to help with sets and costumes while we wait for the gobos we ordered to come in.

Publicity update:

- BIG NEWS: Tyler arranged for us to do a flash mob performance of "One Day More" at the pep rally before opening night (the same Friday as the sitzprobe, so it will be a busy day). This should hopefully generate a LOT of ticket sales and if we're lucky, maybe even a viral video.

Thank you, everyone! —Mel

—Also stored on BHS performing arts department shared drive.
Created by: Melody McIntyre, stage manager, class of 2021
Viewable to: Directors and crew heads
Editable by: Current SM ONLY

Scene 10—The McIntyre-Perez House

DAYS UNTIL SPRING MUSICAL OPENS: 67

"Why do you need muskets anyway?" Pops asks, licking his fingers. "Can't you get by with swords and a few cannon sound effects?"

"Have you *seen* this show?" Will sighs and stirs his pan of carrots. "There's more onstage gunfire than I prefer to think about. One of the many reasons I lobbied against doing *Les Mis*."

"But your veto was overridden, and now we're all suffering." I slump across the counter in feigned exhaustion. "It's going to take me all week to recover from that rehearsal today. We spent an hour moving different factory workers from one end of the stage to the other. And then another hour after that watching Nick pretend to lift an invisible cart while Kyle flailed under it."

"Oh, don't act like you don't love every second of blocking, Mel." Odile laughs. She's perched on a stool on the opposite side of the counter, sipping a glass of seltzer.

Jasmin and Dom both raise their eyebrows at me from

behind her. They've been teaming up like that a lot tonight. I can only assume their goal is to make me as self-conscious as possible about the weirdness between Odile and me. As if I'm not self-conscious about it enough already.

I've tried to avoid her since that flirty "Lovely Ladies" rehearsal, but it's been hard. Largely because avoiding her is the last thing in the world I actually *want* to do. The good news is, our schedule has been too intense for me to see much of anyone, and the teachers have been keeping our breaks short so we can get through as much material as possible. So I don't think she's noticed me acting weird. At least, I hope she hasn't.

I know I'm not supposed to like her, but . . . she's just so darn *likable.*

There was no getting out of this supremely awkward family dinner, though. If I step one toe out of line, Jasmin will figure out exactly what's going on, if she hasn't already. And Dom already knew exactly how much I liked Odile even before *I* did.

"Okay . . ." I huff, trying not to look at her. It's easier to keep from getting overwhelmed if I avoid eye contact. "That's a kind of valid point."

Nick came back today for his first rehearsal since his doctor-mandated week of silence. Ms. Marcus wanted to take things easy on him, so we scheduled songs where he only has short solos and focused on blocking instead of singing. Even so, it was obvious that his voice isn't much better than it was in that first rehearsal. He cracked on the high notes *and* the low notes, and he still doesn't seem to be bothering with the vocal warm-ups all the actors are supposed to do. When the rehearsal ended, Ms. Qiao took him off for a private talking-to while Ms. Marcus and I redid the week's schedule, *again*.

The worst part is, Nick seems to think *his* voice problems are everybody *else's* fault. Today he yelled at Imani for "distracting" him when he was trying to sing, even though she was in character, *acting*, exactly like she was supposed to. Ms. Marcus gave him a private talking-to after that, too.

"I bet you're glad you get to skip some of these rehearsals," Will says to Odile as he pours melted butter into the pan with one hand and stirs with the other. "There are benefits to dying in act one."

"Actually, I miss it on the days when I don't have to come." Odile rests her chin in her hand. "I don't like knowing everyone else is having fun without me."

Pops laughs. "Spoken like a true stage actor. You're sure you want to get into the movie business?"

Odile smiles again, but it's her wide, sunny smile this time. The one I've learned not to believe.

A *Hollywood Reporter* article came out over the weekend, exclusively announcing that Odile had gotten cast in the Scorsese movie. At school, people came up to her all day to congratulate her and ask if she could introduce them to Leonardo DiCaprio. He's rumored to be playing the lead, even though Odile told me last week that the rumor was bullshit.

"You can always come work on costumes on your days off if you want," Jasmin offers.

"Really?" Odile brightens. "I'm off tomorrow. Could I come then? I love costumes. I've gotten pretty decent at sewing buttons over the years."

Jasmin's smile drops. Clearly, she wasn't expecting Odile to say yes. "Yeah, um . . . I mean, you should probably check with Rachel first. I'll warn you, though, the work she's got us doing is a giant pain in the ass."

Pops coughs and Jasmin giggles sheepishly. "Sorry, Charlie. Pain in the tushy."

"She's right, though," I say, reaching over to refill Jasmin's seltzer glass. I'm trying hard to be as nice to her as possible tonight. "I went in to help on Friday after rehearsal and I wound up buried in sashes."

"Uh, Mel, that's because you're the slowest at costumes of anyone on the crew." Dom takes the bottle from me. "I saw Rachel knock out five sashes before you'd finished *one*."

I stick out my tongue at him, but he's got a point. I'm utter crap at sewing.

The costume demands really *are* extreme for this show. All the actors playing students have to wear vests with red, white, and blue sashes, all the girls in "Lovely Ladies" need to look like sex workers but without actually showing any skin, and the dance troupe in the wedding scene needs to look like they're going to a nineteenth-century prom. And then there's all the *regular* peasant attire every *other* character needs to wear, not to mention the accessories—aprons, top hats, shawls, corsets, military jackets, prisoner rags . . . Even with a whole team under her, it's possible

Rachel's working harder than anyone else on this show.

"But we're all avoiding the real question, which is, who's going to help me make two dozen muskets?" Will acts like he's talking to all of us, but he's only looking at Dad. "I have my stagecraft classes cutting up scrap shelving, and Estaban and Matt are all set to attach the clamps and paint, but I need a few hours from someone who can handle a sander."

Dad folds his arms across his chest. "And after the two dozen muskets are ready, I'm sure that barricade's going to build itself."

"Doubt it." Will shrugs a what-can-you-do shrug. "But I was banking on locking in some musket help first, then holding off on asking for more favors for another week or so."

"Ooh, are you building the barricade, Dad?" I hop up onto the stool next to his. "Can I help? Remember how much fun we had on the sets for *Joseph*?"

"We made snow angels in the sawdust." Dad smiles.

"I *love* doing that," Odile says. All five of us turn to her at once, surprised. "I used to hang out in the scene shop freshman year. Wes was the set head then, and he taught me how to use the power drill. I'd come home wearing so much sawdust my sister would get sneezing fits, but I liked how it smelled."

"Ooh, me too. When I was on set crew, I basically breathed sawdust for two years straight, so . . ." I cut myself off before I can say *You should've smelled me then*.

"Well, Odile, if you ever have a free moment in between acting and helping with costumes and waiting to hear back on your college applications, you're welcome to join us in the shop again." Will smiles at her and passes me a bunch of parsley to chop. "Especially now that I know you can use a drill."

"But as for you, Mel . . ." Dad shakes his head. "I know working with the tools is fun, but you aren't the set head anymore."

"Come on, I have an *excellent* barricade design I've always wanted to try." I hold up my hands, trying to act out what I mean, but I'm still terrible at charades, so it probably just looks like I'm waving herb fragments randomly in the air. "We'll use A-frames with burlap sacks on top and put barrels on the ends, and rip up those old pallets in the garage so they'll look distressed, and—"

"I need those pallets for work." Dad shakes his head. "Not everything in this house exists solely for school theater purposes."

"Your dad's right. Besides, SMs don't have time to do construction." Will tastes a spoonful of something and wrinkles his nose. "It's the price you pay for getting promoted. Plus, Fatima needs to be empowered to manage her team. If you're in the shop all the time she'll feel like she has to defer to you."

"It's not *my* fault you waited until this year to do *Les Mis*." I cross my arms over my chest.

"Fatima's set designs are fantastic," Jasmin says, popping a mint into her mouth. "We just tested out the LED lights they ordered for the gunshots. They look awesome."

"Well, that'll be cool." I exhale sharply. "I'm still annoyed we can't have the star drop, though."

"What?" Odile looks up. "We're not doing the star drop?"

I purse my lips and fix my gaze directly over Odile's right shoulder. *No eye contact. No eye contact.* "It was too expensive.

Like, more than our entire budget for the show. I guess it was always a pipe dream, but I'm kind of devastated."

"Enough complaining. It's time to eat." Will waves his fingers at us. "Everybody into the dining room while I put on the finishing touches."

"Could you use another pair of hands?" Odile studies the various pots still simmering on the range. "I can stir the risotto if you need to finish the sauce."

"I'm glad we invited you over, Odile." Pops gathers up the glasses. "This is officially the first time we've had a dinner guest who knew how to stir risotto."

"It's the first time we've had a guest who knew what risotto *was*," Dad adds.

"I will repeat my request and make it a command." Will points his wooden spoon toward the dining room. "I appreciate the kind offer, Ms. Rose, but I still need everyone out, now."

We shuffle into the dining room. Dad and Pops set the table, and Jasmin and Dom reach for their usual seats—they've both been regulars for dinner at our house since freshman year. Odile stands as awkwardly as she's able to stand, which is to say not all that awkwardly, until Dad directs her to a chair.

"So how's the acting life treating you, Dom?" Pops asks.

Dom tries to laugh, but it comes out as a mildly strangled chuckle. "It's a lot of fun. But it's nerve-racking to think about actually singing in front of a whole auditorium full of people."

"I always wanted to play Enjolras," Pops says, staring wistfully toward the dining room window.

Now *I* start laughing. "You're making that up."

"I assure you, he's not." Will strides into the dining room with a giant bowl of steaming risotto and platter of fish. Mmm. Dad grabs them and starts passing the food around immediately. "He used to talk about it all the time."

Will goes back for the carrots and Brussels sprouts while Pops launches into the first chorus of "Do You Hear the People Sing?" I groan, and mercifully he stops two lines in. Jasmin and Odile both clap, but the rest of us react with a variety of eye rolls and embarrassed head tilts. Dom squirms in his seat.

"This looks incredible." Odile gazes down at the parsley artfully dotting the risotto and breathes in the smells coming from the roasted veggies. "And the carrots smell divine."

"Mr. Green's a cooking wizard," Jasmin tells her, helping herself to an extra-large serving of risotto. "You remember his special brainstorming brownies?"

"Very much so." Odile takes a huge bite of risotto and shuts her eyes, like she's on the verge of moaning.

Too late, I realize I'm staring at her. By the time I avert my gaze, Jasmin's studying me way too closely.

"Anyway, back to Enjolras." Dad points his fork at Will as he settles into his usual seat. "Wasn't that the role *you* played in that production? The one right after college?"

I assume he's joking until Will gives him a haughty look. "I'll have you know, I was Valjean."

I wait for Dad and Pops to start laughing, but they just nod. "Right," Dad says.

"Hilarious, you all," I say.

But Will only holds my gaze and takes another spoonful of carrots.

"Wait, are you serious?" My jaw drops to the floor. "You were an *actor*?"

"No way!" Jasmin laughs. Next to her, Dom's still squirming.

"Not only was I an actor . . ." Will grins, clearly delighted at my devastation. "I was the first black Valjean in a summer stock production in all of western Massachusetts."

I shake my head. I can't even eat, I'm so shocked. "You're messing with me."

"I'm not." His grin widens. "I was the first black Curly in *Oklahoma*, too."

"Actors aren't quite the evil subspecies you've imagined, Mel," Dad says. "There are worse things than standing in a spotlight having hundreds of people hang on your every breath."

Dom stands up. The greenish tint he had at auditions is creeping back around his eyes. "Excuse me. I'll just be a minute." He heads for the bathroom down the hall.

"I've been thinking about talking to the crew about that, actually," I tell Pops. "Sometimes the way we talk about actors seems kind of rude. Maybe we should try to cross-socialize more. Or at least not talk behind each other's backs so much."

Jasmin's staring at me from across the table like I have three heads. I take a big bite of fish to keep myself from saying anything else that could get me into more trouble.

"So, Odile, is your whole family in show business?" Pops

asks, neatly changing the subject.

"Pops," I chide him. "No one calls it that anymore."

"It's okay." Odile smiles at him and then at me. Ugh—when she does that, it's physically impossible for me not to blush. "My parents aren't very interested in theater, but my little sister's getting into it. I tried to convince her to stick to dancing, since she's wonderful at ballet, but she wants to act."

"Like big sister, like little sister," Dad says, sipping his wine.

"I hope not." Odile's smile doesn't fade, but she's gone a little stiff. "But it's not up to me."

"Why don't you want your sister to follow in your acting footsteps?" Pops asks, because both my parents have to phrase everything in the cheesiest way possible. "How old is she, anyway?"

"Eleven. And it's not that I think there's anything wrong with acting, but I hope she doesn't wind up missing so much school the way I did. I was homeschooled for all of eighth grade while I was in New York, and I wish so much that I could have that year back."

"You do?" Jasmin seems startled.

Odile nods. "At the time I was excited to be part of a big show, but it turned out that just meant working in a job, with adults working in *their* jobs. And work is work, even when you're thirteen. I'd rather have just had a normal school year with my friends."

Huh. Now that I think about it, I guess my eighth-grade year *was* pretty cool. That was the year I figured out I was queer for real, and subsequently discovered how much fun kissing was. Plus, I was finally old enough to go places on my own sometimes. And my project on stem cells came in first at the district science fair.

I still think I'd rather have done a show on Broadway, though.

Will and Jasmin switch to talking about lighting, since this is officially supposed to be a mentorship meeting, and soon they're having an in-depth discussion about gobos. I don't have much to contribute, since they both know a lot more about lighting than I do. Apparently there's a specific gobo they both want for the inn scenes that's hard to find, and Odile jumps into the conversation, offering to call someone she knows who might be able to track it down. Jasmin grudgingly agrees with Will that it's nice of her to offer.

Dom comes back to the table just as the gobo discussion is winding down. "Sorry I was gone so long. Is there any food left?"

"Please, take it." Dad holds out the fish platter. "Otherwise we'll have leftovers for days."

"That's not true at all," I say. "Leftovers never stay in our fridge more than twelve hours when Will made them."

"Quiet, Melody," Pops says. "You'll give him an even bigger head about his cooking than he's already got."

"I've always found having a hobby to be an excellent form of stress relief." Will smiles as Dom digs into another piece of fish. "If there's one lesson I'd impart to your overscheduled generation, it's that."

I hate it when people talk about how you have to have a bunch of hobbies, as if there's something wrong with being passionate about one particular thing, but Odile nods seriously. "My parents say that too."

"I'm glad to hear that." Pops flicks his eyes from Odile to me and back again. "Speaking of future plans, I've been curious, Odile—*are* you planning to go to college?"

"Pops!" I plead. He's obviously trying to use this conversation to *impart a lesson*, and the last thing I want is to get into the college discussion again. We already spent two hours this weekend watching promotional videos for a half-dozen liberal arts schools that my parents seem to have chosen specifically because they don't offer stand-alone majors in stage management. "We're having dinner. You don't need to interrogate her."

"It's all right." Odile nods. "Yes, I applied to a few schools. I should hear back in April."

"I thought you had to go to London to film that movie after graduation?" Jasmin asks.

"Well, I might need to defer for a semester or two. There's a lot that's still up in the air." Odile sips her seltzer. I can't believe how calmly she's talking about this. If I had to think about college *and* school *and* a real job at the same time, I'd be freaking out.

"Do you have a first choice school?" Dad asks her.

"I'm hoping to get into NYU."

"That's my top choice, too." Jasmin smiles at her. A genuine smile. Odile smiles back.

"You could continue working if you're in the city." Pops nods knowingly, as though he's an expert on acting careers.

"Maybe." Odile tilts her head to one side. "I guess I'll see what happens with this movie and take it from there."

I shift in my seat. Suddenly I kind of like knowing that I still have another year of high school, and that I'll definitely go to college after that. I don't know all the particulars of my future, but I know the general outline, which is apparently more than Odile knows. And her future is a lot closer than mine.

"Seems very reasonable." Dad takes another spoonful of Brussels sprouts. He and Pops both look happy now. I guess Odile is sufficiently levelheaded by their standards. "It's got to be exciting to know you're working with someone like Martin Scorsese."

"Yes. I'm nervous, but I'm also quite chuffed about it."

"*Chuffed?*" I smile. "How very British of you."

"Well, I *am* British." She never stops smiling. "Half, anyway."

"Oh, right. I think I—um, I heard that somewhere." I manage to catch myself before I can say the more embarrassing version of that sentence, which is that I read it on Wikipedia. "One of your parents is British and one's American, right?"

She nods. "My mother's from Southampton, and we spent a few years there when I was younger. I used to speak with a full English accent, but it only comes out now on certain words."

"*Schedule?*" Dad says, pronouncing it the weird way, as if there's no *c* in it.

"No, I say that one the American way. But I always forget how Americans say *aluminium*. In my house everyone says it the British way, even my dad." She takes another bite of risotto and turns to Will. "I don't suppose you'd ever share your risotto recipe, Mr. Green?"

He chuckles. "Absolutely not."

"Speaking of which," Pops tells him, "I know I say this every time, but your Brussels sprouts are divine."

"You *do* say it every time, and it never gets old."

Jasmin and Odile insist on doing the dishes at the end of the night, which means Dom and I are stuck helping too. Dad, Pops, and Will head down to the basement, claiming they're going to watch *RuPaul's Drag Race*, which they know I can't stand. I bet their real plan is to talk about us where we can't hear them.

"See you at school, everyone," Will says before he goes downstairs. "Oh, and I meant to say, Mr. Connor, let me know if you want to set up any extra practice sessions for your songs. It's too bad Ms. Qiao won't have as much time to work with you under the new schedule."

Dom, who never really stopped looking green even after he came back from the bathroom, now goes white. "She won't?"

"Probably not. She's got to spend more one-on-one time with one of the other actors than she'd planned. But I'm happy to work something out if that would help. Just let me know."

"Okay." Dom puts down the plate he was scraping off. "Thanks. Excuse me, I think I need to—um. I'll be right back."

He disappears down the hall again as Will heads downstairs.

"Yikes," I say when he's out of earshot. "I didn't know he was still so nervous."

"You didn't?" Jasmin glances up from where she's leaning over the dishwasher. I don't know if there's judgment in her eyes or if I'm imagining it.

A phone buzzes. We all automatically check our pockets, but it's Odile's. When she glances at the screen, her eyes darken. "Sorry. I should go out and take this."

"No worries."

She pulls her coat off the rack and vanishes through the front door, leaving me alone with Jasmin. I turn, ready for her to lay into me for all my wrongs, but all she says is, "Pass me those forks?"

"Sure." I rinse them under the tap first, trying to make sure they're squeaky clean before I hand them over.

"You don't need to do that." She half glances up at me.

"Do what?"

"You've been extra nice to me all night. Hoping for a get out of jail free card?"

"I . . ." I have no idea what to say.

She laughs. "Relax. I'm sorry I gave you a hard time earlier. She isn't actually that bad. And it's cool if you're friends, even though you also happen to think she's hot."

"I . . ." I blush, but she just laughs again.

"Anyway, I was hoping we'd be alone for a second, because I wanted to say that I really appreciate you resisting temptation for the sake of the show. I know how much you hate being single. But if you've held out this long, I know we can trust you to make it to May." She glances at the clock on the microwave. "What's taking Dom so long? I'm supposed to give him a ride, and if we don't get going I'll be up half the night finishing my problem set for calc."

I crane my neck down the hallway, but the bathroom light

is out. That's weird—if he'd come out, he would've walked right past us. "Maybe he went out the side door?"

"Figures he'd want to skip out on doing dishes." Jasmin slides the last plate into the rack. "Let's go check."

It's freezing outside, so we both get our coats. When we first step out onto the front porch, a truck is driving by and there's no sign of anyone in the yard, but a moment later soft voices float over the hedge.

"Seriously, it's so normal you wouldn't believe it," Odile is murmuring quietly. They must not have heard us come out over the truck noise. "There's only one trick I know. Whenever you get caught up in it, you've got to force yourself to focus on something completely different."

Dom's voice is even lower than hers. They're sitting on the grass next to the porch, under the dining room window. It's so dark I can only see their faintest outlines. "Like what?" he murmurs back.

"Well . . . if I show you something a friend taught me, do you promise not to laugh?"

"Promise."

"Okay . . ." Odile lifts her hand, and the next thing I know, she's singing. "*Baby shark, do do, do do . . .*"

He starts laughing. "*What?*"

"I'm serious. If you're singing 'Baby Shark' in your head, it instantly knocks everything else out. It's impossible to focus on being scared. Plus, if there's no one around you can do the motions. Here, try it."

Jasmin looks at me. We both laugh too, silently, as Dom starts doing the chomp-chomp motion with his fingers. *"Ba-by shark, do do, do do do . . ."*

They get through Mama Shark, but by the time they're onto the next verse Jasmin and I can't take it anymore. We both step up to the edge of the porch, holding out our arms in giant chomps as we lean over the edge. *"Daddy shark, do do, do do do!"*

"Oh my God." Odile giggles, but Dom grins and keeps singing with us.

Jasmin and I climb down and we all go through Grandma Shark and Grandpa Shark together, but then we can't agree on whether the sharks go hunting next or whether there's a swimmer who gets eaten, and we're laughing too hard to finish the song anyway. At least Dom looks like himself again.

"We've got to jet." Jasmin points to Dom. "You didn't puke in Mel's bushes, did you?"

"Uhhh . . ." He pauses, and for a moment I'm alarmed—Pops will be highly displeased if I have to report the presence of puke in his rhododendrons—but he shakes his head. "It was a close call, though."

"Gross. Do the shark thing next time." Jasmin holds out her hand to help him up. I think about doing the same for Odile, but I don't know if I could handle the physical contact. "See you tomorrow."

"Bye. Thanks for coming over."

Odile and I wave as they head toward the curb. A moment later they're driving off in Jasmin's mom's Corolla, and Odile and

I are alone on my front porch. Again.

I shift on my feet. I've thought a lot about how tonight would go, but I'd been focused on how painful it would be having everyone here at once. It hadn't occurred to me that I might wind up face-to-face with Odile, with no one watching. I shiver, and not just from the cold. "So, uh . . . Was everything okay with that phone call?"

"Oh, it was fine." Her smile fades. "My agent's trying to put me in touch with the producer on that Netflix show."

"Oh. I thought it would've been about the Scorsese movie."

"No, it's always about what's up next. My agent calls it 'parlaying this success into future projects.'"

I wince. "That sounds painful."

She laughs. "I agree. But she's excited about this show, so I guess I'll get excited too."

"Is that how it usually works?"

She shrugs. The light from the half-moon shines on the wavy hair that spills over her shoulders. "I don't know."

We're both quiet for a long moment. Then Odile tucks her hair behind her ear and takes a long breath. "Mel . . . could I tell you something?"

I take a long breath too. I want to say *Yes*.

I want to say *Yes, please*.

I want to say *Please, tell me anything you want to tell me. Please, tell me the words I desperately want to hear you say.*

Except—she's asking my permission.

Which means I can stop this, right now. I can say no, and nothing more will ever have to happen.

I'll be safe. My friends will be safe. My *show* will be safe.

But I'm already nodding. "Yeah, um . . . if you want to, I mean, sure, I . . ."

"I really like you," she blurts.

I'm still trying to register that when she lifts her fist to her mouth, her eyes widening.

"I'm sorry." She presses her knuckles to her lips. "That wasn't what I meant to say. Or, well, I suppose it was, but . . . I meant for there to be more buildup."

I don't say anything. I'm not sure my brain is capable of forming words. My conscience is shouting at me loud and clear, though.

The curse. The curse! Mel, you promised!

"I hope, well—I hope that doesn't make you uncomfortable." Odile looks down and slides her fingers into the hair at the nape of her neck. I can't stop watching. Her every movement is mesmerizing. "I know you didn't seem interested during your party when we—I mean . . ." She covers her face with her hand. "Forget I said anything. You don't have to—"

"I really like you too."

I inhale sharply as soon as the words are out of my mouth. Someday my lack of filter around Odile Rose is going to be the end of me.

I don't regret saying it, though.

I should. I *will*, once my friends find out.

(Oh, God. My friends can never find out.)

But in this moment, with Odile standing in front of me,

looking so hopeful, I want to forget all about the stupid curse.

After all—it might not even be real. And regardless, as long as I don't fall in *love*—real, deep, fairy-tale love, not the garden-variety head-over-heels teenage infatuation this has got to be—we'll be safe. Right?

"I have to admit . . . I lied to you." She's smiling her softest smile. "When I came here that first time, I—well, I knew that party was only for the crew. And . . . I didn't need to get a ride from my parents, either. I could've driven my car. I just . . . I wanted an excuse to see you."

I laugh, but I'm so giddy I could cry. "You're going to see me every day for the next two and a half months."

"I know." Her voice sounds so different than it did all through dinner. Open. Almost raw. "It's hard to pay attention in rehearsal when you're in the room. You're very distracting."

I blush. "Um. Thanks, I guess?"

"You don't hold back when you're passionate about something. It's wonderful." She's blushing too, but she doesn't try to hide it the way I always do. "I'm constantly afraid people will judge me if I say what I'm thinking. I love that you aren't like that."

She's wrong. I hold back all the time. I'm careful with what I say. You have to be, when it's your job to tell people what to do.

But I've never felt that way around Odile. The opposite, in fact. I *have* to tell her what I'm thinking. What I'm feeling.

"While I'm admitting things . . ." She tugs on her gold hoop earring. It's stupidly adorable. "I'm not sure if you even knew who

I was before this year, but, well . . . I've been wondering about you for a long time. Whenever I saw you backstage, I'd wonder . . . but every time I asked, people always told me you had a boyfriend, or a girlfriend. I guess you could say . . . I've been waiting for my chance."

I giggle so sharply my dads can probably hear me in the basement.

I take a step toward her. The curse thing, the superstition—it's not real. It *can't* be real.

"I, um." I try to find the right words, but as usual, the wrong ones come. "I should probably warn you, I'm not actually that exciting."

"I think I should test that theory for myself."

Then she kisses me, and I can't think about words or rules or curses or anything at all. Somehow I'm still standing, even though it feels like the earth just disappeared beneath my feet.

She tastes like magic. Kissing her feels like standing in front of a dark curtain with the spotlight closing in, until the whole world is nothing but her and me.

Her lips on mine. My hands in her hair. Her fingers tracing my spine.

No one's *ever* kissed me like this. I'm *always* the one who kisses first.

I've lost control. If I ever had it to begin with.

It's too late to hold back. And I wouldn't want to even if I could.

INTERMISSION

<u>ATTENTION!</u>

Rule 1: If this door is closed, YOU SHOULD NOT COME IN.

Rule 2: If this door is closed and you MUST come in, KNOCK and wait to be admitted.

Rule 3: All requests for entry by anyone other than the SM, ASM, TD, LD, or SD must be accompanied by either the performance of a quirky set of dance steps OR the singing of at least EIGHT bars of a musical theater song (your choice, but be warned that songs from the show currently being performed OR from *Hamilton* or *Dear Evan Hansen* will be considered cheating, though exceptions may be made for the "Guns and Ships" rap).*

*Please note: This rule is to be enforced at the SM's discretion. Sometimes the SM might be too busy or tired to properly judge the quirkiness of your dancing ability. Give them a break, they've got a lot going on.

—Sign taped to the Beaconville High School tech booth door

Tech Booth, Beaconville High School Theater

DAYS UNTIL SPRING MUSICAL OPENS: 66

"Can I tell you something?"

"Of course."

"It's embarrassing."

"Embarrassing things are my favorite."

"Okay, but it's *dorky*-embarrassing."

"Even better."

"Okay, well, it's just that I've always kind of had this . . . um. This fantasy."

"Ooooooh."

"No, no, it's not like that. I've just kind of always, um . . . wanted to make out with someone in the booth during intermission on a show I was calling. . . . Okay, you can stop laughing now."

"I'm not laughing! I mean, okay, I am, but I get it. It's really cool up here, especially now that rehearsal's over. It's like our own little world, isn't it?"

"Exactly. That's *exactly* how it's always felt to me."

"Well . . . I know it isn't intermission during a show right now, but would you want to, perhaps, practice? For your fantasy scenario?"

"Um . . . yeah. That would be really, um. Helpful."

" . . . "

" . . . "

" . . . "

" . . . "

"Hi."

"Hi."

"So . . . how long do you think we can stay up here without someone getting mad at us?"

"Forever, in theory. I have keys to the theater."

"Who else has keys?"

"Just the teachers."

"None of your friends on crew?"

"No . . . why? Hey, is something wrong?"

"No, no. I was just wondering, if . . . I noticed you were being quiet when I came up to you during rehearsal today. I wondered if it was because you didn't want your friends to know . . . about this."

"Oh. Yeah . . . what do you think about that? Telling people, I mean?"

"Actually, I thought it might be fun to keep it a secret. Then it really would be our own little world. Plus, no one could say there was a conflict of interest, since you're the SM and I'm in the cast. Only if you thought so too, though, of course."

"Oh, um . . . you know, I hadn't thought about that much, but now that you mention it, that's a good idea. You know how people are. They'd just tease us and stuff."

"Really? You don't think it would be strange?"

"No, it's cool. It'll be something special just for us. Besides, it's not like you really believe in the superstitions anyway."

"What?"

"Nothing. Sorry, my mind just started wandering randomly. What time do you have to be home tonight?"

Tech Booth, Beaconville High School Theater

DAYS UNTIL SPRING MUSICAL OPENS: 52

"Ooh, hi. I was afraid you wouldn't be able to come today."

"I stayed in the library working on my government paper. I thought it might look odd if I was around the rehearsal since I'm not in any scenes today."

"You stayed in the library for three hours?"

"It's a long paper. Also, I had to take a phone call halfway through."

"The Netflix show again?"

"Yeah. My agent's pushing me to meet with the producer. But I'd have to fly out there, and we're in the middle of rehearsals."

"To LA?"

"Mm-hmm."

"We can always redo the rehearsal schedule if we need to. We've certainly done it enough times for Nick. How long would you be there?"

"Just a day or two. But . . . honestly, I'd rather not have to do it. Out there, everyone acts like that's the entire world. You're not allowed to acknowledge that there's life outside California. And they're all completely allergic to the word *theater*."

"Ugh. That sounds awful."

"I wish, just for one day, I could do the opposite of all that. Pretend my life *here* is the entire world. That all I'm responsible for is turning in my government paper and making sure I'm ready for rehearsal, without having to be ready to jump into LA mode at any second."

"Could you do that?"

"I probably wouldn't even know how. But I do know . . . this is nice. Being here with you is nice."

"Yeah . . ."

"Do you want to go back to the scene shop? We could write our names in the sawdust again."

"Ha, sure. We just have to make sure we remember to sweep it up before someone sees."

"We could leave the hearts this time. They don't have any identifying details."

"I mean, they identify us as cheesy."

"This is theater. We're all cheesy."

"Good point. So should we go?"

". . . In a minute, maybe. First I thought maybe we could . . ."

"Okay . . ."

" . . . "

" . . . "

" . . . "

Scene Shop, Beaconville High School Performing Arts Wing

DAYS UNTIL SPRING MUSICAL OPENS: 45

"Ms. McIntyre . . ."

"Mr. Green?"

"May I make an inquiry?"

"Sure."

"Do your parents know about your . . . *situation*, with Ms. Rose?"

"Uh . . . pardon?"

"I respect your wanting to keep things under wraps here at school. I just want to make sure everyone who needs the information has it."

". . . How did *you* find out?"

"You aren't the only one who stays after rehearsal, Ms. McIntyre. The lights in the booth are hard to miss when the rest of the theater's dark."

". . . Am I in trouble?"

"No, I only want to make sure your parents know why you're

staying at school so late."

"Uh . . . yeah. I told them. Pops said he hopes she'll be a good influence because she's so dedicated to her goals. . . . Yeah, I know, I thought it was funny too."

"All right. Just keep in mind that your first obligation is still to everyone's safety."

". . . What are you saying, exactly?"

"As stage manager, you've got to make sure the other students are following protocols. It's easy to lose sight of that responsibility when you're distracted."

"Oh. Okay. I thought you meant . . ."

"What?"

"Never mind. Thanks for the warning. I promise, I'll be extra careful. Also, I've been wanting to ask, how come you never told me you used to be an actor? You're like a traitor to tech kind."

"I contain multitudes, Ms. McIntyre."

Dance Studio, Beaconville High School
Performing Arts Wing

DAYS UNTIL SPRING MUSICAL OPENS: 30

"Whoa, this is cool. I've never come here except when we needed it for extra rehearsal space. It's bigger than I remember. Or maybe it's just all these mirrors."

"I've always loved it here. The same way you love the tech booth, I think. I come here sometimes when I need to be alone."

"For extra dance practice?"

"Yes, but mainly I just come to get away. Sometimes I like to turn out the lights and lie back on the mats and stare up at the ceiling. With all the mirrors, it's like being in space."

"That's so cool. . . . Anyway, I wanted to say, I'm sorry about earlier."

"It's all right."

"No, it isn't. I shouldn't have pushed you about the college stuff."

"You didn't push. Really, it's fine. I know it's all anyone's talking about today."

"Yeah, every year the seniors all find out where they got in around the same time, so . . ."

"I'm sorry I acted strange about it."

"You didn't act strange. I was surprised you didn't want to talk, but that's okay."

"Thanks . . . I've just been trying not to think about it."

"It's totally cool. You don't have to tell me."

"Well, it's not a secret. I got into a few schools. Emerson, Ithaca, and NYU."

"Wow, that's great! NYU's what you wanted, right?"

"Yes, but . . . I'm almost definitely going to defer. If I accept in the first place."

"What do you mean, *if*? When we talked about it at my house, you didn't say anything about not accepting."

"I didn't want your dads to think I wasn't serious. But my agent keeps sending me out on more auditions, and if I get this show, or another role after this movie ends, I don't know how I could work and take classes at the same time. Even if I did, I don't know how many years it would take to get a degree. And I'd be taking a spot from someone who could actually use it. Again."

"Again? What do you mean?"

"It's like with the show here. Christina would be playing Fantine if it weren't for me. And then someone else could've been Factory Girl, and that would've been *their* first big role, and . . . no matter what I do, I'm messing things up for someone."

"You're not making any sense at all. Christina's barely even a singer, and it's not *your* fault you're talented. Why shouldn't you get to be in your school musical? Or get into NYU, for that matter?"

"I don't know if NYU would even have let me in if it wasn't for all this. Besides, some days I don't know what the point is of thinking about college if I'm on this trajectory in the opposite direction."

"Oh. Wow. Well . . . what do you *want* to do? Go to college, or be in movies?"

". . . Do you know you're the first person who's actually asked me that?"

"What? What about your parents?"

"They assume I want to go to college. And my agent and everyone else assumes I want to be in movies."

"Then what's the truth?"

"I don't know. That's just it, I feel as though I can't commit to either. And of course acting's not even a real *commitment*, because there's never any guarantee there will ever be another role. What happens if I wind up with a pile of negative reviews, or get on the bad side of some important studio executive, or . . . look, do you think we could talk about something else?"

"Oh. Sure, of course."

"Tell me more about your dads. How did they get together?"

". . . You seriously want to know?"

"I want to know everything about you."

". . . Wow. Okay. Well, it isn't really interesting. They met when Pops was working for a nonprofit in Jamaica Plain—before he turned all boring and got a consulting job—and Dad was finishing college. It was Will who introduced them, actually. We've got an old album full of pictures of the three of them wearing punk band T-shirts. It's all very nineteen nineties."

"Ha. And then you came along?"

"Yeah, after they'd been together a few years, my dads put in with an adoption agency. That was before marriage was legal, but a lot of the agencies were doing adoptions for gay couples anyway."

"I forget sometimes that marriage used to be illegal."

"I know, me too."

"So they adopted you from an agency?"

"Yeah. My bio-mom was in high school when I was born. I met her a couple of times when I was little, but then we stopped doing that. I don't remember much about her."

"Did your dads get married later? Is that why you just have one last name?"

"They got married, yeah, when I was still a baby. We've got a photo album of that, too. I look really confused in all the photos. Dad said they wanted to make me the ring bearer but they had to fire me because I kept trying to eat the ring box. But the reason my last name's just McIntyre and not McIntyre-Perez or something is because back when they first got together, neither of my dads' families were okay with them being gay. It took them both a long time to warm up to the idea, but Pops's family took longer. When I was born, my dads were afraid his parents might try to challenge them for custody one day. So they gave me Dad's last name because they trusted his side of the family more."

"Oh my God. I'm so sorry, I had no idea."

"No, no, it's okay now. I know it sounds really dramatic, but I don't remember any of that. I actually see *more* of my grandparents on Pops's side than on Dad's now, because they live closer. Pops says adorable grandchildren are the ultimate family icebreaker. They renewed their wedding vows when I was in middle school, and all four of my grandparents came and lit sparklers with us."

"Ha. That's wonderful."

"What about you? Your parents are more conservative, right?"

"I don't know that I'd call them conservative, exactly, but they're . . . traditional. As far as they're concerned, everyone should aspire to stability and security and that's all there is to it."

"Why did they let you start acting, then?"

"At first I think they just saw it as another activity, like being on the soccer team or something. By the time it got more intense, I'd proven I could do it and keep my grades up at the same time, so they let me continue, but they still don't really understand it. Did I tell you they made plans to be out of town the night *Les Mis* opens?"

"What? No way!"

"They'll be back to see it the next weekend, so it's fine, but . . . they just don't understand theater."

"Wow. I can't imagine. My dads come to every performance of all my shows. But then, usually they're working at concessions or the box office or something."

"As far as I can tell, your dads are generally . . . awesome."

"Ha. I guess they're okay. . . . Can I ask an awkward question?"

"Of course."

"I think this is something I heard somewhere—or maybe I read it. But is it really true you were discovered at your middle school choir recital? . . . Sorry, was that rude of me to ask?"

"No, it wasn't. Sorry, I didn't mean to make a face. I suppose that's true, but that word, *discovered*, is silly. In any case, I had a solo in the winter concert in sixth grade, and Rami—he became my first agent—was there, because his niece went to my school. He came up to my parents after the show and asked if he could introduce me to a voice teacher he knew to prepare for an audition. Just regional theater, but he said it could lead to other things. And it did."

"Wow. It's the kind of story you read in celebrity bios."

"Rami was very nice, and he understood why I wanted to do theater. He's the one who got me the audition for *Annie*."

"I still can't believe you've been on Broadway already."

"Well, one show there was enough for me. I bet you'll like it, though. The crew on that show seemed to have a lot more fun than the cast. I made friends with the sound mixer, and he'd let me sit in the booth during rehearsals when I didn't have anything else to do. The stagehands were great too. Sometimes I'd help them sweep up sawdust backstage. They said it was against union rules, but I think that was a joke."

"You . . . sat in the booth. Of . . . a Broadway show."

"Well, not during *performances*."

"I am still absolutely seething with jealousy right now. I'd *pay* to sweep up Broadway sawdust."

"It's no different from sawdust here. Besides, they'll pay *you* to do that in a few years."

"Ha. I wish my dads had your faith in me."

"Oh, they do, I can tell. They just feel like they have to push you in another direction because that's the kind of thing parents do."

"Seriously, though. Even if you didn't like working on Broadway, your agent must've been thrilled."

"Well, yes, especially because it paid well. But when I told him I didn't like it, he switched me to doing commercials. That was the other best way to make money, for a while at least."

"You made my dad cry. In that dog food ad."

"That shoot was fun. They let me play with the dog between takes. We can't have one, because my sister's allergic."

"Did you have to miss school for it?"

"I don't remember, but probably. That was always the worst part. I never got to do normal school things."

"Like what?"

"Oh, you know. Have a big group of friends. Go to prom, with a date and a corsage and everything. Eat cafeteria food."

"You aren't missing much with the cafeteria food."

"You know what I mean."

"Yeah. Do you, um . . . sorry, this is another personal question."

"You can ask me personal questions. We're lying on mats in

an empty dance studio with the lights off an hour after everyone else left rehearsal. I think we can safely say what we want to say."

"Okay, good point. So . . . do you think you'll come out to your parents eventually?"

"Yes. My great-aunt's married to a woman, and my parents get along fine with them. And my dad gave my sister and me a speech a few years ago about how it's fine to be gay. I don't know how they feel about being bi, specifically, since that's probably closer to what I am, but I don't think they'll mind. Maybe I can just slip it into a conversation and be done with it. Or maybe I'll get lucky and they'll figure it out on their own somehow. I don't like the idea of having to sit down and have a big conversation about it, as if it's some dramatic development, when really, it's just part of life. I wish I didn't have to think about it so much."

"I know what you mean. How tired you can get of having to think about something over and over, when all you want is to have that space free in your brain so you can finally think about something else."

"What do you want out of your brain?"

"Oh, I just meant in general. So, uh . . . I know this dance studio is one of your favorite places, but is it, like, sacred space to you? Like, would it mess up the vibe for you if we made out in here a little?"

Back Bay, Boston

DAYS UNTIL SPRING MUSICAL OPENS: 12

"You've *got* to tell me where we're going."

"That would defeat the entire purpose! Keep your eyes shut. Unless you want me to get the blindfold back out."

"If I wear that out here on the street, people will think you're kidnapping me."

"How do you know I'm not?"

"Mel . . ."

"Kidding, kidding. Okay, we're here. You can open your eyes."

"Are we in—wait. Is this the restaurant you were telling me about?"

"Yep! The one where you tell the waiter what mood you're in and they custom-blend you a milkshake that's guaranteed to make you at least fifty percent happier, or you get your money back. Apparently they'll do it with alcoholic drinks too, but that's the underage version. Also, the burgers are incredible."

"Mel, I knew we were in that Uber for a long time, but did you really bring us all the way into the *city*?"

"Uh-huh. And I did you one even better—look in your purse."

". . . Where's my phone?"

"Somewhere safe, I promise."

"You *stole* my *phone* while I was *blindfolded*?"

"It's for a good cause! Anyway, did you find anything else in there?"

". . . Is this a flower?"

"It's a corsage. You wear it like a bracelet. Here, let me put it on you."

"Awww. You got me a *corsage*?"

"Hey, you already know how cheesy I can be. And I guess I kind of thought . . . maybe tonight we could do some of the stuff you said you'd never gotten to do. Like go out on a date and wear a corsage. And not have to be constantly waiting on the edge of your seat for phone calls. I thought tonight we could drink milkshakes and eat burgers and just be normal teenagers without counting calories or being paranoid."

"That's so sweet! I'm so happy. Thank you. Oh, but for the record, I don't count calories. And I don't think I'm paranoid most of the time either."

"Good. When's the last time you had a milkshake, though?"

"Ah, well . . ."

"That's what I thought."

"In all seriousness, though, if I get a call, I'll have to take it."

"It's Sunday night, you're not going to get a work call. And if you do, I've got your phone and I can give it to you, but for now, let's have one night when we don't have to worry."

"Thank you. For planning this all out. No one's ever done anything like this for me. . . . Ah. I love it when you blush."

". . . Okay, I'm going to go hide somewhere now."

"No, you're not! We're going to find a booth and order life-changing milkshakes. I think there's one in the back."

"Oh, I see it. Wait here in case something else opens up first, and I'll run and grab it."

"All right."

". . . Hey, is this table free—oh. *Oh.* Oh, hiiii, Rachel."

"Mel. Hi. This is . . . random."

"Yeah, I know, right? Are you here with—um, who are you here with?"

"Why? Who are *you* here with?"

"No one. I mean . . . I'm here with my dads."

"Oh, you are? Where are they? . . . Wait, is that Odile Rose by the door?"

"What? No. Oh, wow. Um, yeah, I guess it is. Hey, who's that guy who's turned around waving at you? Over by the bar, with his back to us?"

"Uh . . . just somebody I know from swimming."

"Oh. You know, it's cool if you're here with a guy. You don't need to be embarrassed or anything."

"I'm not embarrassed at all. . . . Oh, hi, Odile. We just spotted you over there. Wow, is that a *corsage*? You must be going
somewhere exciting after this."

"Hi, Rachel. So nice to see you! It's so funny that we all
wound up here tonight, isn't it?"

"It really is! Hi, Odile, I'm Mel, by the way. We've, um, met
before, but just in case you forgot. I'm the stage manager."

". . . Hi, Mel."

"Anyway, I've got to go. Nice seeing you, Rachel. And you
too, Odile."

"I thought you just asked if this table was free?"

"Oh, yeah. Sorry, I got confused. I have to go, um, meet my
dads outside."

"I should be going too. Rachel, is it all right if I come by the
costume room Wednesday after rehearsal again, if you still need
help?"

"Sure, that's fine. We always need help."

"All right. See you then."

". . ."

". . ."

". . . Okay, I don't think she can hear us out here. Odile, I'm
so sorry. I didn't know what to do. I just blanked completely. I
know we said we were going to keep things secret, so . . ."

"That's all right, but . . . Rachel's got to know you were lying.
She's seen us talking before. Everyone has. We might as well go
back in and tell her the truth."

"No, no, we can't. It's fine. There's another restaurant down the block that's just as cool—it's got a tiki theme and all the drinks come with umbrellas. I bet they've got good burgers, too."

"I don't feel right about this. We're both working with Rachel on the show, and you're her boss. Keeping this quiet was fun at first, but this kind of thing is how rumors get started."

". . . I mean, she's also my ex. And that whole situation is . . . complicated."

"I know, but—"

"Look, I'm really sorry. I don't want this to ruin our night. Can we please just pretend it never happened?"

". . . All right. Where's this tiki place?"

"Down this way."

"Let's go, then."

"So in the interest of pretending that whole thing never happened . . . can I tell you something embarrassing I've always wanted to do?"

"Of course."

"And maybe it'll turn out it's something you want to do, too."

"Maybe . . ."

"I've actually never walked down a street in the city holding someone's hand."

". . . You mean, like this?"

"Yeah. Like this."

". . . I love seeing you smile like that."

"I love being here with you like this."

"Good. Now . . . can I tell *you* something embarrassing?"

"Hell yes. I feel like such a loser tonight, that might actually help."

"Please don't feel like a loser. I love that you came up with this plan. And here's my embarrassing thing . . . I've never walked down a street *anywhere* holding *anyone's* hand."

". . . Really?"

"Really."

"I'm your very first?"

"You are."

"Wow. I . . . I really love being here with you."

"You said that already."

"I know, but . . . I'm sorry again about before."

"Don't be. This, you and me—this is what really matters. All the rest of it is just . . ."

"Sawdust. Right?"

". . . Exactly."

ACT 2
April

LES MIS REHEARSAL SCHEDULE
APRIL 20–24

Reminders:

- All actors are now required to be off-book. This is the last week the SM will provide your lines if you forget them. Next week in dress rehearsals you're on your own.
- NO ACTORS ALLOWED in the auditorium on Friday. The crew will be installing the turntable and if you enter without permission you most likely WILL GET HURT.
- All cast and crew are required to report to school on Saturday and Sunday for tech starting at 9:00 a.m. and continuing through 5:00 p.m. (later if necessary). Tech may continue through Monday if we can't wrap it up over the weekend, so please please please be on time both days.

Monday, April 20—No school, no rehearsal (Patriots' Day—go, marathon runners, go!)			
Tuesday, April 21			
Time	**Who**	**What**	**Where**
3:00–6:00 p.m. (later if necessary)	Full cast	Run through "At the End of the Day," "Lovely Ladies," "The Runaway Cart," "Master of the House," "Look Down/ The Robbery," "One Day More," "The First Attack," "The Second Attack," "The Final Battle," "Wedding Chorale/ Beggars at the Feast," "Epilogue"	Auditorium

Wednesday, April 22			
3:00–6:00 p.m. (later if necessary)	Full cast	Act 1 run-through	Auditorium
Thursday, April 23			
3:00–6:00 p.m. (later if necessary)	Full cast	Act 2 run-through	Auditorium
Friday, April 24			
12:00–12:45 p.m. (lunch)	Full cast (except Fantine)	Pep rally rehearsal—"One Day More" flash mob	Gym
2:00–2:45 p.m. (seventh period)	Full cast (except Fantine)	Pep rally—"One Day More" flash mob	Gym
6:00–9:00 p.m.	Full cast & orchestra	Sitzprobe	Band room

—Distributed by hard copy and emailed to all cast, crew, and directors.

Also stored on BHS performing arts department shared drive.

Created by: Melody McIntyre, stage manager, class of 2021

Viewable to: All cast, crew, and directors

Editable by: Current SM ONLY

Scene 1—Beaconville High School Theater

DAYS UNTIL SPRING MUSICAL OPENS: 10

"Nick missed that cue," Ms. Marcus whispers. "And tell Alejandra to work on that line. She should go the whole phrase on one breath instead of pausing between *soon* and *to*."

I nod and jot it all down. I won't actually be *telling* anyone any of this myself, which is good, since if *I* had to personally break the news to Alejandra that her singing was off, we'd both probably wind up in tears. Instead I'll hand over my notes to Ms. Marcus at the end of rehearsal, and she'll decide what to do with them. It's still kind of weird being the only one who knows exactly what all the actors are doing wrong, but I'm used to keeping secrets.

The ensemble joins in to sing the finale. It's almost seven at night, and we're at the end of another epic rehearsal. All the rehearsals are epic now that we're this close to tech. Logically we should all be exhausted, but the actors' giddiness is shining even through their fatigue. I spotted the same light in Gabby's eyes last time I caught sight of her backstage, and it's there on Ms. Marcus's face, too.

It's all coming together now. After weeks of running these songs, endless production meetings agonizing over every detail, hours upon hours spent discussing every sound and light and set cue, our show is actually, finally, getting *good*. The harmonies are soaring, the blocking is solid, the emotional scenes are emotional, and the sets and costumes and props look real. The actors are even mostly remembering their lyrics without my help.

Best of all, we haven't had any real crises, apart from the catastrophe that Nick's singing voice wrought on us all. Fortunately, he's gotten better thanks to lots of diligent tutoring by Ms. Qiao, who should seriously get a raise for having to spend so much time with Nick the Dick. She somehow convinced him to start drinking hot water with honey before every rehearsal, *and* made sure he knew the crew wasn't going to pour it for him.

We've still got a ton of work to do, but this show is already going to be *incredible*. The best musical BHS has ever put on. And it's all happening under *my* watch.

Best of all, the curse hasn't reared its head once. All that worrying over nothing.

I just wish I didn't have to keep this thing between me and Odile secret from my friends. When we ran into Rachel at that restaurant Sunday night, I was sure it was all over. But we've had two rehearsals and a production meeting since then and no one's looked at me any weirder than usual. Besides, Rachel seemed distracted. She probably didn't pick up on what was going on.

Plus, it's not like I'm planning on lying to the crew forever. I'll tell them at the cast party, once the show's safely closed. Odile and I can pretend we just got together after exchanging lots of flirty glances from afar.

For now, though, we've actually got a shot at pulling off a perfect show on opening night. Which means we can't risk anyone getting worked up over nothing. If the crew knew what's been going on, it could mess with their heads and affect their work. It's like Will said—fear of the curse is worse than the real thing.

The whole cast belts the last line of the song together, and as the final notes of the piano trickle out, Ms. Marcus claps harder than I've ever heard her clap.

"Terrific, everyone! Terrific!" She climbs to her feet, still clapping. "It's late, so let's hold off on running the curtain call until Thursday."

A few of the cast members make big shows of acting disappointed—actors will rehearse bowing until their heads fall off if you let them—but I'm relieved. Ms. Marcus decided to add a final "One Day More" reprise at the end of the curtain call, so rehearsing it always takes forever, and we've still got a lot of set pieces to paint tonight.

I clap along with Ms. Marcus and wait for her to call the cast to the edge of the stage so she can deliver the notes. Usually we go straight into them as soon as the rehearsal ends, so I don't know why we're spending all this time clapping. Sure, the singing was good, but the actors obviously know that. They're even clapping for themselves.

That's when I realize I can't see Gabby. She always stays in the wings during full-cast run-throughs, but there's no sign of her now. And, even weirder, Odile is gone, too. She should be up front with the other principals, but there's a hole in the lineup at her usual spot.

"I think Gabby might be dealing with a problem backstage," I tell Ms. Marcus, but she doesn't meet my eyes. "Is it okay if I go check on her?"

"Please wait here for now," Ms. Marcus says without looking at me.

Okay, this is getting *really* odd.

I shift in my seat, trying to get a better look into the wing where I last saw Gabby. There are few things I hate more than not knowing what's going on.

That's when I notice a dark, unfamiliar shape above the stage. A *moving* shape.

Something's come loose. It's slowly falling down from the rigging with the entire cast on the stage below it.

Oh my God—this is the worst possible thing that could happen.

The curse! It's finally here!

I'm about to leap to my feet when I realize the dark shape isn't falling—it's moving too smoothly for that. Someone's got to be *lowering* it. One of the curtains, or a scrim, maybe—it's too high up for me to be sure.

"Somebody's using the flies." I sit straight up. It could only be Gabby, since no one else on the crew is here—but Gabby hasn't been fully trained on the flies yet, and she'd never use the equipment without telling me. "I should go—"

"Please stay in your seat, Melody." Ms. Marcus's eyes are locked on the moving shape, and she's wearing a mysterious smile. "You'll appreciate this more from the house."

"*Appreciate* this?" Something's happening in my theater, and I don't know what. I don't appreciate anything about it.

Onstage, the actors are craning their necks, watching the curtain come down with mild curiosity. A couple of them have their mouths open in little Os. A few seconds later, I see why.

The curtain that's descending upstage is dark—as black as the night sky—but all over it are twinkling stars. *Hundreds* of them.

It's a star drop.

Thirty seconds ago we were winding down a garden-variety afternoon rehearsal. Now it's midnight in the middle of a gorgeous, bare landscape, with nothing in view for miles around but starlight.

It's breathtaking.

It's exactly what I wanted to rent for this show. It's *perfect* for Javert's big solo, but the cost would've blown our budget completely. Or that's what Ms. Marcus told me.

"Oh my God, this is unbelievable! Did you find the money after all?" I turn to her, nearly panting with excitement. "Would it be unprofessional to hug you?"

"I had nothing to do with this, beyond giving my consent."

She holds up her hand with a laugh. "Your gratitude's due to a member of your cast."

"Wait, *what?*"

I turn back to the stage—and that's when I get my first glimpse of her. She's peeking out at me from the curtain, watching for my reaction.

It's Odile. *She* got us the star drop.

I don't deserve this. I don't deserve her.

I am the luckiest person in the *world*.

"Oh my *God*!" I leap to my feet and run toward the stage. In this instant, I couldn't care less that there are other people in this room besides her and me. "*You* rented this thing?"

"Well, not exactly, but—" She's grinning, practically *squealing* as I climb the steps up to the stage, her shoulders scrunched up around her ears and her teeth digging into her bottom lip. "It's ours—the school's, I mean. It's custom-sized for this theater, so we can save it and use it for other shows. Or for concerts, or— anything, really. Do you like it?"

"Are you serious? I *love* it!" I'm about to throw my arms around her when I catch up to the fact that we have an audience.

When I turn around, the entire cast is staring at us. Everyone except David, who's staring up at the star drop like his birthday's come early.

The actors—except Dom, who's looking pretty delighted about the star drop too—don't know about my so-called love curse. But they don't know about me and Odile, either, and I have to keep it that way. Once the cast knows, the crew will find out in a microsecond.

"This will be incredible for the show." I raise my voice. "It's so generous of you. Gabby, did you see—"

Gabby steps out of the wing behind Odile, grinning. "Of course. I helped Mr. Green get it set up."

"She and Mr. Green have been my partners in crime, getting this in and keeping it a secret." Odile is still beaming, and I probably still look just as ecstatic, with or without all the eyes on us. "It was *so* hard not to say anything."

"I can't believe you all did this." I laugh. If you'd asked me yesterday, I'd have said there was no way in hell I'd be okay with this kind of subterfuge in my theater, but right now my heart is pounding with pure joy. I can't believe she did something so huge, just for *me*. "You were so sneaky!"

"Well, *I* didn't know you wanted it *this* much." Gabby's still smiling, but there's a confused crinkle between her eyebrows, as though there's a lot she's thinking but not saying. "I know you said it would be cool, but . . ."

"It's just astonishing to *see* it, you know?" I'm talking too fast. I've been talking too fast ever since I reached the stage.

"I can't *wait* to rehearse with it," David says. Next to him, Dom's eyes flick back and forth between me, Odile, and Gabby.

"Good. We'll unveil it for 'Stars.'" Ms. Marcus must have climbed up onto the stage at some point in the past few minutes when I was too distracted to notice. "We might use it again for your suicide, too—we'll see how it looks at Thursday's rehearsal. First, though, we need to go over today's rehearsal notes. I know everyone's excited, but let's try to focus."

I will my heart to stop thumping so fast as the cast assembles, sitting down and dangling their legs off the edge of the stage.

"Mel?" Ms. Marcus turns to me with an impossibly patient smile.

"Yes?"

"The notes, please?"

"Oh. Right! Sorry, sorry!"

I try to focus on not tripping as I run back up to the table where I left my notes. Most of the cast smiles good-naturedly as I run back down and thrust them into Ms. Marcus's hand, but Dom is watching me with a decidedly neutral expression on his face, and Gabby still looks concerned.

Ms. Marcus starts delivering the notes, which is going to take forever since I just handed her five entire pages full of scribbles. I sit on the edge of the stage, only leaving a few feet of space between Odile and me. She smiles, and I answer her smile with one of my own.

Being with her is nothing like I ever imagined it would be. She's so warm. So smart, too, and so funny. I don't think I've ever liked any other human being as much as I like her.

I can't get over how she surprised me today. All *I've* managed to do, romantic-gesture-wise, was steal her cell phone and take her out for drinks with paper umbrellas. I need to do something big and exciting for her, too, in front of everyone.

Wait—prom!

She said she's always wanted to go. I could ask her. I could do a big promposal, something grand and theatrical, to make her feel the way she made me feel today. The night of the cast party, maybe.

I dip my head, grinning at the thought. Then I notice Rachel.

A few of the crew members have arrived backstage to start the painting shift. I spot Fatima, too, and Jasmin, and some of the others from the set crew walking around quietly, studying the star drop and moving painting supplies into place.

But Rachel's looking right at me. Glancing back and forth between me and Odile, in fact.

The crew's probably heard that we have the star drop because of Odile. Word travels fast in theater land. They all knew how much I wanted it, too.

But thanks to our run-in on Sunday, Rachel knows something the others don't. And from the calculating steadiness in her dark eyes, I have a feeling she's put it all together.

Rachel knows.

Shit, she *knows*.

I scramble up from my seat. Odile glances at me, her eyebrows knitting in confusion, but I don't meet her gaze. Instead I step carefully through the group of actors and drop down to sit next to Ms. Marcus.

None of the others seem to notice, but when I look up again, Rachel's still watching me. She finally steps back behind the star drop just as Ms. Marcus finally gives the last of the notes and tells everyone who didn't sign up for tonight's painting shift they can leave.

"Ms. Marcus?" Leah raises her hand from her seat next to Nick. "I need a Band-Aid for my shoulder."

"Of course." Ms. Marcus nods to me. "You have some, right, Mel?"

"Yep." I climb back up to my feet and try not to think about Rachel's harsh gaze as I lead Leah down the steps toward my SM kit.

She takes her time following me, pausing to pull back the neck of her sweater to show Malik whatever it is that's bothering her. When she finally climbs down into the house and flounces toward me, she grimaces for the maximum possible drama. "Do you have anything for this, or should I go see the nurse?"

"The nurse's office closed hours ago." I study the spotted red rash on her shoulder. It's hardly a rehearsal-related injury, but I pull a tube of hydrocortisone cream out of my first aid kit anyway. "What did you do, stick your shoulder in poison ivy?"

"*No*, I haven't even been near any bushes!" Leah scratches the rash again. She angles her shoulder toward me like she expects me to put the cream on it myself, but for all I know it's catching.

"Here you go." I offer her the tube, then reach for a bottle of hand sanitizer. "Actually, on second thought, use this before you touch anything."

"That's creepy," Nick says as he climbs down from the stage. "You should see a doctor. It could be scabies, and that's highly contagious."

Leah blinks rapidly, looking terrified. "How do you know?"

"Yeah, how *do* you know that, Nick?" I ask, not bothering to hide the sarcasm in my voice. We don't need our cast getting paranoid about contagious skin diseases a week before opening. "Do you have a secret dermatology degree?"

Nick folds his arms. "I get why you boss around all the stoner techies, but tell me again why we're supposed to act like you're in charge of *us*, too?"

"Because the teachers made me stage manager, which means it's my job to control what happens in this theater whether I enjoy it or not?"

Leah backs away, carefully unscrewing the cap of the tube I gave her.

"Mel . . ." Ms. Marcus waves. "Do you have the updated costume matrix?"

I leave Nick with a mutual glare and hand the printout to Ms. Marcus with a flourish. It's a ten-page spreadsheet listing every costume piece in the show. Rachel and I spent three only-semi-awkward hours working on it last week. With sixty cast members, some of whom have six or more clothing changes over the course of the show, the costume team is wrangling hundreds of shirts, skirts, dresses, hats, pairs of pants, and accessories, and we have to keep track of every single one.

Ms. Marcus and I go over the week's schedule after that, and then she heads backstage while I go around with my shiny set of keys, checking and locking each room. When I'm finally done, I head over to where Odile's stepped into the wing, turning my back so the others won't see us talking.

"Thank you, again." I smile at her. "I can't even tell you how much that star drop means to me."

She smiles back. "I'm so glad."

"Are you heading out?"

"Well, my parents probably want me to have dinner with them, but . . ." She trails off. "Are *you* staying?"

"Yeah. I signed up to paint tonight." Everyone on the cast and crew has to do at least two painting shifts during the run, but I signed up for all of them. Which, granted, is a little much, but every time I see a set piece I worked on, I feel this intense wave of satisfaction. As though I'd painted the words "MEL WAS HERE" on every tree or sign post or palm frond.

"Well, *I* didn't sign up for today, but suddenly I feel like adding on an extra shift." Odile grins. "If that's all right with the boss."

"Of course it's . . ." I stop myself before I can say more. I *want* to spend more time with Odile tonight. I want that a lot.

But with the way Rachel was eyeing us . . . plus, Jasmin's here too, and she's been onto us from day one . . . and then there's that strange look Gabby gave me . . .

But I can't tell Odile any of that. Besides, I *want* her to stay. I'll always want her to stay.

"Yeah." I nod. "That's very much all right. You might want to see if we have any spare painting clothes, though, because . . ." I grin and gesture to her black-and-white polka-dotted jumpsuit, which I'm pretty sure came straight from some Fashion Week runway. Odile grins back.

It turns out Daniel has a suitcase full of old clothes he brought in with the other supplies, so Odile goes to the bathroom to change. I get an assignment from Fatima—the gate trim needs touching up, which is perfect, since I love painting trim—so I grab a detail brush and set to work.

Odile comes out of the bathroom shortly afterward wearing a pair of sweatpants that are just a little too short for her and what looks like Fatima's dad's old Bruins jersey. It's a good look on her. A very good look. She gets assigned to help with the bridge on the opposite side of the stage from me.

Whenever I steal a glance at her, that same rush of feeling I had when I first saw her peeking out from behind the star drop surges up all over again. I smile goofily and have to stop myself before someone notices.

Someone like Rachel. All through the shift, she keeps hovering in the edges of my peripheral vision, like a creepy guardian angel.

Or maybe I'm overthinking things. Rachel's got an agenda tonight, a legitimate one. Her team has wrapped up most of their major work, and now they're doing the final fittings for the principals and featured soloists, so she keeps coming to the stage to pull actors away to try on their costumes. That's got to be the *real* reason she keeps popping up. It isn't like her to be intentionally sinister.

Like always, the actors are psyched about their fittings. Dom gets to try on his special red vest for the first time, and he spends the rest of the shift gushing about it to anyone who'll listen. Even Odile comes back beaming after trying on her "I Dreamed a Dream" dress, and there's no sign that Rachel said anything weird to her while they were alone.

Before the painting shift ends, I head back to the scene shop to check out the still-in-progress barricade. It's awesome, how good a bunch of old props and scrap wood can look when they're thrown together onto a wheeled platform in a design that's carefully calculated to look haphazard. When I come back around the corner, jogging because I want to make sure I reach the stage in time for Fatima's official dismissal, I hear voices.

"I just want to know what's going on," Gabby's saying quietly. "I don't like all this—"

I don't want to eavesdrop on her, but I'm moving too fast to stop subtly, and I'm also wearing sneakers with rubber soles. Which means I skid into the narrow hallway outside the otherwise deserted scene shop just in time to see Gabby and Dom with their arms around each other and their faces inches apart.

Oh my God. Because there wasn't enough awkwardness in life already.

They've seen me too. They spring apart, even though clearly there isn't much point.

"Wow," I say, very articulately. "Hi. Sorry, I was just in the scene shop, and . . ."

"Hi, Mel." Dom rubs his hand over the back of his neck, looking only mildly sheepish. Gabby, though, steeples her hands in front of her face, as if she can't bear for me to see her. Or maybe it's the other way around.

I have no idea know what to say. It's fine for Gabby and Dom to hook up, or whatever it is I stumbled into. It's kind of shocking, though. I know Gabby's only two years younger than Dom and me, but I think of her almost as a kid sister. And it's hard not to feel a little betrayed that they kept this a secret from me.

Except for the part where I'm keeping a secret from them, too.

"So." I try to think past my panic. "Don't worry, everything's cool. I'm just going to . . ."

And then I leave without trying to come up with an explanation of what, exactly, I'm going to do.

To my relief, there are no footsteps in the hall behind me. By the time I get back, the others are packing up.

I help Daniel seal up the paint cans, and as I'm hauling them off I spot Odile rolling up drop cloths in the wing. There are paint splatters in her hair, and her makeup has faded, leaving her face fresh and open. Somehow she looks prettier right now than she ever has onstage, even with all the lighting and costuming and theater magic in the world.

"Hi." I grab the opposite end of the cloth she's holding. "Can I help?"

She smiles. "Of course."

I keep my eyes focused on the drop cloth as I roll it toward her, still trying to sort out the jumble in my head. People are leaving and calling out goodbyes, and I turn to wave without meeting anyone's eyes.

They can all see me with Odile. I'm letting them see.

Because the truth is, I despise secrets. I always have.

Theater is all about trust. I trust the crew to follow the cues I call, and they trust me to call them right in the first place. That's the cornerstone of any successful production.

But it's bigger than that, too. The actors trust me and my team to keep them safe. We trust the actors to learn their lines, and to do whatever it is they do that makes audiences so happy.

It's really, really hard to trust someone who's been keeping secrets.

I meet Odile's eyes over the drop cloth. She's smiling at me again.

And I remember that I'm keeping a secret from her, too. She has no idea that all this time, the real reason I didn't want to tell anyone about us is some stupid curse that isn't even real.

I have to be honest with her. Tonight. As soon as the others are gone.

I glance over my shoulder. Fatima and Daniel are still packing up. I didn't see Dom and Gabby leave, but they've got to be gone by now, like everyone else.

Maybe they left together. Maybe they're talking about me. Maybe they talk about me all the time. Maybe I can't trust *them* anymore, either.

I step out of the wing and make a big show of checking the

placement of the glow tape on the stage. Odile's eyes flash with something I can't quite make out, but it's too much of a risk for me to tell her anything until the others are gone.

A few minutes later, Fatima and Daniel climb down the steps. Fatima looks over her shoulder at me, but I can't read the expression on her face. She waves and glances back toward the wing.

"See you tomorrow," I call, trying to act normal. Fatima just nods.

I wait until I'm sure the door is firmly closed behind them before I sigh and step back toward Odile.

I shut my eyes and breathe in the moment. *This* is what I've needed all night—to be alone with her. When it's just the two of us and all the complications can fade away.

"So, um . . ." I open my eyes and meet her gaze. There are only inches between us. "I know I already said this, but . . . thank you, again, for the star drop. No one's ever done anything like that for me."

"I loved doing it." She smiles again and reaches for the end of my ponytail. "There's sawdust in your hair."

"Sorry. I went by the scene shop."

"I like it. It smells nice."

"I . . . um, there's something I should say . . ."

"What?" She never stops smiling that soft smile.

"I trust you." That isn't what I meant to say at all, but now that the words are out there, I'm astonished by how true they are.

I'd trust her with anything. I'd trust her with everything.

Odile's smile widens, and she loops both arms around my

waist. I shut my eyes and lean against her. The next thing I know I'm collapsing into her, and she's laughing, rubbing her hands over my back as she takes on more of my weight. "Now you can't let go, or else I'll fall," I say, and she laughs again.

It's the truth, though. At some point, when I wasn't paying attention, Odile became a lot more important to me than I'd ever planned.

It feels like I'm giving up control. But this time, weirdly, I *want* to give it up.

"So . . ." Odile pulls back a little, and I look up at her. She's still smiling. "We could go to the dance studio."

I nod. Honestly, I don't care where I am right now, as long as I'm with her.

"But—wait." She freezes, her smile fading.

I take a small step back. "You're right. There's something I have to tell you first."

"No, it's not that. Do you—" She inhales sharply, then wrinkles her nose. "I smell something."

"What? You *smell*—?"

Then the alarm goes off, and I smell it too.

Smoke.

Something's on fire.

GROUP TEXT THREAD FROM
EARLY WEDNESDAY MORNING

Christina:
HEY EVERYONE

Christina:
I'm sorry to send a big group text like this but
DID YOU KNOW THERE WAS A FIRE IN
THE THEATER

Fatima:
FIRE? What???

Fatima:
Are the sets okay????

Fatima:
We had the barricade almost done!!

Gabby:
Mel what's going on?

Christina:
I got to school early for cheerleading practice
and there's a FIRE TRUCK outside the
performing arts wing

Christina:
There's police tape around and no one's being
allowed inside

Mel:
Hi, everyone. Don't worry, it's under
control. The fire department came, and the
auditorium's still standing.

Mel:
Crew heads & Gabby, let's meet
quickly at lunch to discuss next steps.
Cast, I'll let you know as soon as
I hear the plans for today's rehearsal.

Estaban:
Wait was there seriously a fire?

Alejandra:
Is everyone all right????

Christina:
Okay look you all this is clearly the curse

Christina:
I don't know why everyone is so afraid to say it so
I'll say it. Something must've set off the curse.

Mel:
Relax, everybody, no one was hurt

Mel:
These things happen. There's a long tradition of theater fires going back to, like, ancient Greece

Christina:
WE KNOW

Christina:
THAT'S WHY WE'RE CONCERNED

Lauren:
Is the opening going to be delayed?

Mel:
Look, the fire's out now and no, nothing's delayed. Remember the first rule of theater: the show must go on!

Mel:
I'll text everyone as soon as I know the plan for this afternoon

PRIVATE TEXT TO MEL, LATER THAT MORNING

Gabby:
Seriously, could you tell me what really
happened last night? Please?

Scene 2—Beaconville High School Cafeteria

DAYS UNTIL SPRING MUSICAL OPENS: 9

I turn off my phone and slide it into my backpack as I step into the back of the lunch line. I have no idea what to tell Gabby. I don't know what to tell any of them.

I can't believe Christina just threw out the word *curse* in that text thread. Like it was nothing.

"So what exactly *is* going on?" Dom jogs up and ducks into the line behind me. The two texting baseball players he just cut in front of eye him warily, but he ignores them, and they roll their eyes and go back to texting. "Nick's telling everyone the whole theater melted down."

I sigh. "Nick just wants a day off from rehearsal."

"What *really* happened? You were there when the fire started, right?"

"What? Where did you hear that?"

"Fatima said you and Odile were still in the theater after everyone else left."

"That doesn't mean we were there when it—"

"Okay, but were you?"

I cross my arms and try to think. I don't want to lie to Dom, but I don't want to admit that Odile and I were alone together when the smoke alarm went off.

"I don't know any more than anyone else," I say without meeting his eyes. "There was smoke out of nowhere, and then the alarm went off and the sprinklers came on, and we ran outside and called 911. It was scary."

"Hell, I'm just glad you didn't try to put out the fire yourself with that water bottle from your kit. I wouldn't put it past you to go into *seriously* full-service stage management."

I force a laugh, but after that we both get quiet, shuffling forward as the line creeps toward the front.

There's so much we aren't saying. He isn't asking about Odile, and I'm not asking him about Gabby, either.

I wish I'd told him everything from the beginning. He's the one person who might not've thought I was a horrible person. But now he's doing—whatever it is he's doing with Gabby.

Gabby, who was already worried about the moral implications of not telling the cast every detail of my so-called love curse. Gabby, who maybe actually kind of looks up to me a little bit. Or used to.

I have to tread carefully. Anything I tell Dom could get back to her.

Which means there's *no* one I can talk to about what's really happening. My dads are furious with me for hanging around in the building so late, and, as Pops put it, "Nearly getting burned to a crisp because you couldn't be bothered to come home and kiss your girlfriend in our perfectly safe, well-appointed, fire-hazard-free living room."

Even the teachers seem mad. I emailed Will and Ms. Marcus and Ms. Qiao this morning asking how I could help deal with the fire's aftermath, but none of them responded. There was an announcement over the intercom that today's theater and stage-craft classes had been moved to the auxiliary gym, but that was as much as anyone's said.

Worst of all, I can't even talk to Odile. I never got a chance to tell her about the superstition. And now, with what Christina said on that all-cast, all-crew text thread . . .

Could she be right? *Did* I set off the curse last night?

All those feelings . . . stuff I've never felt before, about any-one . . .

If I triggered the curse, that means I've fallen in love with Odile. Doesn't it?

Have I?

No. Yes. I don't know.

It's too much to think about. I need to focus on something else.

Like making my cast and crew calm down already. Rumors are clearly going around fast. Lauren even asked if the opening was going to be *delayed* over this, and that's exactly the kind of story we can't have spreading. I've got to contain this ridiculous-ness, now.

Moving our performance dates is a nonstarter. As soon as we strike, the dance company in downtown Beaconville has the auditorium rented for the next four weeks for their annual recital, and they're paying the school system way more than our show could ever earn in ticket sales.

I've got to calm everyone down long enough to get through the last few rehearsals, then tech this weekend and dress rehearsals next week. Surely that's doable. There are still nine days until we open, and the theater looks fine. From the outside, anyway.

As I'm leaving the lunch line with my plate of salad and mac and cheese, I spot Ms. Qiao heading for the door. I run up to her, fighting to hold my tray steady.

"Ms. Qiao!" I wave, but she doesn't seem to notice me. "Ms. Qiao, please!"

When she turns around, there are bags under her eyes. "Can it wait, Melody?"

"Oh, sorry. I, uh." I'm used to the theater teachers looking at least somewhat happy to see me. "Sorry to bother you, I just . . . no one seems to know what really happened—how bad the fire was, I mean—and there are a lot of rumors spreading. I want to tell everyone not to be so worried, but it would help if I could give them some real facts."

"Well, I'm afraid we don't have many of those yet." She glances out into the cafeteria. The theater section in the middle of the room is packed. Everyone's leaning into their tables, talking urgently, cast and crew alike. Ms. Qiao sighs. "All right, here's one thing you can tell them. The fire seems to have been largely contained to one room backstage, but the smoke damage was extensive, and the sprinklers soaked everything. There's a cleanup crew working around the clock, but we don't know when students will be allowed back into the performing arts wing."

"Okay." That sounds . . . not as bad as it could, I guess, but still not good. "It won't jeopardize the show, will it? We'll still be able to open next week like we're supposed to?"

"It's too soon to know those particulars."

I swear my heart stops beating. "You don't think there's a possibility we'll have to *cancel*?"

"As I said, it's too soon to determine." She sighs again. "But keep that to yourself, please. No need to cause a panic."

Too late for that. "Is there anything I can do to help?"

"No. As I told you, it isn't safe for students to go in the wing until further notice."

"Well, which room was the fire contained in? I could tell the crew that at least."

She nods heavily. "I suppose you might as well. It was the costume room."

Oh no. Oh *no*. "Are the costumes toast?"

"I don't have any more information, Melody. All we know right now is, that's where the most extensive damage was."

"But we had *hundreds* of pieces in there. It took the team *months* to make everything."

"We're aware of that."

"How could that have even happened? I locked all the rooms myself at the end of rehearsal. Did the fire start *outside* the closet?

But then why would it have been *contained* . . ."

"I really need to get back to work, Melody." Ms. Qiao unscrews the cap of her water bottle and takes a long swig. A thin trickle drips down her chin. It's the first time I've ever seen Ms. Qiao look anything less than totally composed. "Please, try to keep the cast and crew as calm as you can, and tell them there'll be no rehearsal today. When we have news to share, you'll know."

"I . . ." Oh, God. This is much worse than I thought. "All right."

I glance back to the middle of the room. My usual table is packed with all the crew heads, plus Gabby. There are more of them than our table has seats, so people are sharing chairs and sitting on each other's laps. Still, there's none of the happy, giggly vibe you'd usually get from that kind of setup. In fact, no one seems to be talking at all.

Instead, they're all watching me. They've left my usual seat open.

They saw me talking to Ms. Qiao. They'll be waiting for a report.

I swallow, my tongue thick and unwieldy in my throat, and make my way toward them, still clutching my tray of cold mac and cheese.

"Is it true?" Fatima asks before I've even put down my tray.

"Is what true?"

"About the costume closet." It's Jasmin who answers. "Devin heard it was completely destroyed. *All* the costumes are gone."

"Where did he hear that?"

"It doesn't matter." Dom's voice takes me by complete surprise. When I turn his way, there's none of the easygoing vibe he had when we talked just a few minutes ago.

He looks deadly serious now. But then, I probably do too.

"Where Devin heard it isn't important," he says quietly. "Please just tell us if it's true."

"I don't know exactly how bad the damage is, but . . ." I sit down heavily. "Ms. Qiao said the fire hit the costume room, yeah. The good news is, it was contained there. The damage to the rest of the building is just water and smoke, but we have to stay out of the whole wing until they're finished cleaning it."

No one looks like they consider any of this good news.

My eyes slide over to Rachel. She hasn't spoken since I got here. She hasn't even looked up. But she's sitting sandwiched between Fatima and Jasmin, and there's a pallor to her face that I recognize.

It's the same way she looked when she came into the booth that night during *R&J*. There's anger there, it's true, but more than that she looks . . . empty. As though she's already given up.

I lean across the table to touch her hand, to make sure she knows I understand, but she pulls away before I can reach her.

"Be honest, Mel," she says, her voice flat. "Is this the curse?"

I shake my head, but everyone's already talking at once.

"They're going to cancel the show," Tyler mutters. "They have to, if we can't even get in the theater."

"You know how we found those old swords we thought were from *Shrek* in the sub-basement?" Estaban asks. "Jacob checked the inventory and found out they were really from the Scottish Play. I told him to toss them, but we've already been using them in rehearsals for weeks."

"Plus, Leah's still got that weird rash," Fatima adds.

"You know . . ." Jasmin scratches her neck. "I heard Beth thinks she's getting it now too."

"How's the team going to start over on all those costumes?" Dom asks. I give him a pleading look—he's supposed to be on *my* side, and besides, this is a crew meeting; he doesn't even need to *be* here—but he won't meet my eyes. "It'd take months to make everything again, and the budget's already shot."

"Fantine's wigs were in the costume closet." Shannon rubs her forehead. "The long one *and* the short one. Even if they didn't get burned, the smoke will have ruined them. We're going to have to put her hair up in a stupid mop cap and it'll probably fall off in the fight scene."

"Hey!" I raise my voice just enough to get their attention, then drop it again so the other tables won't hear. "You've got to stay calm, everybody. We're supposed to be the leaders here. We can't lose control, or the whole show will fall apart."

No one answers. But Gabby looks right at me for the first time since I sat down.

She shakes her head, slightly. It's the closest thing to outright disagreement I've ever seen from her.

"Look." I scoot forward to the edge of my chair, my lunch— and everyone else's—pushed to the middle of the table, forgotten.

"This is bad. I'm not pretending it's not. But we've dealt with crises before. This team is a well-oiled machine, and we can handle *anything*. Besides, it isn't a BHS show without some kind of last-minute emergency."

"Sure, we've had problems on our other shows." Tyler leans across the table, his shoulders slumping. "But the theater's never outright *burned down* before."

"And it didn't burn down this time either!" I take a deep breath. Stage Manager Calm. "Seriously, it's just one room backstage. An important room, no question—but it's not the stage, and it's not the house. Rachel and Devin and the rest of the costume team stored all their sketches and photos on the shared drive. I'm praying at least some of the clothes are still usable, but even in the worst-case scenario, we've still got their designs. All that's left is the execution."

"You say that like it's easy," Jasmin says, but she doesn't look quite as ready to kill me as she did a second ago. "Even if we got the *entire* crew to drop everything else on our plates and do nothing but sew all-new costumes for the entire show, we've only got nine days until opening. Not to mention that we don't have any materials, because we don't have any *money*."

"There's still the emergency fund we always keep in the budget." A plan is rapidly forming in my mind. "We can't go in the performing arts wing after school today, but we *could* do a thrift store run. Who's in?"

My friends glance at one another uneasily.

I watch, trying not to let on how nervous I am. It would be so easy for them to say no.

"I could drive," Bryce offers after a minute. "I've got my mom's Tahoe."

"I could take my car, too, if we want to split up and hit more places," Tyler says slowly.

"That's a good idea." I nod confidently, as though I never doubted they'd agree. "Maybe Rachel could go in one car and Devin could go in the other. I can pull the costume matrix off the shared drive and we can divvy it up between the groups."

"I was just at Filene's with my mom last night, and the clearance bins were overflowing." Dom nods at me, and I can't resist breathing out a sigh of relief. Him being mad at me is worse than anyone else being mad at me. "They've got to have some jackets and skirts we could work with."

"Excellent. Let's write this down. Who wants to go in which car?"

I take out a sheet of paper and start scribbling notes. Soon the others are volunteering ideas. I originally brought this up just to calm everyone down, but it's already forming into an actual plan.

Maybe we really can put together all-new costumes for an incredibly costume-heavy show in nine days. I never, ever would've chosen to do this, but what I told the others is true—we have it in us to do absolutely anything to make the show work. That's what theater's all about.

By the time the bell rings, no one's side-eyeing me anymore.

We've all got our assignments. We'll rendezvous at my house at the end of the day.

The only person who still hasn't spoken is Rachel. She listened while we were making plans, and she didn't try to stop us, but she never said she agreed, either.

When we get up to dump our untouched lunch trays, though, she finally catches my eye. There's an unsettling heaviness in her gaze.

I can only guess what she's thinking. And none of my theories are comforting.

From: Jennifer Marcus

To: All cast and crew

Date: Wednesday, 4/22, 6:52 p.m.

Subject: Performing arts wing cleanup

Hello everyone,

I know there's a lot of concern about the performing arts wing. I wish I had more information to share, but right now we're still waiting for assessments from the fire department and our insurance provider. We'll send out more information as soon as we can.

Theater and stagecraft classes will continue to be held in the auxiliary gym until further notice.

We hope to have an update by midday tomorrow regarding the spring musical. Please continue to check your email for more information.

Best wishes,
Ms. Marcus

—Also stored on BHS performing arts department shared drive.
Created by: Melody McIntyre, stage manager, class of 2021
Viewable to: All cast, crew, and directors
Editable by: Current SM ONLY

Scene 3—The McIntyre-Perez house

"Success!" Pops's voice booms as he staggers down the steps carrying my old sewing machine. "Found it in the attic, but it should still work."

"Let me see it." Devin hurries over to grab the other end. It's an ancient machine my grandmother handed down to me years ago, saying if I ever wanted to save money, I could learn to make my own clothes. I never did, but I'm glad we kept it. Maybe I had a sixth sense that someday I'd need to host an emergency costume sew-in in my basement.

Pops and Devin maneuver the sewing machine into a corner and Devin bends down to examine it. Rachel crosses the room and kneels beside him. She wound up directing our afternoon shopping trip, so clearly she's on board with this plan, but she still hasn't made eye contact with me since lunch.

We had a good haul, though, and two dozen members of the crew, plus Dom, are currently gathered in my basement, sorting through the bags full of clothes we dug out of clearance bins and thrift-store racks. It's mostly long skirts and clothes and accessories that were fashionable a decade or so ago, so it'll still take a ton of work to transform them into usable costumes, but it's a start.

I texted Will to tell him what we were doing, and he texted me back a thumbs-up, but that was it. Pops said he's been in the performing arts wing all day with Ms. Marcus and the cleaning crew, and he'll probably be there all night, too. Dad even left work early to go help.

We got a very stressed-sounding mass email from Ms. Marcus a few minutes ago, but she didn't say when we'll be allowed back in the auditorium, or if the show's still on in the first place. I only have one mode during a theater emergency, though, and that mode is action. Even with most of the crew, plus Dom, putting in as many hours as we can physically manage, it will still be a miracle if we can assemble enough costumes for a halfway decent show in time for opening, let alone tech.

Still, there's nothing we can do but try.

"One sewing machine," Rachel mutters. "Well, looks like it works, at least. Do you have any thread?"

"Some," I say, trying not to let on how shocked I am that she actually spoke to me. "We'll have to triage. What do you think, one costume for each principal?"

"Won't work." Rachel shakes her head. "Valjean alone has to change at least three times, and Cosette can't exactly wear her wedding dress for the entire show. And Fantine can't go to the factory in her 'Lovely Ladies' costume."

"If we cover her up with a sheet for the hospital scene, we can get away without a costume for that," I suggest.

"You want her to die in her sex worker corset?" Rachel glances up at me, meeting my eyes for the first time since lunch. Her jaw is clenched tight.

Wow. That's pure, undeniable loathing on her face.

"Fine." She turns back to the sewing machine. I'm clearly dismissed. "You're the boss."

"No, I mean, I only—"

"More help has arrived!" Pops booms from the top of the basement stairs. "Go on down, you all."

Rachel glances up suspiciously, and so do I. The whole crew's already here. It's seven o'clock and we're planning to be here for hours yet, ignoring homework and families and everything else in our lives. No one but us would drop it all to sew costumes for a show that may or may not be going up next week.

The footsteps that come down the stairs are quiet at first, but they quickly get louder. It sounds like at least half a dozen people are coming down.

"Hey, everybody," David's richly resonant voice calls out. "I brought my mom's sewing box in case we need it."

I catch Rachel's eye again. She looks as wary as I feel. What are *actors* doing here?

"I've got all my brothers' old Halloween costumes," Beth calls behind him. "Most of them are crap, but maybe we can cut them up or something?"

"I have some random stuff." Odile comes down next, holding

up two bulging shopping bags from Joann Fabrics. "I didn't know what we needed so I got a little of everything."

Now Rachel's outright glaring at me, but Devin rushes up to Odile. "Did you get machine thread?"

"I got so much thread." Odile steps forward and opens the bags so Devin can see. Behind her, Malik, Lauren, and Alejandra are trooping down the stairs, all of them carrying boxes and bags.

"How did you know we were . . ." I stare at them stupidly for a moment. Then I make the connection, and I turn to Dom.

"I told some of the cast what was going on." He glances up from where he's sorting thrift-store vests into piles. "It was Odile's idea to bring stuff over."

"I asked him not to say anything." Odile shrugs sheepishly as she bends to unload her bags. "I . . . was afraid you might not want us to come."

"We definitely would've wanted you to if we knew you were bringing thread," Devin says.

"I got a portable sewing machine, too." Odile pulls a brand-new box out of the bottom of her fattest bag. "It's a cheap one, so I don't know how much help it'll be, but . . ."

"Cheap is better than nothing." Devin rips open the box, which doesn't actually look that cheap to me.

I step forward to help Odile with her bags. Just like she said, they're full of random odds and ends—thread and needles, buttons and zippers and snaps, half a dozen hot glue guns, and bags and bags full of lace and trim and beads. It's *exactly* what we need to turn our pile of thrift-store finds into actual, period-appropriate costumes.

"You're incredible," I whisper as the rest of the actors make their way into the room, the crew members eagerly reaching out to see what they brought. "Seriously. Do you have any idea how incredible you are?"

Odile steps forward and tilts her head onto my shoulder, which catches me by surprise. I want to put my arm around her and keep her in exactly this spot, just for a moment.

But we're surrounded by crew members, and even though everyone's distracted right now, this is exactly the kind of risk we can't take.

I pull away.

"We should ask how the costume team wants to use you all," I say loudly to the actors, moving over to where Rachel's winding thread into my grandmother's sewing machine. Before I reach her, a light hand lands on my elbow.

"Hey, Mel?" I turn to see Gabby biting her lip. "Could we talk for a second?"

"Yeah. Yeah, of course."

I can tell she wants to be alone, so we climb the stairs to the kitchen as Devin starts loudly assigning jobs to the actors. Pops has gone upstairs, but the bread and cold cuts and protein bars he set out for us earlier are still on the counter. Hunger gnaws at my stomach, but the serious look in Gabby's eyes makes me wait to touch the food.

"So I, uh . . ." She crosses her arms. "I wanted to ask if it's true."

Uh-oh. "If what's true?"

"You're with her, right? You have been for a while."

I swallow.

"Please don't lie." Gabby swallows too.

I shut my eyes. Then I nod. This is over. "I'm so sorry."

"What about the curse?" Her voice is creeping higher. When I open my eyes, her lip is trembling. "What we talked about at strike—how you weren't going to go out with anyone because that might trigger it . . ."

I shake my head. "I know. I'm so, so sorry."

"So you've just been—doing it anyway?" Gabby's lip is full-on shaking now. She looks seconds away from outright crying. "And what, hoping none of us would notice?"

Now I want to cry, too. "I didn't think of it like that, but . . ."

She turns away, intently studying a loaf of multigrain bread. I try to think of something I can say to make this better, but there's nothing.

"It's not as if I planned it. It just sort of . . . happened." But I know that doesn't make it better, and it's obvious Gabby doesn't think so either. "It was one of those things. Like you and Dom."

"I didn't want you to know about Dom and me because I thought you'd say it was unprofessional. You're always talking about how we need to keep a safe distance from the actors."

"Well . . . I mean, that's true, but it's fine in this case. I don't really care if you and Dom go out."

"I'm not sure what you *do* care about anymore."

It feels like she slapped me. Before I can come up with a response, she keeps going.

"Did you mean it when you first agreed? During strike?" She turns around and looks straight into my eyes. That makes this worse, somehow. "When you told us you wouldn't go out with anyone, were you being serious? Or did you figure you could do whatever you wanted as long as you kept it a secret?"

"I *never* thought that. I wouldn't have agreed if I didn't mean it."

"But clearly, you *didn't* mean it. It's not like someone *made* you go out with her."

"Gabby . . ." I hate everything about this conversation. But most of all, I hate the way she's looking at me, with her head tilted down and her lips half-parted. Disappointment and disbelief and disgust all rolled into one. "The curse, the superstitions—we don't have proof any of it's real. Accidents happen in theater all the time."

"But accidents happen in *our* theater way more often than other theaters, don't they? Because of that fire a hundred years ago, and everything?"

"That's only a theory. And the idea that it has anything to do with my *love life* is just—"

"But your love life *did* screw things up on the last show. I was there."

I nod, remembering with perfect clarity how Gabby saved me that night. *She* was the one who brought me back from the brink.

"That was a coincidence," I say, but my voice sounds hollow.

"Okay, but you and Odile . . . it's obvious you're serious. I could tell when she brought in that star drop. You looked like you wanted to marry her then and there."

I can't argue with her. "But that doesn't mean—"

"I had a feeling this was happening. *Weeks* ago. I saw the way you kept looking at each other in rehearsals, but I didn't say anything. Maybe if I had, the fire wouldn't have happened." She wipes a tear off her cheek. "But I didn't, because I trusted you."

For the second time today, my heart stops.

I thought the fire was the worst thing that could happen. I was wrong.

"Look." I keep my voice measured and professional. It's all I have right now. "You didn't break any rules, and neither did I— not real ones. The superstitions aren't what matters. Our *real* job is putting on the best show we can and keeping everyone safe."

"And thanks to the fire, we're not doing either of those right now." She's speaking calmly and quietly, too. It only makes what she's saying that much worse.

That's when a sound behind her makes us both turn. A voice on the basement stairs.

"Who else wants chips?" David calls. Several voices answer, and he laughs. "Okay, be right back."

"Please, Gabby." We only have a few seconds before he gets

up here. I have to fix this, *now.* "You can't tell anyone. If this crew stops trusting each other, the whole show will fall apart."

"It's already falling apart. You're the only one who doesn't see it."

I fight the urge to cry again. *"Please."*

"Fine." She sighs. "I'm pretty sure Dom's known longer than I have, though, and I'm not sure who else suspects. I overheard a few of the actors talking yesterday, and—"

A shout from the basement stairs cuts her off. Then a scream.

We both bolt forward at once as feet pound on the floor above us. Pops shouts something, but I can't make it out over the din from the basement. Dozens of voices coming all at once, a mix of hushed tones and shrieks.

I yank open the door to the stairs. There's a knot of people clustered around the bottom.

"Who's hurt?" I try to run down the steps, but I only make it halfway before I hit a wall of people. "What happened?"

"What's the address here?" Odile's voice rises up above the others, but I can't see her. Dom tells her our address, and she repeats it shakily. I've never heard her sound so afraid. "An ambulance, please. He's—there's a lot of blood, and I heard—there was a snapping sound . . ."

"Everyone move, quickly." Pops pushes past me down the stairs and plunges into the group of people. "Ohhh. Hey, it's all right, you're gonna be all right, try to stay calm . . ."

I follow him, my heart pounding fiercely. That's when I see

David crumpled on the floor. He must've fallen through the gap between the stairs and the banister somehow. His leg is bent at a sickening angle.

"Should we make a tourniquet?" someone asks, and I have no idea if we should or not, but I run back upstairs to look for a scarf. Standing still is impossible right now anyway.

I brush past Gabby, but I don't look at her. I don't need to. I already know how she's reacting to this, because I'm reacting exactly the same way.

She's right. I did exactly what I swore I wouldn't do. I fell in love, and now everything's falling apart.

From: Melody McIntyre
To: All cast and crew
Date: Thursday, 4/23, 7:56 a.m.
Subject: Update

Good morning everyone,

The teachers asked me to send out a quick update.

For those of you who haven't heard, David broke his leg last
night. He's still in the hospital, but he's being discharged
today. The doctors don't think he'll need surgery (yay!).
He hopes to be back at school tomorrow, at least for the
afternoon pep rally. He'll either be on crutches or in a
wheelchair, so we'll adjust the choreography accordingly.
We'll wait to reblock his scenes in the show itself until we're
allowed into the auditorium again.

The good news is, the black box has been declared safe and
the teachers said we can rehearse there this afternoon,
with a tentative goal of sticking to the original schedule for
tech, dress rehearsals, and performances. Ms. Marcus and
Mr. Green will be busy working in the auditorium with the
cleaning crews, so Ms. Qiao will direct the rehearsal. All cast
members, please report to the black box no later than 3:00
p.m. Be prepared to stay late.

Crew members, as you know, we still can't get to the sets or props, but in the meantime we have a ton of costume work to do. So all crew, please report to the black box at 3:00 p.m. as well. We're hauling in all the supplies and materials we gathered yesterday, and we'll move out some of the seats so the crew can sew on the far side of the black box while the cast rehearses in the middle. It'll be close quarters, but we'll make it work.

Thank you, everyone! —Mel

—Also stored on BHS performing arts department shared drive.
Created by: Melody McIntyre, stage manager, class of 2021
Viewable to: All cast, crew, and directors
Editable by: Current SM ONLY

Scene 4—Black Box Theater, Beaconville High School Performing Arts Wing

DAYS UNTIL SPRING MUSICAL OPENS: 8

"But what was David even doing at your house?" Christina taps her jaw testily, leaning back into the circle of actors around her. "Malik said a bunch of people from the show were there last night, but I didn't hear about it."

"It was a last-minute thing." I hunch my shoulders and grab my elbows. "They came to help make costumes."

"Isn't there a whole costume department for that?"

I sigh.

We're an hour and a half into rehearsal. Ms. Qiao just called for a break, but she's the only one who actually left, so the rest of us are still crammed into the black box. Normally this is my favorite place in the whole school, after the tech booth—it's down the hall from the auditorium, and it's a wide-open room that can be configured in a dozen different ways for shows and rehearsals and classes. It's also a great spot to chill with theater friends when it isn't being used for official purposes. Right now, though, it's way too full of people and anxiety for any of us to relax.

The entire crew, except for Estaban, Jacob, and me, is jammed into a narrow space on the far side of the room, sewing frantically. Will just gave me a status report on the major set pieces, and I emailed it out right before rehearsal started—basically, some are salvageable and some aren't—and told us we were allowed in the subbasement again, so Jacob and Estaban are down in the storage room checking the props. We're hoping to get the all clear for the scene shop soon too, but for now I'm trying to use the break time to calm the cast down. It isn't working.

"What's the deal with the costumes, anyway?" Leah leans forward. "I heard they were all destroyed."

"Not *completely*," I tell her. The other sixty actors hang on our every word. "Mr. Green said we can still use some of the pieces. Maybe ten percent."

"So which of us have to wear crappy thrift-store costumes now that the good ones are toast?" Nick asks.

Something clatters sharply on the far side of the room. The crew's eavesdropping on us.

"The *good* ones were made out of thrift-store materials too." I roll my eyes at Nick. "The entire tech crew is working day and night to make new costumes for all of you, so I recommend you give them a break."

Nick rolls his eyes right back. "And *I* recommend you give *us* a break. If you haven't noticed, everyone's stressed out about the whole theater-burning-down thing. Not to mention our costar nearly dying at *your* house."

"Hey . . ." Odile's voice is soft and soothing. She's been sitting off to one side behind me, but now she leans into the middle of the group. "Everyone's stressed, the cast *and* the crew. We all ought to cut each other some slack."

Nick and Christina and some of the others give her a mild side eye.

"Tell us the truth, Mel." Beth leans in now, looking more serious than I've ever seen her. "Are they going to cancel the show?"

I shake my head. "That isn't going to—"

"Hey, no, no, you have to do it," a raised voice calls from the other side of the room. We all look up to see Gabby pointing at Tyler.

"Come on, I didn't say it to one of *them*." He turns to us, heaving a dramatic sigh. "Mel, back me up. Isn't it okay to say— the G-L words, as long as I don't say them to an actor right before a show? I was only telling Devin I hoped he could get the sewing machine to work. Besides, it's not like I'd tell someone to 'break a leg' after what happened."

"You still have to do the countercurse." The needle in Gabby's hand never stops moving, but she gives Tyler, and then me, a dark look. "We can't afford to take chances."

Any other day, I would've agreed with Tyler's interpretation of the rules. Besides, the last thing I want to do is draw *more* attention to all our superstitions. But I can't argue with Gabby after last night.

I nod. "Go ahead. Countercurse."

Tyler sighs and climbs to his feet. "This is ridiculous, but . . ." He steps carefully over the huddle of crew members and walks out the main door of the black box, then knocks on the frame. "May I please be invited back in?"

Gabby's still glaring at me. Clearly, I don't have a choice but to enforce *every* rule. "Close the door first," I call.

Tyler sighs again, but he shuts the door and knocks again. "Hello? It's Tyler? Your publicity crew head? May I please be invited back inside so I can help sew fifty million costumes for a show that supposedly starts next week?"

Gabby stands up, climbs over the others, and opens the door. "Okay."

"*Thank* you." Tyler huffs to his seat. I turn back to the actors, who haven't said a word the whole time.

"Anyway." I try to smile, as though all this is amusing instead of absurdly tense. "Try to relax, everyone. This theater's made it through bigger problems than this."

"But we still have *so* much work to do, and now we can't even rehearse on our own stage." Andrew's voice carries sharply through the room. The crew's silent, but I know they heard him. That's what we get for having perfect acoustics. "And scary shit keeps happening. Leah got poison ivy in the middle of winter. And remember when Julio got hurt?"

"Uh-huh." Peyton nods. "I thought all this curse stuff was bullshit, but this is getting bad. Fires are *not* a good sign."

"Look, all these things are problems, but they're coincidences, not a curse." I shake my head, forcing my voice to stay steady. Stage Manager Calm. "There are problems on every show. When we did *Midsummer* we didn't have the new hazer yet so we had to keep dry ice backstage, and it bubbled so loud in the dress rehearsals the fairies had to yell their lines, but it worked out fine. The audience thought it was a spooky sound effect."

"I remember that." Peyton frowns. "I was hoarse for the whole run."

"Right, well, sorry about that, but I'm just saying." I'm about to roll my eyes again when I remember that I broke up with Isabelle hours after the *Midsummer* invited dress rehearsal. The dry ice stopped giving us trouble after that.

"Anyway, aside from the fire, these aren't catastrophes." I concentrate on using my most diplomatic voice to cover up the fact that I'm currently trying to calculate exactly how many crises I could've been responsible for over the past three years. "Leah, your rash is getting better, right?"

She scratches her arm. "A little."

"I might be coming down with it too, actually." Peyton scratches her knee. "I was itching the other day."

"Maybe you got it when you had to help paint the sets," Kyle says. "A lot of those chemicals aren't safe to breathe in."

"You can't get a rash from painting sets." Dom, who's been quiet through this entire conversation, finally lets out an exasperated sigh and climbs to his feet. "The crew paints sets *every single day*. You all need to stop being such assholes. Mel, I'm going to the bathroom, I'll be back before break ends."

As much as I appreciate Dom's support, I wish he'd use more diplomatic language. Nick and Christina are both shifting in their seats, shooting daggers from their eyes at Dom's back as he turns away.

"Anyway, I promise we'll get through this," I tell the others as calmly as I possibly can. "We're going to have an awesome show. All you need to worry about right now is working hard in rehearsals."

"Mel's right." Odile nods. At least I can count on *her* not to curse everyone out. "Our show's in good hands. The crew and the teachers know what they're doing."

Then, as she leans back into her seat, she lays a soft hand on my arm.

I stare down at her French-manicured fingers resting on my sweatshirt sleeve. I'm not the only one.

Leah and Christina both draw in quick breaths. Andrew and Beth glance at each other. Peyton scratches her elbow and raises her eyebrows sky-high.

I don't dare look at the crew side of the room to see if anyone's watching, but it doesn't matter. They'll hear about it soon enough.

Oh, God. This is my own fault. I never told Odile the truth, and now it's too late.

"Careful!" someone shouts from the door behind us. I turn just in time to hear a loud thump followed by the sounds of breaking glass and a phone ringing.

Estaban charges around the corner, his eyes wild.

"What was that?" I jump up.

As I'm running toward him, Odile ducks past me with an apologetic wave, holding her phone to her ear. That's when I spot the pile of shattered, spray-paint-covered glass by the door.

"The bishop's candlesticks." Jacob looks like he's on the verge of hyperventilating. "We brought them up from storage to check them and I swear—they were just *sitting* here. I don't know how they could've fallen."

Estaban looks like he might hyperventilate, too.

Okay. So. Stage Manager Calm.

Those candlesticks are the most important prop in the show. Estaban and his team spent weeks getting them exactly right. They've kept them carefully wrapped in tissue paper every time they had to be moved. They *couldn't* have randomly capsized.

Still, I can't let anyone get the idea that there's some grand cosmological significance in this. Props break. It's the first rule of theater.

This is a fixable problem. Stage Manager Calm.

"We have backup candlesticks, right?" I ask.

"Yeah, but they're crap." Estaban rubs his forehead. "They're the gold ones we tested with the foil wrapping. The silver spray paint on the glass looked a thousand times better under the lamps. We'll have to go back to IKEA to make a new set, and there's no time with tech this weekend."

"It'll be okay." I check my timer. Break's almost over. "Jacob, could you please go get the backup set for now, and grab the dustpan while you're at it? Estaban, I'll talk to Ms. Marcus about the budget, but I think we can order a new set of glass candles with rapid shipping and switch them out when they get here. Don't worry, we'll figure it out."

"Could you please stop pretending everything's going to be fine? Because you *know* it isn't. None of this would be happening at all if it wasn't for you."

A hush falls over the black box. When I turn around, Nick, of all people, is standing in the middle of the room, his arms crossed and his eyes locked on me.

The hell?

He's got to be talking about the curse. But since when does Nick the Dick even *know* about the curse, much less care?

"Don't be ridiculous." I force a laugh. The crew has frozen, their needles still in their hands. They're all watching Nick.

Except for Rachel. Her steely gaze is leveled straight at me.

"Mel wasn't anywhere near the candlesticks." Estaban sounds confused. And maybe a little suspicious.

There's got to be a way to fix this. But before I can think of it, Nick the Dick opens his mouth again, and starts whistling.

The *asshole* is staring right at me, whistling "One Day More."

"Stop and do the countercurse." I put my hands on my hips. "*Now.*"

He keeps whistling.

"*Stop* it." I turn, trying to catch the others' eyes for backup, but the rest of the actors are glancing back and forth between Nick and me uncertainly. Even the crew is quiet.

He finally stops whistling. I exhale, thinking he's done what he set out to do, but then he opens his mouth and shouts, "*Macbeth!* Macbeth, Macbeth, Macbeth!"

"What the *hell!*" I can't *believe* this. "Shut *up!*"

"Come on, you don't actually think any of this matters, do you?" He takes a step toward me.

"What are you talking about?" I cross my arms, but it feels like I'm walking into a trap.

"While *she's* got us busy doing stupid tricks, our show's on life support." Nick's words boom out, directed at everyone in the room at once. The way he's holding himself, the passion in his voice—he actually sounds like a lead actor for the first time. Oh, the irony. "Our costumes are toast. David's in the hospital. Our theater's shut down. We all know there's a bigger problem here than some crew guy saying 'good luck.'"

There's a collective sucking in of breath from the crowd around us. I glance from face to face, trying to figure out what they're thinking, but there's no way to tell.

"You make *us* follow every single rule, but you think you're above it all." Nick lifts his chin, the same way he always does during his first big solo in rehearsals, except this time he's looking right at me. "You're going out with that girl even though you *know* it means the rest of us could get hurt."

"I'm not—I wouldn't—" But I can hear my voice waver, and I hate myself for it.

"Everybody knows." Nick looks around at the group. Christina and a couple of the other actors nod, but most of them are still swiveling their heads back and forth between Nick and me. "There *is* a curse on our theater, and it's all because *she's* a slut."

"Hey!" I shout, and it's comforting when a handful of people—actors and crew both—chorus "Hey!" and "Don't!" at Nick, too.

But my relief only lasts a second, because right away, it becomes clear that all they're mad at him for is the use of that one particular word. And as soon as they're done complaining about it, they fall quiet again. No one's actually come over to my side.

"Is it true, Mel?" Jasmin asks in the sudden silence. "You're with Odile?"

"I . . ." I can't keep this up. I've *hated* lying to them.

I shut my eyes and nod. It's a relief not to see anything while I listen to the chorus of whispers and sighs that follows.

"Tell them the rest," Nick adds. When I open my eyes, he's sitting back in his seat, a triumphant grin on his face. I turn away, but that only leaves me facing the crew side of the room, where dozens of incredulous mouths are hanging open. "About how the curse works."

I shake my head. "I . . ."

"So the theater's cursed because of that fire a hundred years ago, right?" Nick sounds absolutely delighted to explain this. "So what the techies do is, they get together and secretly pick a rule for every show. If we don't follow it, the show's ruined. This year they told us the rule was we couldn't say *thirteen*—oh, and by the way, *thirteen, thirteen, thirteen*! Yeah, just like I thought, nothing happened. See, they didn't tell us they'd already come up with a *secret* rule already. *She*"—and here Nick points at me, his grin widening—"wasn't supposed to go out with anyone. But she did it anyway and then lied to everybody."

"Those two have been screwing us over all along." Christina smirks, and it occurs to me, dimly, that she's Odile's understudy. She probably thinks if she goes along with this, somehow it'll translate into *her* getting to be the star.

This whole thing is so *gross*.

"God, look at her—she isn't even trying to deny anything," Leah murmurs. "I didn't want to believe it, but . . ."

"Now we know why so many things have been going wrong." Nick's voice is still booming, but he isn't looking at me anymore. He's roving his eyes over the others, and they're hanging on his every word.

He thinks he can convince them that *me* being with Odile is why *he* lost his voice and nearly ruined everything. Hell—maybe he even believes that's the truth.

"She's supposed to be our *leader*, right?" he booms on. "She can't let her personal feelings take priority over the show."

The way he says that word, *leader*, drips with condescension. I want to scream at him, but that isn't what an SM does.

"Everyone." I'm shaking, but I try not to let it show. "Think about this. We've had plenty of problems when I *wasn't* dating anyone. Remember when Julio got a bloody nose out of nowhere?

That happened *before* Odile and I started going out."

Except . . . it happened while Odile and I were blatantly flirting a few feet away.

It's true. God, it's true.

The curse, the superstition—I knew it all along. I just didn't want to believe it.

For years, I've lived and breathed theater. All I cared about was putting on a perfect show.

It never could've happened. I've been messing it up for everyone all along.

What if we can't ever get back into the theater? Or worse—what if someone else gets hurt?

This can't keep going.

"I'm sorry." I stand up. I can see Ms. Qiao just outside the door of the black box, thumbing her phone. The break time must be up, but I don't look down at my timer. "I'll be back soon."

I charge through the group without making eye contact with anyone and stop Ms. Qiao as she's walking inside. "Hi. I'm really sorry, but would it be all right if I missed the first couple of minutes back from the break?"

Ms. Qiao nods, frowning. "If absolutely necessary. Is something wrong?"

"I . . . no. I'm really sorry. I'll be right back."

I'm not conscious of where I'm going until I'm already halfway to the dance studio.

I have to do *something*.

I have to fix this.

From: Melody McIntyre

To: All directors and crew heads

Date: Thursday, 4/23, 3:07 p.m.

Subject: Damage to Set Pieces Due to Backstage Fire—
Preliminary Assessment

List compiled based on verbal report from Mr. Green:

- Turntable—Some visible smoke damage but shouldn't impact functionality and doesn't require repair (hallelujah).
- Barricade—Two barrels were soaked by the sprinklers and will need to be replaced (or removed) before tech. The rest has some visible smoke damage, but to quote Mr. Green, "It adds verisimilitude."
- Cart—Too much smoke and water damage; declared unsafe and removed by the cleaning crew. A parent* volunteered to build a new one out of the old Tevye cart from storage.
- Gate—Structurally sound. Needs complete repainting.
- Bridge—Structurally, looks sound but needs another round of testing. Also needs complete repainting.

*Incidentally, the parent of the SM writing this list.

Thank you, everyone! —Mel

—Also stored on BHS performing arts department shared drive.

Created by: Melody McIntyre, stage manager, class of 2021
Viewable to: Crew heads and directors
Editable by: Current SM ONLY

Scene 5—Dance Studio, Beaconville High School Performing Arts Wing

DAYS UNTIL SPRING MUSICAL OPENS: 8

I find her here, like I thought I would. The lights are off, so I can just see her silhouette. She's standing by the bookshelf with her back turned, the phone to her ear.

My heart thunders in my chest. I should've come into this with a plan—but I'm not used to meticulously planning conversations with her, the way I do with other people. She's the one I actually take risks with.

Or she was.

"Thank you," Odile's saying into the phone. "No, I can't wait. I just have a few things to wrap up here and then I'll be set." There's a pause, and she laughs. The same full-throated, genuine-sounding yet totally fake laugh I've heard her use on a dozen phone calls before. She's acting.

"Yes, certainly, let's catch up on Monday," she says, turning around and spotting me in the doorway. She smiles and holds up one finger. "Thank you again. Of course. Goodbye."

I wait until I'm positive she's off the call before I say anything. When I do, my voice comes out in an embarrassingly fragile whisper. "Odile?"

"Hi." She looks tired, but she smiles when she meets my gaze. "The Netflix show is a go. I don't have to meet the producer after all. I guess that's good. But . . . anyway, has rehearsal started back yet?"

"Yeah, but we've got a few minutes. They're starting with 'One Day More,' so they won't need you for a while."

"Still, I should be there, and so should you. . . . Right?"

"I'll head back soon." I shut my eyes. All I can see is the quiet, pale faces of the crew realizing what I'd done.

I can never let anyone look at me that way again.

I open my eyes and stare down at the shiny wood floor, shoving my hands into the back pockets of my jeans. I'm wearing my *Midsummer* shirt, which might not have been the best choice. Every time I look at it, I remember how ethereal Odile looked in her shimmery fairy queen gown.

"There's sawdust in your hair. How'd you manage that, with the scene shop closed?" Odile smiles and steps toward me, like she's going to pluck it off my head, but when we're three feet apart and I still haven't moved, she drops the smile. "Is something wrong?"

"Um." If I just say the words, maybe this will get easier. "There's something I should tell you. Some of the crew—and now the cast, too—well, they've got a new superstition, and it involves, um . . . me. And you."

"Right." She nods, a short, heavy movement. "The rule about you not dating during shows?"

I freeze. "What?"

"David mentioned it a while ago. He said Nick was trying to spread some idea around that you were trying to sabotage the production by going out with me, but no one actually believed it. He wanted me to know so I wouldn't be confused if anyone looked at me strangely, but I told him they already did that anyway."

She *knew*? "Why didn't you tell me?"

"Why didn't *you* tell *me*?"

"I—I tried. I mean, I was going to. But . . ."

"I understand." The corners of her lips turn up again. "You have to look like you believe in this stuff for your team's sake. You're the one who has to keep things going, whatever it takes. The show must go on, right?"

I have no idea what to say.

"I wish the whole world was only you and me." She sighs. "Like that night before the fire started, when it was just us on that empty stage. It was only a couple of minutes, but it felt so good. As if the outside world didn't exist. I wish it could always be like that."

"Me too." I reach forward and thread my fingers through hers. Even though I shouldn't.

"I know you love the crew, and I do too, but I can't believe they made you do that." Odile shakes her head, still smiling softly. "I know they take the superstitions seriously, but that one crossed a line. They're your friends. They had to know they couldn't hold you to an expectation like that."

"Well . . ." I swallow. "It's just that it looks bad, you know? I'm the one in charge of making sure everyone follows the rules, and here I am, breaking one."

She raises her eyebrows. "Did something happen after I left rehearsal?"

"Nick kind of . . ." I shake my head. "It doesn't matter. I shouldn't have lied to my team. I've got to do something to make them trust me again."

She nods, squeezing my fingers in hers. "You're right. I wanted to keep things quiet at first, but it's gotten too complicated. It's time to tell them the truth. No more worrying about rumors."

"They already know." I glance down at our intertwined fingers, then pull my hand back. "It's too late."

"Wait." She peers at me through the wispy curls that frame her face. "What are you saying?"

"I'm saying I have to fix this."

The words hang in the air between us, clogging up the space. Odile bites her lip. "Fix it . . . how?"

"I need to come up with something that'll make them leave us alone." I shrug, but I'm trembling. "I don't know. Maybe we should pretend to break up."

"You want to *pretend* to break up?" Odile blinks, hard, then nods, short and heavy, all over again. "Okay. Right, okay. Is . . . this your way of letting me down easy?"

I freeze again. "What?"

"If you want to end things, you don't need to make up some excuse." She reaches back and tugs on her long wavy hair, as though she's going to pull it into a ponytail, even though she doesn't have a hair tie in her hand. "I know I'm not like the other people you've gone out with. Everyone at this school has always thought I'm strange. But I thought things were different with you and me."

Rachel's voice echoes in my ears. She said exactly the same thing.

"They *are* different." I swallow.

"Then why are you suggesting we *pretend* to break up? And please don't tell me it's about getting the crew to trust you. You don't make up for lying to someone by lying to them *more*."

She's right. It's just that I can't bear to think about breaking up for *real*. "I don't know. I barely understand any of this."

"Do *you* believe the curse is real?" She shakes her head. "Because if you *do*, then us *pretending* to break up won't do any good, will it?"

She's right, again.

I don't want to be standing here. I don't want to be saying these things that are making her look at me this way.

I don't want any of this to be happening. I want to wake up and have everything be the way it was.

"You could tell them it's none of their business if you want to date someone, and that this superstition has gone too far." She shakes her head. "Of course, you can't say that if you don't believe it's true. So do you?"

"I . . ."

"You know what, actually—I just realized I'd rather not know."

"Odile, I . . ."

I don't even know what I'm trying to say. All I know is, she's turning toward the door, and that isn't what I want. It's the *opposite* of what I want.

"The way I feel about you—" I stumble over the words. "I've never felt like this about anyone."

"All right, well, it would be nice to believe that, but you're clearly very good at lying." She shoves her phone back into her pocket.

"Wait. *Please.*"

She doesn't look at me. Just shakes her head again.

Some part of me is thinking, *Okay. So we're breaking up. I can deal with the breakup kind of pain. I know how to do that.*

But I already know this is different.

I'm trying to focus on breathing—in, out, in, out—when the door behind me slams open.

Bryce runs inside. When she sees us, her face goes slack. "Mel! We've been looking everywhere! Do you have your first aid kit?"

Oh, God. "It's in the black box. What's going on?"

"It's Fatima." Bryce looks like she's about to throw up. "We were in the scene shop. There's been an accident."

LES MIS CRISES TO DATE

Victim	What Happened	Cause
Julio	Somehow got hit in the face without ever actually getting hit in the face	Completely random—no natural explanation (in other words . . . totally could've been the curse)
Leah (Beth and Peyton have also theoretically gotten it, although I haven't seen evidence of this)	Weird rash	Completely random—no natural explanation (in other words . . . totally could've been the curse)
Nick (also perpetrator)	Got laryngitis right before rehearsals started	Yelled at a hockey game (in other words, being a dick)
David	Broke his leg (in *my* house)	Completely random—no natural explanation (in other words . . . totally could've been the curse)
Gabby	Got a cold (which is weird because she said she *never* gets colds)	Completely random—no natural explanation (in other words . . . totally could've been the curse)

Fatima	Got her hand caught on the turntable (she doesn't need stitches and apparently it could've been a lot worse, but *still*)	Completely random—no natural explanation (in other words . . . totally could've been the curse)
Kevin	Got stomach flu the day of the pep rally/sitzprobe	Completely random—no natural explanation (in other words . . . totally could've been the curse)
Only logical conclusion:	I, Melody McIntyre, have cursed my own show.	

—Stored on Melody McIntyre's home laptop hard drive and Melody McIntyre's home laptop hard drive only.

Scene 6—Beaconville High School Gymnasium

DAYS UNTIL SPRING MUSICAL OPENS: 7

"The battery needs to clip onto your back." Dom holds the wireless microphone pack above his head so the other principals can see. "The crew will keep them wrapped up, so don't worry if you get sweaty. During shows they'll clip onto your costume, but for today just stick them on your belt loops. You switch them on and off at the top."

"Like this?" Alejandra tries the switch, then taps the mic to see if it's working.

Feedback whines out through the gym, and we all cringe. Then, of course, two more actors immediately tap their mics exactly the same way, as though they're expecting a different result. Dom waits for the feedback to end before he answers.

"Yeah, that's the right switch, but try not to tap the mics." Dom sounds a lot more patient than he probably feels. I can't believe I never noticed how good he was at acting. "In fact, it's best not to touch them at all."

"Sorry." Alejandra looks as though she wants to melt into her shoes.

"No worries."

"Why are you telling *us* this?" Nick interjects. "Isn't dealing with these a *techie's* job?"

The cords on Dom's neck start to swell, so I jump in. He only offered to help with mics today because Kevin is out with the stomach flu, but the rest of the cast doesn't need to know that. We don't need yet more rumors spreading about communicable diseases, especially since Fatima's injury is still fresh in everyone's minds.

Besides, it's not as if it's beneath an actor to help with mics, for God's sake.

And I'll never forgive Nick for that whole scene yesterday in the black box. Okay, so maybe I *did* trigger the curse, but that didn't give him the right to act as if I'd done it on purpose. As if I *wanted* to hurt my friends. To hear Nick talk, I might as well have made some sort of demonic pact, and only *he* could save the show from destruction. As though he's ever actually cared about anything but himself.

"The crew will help you attach the mics during tech and shows, but keep in mind you're literally going to have a microphone taped to your face for most of the next two weeks." I'm talking to the whole group, but I keep my gaze focused squarely on Nick. "So it's to your benefit to know how to switch it on and off. Unless you want everyone in the auditorium to hear you pee."

There are a few giggles, but most of the actors don't seem to know if it's okay to laugh. Since yesterday, the tension's been overwhelming. After I ran to the scene shop to make sure Fatima was all right, I had no choice but to go back to rehearsal and avoid looking at anyone—most of all Odile, but also Gabby and the rest of the crew. And since we still had to slog through another three hours of rehearsal, that added up to a *lot* of staring down at my binder.

"What are these things covered in, anyway?" Leah holds up her plastic-wrapped battery pack, wrinkling her nose.

"Condoms, obviously," Malik says, which is cheating since he was a featured soloist last spring and thus already knew that. Most of the other principals haven't used the wireless mics before, though, and they all laugh harder than really seems necessary when they realize each of them is holding a battery pack carefully wrapped in an unlubricated Trojan. Nena, the assistant sound head, bought a bunch of them at Target last night and carefully slipped them into place during the break before third period.

"See?" I say, patting Julio on the back, since he's doubled over laughing. "Everyone thinks I keep condoms in my kit as a joke, but they have a practical application."

"Yeah, that's *totally* why we thought you had them." Nick tilts his head. "A *joke*."

I wait to see if everyone will leap to my defense like they did when he slut-shamed me yesterday, but only Dom shakes his head this time. "Leave her alone, man."

Nick scoffs, and an awkward silence hovers until the

cheerleaders practicing on the opposite side of the gym shout, "*Go! Bulldogs! Go!*"

"Do we have enough mics, or should I get some from the black box?" Gabby asks as I sink back into my seat beside her on the bleachers. She doesn't meet my gaze.

"We should be all right."

"Could we get away with not using them at all?" Tyler mutters on my other side as we watch Nick breathe heavily into his mic. Dom catches Nick's eye and makes a slashing motion across his neck. "What if something goes wrong with the gym's sound equipment?"

"We have to use mics in here." I gesture to the wide-open gym. "The acoustics are crap. None of the soloists could project without amplification."

"Odile could." Tyler drums his fingers on his chin. "Maybe we could add Fantine to 'One Day More.' They did that at the Oscars."

"There's no time," I say quickly, before he can start running with that idea. "We're strictly cut off at three minutes."

Tyler grumbles about how the baseball team could probably run around the pep rally for three *hours* if they wanted to, but I don't join in. I'm just relieved he's not talking about Odile anymore.

No one knows what happened between us in the dance studio. Yet.

But I can't focus on that now. Our pep rally flash mob is

in two hours, and we've got it planned down to the microsecond. At the beginning, the cast will be scattered throughout the bleachers, and just as the vice principal starts to launch into a fake speech about school spirit, Nena will start piping in the music to "One Day More." The soloists will stand up one at a time to sing their parts, and as the song builds, the ensemble will start streaming down the aisles in their official *Les Mis* T-shirts until they're all gathered in the middle of the floor, marching in unison, with Lauren perched on Adam's shoulders waving the school flag.

It'll be our first time performing in front of a real audience, which is equal parts exciting and stressful. Either way, it's a welcome distraction from all the curse talk. We might even be allowed into the auditorium tomorrow, too.

Something needs to start being normal again.

"Soloists!" Ms. Marcus calls from the middle of the gym floor. "Places, please."

Nick taps his microphone again as he sprints up the bleachers. Feedback whines out, and I fantasize about running up after him and snatching the mic pack out of his hand.

But when Ms. Marcus gestures for Nena to start the music, the entire atmosphere in the gym turns upside down. The song's opening notes are light, quick, and so pretty they're almost magical. The cheerleaders pause on their way to the locker room, their pom-poms dropping to their hips.

"One Day More" is the biggest, most exciting group number in *Les Mis*. Most of the principals have solos in it, but Nick's the one who kicks it off. And when he starts singing into his mic in the pompous, overly dramatic way he always does (which, to be fair, is also how every Valjean in human history has always sung this song), I have to admit he sounds good as he slowly climbs down the bleachers, lifting his chin to sing up into the beams that crisscross the gym ceiling.

The cheerleaders gasp. Even the other actors, all of whom have heard Nick sing this song approximately fifty million times, look impressed. His last traces of laryngitis finally seem to have subsided, and having an audience clearly adds something to his voice, too, or maybe just to his ego. A few of the cheerleaders look ready to swoon.

I've never understood why audiences fall all over themselves around guys who are halfway decent singers. Women can perform astonishing vocal feats and no one blinks an eye, but when guys do it, people act like they just cured cancer.

When Nick wraps up, Malik and Alejandra stroll out from opposite ends of the gym floor, singing their duet. They've struggled with this harmony for weeks, but I guess the presence of the cheerleaders is good for them, too, because they sound fantastic right now.

Maybe the curse is subsiding. Maybe Odile and me breaking up really did fix everything. Maybe all I had to do was rip my heart out of my chest and stomp on it to get the success I've always dreamed of.

Leah climbs down the bleachers next, singing her solo under

Malik and Alejandra's harmony. The sound fills up the gym. I decide it's the harmony, rather than my own personal romantic devastation, that's making me totally teary-eyed just as Alejandra trips over an empty McDonald's cup in the middle of the gym floor and comes down hard on her hands and knees.

"*Hold!*" I shout, grabbing my kit. Ms. Marcus signals for Nena to pause the music.

I run straight up to where Alejandra's sprawled out on the floor, trying to get a look at her wrists and ankles to make sure she didn't twist anything.

This is my fault. I should've checked the floor for trip hazards as soon as I got to the gym.

"Are you okay?" I ask, carefully scanning her limbs.

"Did I mess up the whole song?" Alejandra sits up, her eyes darting around the gym. "We don't have to stop. I can keep going."

"It's fine, don't worry. Can you move all your fingers and toes?"

She wiggles her appendages, still casting anxious glances over my shoulder. The ensemble members on the bleachers are watching us and talking behind their hands. Someone stage-whispers, "*It's the curse!*"

"Everything all right, Mel?" Ms. Marcus calls.

I glance at Alejandra, who nods quickly. I give Ms. Marcus a thumbs-up.

"All right, from the top!" she calls, clapping her hands. "Places!"

The music starts again, and Nick climbs back up to the top of the bleachers. This time, though, when he goes to sing, his voice croaks on the third note, the way it did in those earliest rehearsals.

Shit. Is *this* the curse, too?

He sings another line and croaks again. The cheerleaders watching from the floor start to giggle. Anyone else would be embarrassed, but Nick just looks pissed.

But the music doesn't stop, and he finishes his lines, sounding relatively decent by the end. When Malik and Alejandra come in, they're even better than they were before, and this time, to my immense relief, no one trips over anything. Leah joins in, and all three of them hit every note perfectly.

Dom's big entrance is next. It's his most dramatic moment in the whole show, aside from his death scene, and before he's sung a note, it's clear he's already relishing it. He runs out to the top of the bleachers on the far side of the gym, singing at the top of his voice and waving a purple foam finger over his head. The foam finger was my idea—he's supposed to wave a musket during this bit in the show, but there was no way we'd have been allowed to use even an obviously fake musket in the gym, and besides, the foam finger is a guaranteed crowd-pleaser.

But his singing is even more striking. Dom's never sounded better. For a second, I'm so happy for him I almost forget how stressed I am about everything else. He and Malik trade solo lines after that, but the glory is all Dom's, and his voice rings out as he storms down the steps, waving that foam finger over his head.

The cheerleaders' gaping expressions are fixed squarely on

Dom now, and half of them are already whooping and waving their pom-poms. When he realizes what's happening, Dom's eyes widen for a fraction of a second—he isn't exactly used to this, since working in the tech booth and drumming in a not particularly successful band called the Honey Badger Liberation League don't tend to generate pom-pom waving—but he disappears back into his character just as quickly, and soon he's passionately calling his troops into battle.

By the time he reaches the gym floor and the ensemble has joined in, all the cheerleaders are clapping, even the guys. A moment later, as David climbs to his feet on his new set of crutches and joins in for *his* solo, his voice is exactly as dark and scary and startling as it's supposed to be, and this feels less like a rehearsal and more like a performance. Our first *real* one, with a real audience. It's very, very cool. When we reach the finale, with Lauren riding on Adam's shoulders and waving the flag as the whole cast sings the last few lines, all the cheerleaders are roaring, and I can't resist clapping along.

Ms. Marcus calls a three-minute break, and we all troop out into the hall, still reeling from the performance high. Dom bounds over and hugs Gabby and then me. "That was good, right?" he says into my ear, breathless.

"It was *great*," I tell him.

Two of the cheerleaders glance back at us on their way to the locker room. Dom blushes. Gabby pokes his arm, and he blushes harder.

"Hey, listen . . ." He lowers his voice and turns back to me. "I tried to find you yesterday after rehearsal, but . . ."

"Yeah, sorry. I was in a rush to get home."

"I just wanted to tell you, I heard about what happened from a bunch of different people, and it doesn't sound like most of them really believed Nick. He was so over the top, trying to get people to think you *wanted* to cause problems on the show. Like a successful run of *Les Mis* hasn't been your lifelong dream."

I shake my head. "I don't want to talk about this right now."

"No one who actually knows you wanted to buy what he was selling. The problem was, you let him get to you. From the way you were acting, people thought you were saying he was right, and that confused some—"

"What are you talking to *her* for?" We all turn at the sound of Nick's voice. He's walking past us with Christina and a couple of the ensemble girls. There aren't any gym classes scheduled during lunch and the cheerleaders have finally vanished back into the locker rooms, so we have the hallway to ourselves. "Didn't you get the memo? Even the techies don't like her anymore. Keep it up with the singing, though. Maybe your little band's next video'll get twenty whole views."

Dom turns sheet white. I'm so stunned that for once, I can't think of a single thing to say. Only Gabby seems to have maintained her composure.

"Yeah, Nick?" She stands up, squares her hips, and lifts her chin, exactly the way Nick does when he solos. He's probably a foot taller than Gabby, but she's looking up at him coolly, as though they're on exactly the same level. "You might want to try chugging some more of that honey water next time, because my neighbor's cat sounds better than you just did. Or you could go back to sitting on the bench for Coach Polakowski instead of getting mad at everybody else for being better than you."

Whoa.

"Go, Gabby," I mutter, but if she heard me, she doesn't turn around.

Nick just stares at her in stunned silence. Then his gaze shifts to me, his eyes narrowing.

"I can't believe you still have the nerve to act like you're our boss." He raises his voice again. "Bad shit's still happening, and everyone knows you're the reason why."

I toss my head to the side, like he couldn't possibly be getting to me. "I know you want everyone to think *your* vocal problems are happening because of *me*, but this cast isn't stupid."

"Well, from where I'm sitting, it looks like *another* one of our stars just almost broke a bone on your watch." Christina's raising her voice, too. "While *you're* still screwing us over for *her*."

"You lied to us all for weeks and you're not even sorry." Nick curls his lip up in what I think might actually qualify as a genuine *snarl*.

"What did I do, Nick, poison your puppy in a past life?" I ask him. No one laughs.

He takes a step forward. I move back, turning to face the rest of the crowd, but my vision's getting blurry. All I can see is an ocean full of cold, silent faces.

"Look, I shouldn't have lied." I swallow. "That's true. I'm sorry."

"They should both be kicked off the show," one of the other actors mutters behind me. I don't know which one, and I'm starting to panic a little.

"There's no reason to be mad at Odile." I gulp in a thick breath. "She didn't know anything about the curse."

"Well, she's got to now," Christina snaps. "Which means you're both to blame."

"Well, we *broke up*, okay? So, can everybody please just shut up?"

I practically shout the words.

No one says anything, but Nick's eyes widen. Even Christina seems to be at a loss for words.

That's when my timer goes off.

"And we're back!" I yell at the top of my lungs. I'm trying to sound commanding, in control, but I'm not fooling anyone. "We need to run this song at least three more times if we're going to be ready for this afternoon."

The actors filter back toward the door, but I can feel their eyes on me. There are murmurs, too, but I try not to listen.

"Um, Mel . . ." Naturally, Gabby's the only one who'll actually speak *to* me instead of *about* me.

I turn to her with a grateful smile. "Hey. What's up? We need to get back inside."

"I . . . I'm not going back in."

My smile falters. "What?"

"I've been thinking about it—a lot, actually, ever since that night at your house when David, um—and . . . I think I need to quit."

I blink at her. I can't find any other words. "What?"

"I can't keep working with you." There are tears in her eyes. "I'm sorry."

I swallow, but I know I have to speak. I have to find a way to talk her out of this. "If this is about the curse, we don't even know if that's—"

"It's not the curse. It's the way you lied to us." She bites her lip and looks down. "To *me*. You need an ASM who'll do what you say without questioning it, and I . . . can't be that anymore."

"Gabby, please, let's talk about this. It's okay if you need to—"

"Goodbye." She turns and walks, then runs, down the hall toward the cafeteria.

What the hell is *happening*? I'm not even with Odile anymore, but my life just keeps getting worse.

I never should've been with her in the first place. I ruined *everything*.

My show really is falling apart, and it's all been for nothing.

Attention, Beaconville Middle School Students

Welcome to the invited dress rehearsal for *Les Misérables* at Beaconville High School!

A word of warning: an IDR is not necessarily a completed show. By the time our spring musical officially opens tomorrow night, things will be running perfectly (we hope). This rehearsal is our last chance to work out any kinks, which means you may witness a few minor hiccups during the performance this afternoon. We request that you bear with us.

Now—to the barricades!

—Sign displayed in BHS Theater lobby.
Photo taken by Melody McIntyre and stored on BHS performing arts department shared drive.
Viewable to: All cast, crew, and directors
Editable by: Current SM ONLY

Scene 7—Tech Booth, Beaconville High School Theater

HOURS UNTIL SPRING MUSICAL OPENS: 28

"*HOLD!*" I shout the word into my headset, then lunge for the God Mic.

When I press the button my voice echoes out from the booth into the entire auditorium. Hundreds of middle schoolers all look up at once, astonished.

"*HOLD!*" I shout again. "Clear the stage!"

David, who's the only person on the stage just now, swings toward the wing as fast as his crutches will carry him. It's a good thing he's gotten plenty of practice at that this week. The orchestra stops playing mid-note, and a hush falls over the theater.

My heart thuds as I sink back into my seat. I've never had to use the God Mic with an audience in the auditorium before. But then, I've never seen anything like this happen.

Below me, the hush evaporates and the house begins to buzz with dozens, then hundreds, of preteen voices. Some of the middle schoolers sound alarmed, but most just seem amused. They wouldn't be if they knew what actually just happened.

In this scene, a 150-pound bridge is supposed to float gently down from far above the stage to upstage center, courtesy of several sturdy cables connected to the fly system. But at this moment, that bridge appears to be *literally flying* in midair. A cable snapped when it was halfway down from the rigging and now the neatly repainted white bridge is spinning slowly over the stage, where it's in legitimate danger of crashing down. Fifteen feet above where David's head just was.

Clearly, it doesn't matter how much I give up. The stupid curse *still* won't let go.

"*Shit!*" Bryce bellows into my headset. "I'm so sorry! We had to reset the bridge after yesterday's dress and it got all screwed up!"

"Ms. Teitelbaum and I are heading to the catwalk, Mel." Will sounds astonishingly calm considering that only through the grace of God and the other three cables is David not dead.

"Thank you, catwalk," I say, because I'm not sure what the protocol is for an SM responding to the news that a couple of crew members are heading out onto the narrow stretch of wire fifty feet above the stage to rein in a flying piece of scenery. All I know is, when you need to register that you heard something, you start by saying "Thank you."

"All right, everybody!" David calls from below. The body mic taped to his cheek makes his voice echo around the auditorium. He cleared the stage, as instructed, but instead of going backstage like I meant for him to do, he's climbed down the stairs to the house—on his crutches, no less—and now he's swinging his way slowly up the right aisle. He's in his full last-minute Javert costume, with the braided jacket and the ridiculous triangular hat Rachel just finished making this morning, not to mention the layers of caked-on makeup and the powdered gray ponytail that are supposed to make him look old and sallow. He's got a tall brown leather boot on one foot and a thick white cast on the other that his doctor forbade us to cover up.

But he's smiling in a way Javert never would. All sunny and devious, like he's plotting something that amuses him a *lot*.

"Looks like we've got some time to kill," David calls out to the audience of middle schoolers, "so . . ."

We absolutely do not have time to kill. We need Will and Bryce and any other human who knows how to handle rigging to *immediately* fix the problem with the bridge before it takes out the entire stage. I want desperately to go up there myself and help, but an SM can never leave the booth.

Besides, the very second the hazard is cleared, we need to get on with the IDR. The school day's almost over. If the final bell rings while our characters are still dying, the middle school kids will start stampeding for the doors en masse, and the actors will be singing their grand finale to a bunch of retreating backpacks. As if cast morale isn't already bad enough.

This entire rehearsal has been a disaster. *Everything*'s been a disaster for more than a week. With Gabby gone, it feels like my arm's been cut off. All the other crew heads and assistants are slammed, so I wound up promoting Michael Coken from the set crew to serve as a temporary ASM. He's trying hard, hovering backstage with Gabby's old headset, waiting for things to go wrong so he can anxiously report them to me and wait for my instructions on how to handle them. But he's no Gabby, and we've already had to deal with more nightmares today than I've ever encountered in a single rehearsal. The battery on Nick's mic inexplicably died in act one, and we had to switch it out with Lauren's while Nena raced to the scene shop for batteries. The new cart Dad built got stuck when the run crew was wheeling it onstage, and Jasmin had to run the fake strobe light twice while they struggled to unstick it. The actors keep tripping getting on and off the turntable, despite the fact that we've practiced every single entrance and exit dozens of times already. And now, we've got set pieces falling from the sky.

It's obvious we're all in *way* over our heads.

But right now, the middle schoolers couldn't care less. They're all leaning eagerly toward David. Audiences love it when something goes wrong onstage, and they love it even more when actors break the fourth wall. None of these kids has the slightest idea how close we are to a *major* disaster, because when you walk into a room with a stage, you leave fear and normalcy and risk outside. The magic of theater. Unless you're on the crew.

Will and Bryce have reached the catwalk now. I watch anxiously as they tromp back and forth fifty feet over David's head.

"What do you say we mix things up a little?" David calls, and that's enough to make the crowd cheer.

David starts clapping, too, but in that actor way—the one that makes everyone in earshot want to play along with whatever he's doing. He claps out a beat, and the kids quickly start clapping in time.

Then David opens his mouth and starts belting out "If I Were a Rich Man."

"He isn't." Jasmin's jaw drops beside me.

"Oh, he is." I've already registered it and moved on. My focus is still locked on the catwalk and making sure nothing else comes crashing down. But Jasmin starts laughing.

When we did *Fiddler on the Roof* two years ago, David was Tevye. Now he's singing his showstopping *Fiddler* solo while dressed as an ultra-serious French police inspector who's supposed to be jumping off a bridge to his death at this very moment. And who happens to be doing it all on crutches.

The audience adores it, obviously.

The feet on the catwalk have slowed down. A moment later, the bridge gradually begins climbing back into the rigging. The sight of it moving up instead of down elicits a new chorus of scattered laughter from the kids, but David never stops singing.

Will's voice sounds in my ear. "Ms. McIntyre, I think we've got it. Just testing now."

"Thank you, testing," I say, but I'm not ready to believe any problem is actually fixed on this show until I see it for myself.

The bridge starts coming down again as David enters the next verse. They're moving it extra slowly, but the cables hold.

David glances up, and I can tell he knows it's time to wind down.

"Everybody now!" he shouts, launching into the chorus one more time. The kids sing along and on the second line a piano joins in, making everyone laugh even harder. In the orchestra pit, Dr. Benjamin is cheerfully conducting while the pianist plays, and that's when I finally allow myself a second of laughter. If our straitlaced band teacher thinks it's okay to joke around, the crisis might really be over.

"Ready on flies, Mel." Bryce sounds breathless over the headset. "I'm *so, so, so, so* sorry."

"Thank you, flies. Mr. Green, can you confirm?"

"Yes, we're ready. You can give the *G-O*."

"Stand by, Michael, to signal Dr. Benjamin," I say just as David leads the audience into the last line of "If I Were a Rich Man."

"Thank you, uh, Michael," Michael says into the headset, panting as he runs down to the pit.

"*Go!*"

Michael must've given the signal successfully, because the piano switches seamlessly into the opening notes of "Javert's Suicide." In the pause before the full orchestra joins in, David does a mini bow over his crutches. It looks painful, but he smiles anyway.

"Farewell, Anatevka. And now, back to Paris!" He slowly climbs up to the stage, and I can *see* him putting Javert back on as the orchestra comes in. His steps are slower and heavier when he reaches the top of the stairs, and his movements are labored as he takes his place stage right, dragging one of his crutches behind him with tragic flair.

I brace myself for more problems, but the rest of the scene is astonishingly smooth. David picks up where Javert's song left off, and he manages to draw the audience back in right away. When the bridge finally comes down, exactly the way it should, the mood is so appropriately somber that not a single audience member laughs.

We had to modify the end of this scene during the nightmare that was tech weekend. The original plan had been for David to jump through the trapdoor, but that obviously wouldn't be safe now that he's got crutches and a cast to deal with. So now, David stares down mutely into a patch of lighting-effect-created water, somehow managing to convey the idea that he's about to jump without moving a muscle. Then Jasmin cuts to a blackout and the bridge flies back up, just like it's supposed to, and the audience gasps, just like *they're* supposed to.

How is this possible? When so many things have gone wrong, how does this show still make people *feel* so much?

Nothing major goes wrong for the next couple of songs, and the audience seems just as caught up in the story as they were before our bridge disaster. At yesterday's dress rehearsal we had a near-injury during the wedding dance sequence—Imani tripped over a skirt we hadn't hemmed short enough—but today everyone manages to stay on their feet. As the epilogue starts, it occurs to me that we might actually get the audience out of here before the bell.

"Stand by, light sixty-two," I say.

Jasmin nods and hovers her finger over the key without looking my way. We've been working together without any major issues, but we've made almost zero eye contact all week. It's obvious she still feels like I betrayed her. Which is fair, since that's exactly what I did.

Not everyone on the crew is being so professional, though. Most of them are still doing their jobs the way they always have, but I can hear the resentment in their voices over the headset when I give instructions. And all through tech, I got angry looks and eye rolls from the run crew. I wound up eating lunch in the booth both days so I wouldn't have to see all those judgmental faces turned my way.

"Lights, *go*," I say.

Nick steps onto the stage and slumps onto his death bench. Thanks to Jasmin, the special beams down perfectly, but Nick's sitting just to the right of where he should, so his face is half in the dark. Typical. A lot of actors have trouble finding their light, but Nick the Dick is especially bad at it.

I haven't spoken to him since the pep rally, and I'm hoping to get away without ever having to talk to him again for the rest of the show. Ideally, the rest of my life. His singing today has been all right, though.

"Stand by, light sixty-three . . . lights, *go*."

The spotlight comes on as Odile steps out, dressed all in white. I order myself not to react, but it doesn't work. It never does. The only time I see her now is when she's onstage, and every time I watch her enter, I nearly start crying all over again.

It's no surprise we keep having crises. Breaking up with her made me miserable, but it didn't make me any less in love.

The spotlight follows Odile as she glides across the stage and sings her first line, laying a gentle hand on Nick's shoulder. Somehow, she sounds better, clearer, than she ever has, and even though she's singing with Nick, her voice is so pure I forget she's acting. All I see is her, surrounded by a perfect halo of light. There's so much weight in her voice, so much *feeling*, I want to crumble into sawdust.

I can't believe I let her go.

"Stand by, light sixty-four." I swallow, trying to squeeze the tremor out of my voice. I can feel Jasmin's eyes on me, and I summon my Stage Manager Calm with all the strength I have left. "Lights, *go*."

The stage brightens, but my eyes are still fixed on Odile. The calm won't come. I swallow again. "Stand by, light sixty-five."

Somehow I hold it together through the curtain call, and the actors are taking their final bows to raucous applause just as the bell rings. The middle schoolers jump up and all try to leave at once, so I get on the walkie-talkie and tell the house manager to expect some chaos.

Jasmin shuts down the light board. There's nothing else for us to do in the booth, since the sound team is working from their table in the house. Kevin recovered from the stomach flu, thank God, but he's just as pissed at me as the rest of the crew, so it's probably a good thing that he isn't sitting up here with us.

"See you backstage," Jasmin says, nodding at me without meeting my eyes.

I nod back, rubbing my forehead as she leaves. This was scheduled to be an afternoon off, our first in weeks, but instead the whole crew is meeting for another last-minute costume workshop. There are still dresses and pants and prisoner jackets that need hemming.

"Ms. McIntyre?" Behind me, Will steps through the open booth door. He isn't smiling. "I've got an update on the rigging."

"That doesn't sound good."

"We need to triple-check everything before tomorrow. Not just the bridge, either—all the pieces that fly in or out. Ms. Teitelbaum and Mr. Levy said they could stick around. Do you have any veterans on the run crew who could help?"

"Everyone's working on costumes, but . . ." I sigh. "I'll broadcast to the backstage and ask. And I can help, too. I'm better at flies than costumes anyway."

"Good. It's all hands on deck. Keep your headset on when you come back."

Will leaves and I switch my mic to broadcast through the backstage speakers, asking for Rachel to send anyone she can spare to stage right in five minutes. Then I turn off my mic, climb to my feet, and start weaving my way through the house. The time it'll take me to walk backstage will be the closest thing I'll have to a break today, so I'm dragging my feet.

That's when the murmurs in the back row catch my attention. The house manager is long gone, so it's on me to kick the dawdlers out. I sigh and start toward them.

Until I realize one of the murmuring voices is extremely familiar.

"I know what you mean," she's saying softly. "You'd be surprised how common it is."

"But . . ." Another familiar voice sniffles. *Sniffles.* He's literally in *tears.* "I just feel so *useless.*"

"I understand, but the show must go on, remember?"

I'm so close it's a miracle they haven't seen me. But there's no way that's going to last—if I try to sneak away, the movement will get their attention. They'll think I was eavesdropping on purpose.

I clear my throat, and Nick and Odile both look up at once. Her eyes widen, but Nick drops his face into his hands and slowly climbs to his feet, leaving her alone in the back row.

"You might as well tell her too," he mutters to Odile. "I mean . . . please."

She nods. "I will. And my offer still stands."

"Thanks," he mumbles, so quietly I'm not sure he meant to say it out loud at all. Then he shoves his hands under his arms and stalks up the aisle toward the lobby. He's still in costume, and his white shirt is puffed out and drenched in sweat.

"Change into your street clothes," I call after him, because whatever else might be going on, we need that costume. "And give that shirt to Devin for the laundry."

Nick gives me a tiny nod, and then he's gone.

I have no choice but to turn to Odile. It's the first time we've been alone since that day in the dance studio, and everything I felt watching her onstage is bubbling up inside me all over again.

I'm sure she doesn't want me here. But *I* want to be here. I want to be wherever she is, always.

I fold my hands under my arms, the way Nick did. "So, um . . . was there something he wanted you to tell me?"

She tilts her head to one side, looking right at me. Making eye contact with her again after all this time feels like a gut punch. "Careful. Someone could see us talking."

The words hurt, but even so, I glance around the auditorium. Most of the cast is gone—probably in the lower-level dressing rooms, or, more likely, already on their way home, since for them this *is* actually a free afternoon—and only a few members of the run crew are onstage, resetting it for tomorrow. The others are probably back in the makeshift costume area.

"Ms. McIntyre?" Will's voice sounds in my headset. "We're holding on flies. I need to sand this piece down first. I told the others to go back to help Ms. Scott with costumes, but if you could stick around, that would be helpful. We may still need you."

I switch my mic back on. "Thank you, holding on flies."

When I turn it off again, Odile is still watching me.

She's in her street clothes, a surprisingly non-expensive-looking pair of jeans and a plain white T-shirt, but she hasn't washed off the angelic ghost makeup yet. The wigs we'd bought for her were ruined in the fire, so the hair and makeup team wound Odile's actual brown hair into elaborate waves. In this moment, she looks exactly like the glamorous movie star I always used to envision her as, before I really knew her.

"He's having a crisis of confidence." Odile sighs, meets my eyes again, and looks down at the empty seat beside her that Nick just vacated.

I hesitate—is she really okay with me getting that close?—but she nods down at it again. I sit gingerly, making sure not to put my hand anywhere near the armrest between us. Odile fixes her gaze on the stage.

"He is, huh?"

She nods. "Now that he's performed in front of an audience, he's afraid he's making a complete fool of himself."

I nod too. This is pretty standard actor stuff, especially for a first-time lead, but given that it's Nick, I don't feel particularly sorry for him. His voice hasn't cracked in any of the dress rehearsals so far, but I could tell he was holding back today on some of the tougher songs, as if he was afraid to let himself sing full-out. "And he decided to confide in you?"

"Yeah. He wanted me to help him convince Ms. Marcus to put on Andrew instead of him."

"*What?*" My heart starts thumping. No. *No.* This show is already maxed out on crises. My brain starts running a hundred miles an hour. "Oh, God—there's no time. We haven't rehearsed the understudies. I don't think Andrew even knows the *lyrics*. He probably can't do the falsetto, and the costumes *definitely* won't fit him, and we don't have time to rehearse the cart scene again. And we'd have to restage the sewer scene—there's no way Andrew could lift Malik like that. Actually, come to think of it, we could probably put Malik on for Nick, but then we wouldn't have a Marius and we'd be just as screwed—"

"Try to breathe, Mel. I talked him out of it." She meets my eyes again. Her gaze is slow and heavy, and I wonder how tired she is. If she's been having trouble sleeping, like I have. "Relax."

I want to take her hand. I want to take her hand *so much*.

"He didn't think he'd get the lead," she goes on, turning back to the stage. "He auditioned because his parents hired some kind of college counselor after football season didn't go as well as they'd hoped. The counselor said he should try out for the spring musical, to pad his extracurriculars and give him an essay topic. Something about translating his leadership and physical strength from the football field into the arts field."

"That's incredibly stupid."

She chuckles. "He used to sing when he was younger, and they hired him a vocal coach to prep for his audition, but once he got the role he was on his own. He thinks he yelled at that hockey game and gave himself laryngitis on purpose. Subconsciously."

"Great. Did you record him saying that? Because he tried to tell everyone it was *my* fault."

"Yeah . . . he mentioned that. He asked me to tell you he was sorry."

"Sure, I totally believe *that*."

She smiles a little, still looking at the stage. "He overheard you talking to the crew about him back in February. You said something—or he thought you did, anyway—about him not belonging in the show, and it got to him. He started blaming you for everything that was going wrong. Now he's finally figured out that didn't help anything."

"What? I never said anything like that. Or—wait . . ." *Did I?* I've talked to my friends about actors countless times. It never occurred to me that anyone might hear.

Nick may be awful, but we can't do this show without him.

"Anyway," Odile goes on, her voice still slow and heavy, "then he heard about the curse from Rachel, and . . ."

"What? *Rachel?*"

Odile nods. "They were together for a while. You didn't know?"

"*What?* No! I hear *every* rumor."

"They kept it under wraps. I didn't know, either, until we saw them together at that restaurant in the city."

"Wait. *Nick* was there that night?" That's when I remember the guy waving to Rachel with his back turned. He definitely had Nick's football-player frame. ". . . Oh. Oh, shit."

I must've screwed things up with Rachel worse than I realized. I wonder how much else I've ruined without even noticing it.

"For what it's worth, I really do think he feels bad. He knows he messed things up for you." Odile looks down at her hands. "And me."

"Well . . . he's not the only one who messed up."

She shrugs. If she heard the regret in my voice, she doesn't comment on it. "I said I'd help him rehearse one more time this afternoon, to get his confidence up. I hope he agrees. He isn't in a good place right now."

"And that's not good for the show." I meet her gaze again. "That was really nice of you to offer. Spending extra time with Nick the Dick isn't my idea of a fun afternoon."

She finally laughs, a real laugh, and shakes her head. "Is that what the crew calls him?"

"Some of us. I guess we should stop, though. It isn't cool to talk about the actors that way. I mean, if he overheard us back in February and it freaked him out that much . . ."

"Honestly, cliques are my least favorite thing about high school theater."

There's a damp spot on the shoulder of Odile's scoop-neck T-shirt. I want to touch it, badly. "Did he literally cry on your shoulder?"

She brushes at the damp spot. "Professional hazard. Get ready. SMs are most actors' favorite crying targets."

"So whose shoulder do *I* get to cry on?"

Her smile falters. "Mel, I . . . I talked to Dom last night."

For some reason, those words make my stomach give out. "Oh?"

"Yeah. He told me some stuff I didn't know."

"Such as?" But from the way Odile's gritting her teeth, I'm not really sure I want to know.

"Well, he said a bunch of things. But the one that stuck with me the most was that the superstition—the one about you not dating—he said the rule was actually that you . . . you weren't allowed to fall in love."

We're both looking straight ahead from the back row of a cavernous auditorium with the run crew still adjusting the sets on the stage in front of us. Somehow, though, it feels like we're in a tight, dark room, with nothing occupying the space but the two of us.

"He said that if you really believed you'd set off the curse . . . then it must mean you thought you were . . ."

I keep staring straight ahead. "Yeah."

"That you . . . I mean, that you and I were . . ."

"In love." I shut my eyes.

It's strange. This is hardly the first time I thought I was in love. Hell, I even thought I was in love with *Rachel*. I'd said those words to her—"I love you"—when we were still away at theater camp, a week or so after our first kiss.

Jasmin used to tease me about it. During the first couple of *R&J* rehearsals, she said I was as bad as Romeo, thinking he was head over heels for Rosaline and probably a whole parade of nameless girls before her.

Now I know better. I know what *real* love feels like.

But I never got to say those words to Odile. I lost her too quickly.

Stupid. I was so stupid. About so much.

"Yeah." I open my eyes. "I was. I mean . . . I am. In love. With you."

Onstage, someone yells, "Watch out!" I look up, on instinct, but it's just Michael tossing an empty water bottle to Melissa. They're both laughing.

"But you . . ." Odile shakes her head. I can't look at her, but I can feel the movement at my side.

She's so close. I could touch her hand, if she'd let me.

"You still . . ." She's stammering. I wouldn't have thought she *could* stammer. "You acted like the most important thing in the world was dealing with some superstition. You said you had to—to *fix this*. I remember those words so clearly."

"It's not about the superstition, it's about the show. Everything was falling apart. I couldn't let that happen."

"Because fixing the show mattered more than anything."

"I . . ."

"More than love."

I shut my eyes again. "When you put it like that it sounds really horrible, but . . ."

"Yes, it does."

"Okay, but—"

"Mel—for what it's worth, which I guess isn't much . . ."

Soft fingertips on my shoulder. I open my eyes and turn to face her. She's biting her lip. "I was in love with you, too."

She turns away again. And a second later, she's reaching for her purse.

"I—"

"It's okay. I know where I stand." She gets up so fast her purse catches on the armrest. She doesn't look at me as she disentangles it, but she puts on a strained smile. "We can pretend we never had this conversation. Or any other one, if you want."

"I'm so sorry, Odile, I—"

"Yeah, okay." The male voice is abrupt over our heads. I snap around to see Nick, still in his sweaty costume, his hand buried in his dark, curly hair. "Let's run the scene."

Are you serious?! I want to shout. But Odile's already smiling her Hollywood smile.

"Of course." She tosses her hair over her shoulder, as though nothing's wrong. As though nothing's ever *been* wrong. "The docks or the hospital?"

"Both. Hospital first, though, that one's harder." He's bouncing from foot to foot. Pure adrenaline.

I glance back up at the stage, but I can't see Will or Bryce. Well, they can call me on the headset if they need me. Besides, we need Nick as much as we need a functioning fly system.

To be honest . . . we need him more.

"I'll help." I sigh. "We can use the black box."

"Is it open?" Odile asks, still smiling brightly. Still acting.

I dangle my keys and force a smile of my own. Maybe it's time I learned to act. "It is if we need it to be."

Right now, putting on a perfect show is the only goal I might actually be able to pull off.

From: Melody McIntyre

To: All directors and crew heads

Date: Thursday, 4/30, 11:05 p.m.

Subject: Rehearsal report

Today's rehearsal:

- 12:20 p.m.–2:54 p.m.: Invited Dress Rehearsal (full show run-through)

Tomorrow's schedule:

- 7:00 p.m. PERFORMANCE (fight call 4:30 p.m.; all other cast/crew call time 5:00 p.m.)

Actor report:

- No absences
- Late: Noah (3 minutes—excused)

Set updates:

- We're still in the process of double-checking all the flies and related set pieces. Mr. Green or Mel will confirm when we're confident everything has tested safe.

Costume updates:

- Costumes are at long last COMPLETE. Thank you so much to everyone who pitched in to help this week.
- The costume crew is nonetheless expected to be on call

backstage on all show days to deal with the last-minute fixes that always spring up.

Lighting and sound updates:
- None.

Publicity update:
- Advance ticket sales are showing a near-sellout crowd for opening tomorrow. When walk-up sales are factored in, we expect a full house and may wind up having to turn people away (fingers crossed).

Thank you, everyone. —Mel

—Also stored on BHS performing arts department shared drive.
Created by: Melody McIntyre, stage manager, class of 2021
Viewable to: All crew and directors
Editable by: Current SM ONLY

Scene 8—Tech Booth, Beaconville High School Theater

HOURS UNTIL SPRING MUSICAL OPENS: 20

"Mel? You're still here?"

It's always strange to hear Will call me by my first name. "Yeah. Everything all right?"

"I saw your rehearsal report come through on my phone." He ducks into the booth, sliding a C-wrench into his pocket. The house below us is dark, with only the bare ghost light perched on the stage. "Do your dads know where you are?"

"Uh-huh. I've been texting Pops."

"You should get home. Your friends all left hours ago."

That's not technically true, but I don't correct him. After the other actors realized Odile and I were in the black box with Nick, some of them decided to put in extra rehearsal time too. I had to go backstage to work on the flies, but I let the actors stick around.

Dom and Malik wound up being the last to leave, so Dom stopped by the booth on his way out. And we . . . kind of had a fight.

Fine—I started it. I was mad at him for telling Odile about the curse. I thought he'd apologize right away.

But he didn't. In *his* opinion, he'd only been trying to help. And the next thing I knew, we were fighting about *everything*.

He's still angry that I ignored him during auditions. *I'm* still angry he abandoned the crew to act in the first place. *He's* mad I didn't tell him about me and Odile, even though he's been on my side about the curse from day one.

And, okay, he might've had a point about that last one, but there's nothing I can do about that now. All I know is, I'm working on an epic disaster of a musical, I'm in love with a girl who hates me, and my own best friend thinks I'm a screwup.

"I know," I tell Will, wishing I had another rehearsal report to write so I could think about *that* instead of all *this*. "I'm just polishing my prompt script."

He frowns down at my binder. "You've had that done since tech ended."

"We made changes during dress. I needed a clean copy."

"Listen . . ." Will pauses. "I've been meaning to talk to you."

"Oh God, what's wrong? Are the flies in even worse shape than we thought?"

"This isn't about the flies. Or, well, it isn't *just* about the flies." He meets my gaze. "I'm concerned about this show, Mel."

My heart flips over. Will doesn't say things like that without a reason. "Oh crap. Is the turntable having issues again?"

"No. Not yet, anyway. But all told, wouldn't you say we've had a fair number of problems?"

"I mean, yeah. There's a reason everyone thinks we're cursed."

"Yes, there is." Will drops into Jasmin's empty seat beside me. "It's because you're all in high school, and most of you have only worked on a handful of shows at most. You don't have enough context to realize exactly how many things *can* go wrong on a large-scale production."

"Come *on*, Will. Stuff doesn't just drop from the rigging on the regular in other theaters."

"Actually, it does." He nods, his gaze serious and steady. "Generally it doesn't happen during the IDR, and generally it doesn't involve such enormous set pieces, but this is hardly the first time I've seen something like this happen. It's the reason this industry has safety protocols. It's the reason *everyone* involved in a show needs to understand that these things *are* normal, and that the only way to stay safe is to follow the rules. We can't have people believing it's all controlled by supernatural forces, or they won't understand that they actually need to be careful. And that understanding has to start at the top. Which means you, Mel."

"Come on." I hate it when adults talk down to me. "I've poured *everything I have* into making this a perfect show. I've given up things I *really, really* didn't want to give up. I can't possibly work any harder than I already am."

"I'm not talking about working harder, I'm talking about the tone you set for your team. Tomorrow's opening night, and after everything that's happened, the cast and crew need to know they can do this. They need to believe you have faith in them to make this come off right."

I shake my head. "Things *can't* come off right on this show. Every possible thing that could go wrong, *has*."

"Not true. There's always room for it to get worse."

"Don't be ridiculous."

"I'm not being ridiculous." His face is dead serious. "There's a reason superstitions rise up among the people who do this work. It can be overwhelming, and sometimes it can help to believe the threat is coming from outside. All the same, though, we have to keep in mind that the real danger is right here in the real world."

"I mean, sure, we obviously need to be super careful, but there's no way to explain *all* the weird stuff that's happened in this theater. That fire started in a *locked room* for *no reason*."

"That's exactly the kind of thing I'm talking about." Will sighs. "There *is* a reason the fire happened, and it has nothing to do with any curse. The fire department investigated. The spark in the costume room started because of faulty wiring. It's been there ever since this building went up, and it was just a matter of time before it caught."

I pause. I don't have an answer for that. "They're positive?"

"They are. And the investigation found something else, too. The only reason the fire didn't spread was because the costume room was locked. Because *you* followed the safety protocol."

I can't hide how stunned I am. "But . . . but what about Julio getting hurt in that rehearsal? And when David broke his leg at my house, he didn't even fall that far—"

"Mel, we can't spend time analyzing every detail of everything that's ever happened. What matters is what happens next.

We need you to step up and be the leader your classmates desperately want. Not a dictator focused on arbitrary rules, but someone your friends will *want* to get behind and support."

He might as well have punched me in the face. "That's what I've been trying to be. Every single *day*. It's all I want in the entire world."

"I know. I heard you helped Nick get in some extra rehearsal time today, even though he isn't your favorite person. That's the kind of thing I'm talking about—the actions you can take that show your cast and crew you care about *them*, not the show."

"But caring about the show *means* caring about them."

"It needs to be the other way around, Mel. There's no such thing as a perfect show. If you keep striving for that, you'll burn out before you ever make it to your first paid stage management gig."

He's right. I already feel burned out, and I haven't even called my first musical yet. "But I want the show to be perfect."

"Of course you do. You wouldn't be a good SM otherwise." He smiles. "Speaking of which, when you're at camp this summer, you should really sign up for a costume class. I saw some of the sashes you made the other day, and . . ."

"I know, I know. I suck at sewing. Good SMs need to be able to do costumes."

"Exactly. You need to be able to pitch in absolutely anywhere."

"Is that why you used to be an *actor*?"

He grins. "I wondered when you were going to bring that up again."

"Which did you really want to do? When you were my age, I mean?"

"When I was your age, I wanted to be in Boyz II Men." His grin widens, the dimple in his chin flashing. "I didn't discover theater until college. But once I did, I wanted to do all of it, onstage and off. All that mattered was, I'd found my people."

I shake my head. "I can't imagine that."

"Well, you were lucky enough to find your people earlier than I did. And you've still got a long life ahead of you to imagine all sorts of things." He climbs to his feet. "Now, it's time for us both to be heading home. We've got a big day tomorrow."

My stomach roils. "I've just got to send a couple more emails."

His smile fades. "I don't feel right leaving you here by yourself."

"I promise, I'll be fast."

"Well . . ." He glances at his watch. "I'll text your dads and tell them you'll be home in twenty minutes. Sound good?"

As Will knows very well, my house is fifteen minutes from here. I sigh. "Fine."

"Good. See you in the morning. Oh, and watch your step if you go backstage. I tried to sweep up all the sawdust from the sander, but I might've missed some."

"Right." Tears spring to my eyes. "Sawdust."

Will shuts the door to the booth behind him, and I gaze down through the glass at the stage. The sparse prison set stands empty behind the ghost light, waiting for theater magic to fill it up tomorrow.

Unless there's no such thing as theater magic. Maybe that's no different from all the superstitions—something we pretend to believe in to make ourselves feel better.

I have no idea what I really believe at this point. All I know is I ended things with Odile, and it only made this mess get worse.

Maybe Will's right. Maybe all these rules I've been obsessed with following mean nothing at all.

Or maybe love is a kind of superstition, too.

I purse my lips, staring down at the set. The show's opening music is beautiful, and it's been on an unshakeable loop in my head for the past three weeks.

That's when I realize I've been softly whistling it ever since Will closed the door behind him.

And I don't actually want to stop.

The notes are powerful, even if my voice isn't. The simple, wobbly sound of my whistling fills the silent space around me.

All the rules I've been so obsessed with for all this time are meaningless. Arbitrary, like Will said. I gave up the person I cared about more than anything, and all because I was trying to follow those damn rules. Now I've got nothing to show for it but hollow misery.

The curse didn't screw me over. I did that all on my own. Maybe I only followed all those rules so I could tell myself my choices didn't matter.

Falling in love, though—*that* wasn't a choice. It was a gift. And I chose to let it go.

PRESHOW PERFORMANCE TASK SCHEDULE

Time to top of show	Task
2 hours, 45 minutes before	SM opens theater, turns on lights, preps backstage
2 hrs, 30 min before	Fight call (Valjean, Javert, Fantine, Factory Girl, Bamatabois & SM)
2 hrs before	Cast & crew sign in, start prepping costumes & checking equipment
1 hr, 30 min before	Begin hair & makeup for Valjean, Javert, Fantine, Thénardiers, Éponine & Cosette
1 hr, 15 min before	House manager checks climate, etc.
1 hr before	Final checks on costumes, props & makeup; put mics on principals; box office opens; ushers arrive & prep lobby
45 min before	Cast & directors onstage for pep talk & vocal warm-up
20 min before	Orchestra takes places & tunes up
20 min before	House manager opens house; audience begins to enter
15 min before	SM calls, "15 minutes, please" to cast & crew

5 min before	SM calls, "5 minutes, please"
Top of show	SM & house manager confer to set curtain time
Top of show	SM calls, "Places, please"
Top of show	SM & house manager confer one more time to ensure audience is seated; HM closes auditorium doors
5 min later	SM calls for house lights & preshow message, then cues conductor
GO!	*To the barricades!!!*

—Distributed by hard copy and emailed to all cast, crew, and directors.
Also stored on BHS performing arts department shared drive.
Created by: Melody McIntyre, stage manager, class of 2021
Viewable to: All cast, crew, and directors
Editable by: Current SM ONLY

Scene 9—Beaconville High School Theater

MINUTES UNTIL SPRING MUSICAL OPENS: 20

It's opening night.

Holy *shit*, it's opening night. And we're already *way* behind schedule.

"Mel, we need another backup yellow ticket," Michael whispers into the headset. I've learned the hard way that when he whispers, it means he's even more nervous than usual. "The backup Jacob had got used as a Post-it."

"Have him send someone from his team to check the art room." I rub my forehead. Normally, our crew heads and assistants are calm and collected on show nights, but this isn't any other show night. The crew is freaking out on level twenty, and from what I hear filtering over the headset mic whenever Michael gets near the dressing rooms, the actors are, too. "We probably won't even use the backup. We only need the ticket for the prologue anyway."

"Mel!" Bryce shouts, even though shouting over headsets is

very much against protocol. "Fatima says the casters for the stair-cases keep getting stuck."

"Tell her to chill," I say. "You have grease back there, right?"

There's a pause, and I hear Fatima's voice echoing through Bryce's microphone. She must be leaning in beside her. "Yeah."

"Apply liberally. It'll be fine."

"Does that scrim look like it's hanging at a weird angle?" Jasmin squints down at the stage from her seat next to mine.

"It looks fine to me." But now that she brought it up, I'm squinting, too. The last thing we need is for something *else* to come crashing down on us tonight.

The curtain's supposed to go up in minutes, but we've been fielding a pileup of mild- to medium-level disasters ever since fight call. As soon as the cast and crew arrived, the hazer set off the smoke alarm and we had to follow the evacuation protocol, so dozens of half-dressed actors and panicked crew members were halfway out the door before Will declared an all clear. Then, once everyone was back where they were supposed to be, the lace on Alejandra's wedding dress tore and necessitated frantic resewing by three different members of the costume team. Plus, the actors somehow already managed to use up all the cocoa powder we'd stockpiled, and Preston had to make a last-minute grocery store run. I gave him the emergency credit card and told him to buy out all the double-A batteries for the mic packs while he was at it, but he hasn't been seen since.

Worst of all, the turntable's jammed. If we can't fix it, we'll have to shut it down. That would mean improvising every set change all night, which would make the show half an hour longer. Odds are it would also lead to so many actors tripping over set pieces that we'd be lucky if we didn't wind up having to call an ambulance before the final curtain.

That turntable situation is actually a *high*-level disaster, come to think of it.

But I can't focus on it right now. I'm trapped in the booth until the show's over, so all I can do is wait for my team to update me on their progress. We haven't opened the house yet, but I can sense the press of the crowd from the lobby just outside.

"Caroline couldn't find any yellow paper in the art room," Michael reports. "And the original's gone missing, so now we don't have any yellow tickets, period."

"Mel?" Fatima seems to be speaking into Bryce's mic. "I can't get these casters to unstick. The panel for the inn scene won't roll at *all*."

"Imani just puked," Michael adds. "Ms. Marcus took her to the bathroom."

"There's always a freshman who pukes at opening," Jasmin says. I glance over, but she still won't meet my eyes. "Give her a breath mint, Michael. She'll be fine."

"Well, she thinks it might be norovirus."

"David's body mic isn't working," Kevin announces. "I replaced the batteries but it still won't switch on."

"Also . . . hey, uh, Mel?"

Something in Michael's voice now makes me pause. He's been dutifully informing me of backstage crises all night, and he's always sounded somewhere between level one and level five on the panic meter. He's too intimidated by the actors to reprimand them when they do something wrong, and he's too anxious around the crew to try to solve any problem himself. Will said that was the most I could expect of any last-minute fill-in ASM, so I've been trying not to get stressed out, even when Michael describes problems in the most dire whisper imaginable.

Right now, though, he doesn't sound panicky. He sounds genuinely overwhelmed.

I summon my Stage Manager Calm. "What is it, Michael?"

"Something's happening in the girls' dressing room. I think they're . . . fighting, maybe?"

Through the headset I can hear the sound of actors shouting over one another, with the occasional shriek mixed in. I close my eyes and take a deep breath, and I'm about to give Michael intervention instructions when—

"*Hey!* All of you need to chill the H-E-double-hockey-sticks out." A familiar voice rings through my headset. "Curtain's going up in twenty minutes and if you're bellowing at each other now, you won't have any vocal chords left to sing. Jillian, your braid's coming loose, go see Shannon and get her to put it back up. Christina, where's your apron? You should have it on by now. Did you leave it by the makeup table? Go pick it up and pray no one got lipstick on it. Leah, your cocoa powder's smudged around your eye. Don't worry, you've got time to fix it before you need to go on."

Oh my God—it's Gabby.

"Gabby, is that you? Are you back?" Now the voice I'm hearing is Michael's, and the only note in it is pure delight. "Do you want my headset?"

"No, Michael." I rub my forehead again. "I'm sure Gabby just came by to tell the cast to break a leg. Tell her I said hi, please."

The next sound I hear is the awkward rub of someone putting their hand over a mic. A moment later, Gabby's voice comes through more clearly than before. "Watch out, Lauren! David's trying to get by on his crutches. Sorry, Mel—I asked Michael to give me the headset after all."

"You did?" My breath catches, and I allow myself a fraction of a second to feel actual, genuine hope.

"Yeah, I . . . Julio, where's your jacket? Go find it, you should be upstairs. Mel, I was going to ask if it would be okay for me to ASM the show tonight after all. I was talking to my mom about it, and I realized it wasn't cool of me to leave when I did, since I made a commitment. I feel really bad for skipping tech and the last few dress rehearsals and—Katelyn, put that hammer down, you're not allowed to touch your props until right before you go onstage. No, it's okay, just go put on your jacket and get upstairs."

"Thank you, Gabby." I drop my face into my hands. Something good has actually happened. "Thank you, thank you, *thank you*."

"Indeed, you're welcome back, Ms. Piacine," Will says, and I hear a scattering of applause from the other headsets, too.

I grin. "But now, back to work for all of us. Gabby, tell Michael he's back on run crew and to go ask Fatima for an assignment."

"Already did. She's got him greasing the casters."

"And . . ." I swallow, trying not to think about the half dozen other people who can currently hear me. I need to say this, now. "I'm so sorry. You were right, Gabby, about everything. I violated your trust, and there's no excuse for that. I wish I could go back in time and make a different choice, but all I can do is promise that from now on I won't keep anything from you, or anyone else on this team. You're way too valuable for that. I got it in my head that all our problems were about some curse, but the truth is, I'm the one who screwed up." I sigh. "And now we're seventeen minutes to curtain and we still haven't opened the house and the turntable's broken and our Courfeyrac's puking her guts out. All I wanted to do was put on a perfect show."

"I thought you said there's no such thing as a perfect show," Gabby says. "Hey, Leah. No, no, that looks great, keep it exactly that way."

I freeze. "What? *I* said there was no such thing as a perfect show?"

"Yeah, in our very first meeting after I got the ASM job. You said the first rule of theater is that there's no such thing as a perfect performance and that we should just aim to put on something we feel really good about."

It's exactly what Will told me last night.

Maybe deep down, I knew it all along.

"Anyway, thanks." Gabby takes a breath. Her footsteps echo on the stairs—it sounds like she's going to the subbasement storage level. That's where her standard ASM preshow rounds start.

"For saying you're sorry. It might help if you told the others too."

"It might," Jasmin says.

Cautiously, I turn to look at her. For the first time in days, she meets my eyes. She nods, once, then turns off her mic and whispers, "And . . . I'm sorry too. I know you really liked her."

I nod back and bite my lip. I want to shut my eyes, to wallow for a moment, but—

"*MEL!*" Gabby's voice is sharp and sudden in my ear. "We need you, now!"

I jump forward, anxiously scanning the stage. The curtain is down, and I can't see anything happening under it. "What's wrong?"

It sounds like Gabby's running. I've never heard her sound so out of control. "We're in the subbasement! You've got to come, I don't know what to do!"

"Continue to hold on opening the house," I say into my walkie-talkie. I grab my binder, give Jasmin what I hope is a reassuring nod, and direct my smoothest voice into the mic. "Heads up, everyone. This is Mel, leaving the booth."

MINUTES UNTIL SPRING MUSICAL OPENS: 15

"You're here!" Gabby lunges toward me as soon as I hit the bottom of the stairs. "It's Estaban. He got bitten by a *bat*!"

"*What?*"

Everyone I see is running. Will is running toward the storage room door, and Ms. Qiao is running down the opposite set of stairs toward me. Meanwhile, Gabby's running back over to

Estaban, who's cradling his arm.

The subbasement storage room is dark and grimy, full of props from years' worth of shows, but I never thought there could be a *bat* in its depths.

"Oh, God." I run after her. "Estaban, are you okay?"

"It doesn't hurt." His face has gone pale, though. "I reached in to grab a backup sword, and I didn't think to turn the light on, but then—I felt something sharp, and—"

"Go upstairs!" Will shouts. "All of you!"

"How can I help?" I start toward the storage room door just as Ms. Qiao steps through it, raising a prop sledge hammer from *Beauty and the Beast* over her head.

"Stay out of here!" she calls. "I'm gonna get this sucker!"

Okay. Stage Manager Calm. Stage Manager Calm.

I've read every discussion thread there is on stage management best practice, but none of it's prepared me for what to do if my theater is invaded by flying animals and my props head becomes vampiric minutes before opening. I turn to Estaban, blood pounding in my ears. "We've got to wash out the wound. I'll get the first aid kit—the closest one's in the hall closet."

"No, you won't." Will swoops toward us, steering Estaban away. "Mr. Goodwin, you're coming with me. If that bat had—"

Estaban looks terrified. "If it had *what*?"

"Never mind." Will pats his shoulder and points to my headset. "We've got a show to mount. I need all students *off* the sublevel. Ms. Piacine, go wash your hands, *thoroughly*. Ms. McIntyre, remember the first rule of theater. *The show must go on*."

"Right." I nod, even though I'm still panicking. "So the bat won't—if it gets out or something—"

A sharp clatter from the storage room makes us all freeze.

"Almost had it!" Ms. Qiao bellows.

"The lady's got it under control." Will nods. "Go run your show, Ms. McIntyre."

MINUTES UNTIL SPRING MUSICAL OPENS: 10

I haven't even made it one level up before the crises are swelling up again.

"What should we do if Imani can't go on?" Gabby asks over the sound of running water. She's still in the bathroom, scrubbing her hands. "It's okay if she isn't in the scene for 'At the End of the Day,' but we'll need to have someone else do the dance number in 'Lovely Ladies'—maybe Madison could? Either way, someone else will have to go on as Courfeyrac, unless we give her lines to Christina or something. But wait, can Madison do the dance without practicing it at all, or should we change the blocking? Or we could run it really quickly—Michael could take them to the dance studio to work on it during the prison scene. Or Peyton could, since she's dance captain. Should I go ask Ms. Marcus?"

"I—I don't—let me think." I press the headset into my ear. Gabby's mind is already racing twenty steps ahead, and mine should be too—that's an SM's entire job description—but I'm still trying to navigate the stairs back up to the stage level, and *then* I'll have to run back to the booth, and there are already frenzied actors and crew members everywhere I turn.

"Did something seriously *bite* Estaban?" Jacob's the first one who grabs my arm.

"Yep. You're acting props head until further notice."

"Oh, God." All the color drains from his face.

"What the hell is *happening* in this theater?" Christina charges up the steps toward me in her factory worker garb, shoving her cocoa-powdered face straight into mine. Her eyes are bright, and her lower lip is trembling. "We've got *wild animals* in here now? How much else are you and your stupid girlfriend going to *ruin*?"

I think of what Odile said, about actors needing shoulders to cry on. But Christina's makeup is already done, which means I need to fix this without tears.

"Hey. Christina." I switch off my mic and lower my voice, stepping toward her so no one else can hear. "It's going to be all right. You're an amazing actor, and your singing is gorgeous. You got a standing ovation every night as Juliet, and I've heard you in rehearsals—you've hit every note every time in 'At the End of the Day,' and your 'Drink with Me' solo last week was breathtaking. This time next year, you'll be starring in every show your college puts on, and you won't believe you were ever as nervous about going onstage as you are right now."

Christina doesn't move. I don't think she's even breathing. After a long, heart-pounding pause, during which I do my best to keep track of the urgent reports filtering in through my headset about the status of the turntable without letting any of it show on my face, she whispers, "You really thought 'Drink with Me' was good?"

"I'd never say so if I didn't. You trust me, right?"

"I . . ." She holds my gaze. Tears are starting to form in her eyes.

"You *cannot* cry." I reach into my fanny pack for a tissue. "Your cocoa powder is exactly right as it is. If gets tear-streaked it'll be distracting. You're supposed to look like you're pissed at Fantine, not like you just watched the *Friends* finale again."

She starts laughing and dabs at her eyes. "I'm sorry."

"It's okay. Now go get in character. Do some of those vocal trill things Ms. Marcus is always making you practice."

"Mel!" When I finally step back and sync my brain into what's happening on my headset, it's utter chaos. Jasmin's the one frantically reporting now. "The house manager's in the booth. She says we're already ten minutes late and there'll be a stampede out in the lobby if we don't open the house!"

"Tell her two more minutes." I pant into the mic.

"Mel." It's Gabby. "Three of the prisoners' costumes shrank in the wash, and now Julio's jacket won't close and his factory worker shirt is showing underneath. What should we do? Rachel's busy—George's dog stepped on his cape and now it's got a hole so she's fixing it."

"What's George doing bringing his cape home for his dog to step on?" I groan. "Never mind. Tell Rachel we're in triage mode. Convict jackets beat farmworker capes. Tell her—I don't know, tell her the hole will add verisimilitude."

But now the questions are flying faster than ever, from every corner.

"Mel! I can't get that mic to work, I've tried everything—"

"Mel, the casters still won't roll and Fatima's panicking—"

"Mel, the actors are scared to leave the dressing room in case the bat gets loose, and I heard some of the run crew saying they were going outside in case it—"

This has to end. "Quiet," I say into the mic.

Everyone on the headsets stops talking at once. And I do the only thing I can think of—I change the setting on my mic to *broadcast*.

MINUTES UNTIL SPRING MUSICAL OPENS: 6

"Hey, everybody?" My voice echoes in my ears. I'm still on the dressing room level under the stage, but my mic is pumping my words out to the entire team. The whole cast and crew can hear me, in the dressing rooms, in the wings, in the booth, in the prop rooms. Faint strains are probably echoing even into the vast, empty house. "I need your help."

Imani steps out of the bathroom. She's in her peasant gown for "At the End of the Day," a soft layer of cocoa powder caking her cheeks. She's trembling, but at least she isn't puking anymore. "Mel? How long until top of show?"

"Ten minutes, give or take." It's actually now five minutes, twenty-nine seconds, and I *really* need to get back to the booth, and we *really, really* need to open the house if we want to have any hope at all of starting anywhere close to on time. But I don't say any of that. "I need everyone's attention. Cast *and* crew."

Actors spill out of both dressing rooms, and a few crew

members gather around, too, even though most of them are up on the stage level. A few feet down from me, Rachel is crouched in front of Julio, frantically stitching the long prison jacket he's wearing. She glances up at me, two pins sticking out from the corner of her mouth.

In my headset, Gabby says, "I'm stage right. The run crew's listening, Mel."

The crowd around me is growing. Dom steps out of the boys' dressing room into the back of the group. He's in his prisoner garb for the opening scene, and under his cocoa powder his face is as green as it was at auditions. Nick's leaning against the wall opposite him in *his* prisoner garb, looking exactly as terrified as you'd expect a guy who's about to carry an entire show on a less-than-perfect baritone to look. Next to him, three of the freshman ensemble guys are shaking so hard I'm surprised they haven't fallen over. I gaze out across the group, trying to organize bullet points in my head.

That's when I spot Odile.

She's at the very back with Alejandra and Leah, standing silently with her arms folded, looking straight at me. She's in her factory dress and apron, her hair curled and cascading around her shoulders, her makeup muted. She looks absolutely perfect. It's obvious she's 100 percent ready to go onstage, regardless of what Dom told her about me, or what the other actors were fighting about in the dressing room just now, or what she thinks of the bat attack or the puking freshman or the faulty turntable or any other crisis threatening our show.

Odile's here to do her job. She'd never let doubt or fear get in the way when she knows she's capable of something.

Will's words float back to me. *The cast and crew need to know they can do this. They need to believe you have faith in them to make this come off right.*

Forget bullet points. I've got to trust my instincts.

"Okay, everyone." I try as hard as I can to project Stage Manager Calm into the mic. "You all know we've been having a tough time with this show."

"Yeah, 'cause we're cursed," someone mutters. I don't bother turning to see who.

"I don't know if we have a curse or not." My voice echoes from the speakers on the walls. The cast falls silent, the same way the crew does when I call for quiet. "What I *do* know is, it doesn't matter. We have something that's stronger than any curse, and that's *us*. As long as we trust each other, all we have to do is work hard and let theater magic do the rest."

"Okay, but I heard the crew guys saying the turntable's all screwy." Leah doesn't look angry or resentful. Just afraid. "How can we go on without the turntable?"

"Or what if something falls on us, like in the IDR?" one of the ensemble guys asks.

"We'll fix it," I tell them, amazed at how chill my own voice sounds. I don't have to summon my Stage Manager Calm anymore—it's showing up all on its own. "It's on *all* of us to work together to solve problems and follow the rules. That's how we make sure nobody gets hurt, and it's how we put on the best possible show we can. There are hundreds of people out in the lobby waiting to see what we can do, and now we've got to show them exactly how strong we are. Together."

Together.

My eyes find Odile's again.

"Together." Nick nods. He turns to the ensemble guys next to him and raises his eyebrows. "Right?"

"Together," the guy next to him says, a little awkwardly. Then he nods and says it again. "Together."

Nick nods back at him.

"Together," the two guys next to him say, in unison. Then more of the actors join in, and it starts to form a chant.

"Together."

"Together."

"Together!"

On my headset, Gabby joins in. I can hear the run crew behind her, and Jasmin in the booth, and the rest of my crew doing the same thing. *"Together!"*

Rachel snips a thread on Julio's jacket and climbs to her feet. She holds my gaze and gives me a nod. "Together."

"We're the ones in charge of making this show a success," I say, standing taller. The chanting fades out, but the cast and crew members around me look like they're standing a little taller now themselves. "No one else is going to swoop in and save the day. No one but us will be responsible if something goes wrong. This is *our* show, and I know exactly how much it means to every single one of you. Because it means that much to me, too."

They're all nodding now. The cocoa-powdered faces of the actors and the black-clad crew members are all moving as one, for the first time ever.

"Now, I need *everybody*'s help. We've got to find a new yellow ticket, grease the casters so the panels for the inn will roll in, and get David a body mic that works. And we've got to test the turntable again." I take in a long breath. "Actors, I need you to get into your characters and be ready to sing like you've never sung before. And all of us have to do it while the house is coming in. Do you think we can?"

"To the barricades!" Dom shouts. Everyone laughs, and then they start clapping. People are actually *smiling* now, the eager, we're-nervous-but-we-can-*do*-this smiles that always mean a show's going to be good.

"All right." I'm breathing hard, but I nod. *"To the barricades!"*

I let myself steal one more glance at Odile before I take off for the booth. She's still looking right at me. She's clapping, too.

MINUTES UNTIL SPRING MUSICAL OPENS: 4

"Mel?"

I pause midway through running up the aisle and spin around on my heel. Dom followed me out into the house. He shouldn't be here in his costume, but there's no time for reprimands. Besides, come to think of it, I could use his help.

"Hey," he says. "That was a good speech."

"Thanks. It was unplanned."

"All the better."

"And . . . I'm sorry." I shake my head. "I've been a cruddy best friend, but I'm so, so proud of you. I was cheering for you so hard up in the booth in every dress rehearsal during 'One Day More.'"

"I saw." He smiles. "I always look up there. Force of habit. But anyway, I came to say I'm sorry too. You're the only best friend I'll ever want, cruddy or otherwise."

"Mel? Why aren't you in the booth?" Gabby comes running up behind him from the wing, her headset mic bouncing. When she realizes which of the opening-number prisoners I'm talking to she slows down, her expression shifting from stressed to slightly giggly. It's still so weird to see them together. "Fatima finally got the casters unstuck. We can open the house."

"Good. I'm going back up to the booth in seconds, literally. But first I need you two—and it actually has nothing to do with *Les Mis*."

Both of their eyebrows shoot up at once. It's actually pretty funny. I never noticed the way they both do that.

"Or, not much, anyway," I amend.

I tell them what I want to do. At first they just stand in silence, their eyebrows creeping higher. Then Gabby starts laughing. "You're serious."

"Completely."

"Doesn't this go against your entire life philosophy?" Dom tilts his head. "In fact I distinctly remember you once telling me that this kind of thing ruins the entire illusion of theater."

"Yeah, well, it turns out there are more important things than illusions. Are you up for it?"

"Absolutely. I think it's great."

"Me too." Gabby nods. "How much time do we have?"

"None, basically. We've got to do as much as we can during intermission."

"On it." Dom nods too. "I'll talk to Nick and the others."

"And I'll talk to Ms. Marcus," Gabby adds. "When I'm not doing the fifty other things I'm supposed to do during intermission."

"Don't worry, Mel. It'll be perfect." Dom grins.

"There's no such thing as perfect." I grin back. "That's the one thing I know for sure."

Now I've got to show Odile I know it, too.

STAGE MANAGEMENT POSTSHOW CHECKLIST

All tasks are to be executed by SM/ASM immediately following curtain call. NO EXCEPTIONS.

Task
Call final cues (curtain, lights, house lights)
Ensure house manager opened auditorium doors
Ensure actors removed all flowers and other trip hazards tossed by audience from stage
Shut down projector
Direct run crew to clear stage, placing set pieces in safe positions
Reset props tables and move prop bread to teachers' lounge refrigerator
Confirm with sound whether any additional batteries are needed for next show
Ensure mic packs are safely stored
Ensure actors removed and properly stored all costumes, including accessories and wigs
Sweep & mop the stage
Check trash cans to make sure they aren't so bad we'll get in trouble with the janitors

	Empty booth trash
	Make sure everyone's left the building (cast, crew & audience)
	Turn on ghost light
	Turn off all other lights
	Lock doors
	The barricade has fallen

—*Distributed by hard copy and emailed to all cast, crew, and directors.*
Also stored on BHS performing arts department shared drive.
Created by: Melody McIntyre, stage manager, class of 2021
Viewable to: All cast, crew, and directors
Editable by: Current SM ONLY

Scene 10—Beaconville High School Theater

MINUTES UNTIL OPENING NIGHT CURTAIN CALL: 0

The cast is still belting out the last note of their "One Day More" reprise when I spring out of my seat for the second time tonight. Jasmin holds up her hand, and for a panicked second I think she's going to physically stop me from leaving, until I realize she's only trying to high-five me.

"Awesome show," she says. "Almost perfect."

"Uh-huh." I can't think in terms of perfection right now. "Stand by, light sixty-four. . . . Lights, go."

My hands are twitching, and my feet are, too. I need to be backstage. I need to be backstage *now*.

"This is Mel, going off headset," I say into the mic. "Gabby's calling the last few cues from the booth."

"You're doing *what*?" Jasmin's mouth drops open, and now she *does* look like she might try to physically stop me.

"I just—need to do something. Don't worry, it'll be fine." I pull the headset down around my neck, switch off my mic, and lunge for the booth door.

Gabby's there waiting for me. We exchange lightning-quick nods before I take off running.

The house is way too chaotic for me to navigate. The show got a massive standing ovation, and most of the audience is still on its feet clapping and whistling, but as always a handful of people are also charging up the aisles toward the lobby. (When you sit in the all-seeing tech booth, you figure out fast which audience members have the smallest bladders.) So I duck through the side hall. I dodge all the parents carrying flowers, crossing my fingers that my own dads are still in their seats. Fortunately, there's no sign of them, and the audience is still roaring when I push through the back door to stage right and step into the wing.

It's strange being onstage during a performance, even if I am concealed behind the curtain, and even though the actual performing part is over. The cast is just a few feet away from me, and every single actor is basking in the glory of this drawn-out ovation. To be honest, I'm pretty into it, too.

People liked our show. That's rather cool. We had a late start, but the turntable worked, the actors mostly did what they were supposed to, the bridge flew in without killing anyone, and whole chunks of the audience were sobbing at the big death scenes while I called the light cues.

That's not what I'm focusing on at the moment, though. My brain only has space for five words right now.

This plan had better work.

Most of the cast has no idea I'm back here. Actors never look at the wings during curtain call, not when there are adoring fans to look at instead. But a few of the freshmen on the run crew are gaping at me. Seeing a stage manager outside the booth during a show is like seeing a unicorn strolling through Boston Common.

The cast takes one more bow. Another, louder, cheer rises from the crowd, and the actors grin at each other. Ms. Marcus told the cast they should stay in character for the first part of the curtain call, but that after the reprise it was okay to let go a little.

It's hard for me to see the principals from here—they're all downstage, so there are dozens of other actors' backs between them and me—but when two of the ensemble guys step forward to wave to the audience, I get my first glimpse of Odile. She got the biggest cheer during the bows, naturally, and now she's standing between Nick and David, turning around to clap for the others. She's still wearing her white dress from the finale, with her angel makeup and her hair down around her shoulders, giving her a soft glow. I step behind another cluster of ensemble members before she can spot me.

A few of the actors start to ham it up. Julio and Beth do a jaunty little jig, with her swinging him around like they're on one of those shows where dancers wear sequins and spandex and get voted off. David waves a crutch in the air, and there's a wave of laughter along with the cheers as the lights over the stage shift.

That was the second to last light cue of the show. My headset's still hanging around my neck, so I didn't hear Gabby call it, but the stage is washed in a full, wide light.

That's our sign.

I turn back toward the platform at upstage center. Dom's already climbing onto it, the flag gripped tightly in his fists. He's still in his red-and-gold barricade vest, but he washed the fake blood off his face, and as he climbs up above the rest of the cast it looks like his character's coming back to life.

The crowd's laughter fades, awe surfacing in its place. Something new is happening, and they know it.

The cast is starting to figure it out, too. Some have already turned around. A few of the actors know what's happening, but the rest are looking back at Dom in confusion.

I crane my neck for another glimpse of Odile. She looks as puzzled as the others, but she's smiling at Dom anyway.

Then Nick starts to sing again, and everyone—cast, crew, and audience alike—lets out a collective gasp.

"One thing mooorrrrre!" he bellows, just like he did in the real song, but a cappella. His voice sounds better than it has all night, now that the show's over and the pressure's off.

But it's funny, too, and it's meant to be; the audience laughs, and the cast joins in. I even hear a couple of chuckles from behind me—the crew, genuinely amused by Nick the Dick for the first time ever.

Odile is still right beside him, and she gives him a quizzical look, but Nick manages not to give it away. He just claps his hands in front of him and says solemnly, the mic taped to his cheek carrying out his words to the entire auditorium, "We've received an urgent message from our stage manager. It's for Fantine."

He says it in his vaguely British-y Valjean voice, and for a second the audience seems to think he's serious. They get quieter, creating exactly the hush we were hoping for.

That's when Dom waves his arm, exactly the way he does when he gives the signal in the first barricade scene in act two. The cast onstage splits in half, the actors who know what's happening pulling the others aside. When the path is clear Dom jumps off the platform and runs downstage, still waving that flag. It's started to unfurl, but he's moving too fast for anyone to read it.

That's when I step onto the stage, and everyone suddenly turns to look at me.

I'm not supposed to be here. I'm in rumpled show blacks and frizzy hair. My headset's still hanging anachronistically around my neck, and my face is sweaty and makeup-free.

I'm the exact opposite of angelic Odile Rose. But her eyes latch on to me, her lips parted slightly, and she doesn't seem to mind.

Dom runs toward where she's standing at downstage center, waving the flag more slowly. I never would've been able to get the flag done if it hadn't been for Rachel. I didn't plan to ask her for help—when I ran to the makeshift costume area backstage at the start of intermission, I was aiming to throw something together myself with fabric scraps and Sharpies in the couple of minutes I had free before I needed to be back in the booth for act two. But Rachel saw what I was doing, came straight over, took the biggest piece of white fabric out of the scraps basket, and set up the sewing machine without even asking if I needed help. I told her what I was trying to do, and she told me the story of how she'd dumped Nick after she heard the way he talked about the crew. She apologized for telling him about the curse, too. I resisted the urge to ask why she'd ever gone out with him in the first place.

Either way, it's thanks to her that the flag looks so amazing, especially for something made out of scraps in minutes. It's very appropriate for this show, come to think of it.

Dom crosses the stage and passes the flag to me with a flourish. I take it, nodding at him in thanks, and he gives me a sweeping bow, earning another round of cheers from the crowd before he steps off to the side. I can't believe it took me years to realize he was such a freaking *actor*.

I take a deep breath. I know what I have to do, but every cell in my body is resisting it. Even so, I step forward, passing the rest of the cast until I've joined Odile at downstage center, right in front of everyone, as the voices in my head shout *Stop!* and *Hide!* and *Don't you realize THIS GIANT INDISTINGUISHABLE MASS OF PEOPLE IS LOOKING AT YOU RIGHT NOW???*

I order the voices to shut up and I hold out the flag so Odile can read it.

She smiles at me, then turns to stare at the flag. Her eyes go wide. Then she covers her mouth with her hand. Her shoulders begin to shake, like she's laughing and crying all at once.

The audience can see the flag now, too. There's a chorus of "aww"s and cheers, but I ignore them. I only have eyes for her.

"Odile . . ." I have to fight to get the words out, because I'm laughing and crying at the same time, too.

I can barely speak above a whisper. Odile has to step forward to hear. I considered using the mic, but decided against it. I'm not doing this for anyone but her.

As she closes the distance between us, though, the crowd's cheers swell up even louder. Complete strangers are whistling at us. Whistles from the audience aren't bad luck, but they're embarrassing, and I can't help blushing. Odile's cheeks are pink, too, as she reaches around and turns off her mic pack.

The flag is made of white muslin left over from *Fiddler*. Rachel and I hemmed it to put in loops and painted "PROM WOULD BE MISÉRABLE WITHOUT YOU" in red glitter, then attached it to the backup flagpole from the prop closet.

In my opinion, the occasion called for something theatrical.

"Odile, I . . ." I hold up my hands to either side of my face like blinders, trying to tune out everyone else in the room. "I'm sorry. You were right, about all of it. You're so much more important to me than trying to put on a perfect anything. And I . . ." I swallow again. My bright-red cheeks are probably visible from space. "And I love you. Would you be my prom date?"

There's shouting and jostling in the house and on the stage as the cast crowds around us, craning in to hear. Everyone's looking at Odile, waiting for her to answer. Even some of the orchestra members are standing up, leaning back to watch from the pit with their instruments tucked under their arms.

Odile finally pulls her hands away from her face. She's laughing that genuine laugh I love so much.

She nods, and then she's throwing her arms around me, and I'm not sure my life has ever been better than it is in this moment.

The next thing I know the whole cast is on us and we're all hugging at once, Odile and me at the center of it, both of us cherry-red and grinning. Even some black-clad run crew members are laughing in the back of the giant hug pile. They must've come in from the wings, too.

I shut my eyes and collapse against Odile. She's holding me, and I'm holding her, and it's exactly what I need. The *only* thing I'll ever need.

"Mel!" Gabby's voice echoes up from the headset around my neck. She's shouting so loud I could probably hear her from the booth itself if the audience wasn't cheering so loudly. "Get back on headset! I'm glad she said yes and everything but the theater's about to—"

That's when the lights go out.

I leap back, panicking. Is it a power outage? What the *hell*? It's a gorgeous day, there's no reason for the power to—

The curse, the curse, the curse! It's real after all!

I pull the headset back up around my ears and frantically switch on the mic. "Gabby? What's going on? Do we need to evacuate?"

But the crowd is still laughing. That's when I realize the power can't be out, not completely—a few lights are still shining upstage. I was so overwhelmed I didn't even notice.

When I catch my breath and look up at the booth, Gabby, Will, and Jasmin are all pointing down at me through the glass, smirking.

They *pranked* me. Oh my *God*. I want to flip them off, but there are kids in the audience.

They bring the lights back up to a full stage wash, and the audience lets out another roar. Now that I'm seeing them straight-on, the giant mass of people isn't quite so scary. Just faces, beaming at us. My dads are in the second row, both of them holding out their phones to take pictures. That's against the rules and also mortifying, but I don't even care because I'm just so *happy* right now.

The curtain comes down, slowly, with the audience still cheering on the other side. And when I look down, Odile's hand is linked in mine.

I squeeze it and pull her toward the wings, and she follows, still smiling.

EPILOGUE
One Year Later

Good evening, and welcome to the Beaconville High School production of The Phantom of the Opera.

You are now entering nineteenth-century France, so please take a moment to turn off any devices that haven't been invented yet.

There will be one fifteen-minute intermission following the first act. In case of emergency, exit through the marked doors.

Now—to the opera!

—Preshow script recorded by Malik Sexton with Melody McIntyre assisting, to be played before all dress rehearsals and performances.
Also stored on BHS performing arts department shared drive.
Created by: Melody McIntyre, stage manager, class of 2021
Viewable to: All cast, crew, and directors
Editable by: Current SM ONLY

Tech Booth, Beaconville High School Theater

The lights spark. The audience gasps. And, right on cue, the chandelier crashes down.

Or, rather, it *flies* down, looking fast and dangerous, even though it's precisely controlled. We know it's precisely controlled, because we've run this cue at least a hundred times in the past two weeks, but I still hold my breath every time. That chandelier cost more than our entire budget for *Little Women* in the fall.

As always, the cables hold. The chandelier "crashes" onto the stage, a horrified-looking Alejandra darts out from beneath it just in time, and the audience explodes with cheers.

I stop holding my breath and bark out the cues.

"Stand by, curtain and lights to blackout. Blackout—*go*. Curtain—*go*. Stand by, house lights. House lights—*go*."

The lights fade up slowly, but the applause keeps going even with the curtain down.

"We did it!" Bryce bellows into my headset. "Oh my God, *we did it!*"

"Well done, Bryce and team." I smile into my headset. "Imani, tell the actors to take ten. And you can take ten, too."

"Maybe I'll take eleven just to see what happens," Imani chirps back.

I laugh. "Do it."

"Thanks, boss." Imani's been calling me "boss" ever since tech week. Despite her stellar singing voice, she decided the best way to deal with her intense stage fright during *Les Mis* was to switch to crew, and she's the new ASM now that Gabby's been promoted to assistant costumes head. Imani's good at this, too, even with her weirdly formal headset etiquette. "Signing off."

"Same here. This is Mel, going off headset."

I'm exhausted as I stand up to stretch, but mostly, I'm delighted. It's opening night of *Phantom*, and we hit almost every cue in the first act. Aaron's mic stopped working on the first line of "Notes . . . ," so the assistant sound head ran out onstage to give him a handheld mic, but it wound up being cool. The audience laughed, and Aaron swung the mic around and hammed it up like a lounge singer.

It hasn't been a perfect show, but that's okay, because it's been *fun*.

We agonized over every detail of how to stage it for three months, but tonight the acting, the music, the sets, the lights, the sound, and all the rest of it came together exactly as we'd hoped. More or less, anyway. Plus, Malik and Alejandra have *serious* chemistry onstage, and off, too. We'd already decided not to run the actor hookup pool anymore, since it turns out actors are real people and not semi-entertaining Barbie dolls, but even if we'd kept it up, we would've had to call it off for this show anyway since the winners would've been way too obvious. There were several polite coughs over the headset when Phantom and Christine came *way* closer to kissing than my blocking notes said they were supposed to during "The Music of the Night."

But I don't have time to worry about actor drama tonight. There's something I have to do.

I leave my headset on the desk and reach for the doorknob, ready to yank it open. As usual, I'm in my show blacks, and I'm rumpled and sweaty and my hair's a mess, but I don't care. I'm going down into the house, to where I last saw her in row C, and—

But when I fling open the door, Odile's already flinging herself on me.

"Do you hear that?" Her voice is muffled against my hair, and her arms are tight around my neck. She's wearing her old *Les Mis* T-shirt, and her hair's flowing down her back in messy waves. She's never looked better. "They're *still* cheering for that effect. This show is everything you wanted it to be."

"Uh . . ." Jasmin gives us a slightly amused head shake. "Be back in three, Mel."

"Take five."

Jasmin laughs as she edges past us. I wrap my arms around Odile's waist and squeeze her tight. "You know very well this show's ridiculous. It's got more melodrama than *Titanic*."

"Who cares? The cast sounds *amazing*. And that set, and the costumes—and the *chandelier*! Seriously, I've seen *Phantom* on Broadway *and* the West End, and this chandelier crash was the scariest one yet."

I try to keep a straight face, but a giggle bursts out. Odile's still the only one who's ever been able to make me giggle. "Thank you for saying that. I don't believe you at all, but it was really sweet."

I lead her deeper into the empty booth, collapse onto a beanbag, and pull her down beside me.

I kiss her. She kisses me back. And for a few precious seconds I don't think about my intermission task list, or the staircase the run crew is carefully maneuvering into place right now, or whether anyone's trying to reach me on the headset that's still lying on my desk, because in this moment, she's my entire world.

"Listen . . ." I haven't planned what I want to say, but that's probably a good thing. These days, the more I just let things happen, the more I relish every moment. "Thanks for coming tonight."

"Are you kidding?" She sweeps her hand around at the booth, the auditorium, the stage below with the heavy curtain hanging. "This is my favorite place."

"Still?" I prop myself up on my elbows. "What about that black box at Tisch where you did that play with the glitter masks?"

She laughs. She's been doing that a lot more since she came back from London. "That show was so stupid."

"It was awesome. I love experimental theater. Especially when it involves you doing pantomime in a catsuit."

"I'll bet you do." She laughs again.

Odile finally worked up the nerve to tell her agent she didn't want to do the Netflix show—and that she wanted to go to college once the Scorsese movie wrapped. Her agent wasn't thrilled, but as far as I can tell, Odile's been in heaven all semester.

I took the train down to visit her over spring break, and it was quite possibly the most awesome two days of my life. I think Pops was hoping I'd decide to join Odile at NYU, but I convinced my parents to compromise and we agreed on SUNY Purchase. With a double major in stage management and psychology, partly to shut Pops up, but also because I've realized stage management is equal parts technical expertise, organizational skill, and managing other people's moods.

Plus, Purchase is just an hour north of New York. Which means next year I can swing by and watch more of Odile's experimental theater productions, and *she* can come up and watch me scurry around the stage with the rest of the freshman run crew.

We never officially said we were going to do the long-distance-relationship thing. It just sort of . . . happened. When Odile left for the airport last June, we hugged goodbye for ten straight minutes, but we never actually made any out-loud promises. Even so, she emailed me as soon as she got to her hotel that night, and I wrote back the instant I woke up in the morning.

We wrote to each other every day from then on. We still write every day, even when we're in the same city. There have been mornings when I typed out my message to her, silently smiling into my phone while she slept just a few feet away. Even when she sleeps, she looks like she's posing for some glamorous photo shoot. That's just who she is.

I love who she is.

When her movie wrapped, she flew back to the US, did a play down in DC for two months—she'd asked her agent to find her theater work during her school breaks—then came back to Beaconville before she left to start college in January. By then *Little Women* had ended and my college applications were in, and I had a few weeks to actually spend being lazy with her, cuddling in the den and watching movies we didn't pay attention to and talking so late into the night we earned occasional half-hearted reprimands from my dads.

They definitely like having her around, though. Her movie's coming out this November, and Pops has already made elaborate plans to take me shopping on Newbury Street for a dress that's "red-carpet appropriate" so I can be her date to the New York premiere.

"Okay, so it's *possible* I've seen scarier chandelier crashes," she says now, glancing over at me across our beanbags with a soft smile. Her real one. It's been a long time since I've seen Odile smile anything but her real smile. "But not on a high school budget. And I swear, it *was* really and truly scary."

"Do you think we timed it right with the light cues? Jasmin and Will were having a debate about whether to use a special, but I said—"

A sharp knock on the door interrupts us. I roll over and groan. "Who is it?"

"The French Revolution!" a voice calls back.

"And that would be Dom." I sigh. That joke started during *Les Mis* strike and, it seems, will never go away.

Odile laughs. "Are you going to let him in?"

"I think I have to. He's probably still in costume."

He is, of course—Gabby made the trim for his tux herself—but he's grinning so hard I can't get mad at him.

"You were *amazing.*" Odile climbs up from the beanbag and hugs him. "Christine's totally going to pick you. The Phantom's just a whiner."

"Wish you were up there with us." He smiles at her.

"I'm still sad I didn't get to be in your army last year."

"We got to be dead together at the end. It was all good."

"You really have been awesome tonight," I tell him, because it's the truth. After *Les Mis*, Dom decided to go all in on the acting side and signed up for voice classes, and it paid off. On top of the shows here, he got a great part in the community theater's summer production of *Guys and Dolls*. They're starting rehearsals right after we close. He keeps saying it's no big deal, but every time I mention it, he grins from ear to ear.

"Uh-oh." He glances at my timer. "I've got, what, thirty seconds before I need to be backstage?"

"More like twenty. You have to change for the masquerade."

"Well, I wanted to come see Odile in case I don't get another chance. Are you heading back to New York tonight?"

"Unfortunately." She scrunches up her face. "Finals start tomorrow, so this was the only time during the run that I could leave town. But I can't wait to see you dodge those fireballs in the next act."

"Ugh, the fireballs." I roll my eyes. "We had to do the whole thing with a couple of light cues. It's the most anticlimactic fight scene ever."

"Would you rather we used actual pyrotechnics?" Dom raises his eyebrows. "In *this* theater?"

"Well, no. But I'm just saying, we could've painted some tennis balls orange at least."

"Sorry I'm late." Jasmin charges back into the booth, then halts when she sees Dom. "Whoa—shouldn't you be in a dressing room chugging honey water or something?"

I reach for my headset. "Yeah, he should. Break a leg, again."

"And now, back to France." He holds the door open for Odile. She gives me a quick kiss, right in front of the others, and I'm already giggling before she's even let go. "Okay, if you two don't stop, I'm going to have the cuteness police fire some orange tennis balls your way."

I catch Odile's hand as Dom leaves and squeeze it tight. Voices are chattering away in the headset around my neck, but I don't move to put it on. She's holding my gaze, and there's so much in that look—warmth and trust and an openness that I love almost as much as I love *her*. It's that amazing actor trick, where she can say so much without actually saying anything at all. My heart's thudding so loud it might as well be a sound effect.

I still can't believe she's really mine.

"Mel . . ." There's a warning in Jasmin's voice. "I can't flash the warning light in the house until you call five minutes to places, remember?"

"On it." I lift Odile's hand to my lips, kiss her fingers, and slip back into my seat. I hear her laughing as she closes the door behind her, and my face is bright red as I switch my mic on.

I still can't believe, after everything that happened, that we got to start over. Another try, with no curses or secrets to get in the way.

I lean into my mic. "Imani, how many of the actors are back?"

"Almost everyone, but we're still fixing a couple of costumes. Shouldn't be much longer."

"Okay. Where are we on the staircase?"

"Run crew's testing the casters one last time. Nick got them unstuck, finally. He's good with a screwdriver."

"Tell him well done. Nena, are you ready on sound?"

"Ready."

"Okay. Five minutes to places, everyone. Stand by, lights—lights, *go*. Stand by, curtain."

I grin into my mic. Act two is about to start. A new beginning, for all of us.

"And . . . curtain, *go*!"

CURTAIN CALL

CAST

(in order of appearance)

Jean Valjean . . . . Nicholas Underwood

Javert . . . . David Patel

Fantine. . . . . Odile Rose

Young Cosette . . . . Josefina Penoi

Madame Thénardier . . . . Elizabeth Meyers

Thénardier. . . . . Julio Ramirez

Gavroche . . . . Lauren Breen

Cosette. . . . . Alejandra Huston

Éponine . . . . Leah Zou

Enjolras . . . . Dominic Connor

Marius Pontmercy . . . . Malik Sexton

People of France (Convicts, Constables, Laborers, Factory
Workers, Sailors, Inn Guests, Urchins, Beggars, Thénardier's
Gang, Students, Sentries, Sex Workers, Turning Women,
Wedding Guests, etc.) . . . . Christina Leasure

Aaron Crane

Andrew Hernandez

Uri Lee

Imani Miller

Kyle Marckini

Connor Kukovec

Katelyn Landwehr

Noah Mette

Travis Hedstrom

Peyton Tiu

Trent Fairwood

George Vermaat

Madison Rogers

Chad Syring

Adam Nakumara

Kadie Akins

Selah Levi

Jillian Waldrep

Bruce Dickerson

Tasha Barnett

Briony Olson

(continues on page 12)

STUDENT CREW

Stage Manager . . . . .Melody McIntyre

Assistant Stage Manager. . . . . Gabrielle Piacine

Set Designer. . . . . Fatima Pataras

Lighting Designer .Jasmin Bennett

Sound Designer . . . . Kevin Lo

Costume Designer . . . . .Rachel Scott

Hair & Makeup Designer . . . . .Shannon Kardas

Props Designer. Estaban Goodwin

Publicity Manager . . . . Tyler Zumbrun

Assistant Crew Heads, Production & Run Crew Members . . . .

Michael Coken

Jacob Matushek

Devin Schmidtke

Nena Curley

Aya Aljoulani

Benjamin Levy

Daniel Horton

Ellie Nagy

Han Thai

Joey Pytel

Erin Edmonds

Juan Molina

Matthew O'Hara

Morgan Springborn

Amrita Ramanan

Paul Villalovoz
Riya Florence
Zack Nguyen
Cameron Babb
Ellyn Miller
Miranda Craig
Lexi Grenzner
Lilyan Dilay
Kekoa Lauzon
Mick Coughlan
Holly Pounds
Preston Tekmenzhi
Grant Moore
Kelly Brasseau
Lon Bailey
Ian Mitchell
Victoria Jahn
Reaiah Gerstein
Bach Polakowski
Caroline Graham
Lindsey Thaniel
(continues on page 22)

AUTHOR'S NOTE

I didn't intend to set *The Love Curse of Melody McIntyre* in an alternate universe, but as it turned out, that's what happened.

When I was writing it back in 2018 and 2019, it never crossed my mind that by the time the actual dates of the musical production at its center rolled around, the world would be so dramatically altered by a global pandemic that in fact, in most of the United States, no school theater productions—and, for that matter, no school—would be occurring in the spring of 2020.

The world is still in the process of turning upside down as we're sending this book off to print, so I don't know what's going to happen next, but I hope with all my heart that soon we'll all be heading back to school, back to the theater, and, most important, back to each other.

ACKNOWLEDGMENTS

Aside from a few Christmas pageants in my youth, I've never been part of a theater production in any form. In high school, though, I did have an odd tendency to date actors, and when I reached adulthood I had the good sense to marry an actor/singer/ stage manager/managing director who cheerfully served as both the inspiration and the technical adviser for the book you hold in your hands (or on your screen). She's the one to whom I sent a random text one afternoon asking if it would serve as a realistic story premise if I wrote about an extremely talented high school stage manager who was adamantly anti-actor, who then fell for an actor in spite of herself, and she's the one who texted back, "Oooooooh, SURE." And thus, after lots and lots of collaborative brainstorming and trips to watch local productions and an embarrassing number of hours spent watching performances on YouTube, *The Love Curse of Melody McIntyre* came into being. But, as is appropriate for a book about theater, there were a *lot* of people who I depended on throughout the writing process.

First I have to thank my editor, Kristen Pettit—this book was a serious challenge to structure and shape, and it wouldn't be the story it is if it weren't for Kristen's insights. Thank you to my agent, Jim McCarthy, for championing this book (and all my books) and never tiring of discussing technical theater with me. And to the rest of the team at Harper, including Clare Vaughn, Alexandra Rakaczki, Jessie Gang, Alison Klapthor, Josephine Rais, Allison Brown, Jessica White, and Christine Corcoran Cox, thank you so much for helping to bring this book out into the world and make it a real thing.

Thank you to my early readers: Jessica Spotswood, who read an early and very broken draft and somehow proceeded to tell me exactly how to fix it, and Jacob Gerstein, who served as my very first beta reader on the first draft of Act 1, gave me lots of highly useful feedback, and was nice enough to make sure he didn't mark it up with a red pen. Many thanks to Nicole Overton and Lindsay Smith, who gave me excellent suggestions on the manuscript, and to my chapter 1 beta readers, who kindly offered up their last-minute services via Twitter: Mary N.S. Richardson, Ibrahim Chaudry, and Joanna Kanellopoulos.

Thank you to my many theater-inclined friends who offered thoughts, suggestions, and technical expertise, particularly Jarrett Perlow (who also accompanied me to several productions and critiqued them for me, which was extra useful when my reaction to a song might be "Oh that was . . . nice" only to learn that the actor should have been using head voice the whole time and that's why it sounded all wonky) and Cheryl Williams (who let me borrow her stage manager binder for *Bat Boy: The Musical*, which has an utterly terrifying script, but the associated paperwork was indescribably helpful), as well as Emily Hayes-Rowan, Maggie Walker, Josh Adrian, Sarah Chapin, Ben Levine, Maddie McQuade, Michael Dove, and honestly probably at least twenty other people who I begged to answer questions for me at some point. (I'm really sorry if you're one of those people and I forgot to write down the fact that we had that conversation. My memory is awful, but I very much appreciated your help all the same!)

Huge thanks are also due to the casts and production teams behind the many amazing high school and youth theater productions I treated myself to while I was researching *Love Curse*, including Woodrow Wilson High School in Washington, DC (*Legally Blonde*); Winston Churchill High School in Potomac, Maryland (*Joseph and the Amazing Technicolor Dreamcoat*); Albert Einstein High School in Kensington, Maryland (*Once Upon a Mattress*); St. John's College High School in Washington, DC (*Emma! A Pop Musical*); Walter Johnson High School in Bethesda, Maryland (*Mary Poppins*); St. Albans School/ National Cathedral School in Washington, DC (*Leader of the Pack*); Washington-Liberty High School in Arlington, Virginia (*Bye Bye Birdie*); Georgetown Day School in Washington, DC (*Floyd Collins*); and Ovations Theatre in Rockville, Maryland (*Les Mis*). Special thanks go to DC's Sitar Arts Center, which was kind enough to let me sit in on their sitzprobe for *Seussical* and entertained me with more than a decade's worth of summer musical productions, all directed by the incomparable A. Lorraine Robinson.

Fortunately for me, the internet is full of generous people who've staged *Les Mis* in high schools and community theaters all over the country, who then took the time to share exactly how they did it with their fellow artists. I read detailed descriptions of the window gobos required to make "On My Own" look appropriately despondent and found countless video tutorials on how to build turntables, apply peasant makeup, and construct revolutionary student vests, and I'm hereby sending out massive gratitude to the technical theater community for being so willing to share your knowledge and experiences. Plus, another enormous thank-you to the hundreds of high school drama students and teachers who posted *Les Mis* performance videos, memes, and inspired works online. Particularly to the original creators of the "Prom Would Be Misérable Without You" promposal concept (genius) and the incredible "One Day More" pep rally flash mob at a California high school a few years back.

Finally, and most of all, thank you to Julia, my partner in all things, musical and otherwise. From detailing the philosophical principles behind the Thénardiers' existence to patiently explaining how light boards work, you were my alpha reader and in-house expert on everything. You both wrangled our toddler while I furiously drafted, and sang *Phantom* solos for me as a reward when I met my deadlines. I really would be misérable without you.